Scandalous
SECRETS

SYNITHIA
WILLIAMS

HQN

If you purchased this book without a cover you should be aware
that this book is stolen property. It was reported as "unsold and
destroyed" to the publisher, and neither the author nor the
publisher has received any payment for this "stripped book."

ISBN-13: 978-1-335-01399-6

Recycling programs
for this product may
not exist in your area.

Scandalous Secrets

Copyright © 2020 by Synithia R. Williams

All rights reserved. No part of this book may be used or reproduced
in any manner whatsoever without written permission except in the
case of brief quotations embodied in critical articles and reviews.

This is a work of fiction. Names, characters, places and incidents
are either the product of the author's imagination or are used
fictitiously. Any resemblance to actual persons, living or dead,
businesses, companies, events or locales is entirely coincidental.

This edition published by arrangement with Harlequin Books S.A.

For questions and comments about the quality of this book,
please contact us at CustomerService@Harlequin.com.

HQN
22 Adelaide St. West, 40th Floor
Toronto, Ontario M5H 4E3, Canada
www.Harlequin.com

Printed in U.S.A.

For my Grandma Charlotte. Your encouragement during quarantine meant the world to me. I love you.

Dear Reader,

I am a fan of the secret-baby trope, but I haven't written a secret-baby romance. Leave it to me to take a twist on the familiar trope in *Scandalous Secrets*. Byron, the charming dreamer of the Robidoux family, is on the verge of winning an important senate race when the woman he helped years ago by pretending to be her child's father is threatened.

Zoe Hammond has finally learned to stand on her own and go after what she wants. While she appreciates everything Byron did for her, she doesn't want to be dependent on him again. Her past has shaped her view of relationships and not only is trust hard for her, she no longer believes in love. When they come together to protect her daughter, Zoe and Byron not only have to navigate being back in each other's lives, but the sparks still flying between them.

I hope you enjoy this latest installment of the Jackson Falls series. You'll get to see some of the characters you loved in *Forbidden Promises*. Grant is still trying to maneuver everyone's lives, and Elaina is still as sharp-tongued as before. You'll also meet a few new characters, whom I hope you'll love just as much as the rest of the Robidoux family.

After you've finished *Scandalous Secrets*, reach out to me and let me know what you think. I love to hear from readers via email or social media.

Happy reading!

Synithia

CHAPTER ONE

BYRON WAS AT the top of his game.

His heart pumped with exhilaration. The smile that refused to leave his face was beginning to hurt his cheeks. He stared out at the crowd surrounding the stage, and the eyes looking back at him were bright with enthusiasm, hope and determination. Signs with his campaign's green-and-blue logo flowed like waves in their hands. A blend of people from all races, economic classes and social backgrounds packed into the brewery where he'd chosen to hold his watch party.

And he hadn't let them down. The results were in. He'd won.

His supporters' fervor was like a tidal wave, bowling him over with its strength. He'd done this. He'd actually gotten this far. The primary win wasn't a guarantee he'd win a seat in the Senate, but he had lasted long enough to beat out an opponent with experience as a state legislator and a much longer record of public service. Living up to the expectations of the people who'd voted for him, the people who were currently cheering for him, was something he refused to take lightly.

"I promise you," Byron said into the microphone. In his periphery, Roy, his campaign manager, took a step forward. Byron could hear Roy's warning in his head. *Never make promises in a speech. They come back and bite you in the ass.* But Byron didn't care about that right now. This was a promise he planned to keep.

Byron held up a finger and shook his hand with each word. "I promise you I will not forget the trust you all have honored me with tonight. We have gotten this far, and we will keep going all the way to Washington. No more waiting for tomorrow. The time is now!"

The crowd cheered. They held up and waved his signs and repeated his words. "The time is now!" The campaign slogan had come about during a debate after his opponent, State Senator Gordan, insisted the time wasn't right to try and fight the administration on progressive ideas. Byron's immediate comeback had been that fifteen years was too long to wait, and the time was now.

A slim hand slid into his left one and squeezed. Byron turned from the crowd toward his fiancée, Yolanda. Her brown eyes were filled with pride. Tall, graceful and perfectly polished in a tasteful green blouse and navy pants— to match his campaign colors—she complemented him. As Byron wrapped an arm around her shoulders and pulled her into his side, they looked like a young, optimistic couple deeply in love.

But Byron didn't miss how a gleam of triumph overshadowed the pride in her eyes. Yolanda was a woman on her way to making partner at the reputable law firm she worked for. A position beneficial for the wife of North Carolina's newest senator.

Byron leaned down and pressed a kiss to her lips. She placed a hand on his cheek. Her nails lightly scratched the beard he'd grown during the last weeks of the campaign. Her gentle reminder to cut the damn thing, before she pulled back and grinned wider. "We did it," she said.

He slid his arm back and entwined their fingers. "Yes, we did."

They waved and shook hands as they made their way off the stage. The band played upbeat music. Champagne corks popped throughout the building and more beer poured from the tap. The party would start now, along with the real work. He needed to finalize the strategy against his opponent. Brainstorm how to reach the digitally disconnected members in his district. Figure out the best way to utilize his family to spread his message throughout the area. Develop a plan to be more relatable to his constituents. Something even more necessary now that his best friend and former brother-in-law had plans to remarry into the family. This time with a different sister.

"I know that look," came a booming male voice.

Byron shifted and faced his father. Grant Robidoux had a Robidoux Tobacco cigar in one hand, and the other slammed down hard onto Byron's shoulder and squeezed. His dad was what Byron imagined he'd look like one day. Skin the color of dark honey slightly lined due to age, light brown eyes and curly hair with just enough salt and pepper to make people say he looked distinguished. Pride radiated off him like sunbeams as he studied Byron's face.

Byron took the glass of champagne Yolanda handed to him that she accepted off the tray of a passing server. "What look is that, Dad?"

"The I'm-already-planning-the-next-step look," Grant said, pointing his cigar at Byron. "Not tonight. There is enough time for strategy tomorrow. Tonight you enjoy the win." He winked at Yolanda. "Enjoy the company of the beautiful woman at your side. The real fight is about to begin. But give yourself this moment to bask in the glory."

Yolanda raised her glass and tapped it against Byron's. "I agree with that."

Byron forced the massive list of things he needed to do to the back of his mind. Taking a second to enjoy this milestone wouldn't hurt. "Fine, I'll sit back and enjoy this win, but I'm starting early tomorrow." He glanced around the crowd and caught the fierce glare of his older sister. "Uh-oh."

Grant's brows drew together. "Uh-oh? What's wrong?"

"Elaina is scowling. Do you know why?" Nothing good ever followed one of Elaina's scowls. She'd just been smiling and clapping with the rest of his supporters.

Grant's gaze shifted away. He brought the cigar to his nose and sniffed. "No idea."

"You're lying." Byron didn't hesitate to call his dad out. He loved and respected his dad more than any other man in the world, but he also knew when Grant was trying to keep something from him. "What happened?"

Grant shrugged. "Nothing big. India and Travis ducked out right before your acceptance speech, and she's worried they've run off and done something stupid."

Byron relaxed. "They're probably just getting out of here to spend a few minutes alone together. I don't blame them after we spent the last few weeks pretending as if they weren't together. You tell Elaina to do exactly what you told me. Enjoy the win and strategize tomorrow."

Byron wasn't concerned about his younger sister and best friend leaving his party early. They were crazy about each other—God help them—and they wanted to spend time together. Elaina's being upset, well, that made more sense. Even though she'd given her blessing to India and

Travis after discovering they were in love, the situation was still awkward as hell.

"Why do I have to tell her?" Grant asked, sounding genuinely put out.

Byron lightly hit his father's shoulder. "Because it's my party and I don't want to." He wrapped his arm around Yolanda's shoulders and maneuvered her away from his dad in the opposite direction of Elaina.

"You know you were wrong for doing that," Yolanda said, chuckling.

"He's the one who told me to relax. Dealing with whatever is bothering Elaina is not my idea of relaxing."

Yolanda sighed and leaned farther into him. "I still can't believe you're okay with India and Travis. God knows how we're going to smooth over this situation in the media. We don't need anything smearing your campaign."

"Don't worry. This won't smear my campaign. If anything, it'll show how well our family works together." *Or reveal just how cracked we are beneath the polished exterior.*

Byron caught the eye of one of his larger donors. He smiled and waved and moved in that direction. He added *worrying about his family's image* to the long list of items he'd have to overcome if he hoped to win in November.

Yolanda dug her feet in and stopped him. Her eyes were serious as they met his. "I'm not playing about this. We have to be delicate moving forward. I'm with you to win. Not to let the soft spot you have for your baby sister and best friend derail this train."

Yolanda's words were pragmatic as always. Her practicality and ability to strategize was why he'd agreed to this engagement, but that didn't stop irritation from crawling up his spine. Happiness was hard to find. So why get in the way when two people he cared about actually found it? He may not be a proponent of true love, but he also wouldn't begrudge those who were.

"I know why you're here," he said. She reminded him at least once a week. "We need each other, and it'll take both of us to win. Don't worry about India and Travis. Their relationship won't be the thing that kills my campaign."

"Byron! Congratulations!" The happy voice of the donor whose eye he'd caught a second ago.

"Hello, Mr. Sparrow. Mrs. Sparrow, so good to see you again." Byron grinned and shook hands.

Yolanda's face became a mask of blissful happiness as they talked and schmoozed their way through the party. This was their future. He'd known what he was getting into when his campaign manager mentioned that proposing and marrying would make him a more viable candidate.

So why was it bothering him tonight?

Things were going exactly the way he wanted them to. Yolanda's business ties, along with her family's history in politics, combined with his family's wealth and influence, was political gold. On top of that, he liked her. She was driven, attractive, passionate and had let him know from their very first date she wanted to help him on his rise to the top. Yolanda was a woman who knew her own mind and didn't apologize for going after what she wanted. He never had to guess where he stood with her.

Movement in his periphery caught his eye. He turned and his entire body went rigid. Guess everything wasn't going as planned tonight. Dominic Ferrell, the consultant he'd hired to help with his campaign, made his way toward Byron, his expression grim and his dark eyes blank.

Nothing good could come of Dominic's showing up tonight. He'd hired the guy months ago to handle a situation from his past, one that Byron had paid a lot of money to hopefully fix. Dominic kept in touch to let him know if anything popped up. Mostly via email and the occasional phone call. Never in person.

Byron excused himself from the group. Ignoring Yolanda's concerned gaze, he walked up to Dominic. "What's wrong?"

"Someone is here to see you." Dominic's calm expression didn't waver. Dominic was always calm. An observer who could charm as easily as he could intimidate. But the sharpness of his gaze put Byron on edge.

Byron's heart jumped in his chest. "Zoe?" He'd thought he'd protected her. Had something gone wrong?

Dominic shook his head. "No. She's still back home living her life with no signs of any problems. But I don't know if I can guarantee that much longer."

Byron shifted closer to Dominic. He rubbed his beard, a new habit now that he had one, and tried not to let the fear seeping into him show. "Why?"

Dominic nodded his head back toward the door. "Come with me. You don't want him to create a scene."

Him? "Let's go." Byron followed Dominic out of the party, through the kitchen in the back and into an empty office. Once inside, a man he didn't recognize turned and faced him. Slim, with beady black eyes and a shifting stance. Byron immediately didn't like the guy.

"Byron Robidoux, this is Carlton Powell," Dominic said through clenched teeth.

Byron's hands tightened into fists. "Carlton Powell? What the hell are you doing here?" Byron had paid Dominic a lot of money to keep Carlton out of his business. Carlton had been hired to find the same person Byron had been looking for before announcing his run, and Byron hoped the payoff would ensure that he moved on to other things.

Carlton rubbed his hands together. "Don't be so rude. I'm here to do you a favor."

"I don't need any favors from you." Byron glared at Dominic. "You brought him here?"

Dominic shook his head. "No. I've kept tabs on him. When I found out he was in town, I followed him here. Stopped him before he confronted you."

"I'm not confronting anyone," Carlton said with the nerve to sound affronted. "I'm just here because I've got an offer I think the future senator can't refuse."

"What offer is that?" Byron asked.

"An offer to keep what I know to myself instead of telling all those happy people out there." Carlton pointed to the closed door. "About you being a deadbeat dad."

Byron's stomach flipped, and sweat ran down his back, but he didn't flinch. He hadn't become a defense attorney and served a term in the state house without knowing how to hide his shock. "I'm not a deadbeat dad. I don't have any children."

"That's not what I've heard," Carlton said, sounding like he'd gotten the gospel truth on everything Byron Robidoux. "You see, after you sent me on my way I did a little digging on my own. Turns out the woman you told me to stay away from also told a few people you were the father of her kid."

Byron gritted his teeth. He should have known this would come back. He didn't have any children, but thirteen years ago he'd agreed to help a friend out by keeping her secret and going along with a lie. The image of Zoe in his college apartment, her face bruised, and tears in her eyes as she'd clung to him, played like a bad movie in his mind.

Byron, please say the baby is yours. He'll kill me if I stay with him. This is my only way out.

Even now the memory filled him with rage and help-lessness. Zoe had been his best friend. His homegirl. He'd loved her with everything he had, but when he'd told her, she'd tossed his love back at him as if playing hot potato. She'd been in love with someone else. A guy Byron had never thought deserved her. A guy Byron discovered way too late that he'd been right about. So he'd kept her secret. Said the child was his and promised never to say anything.

"You're coming to me with rumors," Byron replied coldly. He wasn't playing his hand without knowing ex-actly what Carlton knew and wanted.

Carlton shrugged. "Rumors can do a lot of damage. You see, I doubt you're really the father. The person who origi-nally sent me to find ol' girl was pretty sure someone else was the father. Now, I took your money to lead them off her trail, but then I got to wondering why so many people were interested in this one woman and her kid. Did a lit-tle research and here we are," he said, sounding pleased with himself.

"Get to the point," Dominic said in a deadly voice.

"My point is regardless of who the baby daddy is, I think word getting out about everyone's favorite candidate possibly being on the birth certificate won't be good for your campaign. You know the early polls show a strong lead over this other guy. Be a damn shame to lose because people think you're an absentee father."

Byron didn't have time for this. "What do you want?"

he asked instead of going with the urge to shove Carlton into the wall.

"A million dollars," Carlton said without missing a heartbeat. "I know you're good for it. Your family is known for its wealth."

"I don't have a million dollars." He did, but he'd be damned if this guy got any more of his money.

"Oh, I don't want it tonight. I'll give you say…two weeks to come up with the money." Carlton spoke as if he were a debt collector who'd done a client a favor by extending the deadline. "Bask in this win. Let it sink in a little what you stand to lose."

Byron was well aware of what he had to lose. He was also shrewd enough to realize that paying Carlton wasn't going to make this problem go away. He needed to know how far this guy was willing to go.

"What if I say no?" Byron asked. He crossed his arms and sized up Carlton. "A DNA test will prove I'm not the father."

Carlton sucked his teeth and shook his head. "But the scandal it'll cause. That, and your playboy ways. Oh, I'm sure there are dozens of other women willing to come forward and claim you're their kid's dad."

The greedy gleam in Carlton's eyes made Byron's stomach churn. He wouldn't doubt Carlton already had managed to find women who'd say they'd slept with him. Even if he had a dozen paternity tests to prove his innocence, the stigma would follow him and cost him the campaign.

"I thought you'd see what I mean," Carlton said. "Just think it over. But not for too long." Carlton put two fingers to his brow in a mock salute and walked out.

Byron punched his fist into his opposite hand. "Fuck!"

Dominic frowned. "You can't pay him again. Guys like Carlton never go away. I never should have taken his first deal."

Byron paced back and forth. His mind raced with what to do next. He couldn't dwell on previous decisions. They were already done and he couldn't change them. He'd have to deal with the consequences of those decisions.

"Protecting Zoe is what matters," he said. "Carlton just proved what I feared most. Her ex is about to get out of jail and he's looking for her. There's no way that man should be able to get close to her."

"If you pay him for this, you'll have a paper trail of past dealings with him. He'll make things worse and won't hesitate to out you as a guy leaving babies all over the Southeast."

Byron stopped pacing and met Dominic's concerned stare. "No, he won't. I have no intentions of paying him."

"Then what are you going to do?"

He was going to outplay Carlton. Growing up as a Robidoux taught him to recognize when he needed to make a big play in order to win. "I'm going to see Zoe. It's time we figured out our next move in this game."

CHAPTER TWO

Zoe placed the last handout for her training class on the last row of tables. With a sigh she clasped her hands in front of her and surveyed the empty room. Five neat rows of six-foot tables and chairs with bowls of candy and an assorted pile of small toys to occupy any fidgeters in the group. The laptop and projector were powered up and ready to go while instrumental music played softly in the background to keep things from being too quiet as people filed in.

Everything was in order. She'd done training presentations once a month for the past six years. She was comfortable speaking to a crowd and knew all the material. Still, her stomach lurched as if she were on a runaway roller coaster. Today's presentation wasn't just any presentation. It was part of the selection process for the new director of the risk-management department. A position Zoe wanted. Not just because her daughter's private school tuition wasn't getting any cheaper and switching wasn't an option because the school's security was the only thing that kept Zoe from being sick with anxiety about Lilah during the day, but also because she just wanted it.

Five years had to pass before she'd felt comfortable acknowledging things she wanted. Another five before she'd learned to be okay with going after her goals. She wasn't going to feel bad for wanting this even if deep, deep down she still didn't believe anyone would trust her judgment.

She strolled to the front of the room to double-check the slides for her presentation. No death by PowerPoint today. Lots of pictures, bullet points to cue her ideas and several places for her to stop and encourage audience participation. She would ace this.

"Damn, you think you've got it cold enough in here?"

Zoe's shoulders stiffened. She commanded her eyes not to roll before raising her head to give a tight smile to the man at the door. Short, with eyes so full of shade she was surprised the room didn't darken, and a personality as greasy as the extra dosing of whatever gel he slicked his curly hair back with, John Bailey was the guy least likely to throw Zoe a cup of water if she happened to spontaneously combust. He was also vying for the director position.

"This room gets hot when the projector is running. The temperature will balance out once everyone enters and the presentation starts." Zoe managed to keep her voice calm and professional even though she wanted to tell John to shut up.

"What is your presentation on?" John sauntered into the room and picked up one of her presentation packets. His nose scrunched up as he read the first page. "Steps to effectively manage risk? Seriously, Zoe, you went with a topic that's so basic."

His comment shot straight at her confidence and threatened to kill it before she even started. Zoe took a steadying breath. Calling John an asshole would give her great relief, but she was pretty sure he'd come back with something equally mean, and regardless of the outcome she wouldn't come out looking good in the situation.

Zoe focused on the reason why she'd chosen that topic. "People often ignore the basics. Everyone is willing to comply with any new requirements, while the everyday items are ignored. I'm going to highlight the ways we've improved the lives of our employees and reduced accidents mostly by going back to the basics."

Although she kept her voice even and confident, John's quiet scoff as she spoke sent her stomach on another roller-coaster ride. What if her topic was too basic? What if the administrators were into new and flashy ideas? Would they look at her as being too simplistic? Unable to step out of the box?

She believed in this topic. Seven years doing regulatory inspections for OSHA before coming here and seeing how many accidents could have been avoided if people followed basic safety principles proved her point. She knew what she was talking about. She wasn't going to cower before John or put up with his hating.

John raised a skeptical, bushy brow and dropped her presentation packet. "If you say so."

Before Zoe could respond the other department managers filed into the room. The director position wasn't officially posted, but the current director had submitted his retirement plans. Valtec Incorporated was one of the largest suppliers of plastics to the automotive industry. Zoe had worked in the risk management department of their Greenville, South Carolina, location for almost eight years. On paper she was qualified for the position. In reality, being qualified for something didn't always mean success.

The assistant administrator came into the room last. A tall woman with an open smile and poised demeanor, Miranda was the type of professional Zoe strived to be.

Confident, assertive, unwilling to back down from ass-holes like John.

Miranda walked over and shook Zoe's hand. "Zoe, I look forward to your presentation."

"Thank you, Miranda. I appreciate the opportunity."

Everyone got settled in their seats. Zoe took one deep, comforting breath. *Don't start off boring. Introduce yourself with an interesting anecdote and no matter what, remember you* do *belong up here.*

After her internal pep talk, Zoe ignored the smug you're-going-to-fail look from John and started her presentation. Two minutes in she was in her zone. The other managers were engaged, and she saw several head nods, even a few surprised widening of the eyes as she went over some of the improvements she'd made. Her jokes hit, her talking points weren't confusing, and based on Miranda's pleased expression, Zoe's confidence soared.

The sour expression on John's face as the other managers clapped when she finished only made her want to jump up and do a fist-pump, in-your-face dance. *Too basic, my ass!* She'd nailed this.

Miranda raised a hand. "Zoe, I do have one comment."

"Yes, Miranda," Zoe said. The rush of victory swooped through her veins and oozed out in her voice.

"I'll agree that you've achieved a lot with your improve-ments and proven how mitigating potential risks with em-ployees has reduced the number of accidents and mishaps, but you didn't go into detail about the accidents that *did* occur after we implemented your program. I would have liked to see an examination of why those occurred and what plans you have to try to avoid similar mistakes."

Zoe's smile froze in place. Heat prickled across her neck

and cheeks. "I chose to focus on the improvements we made to show how we've reduced the number of accidents."

"Reducing accidents is one thing," Miranda said, sounding like a teacher correcting a student's answer. "Having no accidents is another. Employee safety is the number-one priority for the company. In the future don't just pat yourself on the back for doing well. Look at your failures. They're opportunities to improve and you may discover valuable lessons there." Miranda raised one thinly arched brow. "Understand?"

Zoe had a quick flashback to the time her mom yelled at her in front of her entire class during open house for being "sassy" as she talked about her good grades and projects.

Quit acting like you better than everyone else. Any third grader can get an A on a simple project.

The same sick embarrassment that made her want to curl up into a ball and disappear seeped into her veins. Back then she'd cried in front of the entire class. Further driving her into the bin of embarrassment. She didn't cry anymore, but she hadn't discovered a cure for shame.

She forced the corners of her frozen smile up even more and shoved a big pile of brightness into her voice. "Of course. You're absolutely right. I will look into that."

Miranda nodded. "Good. Send me a report outlining what steps were taken after those accidents. I'll need it by Monday."

Zoe internally groaned. This weekend she'd promised to take her daughter to Atlanta to visit the Georgia Aquarium. She already had tickets. Today was Wednesday, which didn't leave a lot of time on top of the safety audits she was overseeing to finish a report before leaving. If she pulled together the incident reports maybe she'd be able to get something together before leaving on Friday. Maybe.

"No problem at all. I'll have it ready," she said.

"Good." Miranda checked her watch. "I've got to run to another meeting. Again, great job."

Miranda stood and the rest of the managers and division heads followed her lead. John meandered by her desk, a smug smile on his face and a gleam in his eye that made him look like a coked-up great white shark. Miranda had drawn blood and he was ready to pounce. Thankfully, someone called his name and asked a question, which forced John to leave with them.

Zoe cursed herself for not going over the accidents in her presentation as she packed up her materials and made her way to the office. She could stay late tonight, start going through the reports and put something together. The good thing was they already had plans in place to prevent further problems; the bad thing was those plans weren't written in a report format fit to go to the assistant administrator.

"Hey, Zoe, you got a second?"

Zoe turned to the female voice behind her. Rose Clarkson from the information technology department jogged the rest of the way down the hall to Zoe, her black ponytail swinging in tandem with the Valtec employee ID around her neck.

"I do." Zoe glanced around the hall. They weren't alone, but no one was close enough to overhear. "What's up?"

"I checked out that email you sent me. All I can tell you is that it originated from Memphis, but that's about it. I don't have the software here to do much more digging. Where did you get it from?"

Zoe licked her lips. Memphis? That didn't tell her anything. "I think it was spam or a phishing thing. I deleted it."

"Did it come to your work email? I can send it to corporate."

She shook her head. She'd gone past her comfort zone asking Rose for help. No way was she about to have corporate digging into her personal life. Not when she was up for this promotion. "No. It came to Lilah. She was worried about identity theft, so I thought I'd have it checked out. It's no big deal."

Rose shrugged then nodded. "Okay, if you're sure. If you get any more let me know and I'll send it to one of my friends. She's better at tracing the source of emails than I am."

"Sure thing. Thanks." She turned away from Rose and hurried to her office.

Disappointment further dampened her mood. She hadn't wanted Rose to confirm her worst fears, that her ex-boyfriend was behind the threatening emails, but she'd wanted something more concrete. Memphis might be a good thing. Kendell was not from Memphis. He wasn't scheduled to get out of prison for another few months. That email could have come to her by mistake.

You're a lying bitch.

That was all it said. Nothing else, but it was enough to make her uneasy. Enough to make her pull from her savings to cover the increase in tuition at Lilah's private school to ensure her daughter's safety. Enough to remind her that she had lied to Kendell, and if he found out she didn't know what he'd do to her.

She rubbed her chin. The dull memory of the pain she'd felt whenever he'd gotten angry or frustrated and lashed out at her with a backslap reminding her just how vindictive Kendell could be. She did not need that secret to ever be revealed.

Her desk phone rang just as she walked to her small office. A quick glance at the caller ID showed it was the front reception desk. Surprising, since they didn't typically call her unless a state or federal regulator was there for an inspection. There were no inspections scheduled for today.

Lord, please don't let this be a pop-up inspection!

She did not need that on top of the crap that was her day. She picked up the phone. "What's up, Kelly?"

"There's a man here to see you," Kelly said, giving no clue as to who said man could be.

"Is he with OSHA?" Just because there were no audits scheduled didn't mean the regulatory agency couldn't just show up.

"No, he says it's a personal visit." Kelly sounded perturbed as she always did when people dropped by the facility for personal visits. "I told him we only allow employees back, so he's waiting in the visiting room."

Since Valtec created proprietary products for various companies, the security around the place was super tight. One of the reasons Zoe had chosen to work there. She wasn't a fan of surprises. She'd spent enough time looking over her shoulder and being afraid someone was going to hurt her.

Her eyes shot to the calendar. *Stop, Zoe, it's not Kendell.* He didn't even know where she worked. She took a steadying breath and hoped her heart would slow its erratic beat.

"What's his name? I don't have any appointments today."

"He says his name is Pretty Ricky, but I don't believe him. You want me to send him away?"

Zoe's jaw dropped then slowly closed as she smiled. Byron was here? Not only was he here, but he was also using the nickname she'd teased him with back in college. She'd suspected this was coming. After he'd sent two private investigators to find her the year before, she'd wondered if he'd ever seek her out himself. She was surprised by how pleased she was to hear his name. He'd been her friend. Her safe harbor. Her escape.

"Zoe?" Kelly said. "Are you coming?"

Her pleasure was short-lived. If Byron was here, and using his nickname, it didn't mean he was here for a social call. He'd sought her out previously to ensure she didn't plan to use the secret he'd kept for her against him. At first, she couldn't believe he'd think she would do that to him. Then she reminded herself who his family was and the world he lived in and felt foolish for thinking he would trust her all these years later. If he was there in person, it either meant he hadn't believed her before or there was another threat to the promises they'd made.

"I'm coming now."

CHAPTER THREE

THIRTEEN YEARS AGO Byron Robidoux had saved her life. He'd been her best friend and the only person she'd known who'd been nice to her without expecting something in return. Believing he was really a nice guy had taken a while, but as she'd worked beside him on various volunteer projects, she'd been pleasantly surprised. She'd never met anyone like Byron before. Stupid rich, suave, super likeable and serious about making a difference in the world. She'd been drawn to his optimism and believed the hype when he said everyone could do something to make society better.

In the years since accepting his help then running away, she'd wondered what her life would have been like if she'd been smarter and fallen in love with him. If she'd chosen Byron instead of believing the garbage example of a relationship her parents had shown her as the standard for "real" love.

Thoughts of what could have been didn't matter now. Too much time had passed and they'd both moved on with their lives. That didn't stop Zoe from hurrying down the hall with barely suppressed excitement at the idea of seeing Byron again.

She walked into the visitors' waiting room at the front of the building. The room was decorated with stark gray walls, two plastic tables with chairs for visitors having lunch with an employee, and a few vending machines.

The place wasn't designed to encourage lounging or long visits. A man stood with his back to the door and faced the television mounted to the far wall with a game show playing on the screen.

Zoe stopped short. He was tall with broad shoulders and stood with his arms crossed and legs wide. He was dressed casually in a pair of loose jeans and navy T-shirt with a baseball cap on his head. In all the time she'd known Byron Robidoux he'd never worn jeans, T-shirt or a ball cap that didn't look as if it had been put together by a personal stylist.

Her heartbeat kicked up a notch. She'd assumed the fake name was for Byron. That assumption could be dead wrong. The threatening email she'd asked Rose to check out could mean someone out there was really pissed at her. What if it had been a warm-up to this meeting?

She slid one foot back, panic and fear she hadn't felt in a long time tightening her throat. She bumped into the trash can by the door. It toppled over, metal clanging against the concrete floor and spilling paper and aluminum cans everywhere.

"Shit!" she whispered. There she went, auditioning for the least graceful woman of the year award again.

The guy spun around. Whiskey-brown eyes met hers and widened. Zoe froze halfway down to pick up the items she'd spilled. Her mouth fell open.

"Byron?" No way. This man in front of her couldn't be the Byron she'd been friends with in college. The few times she'd looked him up on the internet or saw a news clip of him did not accurately reflect how good he looked in person. Seriously, she knew some guys tended to age into sex gods, but this was something different.

Or maybe it's just been that long.

Byron looked the same but more mature. The boyish features that had made him handsome in college had sharpened into a refined, grown and sexy look. His body was thicker, more filled out, and based on his biceps and forearms he'd filled out with muscle. The five o'clock shadow he used to always try to shave, which had given him charm, was now a full-on well-manicured beard that made it damn near impossible for her to not focus on his lips. Had his lower lip always been that full? That…kissable?

"Hey, Zoe, sorry to pop in on you like this."

Even if her eyes didn't want to accept that the fine-as-hell guy in front of her was her good friend from college, Byron's voice got through to her brain. Deep, cultured and smooth enough to make a woman's panties fly off.

The corner of his lip lifted in a half smile. One of his thick brows quirked up. Confusion clouded his eyes. Zoe snapped her mouth shut and straightened quickly. No need to stand there like a deer caught in headlights.

She forced out the fog of desire trying to cloud her brain and reminded herself this was Byron. Way-too-rich, I-easily-get-whatever-I-want Byron. I'm-running-for-Senate and, if she remembered correctly, am-engaged-to-someone-else Byron.

"It's okay. A big surprise, but okay."

When his shoulders relaxed and the easygoing smile she remembered crossed his features, Zoe's earlier excitement about seeing an old friend returned. She crossed the room and automatically opened her arms to hug him.

"It's so good to see you," she said.

Byron hesitated a beat before his arms spread and he wrapped her up in a hug. Not only did he look different, but he felt different, too. Harder, stronger, way more *you know you want to press all up into me* good. Her skin tingled and her nipples tightened. Zoe pulled back quickly before he noticed, the faint smell of his cologne backing up with her.

Byron slid back, too. His eyes skated over her features before he ran a hand over his beard, and did the nervous nose scrunch she remembered that always reminded her of a rabbit. The movement made her smile and pushed away the lingering awkwardness of her reaction. This was Byron. It wasn't as if she hadn't looked at him in college and allowed a few *what if* thoughts to take over. That was all this was.

"Good to see you, too," he said, finally meeting her gaze.

"Is everything all right? After I spoke with the detectives, I thought everything was settled."

She'd been hurt when he'd sent a private detective to talk to her even if she'd understood. She'd run out on him without a backward glance after accepting his help. He'd sent someone to find her to make sure she wouldn't try to come back and ruin his campaign. As much as she'd wanted to call Byron herself and curse him out for even considering she'd do something like that, could she really blame him for not trusting her?

"I thought everything was settled, too. Last night I was approached by someone and now they're making demands."

Zoe crossed her arms. She looked over her shoulder even though they were the only people in the room. Old habits were hard to break. "You know I won't say anything."

"That's the thing." He slid closer and lowered his voice. "I may need you to say something."

"What?" A dozen thoughts raced through her brain. Say something? About the secret they kept? The idea was preposterous. It would make things worse after she'd spent years blending into the background. "No. I'm not about to draw attention to myself. Not now." Not when Kendell was scheduled to get out of prison soon. "I can't get caught up in a political campaign."

"You're going to get drawn in anyway." He sounded sure of himself. Overly sure.

"I'll deny it." As soon as the words were out she realized denying anything would also put her in an awkward position.

"The birth certificate may not be an open record, but we both know if someone wants to see it bad enough, they can. Then what happens if they start asking if I'm really the father?"

Zoe clenched her teeth. A truth she never wanted revealed. She hadn't filled out the line for the father. Telling Kendell Byron was her child's father had gotten her out of the reach of the man she'd once believed loved her. Byron's going along with her lie was all the proof Kendell had asked for. Leaving the father line blank seemed the best way to avoid bringing either of them into the equation after she had Lilah.

"Who knocked over the trash can?" A man's irritated voice said from the door.

Byron pulled his ball cap lower over his eyes. Reminding Zoe he hadn't given his complete name to the receptionist. He wasn't supposed to be here. Things were about to get pretty bad if he'd taken the risk to come see her.

"I did." Zoe turned to face Dave, one of the operators from the assembly line. "Sorry, I'm going to get it up."

"I was about to say. I figured someone was about to get a write-up from you if they'd made a mess and left it like this," Dave said. "My sister is dropping off my lunch. I left it at my place. Figured I'd wait for her up here." Dave looked over Zoe's shoulder with a questioning gaze.

Byron had turned back to the television. Zoe smiled at Dave and pointed at Byron. "We'll get out of your way." She turned to Byron. "You can't come back to my office unless you sign in," she said, lowering her voice so Dave couldn't overhear. "Do you know where I live?"

He nodded. "What time does Lilah get out of school? I'd like to talk to you first."

"She's done at three, but she has afterschool activities." Zoe checked her watch. She really needed to work on that report for Miranda, but this thing with Byron couldn't wait. "Let me wrap up things here and meet you at my place in about an hour."

Dave's sister came into the visitors' room and the two of them greeted each other excitedly. "You'd forget your damn head if it wasn't attached to your body." The siblings laughed and launched into a conversation about what their mother had packed for Dave's lunch.

Byron placed his hand on her elbow. His voice raised enough for her to hear him over Dave's conversation, but not loud enough so they'd overhear. "Zoe, I know you don't want to do this, but there's more at play than just the word getting out. The person who approached me was originally looking for you."

Zoe clasped her hands together to stop herself from wringing them. Emails calling her a lying bitch were one thing. Emails coupled with someone looking for her sent cold chills across her spine. She shook her head. The urge to run a physical tug in her midsection.

Byron's hand squeezed. His eyes hardened. "Don't worry. I've got you."

He did. He would. Even after all these years she saw that truth in his eyes. The thought both warmed her heart and made her want to kick the overturned trash can. She was not the helpless young woman she'd once been. If Kendell was trying to push his way back into her life, he'd best be ready because she was ready to fight back.

She pulled her arm out of his grasp, the lingering heat of his touch like an electric shock to her system. "Thanks, but I can take care of myself now." She didn't bother to feel bad when she saw the flash of hurt in his eyes. Zoe lifted her chin. "My place. One hour."

"WHERE ARE YOU? Don't you know we're in the middle of a crisis?"

Byron ran a hand over his beard and swallowed the sigh creeping up his throat. He'd been sitting in Zoe's driveway for an hour waiting for her to arrive. Dominic had provided her address after Byron told him he had to talk to Zoe in person and was the only one Byron had told where he was going. Hence the reason his campaign manager, Roy, was now having a minor hissy fit at not knowing the where-abouts of his superstar client.

"Something came up that I had to take care of. I won't be gone long," Byron said, trying to keep his voice upbeat and unbothered.

His plan was to make this a quick trip that wouldn't draw much attention. That was why he'd left home before

the sun rose and tried to look as unpolitician-like as possible. He doubted Carlton thought Byron would go straight
to Zoe instead of trying to find a way to deal with him
directly, but in case he did have any ideas, Byron decided
to leave the political entourage of security and advisers
at home.

His plan to be inconspicuous had flown out the window with the insistent administrative assistant at Zoe's
job, who'd eyed him up and down. On top of that his visit
would be documented by one of the various cameras in-
stalled around the exterior of Zoe's home. That was if the
very observant older woman living next door didn't call
the police on him for trespassing. The woman had come
out and peered at Byron suspiciously three times since
he'd parked in Zoe's driveway.

He checked his watch for the tenth time, tried to remember he'd been the inconsiderate one who'd interrupted her
workday and focused on the problem of calming down Roy.

"What could have possibly come up that you couldn't
tell me about?" Roy's irritated voice came through the
phone. "While you're off chasing whatever unicorns you
discovered last night, I'm here trying to prevent a crisis."

That was the third time since Byron answered Roy's
call that he'd referred to a problem. Roy needed to know
about Carlton's blackmail attempt, but Byron needed time
to think of a solution before Roy and his dad swooped in
and tried to dictate his next move. Roy would have been
all on Byron's case if he had any idea of Byron's location,
which meant something else had come up.

"What are you talking about, Roy? What type of crisis?"

"Oh, now you want to show an interest in your campaign."

"Roy," Byron said between clenched teeth. He understood how important the next few days of his campaign were. He didn't need the extra dose of sarcasm.

"India and Travis eloped."

Byron's body went still. He shook his head as the words sank in. *Nah.* They could not have run off like that. Sure, he'd given his blessing to their relationship, but the plan was to come up with the best way to roll things out to the media. Didn't they understand eloping gave the appearance the family was against them? That people would think they'd had to sneak off and get married to avoid backlash?

Byron shifted forward and backward in his seat. He ran a hand over his beard and scowled at the front of Zoe's home. What the hell were they thinking? He'd been the person to support them, and they run off and elope.

"What the hell, India?" Byron said in a disbelieving whisper. He jerked the steering wheel. The inside of the car was stifling. He turned off the car, jumped out and paced from the front to the back. "How did you find out?"

"India called your cousin Ashiya, who told your aunt Liz, who went to Grant, who came to me because no one knows where the hell you are," Roy said as if Byron going out of town was the reason for the entire screwup.

Byron ran a hand over his face. The squeaking of Zoe's neighbor's screen door sounded again. He looked over at the woman. He smiled and waved. She scowled and ran back inside as if Lucifer had offered her a piece of candy. She was definitely calling the police now. *Shit!* If Zoe didn't pull up in the next two minutes he would leave and circle back in half an hour.

"What do you want to do?" Roy asked.

Byron had no clue what to do. Yesterday had been so

great. The joy of the primary win seemed like a century ago. He stopped pacing, took a deep breath and focused on one problem at a time. India's elopement was ill-timed, but it wasn't the worst thing he had to deal with right now.

"Look, I pay you and the rest of your staff enough money to come up with ways to fix this. Start brainstorming ideas. I'll be back in Jackson Falls later tonight. I've got to take care of something and then be back."

"What are you taking care of? Come on, Byron, we've already got an uphill battle with you going against a candidate with a history in national politics already. I don't need you coming with some other new surprises."

He couldn't keep Roy completely in the dark. Not when he was already flipping out about one thing. "Talk to Dominic."

There were several beats of silence. "That situation?" Roy knew about Byron's promise to Zoe. He'd originally expressed concerns Zoe would try and come out with the information during their campaign. Roy recommended Dominic to help Byron find Zoe and discover if she planned to take advantage of Byron's previous generosity during the campaign. "I thought things were taken care of."

"They were. Until right after the results came in. So believe it or not, India and Travis's inconvenient elopement is the least of our problems. Get with Dominic, come up with a plan. I'll be back tomorrow hopefully with Zoe and we'll get ahead of things."

He hadn't originally planned to bring Zoe back to Jackson Falls with him. He wasn't even sure if she'd be able to get away for the weekend, but he wasn't going to make a plan that affected her and her daughter without her input.

The garage door rose right as a large black SUV turned

into her driveway. Zoe sat behind the wheel. She gave him an apologetic smile as she pulled the vehicle into the garage.

"Look, Roy, I've got to go."

"Hold up, wait, we're not done. I need to know what happened," Roy said frantically.

"Remember the part about me paying you a lot of money to help solve my problems? I meant that. Talk to Dominic. I'll call you later."

"Yeah, I'm not a miracle worker," Roy grumbled.

"That's not what your invoices say." Byron ended the call and slid the phone in his back pocket.

Zoe opened the driver's-side door and stepped out as he approached. "I'm so sorry," she said. "It took longer than I expected to wrap things up at the office."

Byron was struck once again by how much she'd changed since he'd last seen her. Not so much her looks, but the spark of mischief that used to always be in her dazzling brown eyes wasn't there. Her thick, curly hair was parted down the middle then braided back into a sleek bun. She used to always wear it out like a halo around her head. The ready smile she'd worn was now more hesitant and guarded. He would have expected the more demur demeanor to have dampened his attraction to her; instead, he only wanted to bring out the Zoe he remembered. To untwist her hair and gently tug on a tight coil the way he used to before saying something to make her full lips part with unabashed laughter.

"No need to apologize," Byron said. "Thank you for taking the time to meet me. I was afraid your neighbor was going to call the police."

Zoe chuckled and some of the old spark came back to

her eyes. "Who? Mrs. Morgan? Don't worry. She called me as soon as you pulled up. I told her I knew you were there and that you were just waiting on me." She turned back to the car and grabbed her purse along with a leather messenger bag.

Byron hurried over and held out a hand. "Well, she eyed me as if I were about to steal something."

She handed over the messenger bag with a grateful look. "That's why I love her. No one is sneaking up on my place. I've got to get something else." Zoe leaned across her driver's seat to reach for something on the passenger side.

One of her legs lifted off the garage's cement floor. The back of her dark purple skirt rose and provided an enticing view of the rich brown skin on the back of her thigh. Byron quickly looked away before his body reacted. Not just his body, but his entire being. One glimpse of those dark brown eyes, and that dimple in her left cheek and he'd been transported back fifteen years. Back when he'd been a college sophomore who'd fallen hard and fast just from a flash of her smile.

He wasn't supposed to still be attracted to her. He'd grown up. He'd moved on. He wasn't guided by his dick. So he shouldn't feel nervous and jittery just because the woman he used to have a crush on was near.

"Got it." Zoe straightened from the vehicle with a stack of multiple folders in her arms.

"What's all that?" He closed the SUV door for her.

Zoe shifted the items in her arms for a better grip. "I've got some work I really need to do."

He averted his eyes. He shouldn't have pulled her away from her job. She had a life, and here he was about to upend everything. When Zoe had walked away years ago, he'd been hurt at first. In the years since, he'd understood why she'd chosen to go away and get her life together on her own instead of taking his offer. He'd promised himself he wouldn't interfere anymore. He'd respected her wishes and left her alone. Yet, here he was about to ask her for something that would change everything.

"Zoe, I'm sorry. I really didn't plan to ever come back into your life."

She paused in the middle of reaching for the door leading from the garage into her house to stare at him over her shoulder, her brows drawn together. "Don't apologize. After what you did for me, leaving work early is the least I can do for you."

Byron nodded and hoped she still believed that after he told her everything. When she opened the door, the alarm beeped and a robotic voice said, "Garage door." Zoe hurried to the keypad across the mudroom they'd entered and tapped a few of the keys. The beeping stopped as the alarm was disabled.

"Come on in," she said.

He followed her into the kitchen where she dumped the files onto the table. Her kitchen was clean. No dirty dishes in the sink or on the table. She'd decorated the space in bright primary colors, red, yellow and blue bowls and plates adding personality to the white appliances and slate-colored countertops.

"Do you want something to drink? I have juice, soda and water. I've also got snacks. I keep them in the house in case Lilah gets hungry after school. Not just chips, but fruit and stuff, you know?"

Zoe went to the pantry and pulled out a bag with an assortment of chips, then to the fridge where she studied the contents inside. Byron smiled to himself and walked over to her. Just like in college, Zoe tended to ramble when she was nervous. As if no time had passed, he did what he'd done back then. He placed a hand on her shoulder and gave a light squeeze.

"Chill, Zoe, we'll figure this out."

She stiffened like concrete beneath his touch. Byron immediately dropped his hand. He'd gone on autopilot instead of being rational. They hadn't seen each other in years. Could they even still consider themselves friends?

"Sorry, I shouldn't have touched you," he said.

She closed the fridge and faced him. "It's been forever. It feels weird. Why does it feel weird?"

"The last time I saw you I'd asked you to marry me. The next day you were gone." He kept his voice even and tried not to show how much her disappearing had hurt.

She raised her brows and gave a soft laugh. "Yeah, that would make this visit kind of awkward." She ran a hand over her hair. "About that…"

Byron shook his head. "Let's not go rehashing the past. You leaving was for the best."

The line between her brows returned. He recognized the look on her face. She hadn't expected that response. Her frown usually meant she was about to argue with him. Would she say she regretted leaving? His breathing stuttered, and a nervous anticipation flooded his veins. What would he even say to that?

Her face cleared, and she placed a hand to her chest. "Thank you for saying that." Relief filled her voice. "You helped me out, and I always imagined you hating me for not going through with things."

His shoulders relaxed, but he wasn't relieved. How often

had he wondered if even a small part of Zoe regretted leaving him? Now, like before, he was reminded that the feelings between them had always been one-sided.

"I couldn't hate you," he said. The words were the truth. He'd been hurt that she'd run away, missed her because they'd been cool, and angry she hadn't told him to his face. But he'd never hated her for making the decision.

"That's what your mother said." Zoe turned back to the fridge and pulled out a pitcher filled with red juice. "She told me you'd eventually understand why I left and that you wouldn't be mad." She held up the pitcher. "Tropical punch-flavored Kool-Aid. I know you can't turn that down."

That was his favorite flavor. Their favorite flavor. She'd always had some in her fridge in college, and she'd pour him a glass when he'd come over to study. Even though good memories tried to come back, what she'd said snatched his attention.

"Hold up, my mom knew you were leaving?" His mom had acted just as surprised to find out Zoe had left as he'd been.

Zoe hesitated as she poured their drinks. "She was the one who talked me into going."

Byron blinked. "She what?" The words burst from his lips. No way. This had to be a mistake. His mother had convinced him not to look for Zoe. She'd said if Zoe was willing to run off without saying a word of thanks then he was better off without her in his life. "That can't be right."

Zoe walked over and held out one of the glasses toward him. "Look, Byron, I don't know what your mom said after I left, but what happened back then is something we can sort out another day. The more important thing is who's looking for me and threatening to reveal the truth."

A dozen questions bounced around Byron's mind. He wanted an answer to every single one, but Zoe was right. They had more pressing issues. He could figure out what had really happened later.

Byron took the cup from her. "His name is Carlton Powell. He's a shady private investigator. At the time Dominic came looking for you to find out if my name was on the birth certificate, someone had also hired Carlton to look for you. We convinced Carlton to say he hadn't found you."

Zoe pulled out a chair at the kitchen table and sank heavily into the seat. "Who sent him?"

Byron sat opposite her. He gripped the cup to stop himself from reaching out to squeeze her shoulder again. His touch was weird to her. He didn't want to invade her space. "We don't know who hired him. He wouldn't tell us."

"It's Kendell. I know it's him." Her voice was steady, but her hands trembled.

"He's still in prison." Byron had asked Dominic to verify her ex's release date. They still had five months before they had to worry about Kendell. Theoretically. First, they had to prove he wasn't bankrolling Carlton's investigation.

"That doesn't mean anything. He had connections with some pretty bad people before he went. His mom blamed me pressing charges against him for domestic violence as the reason why the police found out about the rest of his criminal ties. I'm sure he's the reason she said that." She placed her forehead in her hand. "I knew things couldn't be this easy forever. I'd hoped that after all the time passed he'd get over it."

"We don't know it's him."

She lifted her head and glared at him. "Who else would be looking for me, Byron?" she snapped.

"Who else knows you said I was Lilah's father?" The words came out harder than he'd planned. Her distress fueled his own. He hated not knowing who was after them. Her ex was the obvious choice, but Byron wasn't about to put on blinders and not consider all options. He softened his tone when he spoke again. "Anyone from college who knew could have heard of my campaign and wondered why I didn't have you and a kid by my side."

She closed her eyes and blew out a heavy breath.

"My bad, I didn't mean to sound so…"

"I get it. This is stressful."

Zoe ran a finger over a groove in the white tabletop. Her nails were short, rounded and painted a pastel neutral color. He'd liked that about her. The way her hands were always neat and manicured. Her touch always soft and comforting. "I asked you to say she was yours, and you did. Even though I ran off before I had her, I always understood what a big deal it was for you to go along with my story."

Big deal was an understatement. He'd gotten into a fight with Kendell. His parents had called him young, naive and ridiculously romantic before hiring a lawyer to make sure no charges were ever pressed against Byron as a result of the fight. He'd asked her to marry him, and without an ounce of regret, told his parents they'd have to accept his decision because he loved Zoe and wanted to protect her. When she'd left neither his mom nor dad had ever said *I told you so*, but he'd seen those words in their eyes every time they looked at him in the weeks after Zoe disappeared. He'd never felt so foolish and so inexperienced.

"Lilah knows the truth."

Byron shifted back, stunned. "She does?"

"When she was younger, I didn't answer questions about her dad, but when she turned twelve, I felt she would understand. Plus, I wanted her to know what you did for us. I never told her your name because I didn't want her to go looking for you."

"Why not?" He shouldn't be surprised. She hadn't wanted him to be a part of her life, so why would she want her daughter to be a part of his?

"Even though thirteen years have passed, I always knew in my heart that if something happened to me and she needed something you'd help her. You've done so much for us already, I didn't want you to feel as if going along with my secret came along with expectations of you acting like Lilah's real father."

Byron clasped his hands in front of him. "I would have helped her, and it wouldn't have been because of expectations. We were friends, Zoe. I hope we can still be friends."

She smiled and something in her dark eyes told him she hoped the same. The late-night talks after study sessions, the laughter at their inside jokes, the way she'd call him Pretty Ricky to tease him about his pretty-boy style or a spoiled rich kid whenever he acted like one were things he'd once depended on. He hadn't been aware of that missing piece of his life until this moment.

Zoe cleared her throat and glanced away. "So you think someone could be looking for me to get to you?"

Byron jumped at the chance to get back to the point of this conversation. "It's a possibility. Other people knew the story from college. They heard the lie we told. Anyone could have mentioned it to a reporter, or someone connected to my opponent. This could be a way to dig up old dirt and slander my name."

The idea seemed to take some of the worry out of her eyes. "What do you want me to do?"

He took a sip of the Kool-Aid and wished it was something stronger. He needed fortification for what he was about to ask her to do. "We have to tell the story before anyone else does."

He'd come up with the idea right after Carlton walked away. This was the best way to beat the jerk at his own game. People like Carlton were only pacified for a short time.

She blinked a few times and shook her head. "You want to claim paternity?" She let out a disbelieving laugh. "Seriously?"

He was serious and had no idea how this would play out. He could only imagine the heart attack Roy would have. Not to mention his dad's head might actually explode. Despite all that, this was the only path forward he could see. Not just to save his own political career, but also to protect Zoe. He would never forget the fear in Zoe's eyes the night she'd asked him for help. He couldn't reveal the truth about Lilah's father, and potentially put Zoe and her daughter in jeopardy. He'd won the primary against an opponent who hadn't gone for his personal life. The race to the Senate would be far uglier. If someone started spreading rumors about Byron and Zoe, he'd have to address this regardless. Something had to be said so why not carry out the lie?

"How would we even do this?" she asked, not sounding the least bit convinced this was a good idea. "I don't want to drag Lilah into a political mess."

The tension in his neck eased slightly. At least she hadn't immediately said no. "If we do things the right way, calmly and with a good story, then it'll blow over before the next news cycle."

Doubt clouded her eyes. She was probably visualizing all the complications that might come with being involved in a political campaign. A part of him wanted to say never mind. To tell Dominic and Roy to figure out a way to make any ties he had with Zoe disappear.

The part of him that wanted to win this seat couldn't do that. That part of him also knew his opponent would catch word of this and spin things into something ugly. The opposition would paint Zoe in a negative light, drag the truth of Lilah's paternity through every shady media outlet they could find, and not bat an eye about making a young girl's life a living hell. Byron couldn't afford to let any surprises pop up in his campaign and kill his chances. Not even lingering affection for Zoe.

He went with what used to work whenever he needed her on his side and reached out to place his hand over hers. Her eyes shot up to his. Byron's pulse sped up. He swallowed and pushed away the ridiculous fluttering in his midsection. This was business, not personal. Zoe would make her own choices, and not once had she ever chosen him. He'd be better off remembering that.

"Please, Zoe. I'll use all my resources to limit the impact on you and Lilah. Too much is at stake if we don't do something. I need you to consider this for me."

She pulled her hand back and rubbed the back of her neck. Hesitation still in her eyes before she sighed. "Can you give me until the end of the week? There are some things I need to do before I give you an answer."

He'd come to have an answer before going back to Jackson Falls, but he wouldn't push. "The end of the week it is."

CHAPTER FOUR

ZOE BARELY HAD time to process everything in the short time between Byron's leaving and her needing to pick up Lilah from school. As much as she didn't want to become a part of Byron's campaign, she'd known this day was coming. Known she'd have to contend with leaving the spot blank on her daughter's birth certificate.

Without a father listed Kendell could return, request a DNA test and fight to have himself listed as a legal guardian of their daughter. If she admitted the truth then Byron wouldn't have to be named, his campaign could go on unbothered and he could walk away just as she'd walked away all those years ago. Except he didn't want to walk away. He wanted to continue to keep their secret even though claiming a child now could cost him the election.

The thought poked at the soft spot in her heart she'd always carried for him. Byron was still out to save the world. She'd thought he was full of shit when they'd first met in college. No way the pretty rich boy who had almost every girl on campus tripping over themselves to get close to him was really into community service and volunteerism. In the end he'd proved her wrong. She'd grown to respect and like him. So much so, she'd been willing to accept Kendell's anger every time she brought up Byron's name. Byron's always dating someone from the high society group was the only reason Kendell didn't believe he really was a threat.

Lilah came bounding out of the school in her blue plaid uniform, a bright smile on her young face and her best friend, Julie, by her side. Zoe's heart squeezed with love and a fierce protectiveness every time she saw her daughter. Lilah's dark skin, wide, expressive eyes and ready smile was evidence Zoe had given her child a better life than she'd had. Lilah wouldn't grow up fearing what type of shitstorm she'd walk into whenever she went home. She'd be confident, know her self-worth and what love wasn't, so she'd never become prey to a man like Kendell.

Lilah spotted Zoe in the SUV and waved. She said something to her friend, and they laughed and hugged before Lilah jogged over to the car. Her long, dark braids swung around her shoulders. A boy stopped Lilah on her way to the car. He said something that made her daughter light up like a Christmas tree before giving her a small envelope and walking off.

Zoe's brows drew together. At thirteen, Lilah was definitely at the interested-in-boys stage of her development. That boy, T.J. Dawkins, was the one who garnered all of her daughter's attention. Lilah hadn't claimed T.J. as her boyfriend, but Zoe feared the declaration was coming soon.

God, I'm not ready for that.

Lilah pushed a few braids behind her ear and watched T.J. walk away for a second before continuing to the car. Zoe cleared up her frown and greeted Lilah with a smile and a kiss as she got in the car.

"How was school?" Zoe asked as she eased her car into the flow of traffic leaving the school.

"Same as always. I did great on my science test today

and got an A on my English paper." Lilah tore open the envelope and scanned the small card inside.

"What's that?" Zoe glanced over but couldn't make out anything before she had to focus on the road again.

"An invitation," Lilah said, sounding distracted.

"To what? I saw T.J. give it to you."

Lilah turned in her seat. "Spying on me?" she said in a teasing tone.

"You're mine, aren't you? That gives me the right to meddle in your life as much as I want," Zoe replied, matching her daughter's tone.

Lilah rolled her eyes but laughed. "He's having a pool party for his birthday. He said he wants me to come."

Pool party? Teenagers hopped up on hormones they were still learning how to deal with and bathing suits. As soon as the thought crossed her mind Zoe chastised herself. Lilah and her group of friends were responsible. All of Zoe's internet sleuthing and undercover monitoring of Lilah's cell phone proved that much. She wanted Zoe to go out, make friends and have fun. She wasn't quite ready for an at-home pool party with the boy Lilah was hung up on.

"What did you tell him?"

Lilah raised a shoulder. "I told him I'd think about it, and that I have to see if we have anything planned for that weekend."

Zoe's hands loosened the death grip on the steering wheel. "Let him sweat a little."

"Exactly. T.J. is the cutest guy in school, but I don't want him to think I'm pressed to be his girlfriend or anything."

Yes, yes, thank the Lord, yes! "Well, let me know when you make up your mind." Zoe kept her inner celebration hidden and replied in an even, disinterested tone. Every time her daughter listened to her advice instead of succumbing to the *pick me* attitude toward boys Zoe used to have, was reason to celebrate. Parenting was hard, getting her kid to grow stronger where she'd been weak was harder and Zoe was going to rejoice after every damn win.

Lilah chatted about school and the latest drama with her friends on the rest of the ride home. When they pulled into the garage, Lilah jumped out of the car and rushed into the house to change for archery practice. The previous fall Zoe and Lilah had attended an outdoor women's retreat where they'd tried out a variety of new things like camping, fishing, outdoor cooking and archery. Lilah had fallen in love with the sport, and after begging Zoe for a bow and arrow for Christmas, Zoe decided that lessons would come first before committing to purchasing all the equipment. Six months later and her daughter's enthusiasm hadn't faltered.

Zoe followed Lilah up the stairs. After practice Lilah would have homework before going to bed. If she didn't talk to her about Byron's visit and his request now, she'd keep putting it off.

"Hey, Lilah, you got a second? I need to talk to you about something."

Lilah was rummaging through one of the drawers probably looking for something to change into for practice. She glanced over her shoulder. "Sure. Can we talk while I change, or is this a *talk* talk?"

Zoe sat on the edge of Lilah's bed. "It's about your father."

Lilah hesitated for a beat before going back to pulling things out of the drawer. "My real dad or the guy who agreed to say he was my dad?" Lilah asked with a hint of sarcasm.

Zoe had hoped that by telling the truth and revealing her own mistakes her daughter would avoid similar situations. Lilah had asked a dozen questions. Mostly about Byron, although she hadn't given Lilah his name. A smart decision in hindsight since Lilah wanted to meet him, and a quick Google search could have given Lilah everything she needed to contact him.

As for her real dad, thankfully, Lilah wanted nothing to do with the man who'd hurt her mom.

"Both, actually," Zoe answered. She paused for a heartbeat. Once she gave Zoe his name and what he wanted, there was no going back. "Byron...the man who said he was your father. He was here earlier today."

Lilah spun around. "He was here? Like, in this house?" Her eyes were wide. Her voice high pitched with excitement and disbelief.

"Yes."

"Where is he now?" Lilah looked over Zoe's shoulder toward the hall as if Byron would magically appear.

"He's gone back to his home in North Carolina."

Although Byron had agreed to give her to the end of the week, she could tell he'd hoped for an immediate answer. She appreciated his not pushing her into making a quick decision. She wanted to help Byron, and she damn sure wanted to keep her secret. She just couldn't move forward without thinking about all of the consequences. Not considering consequences when she was younger had been part of her problem.

"What? Why? Mom, did you send him away?" Lilah accused.

"No, I didn't send him away." Zoe didn't want to think about how much a part of her wanted him to stay longer, catch up, talk the way they used to. "He came here because he needs something from us."

"Something like what?" For the first time suspicion entered Lilah's tone. Another thing Zoe had taught her. Always wonder what someone wants when they approach you for help.

"He's running for Senate, and apparently his connection with me, and you, is coming up." She waved Lilah over to sit on the edge of the bed next to her and gave her the quick rundown. Leaving out the part about threatening emails and the possibility her real father may be looking for her. Until they found out who'd hired the other private investigator Zoe didn't want to scare Lilah. She'd left that out with Byron, too. She still wasn't sure if the emails were anything to worry about or not.

"He wanted me to give him an answer today, but I asked him to give me until the end of the week." Before he'd left, Byron mentioned if she wanted to she could come to his home in Jackson Falls, North Carolina, that weekend to talk things out.

Lilah shook her head and grabbed Zoe's arm. "No, Mom, you need to do this. Call him. Go up there."

Zoe immediately regretted mentioning Byron's parting words in her recap to Lilah. She understood his reasoning. Getting ahead of the lie was best for both of them, but that didn't mean she was ready to face that reality right now. "If I go, it'll put a damper on our weekend. I promised you we'd go to Atlanta."

"Mom, who cares about Atlanta," Lilah said with an eye roll. "You have to go."

That was not the answer she'd expected. "Did you not hear the part about a political campaign for a national office? Lilah, if I go and agree to anything then people will dig into our life."

Lilah did not look impressed or concerned with the idea of people looking into their past. "They'll dig and find what? You're a safety person at some plastics plant, and I'm a thirteen-year-old who spends more time with my recurve bow than anyone else. There's nothing to find."

Nothing except Zoe's terrible relationship with Lilah's father, her parents' own rocky marriage and subsequent not quite legal separation. Other than those things Zoe's life was pretty basic and routine. She liked the mundane quality of her life. Mundane equaled structure and security. Being a part of a campaign would be far from mundane, and she'd have to relive all of the mistakes of her past.

"There's the matter of your real father," Zoe said. "If he sees us, he may try to come back."

"Who cares. You already said that your friend Byron wants to say he's my dad. He'll be able to protect me the way he protected you."

Zoe held up a hand and shook her head. "Hold up, let's not get ahead of ourselves. This isn't going to make Byron your real dad or turn him into a knight in shining armor. He's engaged to someone else. He has his own life."

"But as soon as you were in trouble he dropped everything to come here and warn you. I bet he doesn't love her." Lilah jumped up from the bed and went back to the clothes search.

Zoe's mouth opened and closed before her thoughts came together. "Lilah, this isn't something to make assumptions about. If I do this it will only be to help him for the campaign. We'll make it as quick and painless and possible before we go back to our normal lives. Whether or not Byron loves or doesn't love his fiancée doesn't matter. He has one, which means we'll also have to figure out how to get along with her." She stood and went over to Lilah. She placed her hands on her daughter's slim shoulders and made her face her. "This isn't a game or something we can jump into with unrealistic expectations. Doing this changes everything. It'll be several months, maybe even until the end of the campaign, before things go back to normal."

Lilah sighed but nodded. "I understand all of that. I know this doesn't make him my real dad. But Mom, let's be honest. It would be easier for him to just tell the truth and be done with us. He didn't want to do that, and if he wins, he can't just ignore his 'daughter.'" She made air quotes with the word *daughter*. "He'll be in our life."

The idea should have made Zoe panic. She was nervous, unsure and wary, but she wasn't panicked. If the emails were a threat, and if Kendell did consider trying to come back in their life, then having Byron on their side, even if it was superficial, might be enough to keep Kendell away. As much as she hated to have to depend on his help again, she would take whatever options were available to keep Lilah safe.

"He'll be on the edges of our life," Zoe said. "Not all the way in it."

Lilah shifted until Zoe dropped her hands. "Fine. But you need to go up there. Don't just say no and use Atlanta as the excuse. You always complain about Atlanta traffic anyway. At least go and find out what he really wants. Okay? I'm fine with going to the aquarium another weekend."

Zoe watched her daughter closely. She hadn't expected Lilah to be so excited about this situation with Byron. Her daughter was just as private as she was. She'd kind of hoped Lilah would say no way and then Zoe could go back to Byron with a valid reason not to agree with another larger-than-life secret. There was always telling the truth, but the truth came with another set of concerns she never wanted to touch Lilah.

She could go and find out what he had to say. If they agreed that keeping the lie going was the best step, then she'd just have to try and limit the time Lilah and Byron spent together. Her daughter wanted a father, but Zoe didn't want Lilah too attached to a man who was promised to another woman. The last thing she needed on top of all this drama was for Lilah to think something would happen between her and Byron.

Not like that would be such a bad thing.

No way. She was not going there. Today's attraction was a mixture of nostalgia and too long since her last relationship. Byron was handsome and she could appreciate that without losing her mind.

"Fine, I'll go, but I'm making no promises."

CHAPTER FIVE

BYRON DROVE THE three hours back home after leaving Zoe's place instead of going to his family's estate in Jackson Falls, North Carolina. The Robidoux Estate was the place where his grandfather had built the tobacco empire that they all benefited from today and was his unofficial campaign headquarters. He was sure his family's home was buzzing with activity. Roy and his dad strategizing over the latest developments. Dominic updating the family and providing recommendations on the best way to deal with Carlton's blackmail threats. Elaina would be wound tighter than a rusted spring after hearing about India and Travis eloping, and was probably driving the household staff to the brink of revolt with her excessive demands.

Byron didn't want to deal with any of that. He'd called Roy on the drive back home and gotten an update on their thoughts on revealing India and Travis's marriage. Luckily, the family had already prepared for the announcement; they just had to move up the timeline a bit. He'd let Roy know Zoe wanted to help with her part in the story. He left out the part about Zoe needing to think things over before agreeing to go along with the plan. He just hoped she'd take up his offer and come to Jackson Falls that weekend. All he wanted now was to get home, shower and get in his bed. His shoulders ached from the hours of driving, his eyes were tired and he'd sat for so long his back was stiff.

Yet, anticipation buzzed beneath his exhaustion. Something he knew would prevent him from focusing on work or allowing him to shut down his brain and fall asleep. Thirteen years had passed, and he still felt as if he'd been hit with an electric charge after spending time with Zoe.

He pulled onto his street. He lived in a modest townhome closer to downtown. He wanted to be out of the prying eyes of his family and close to the actual campaign headquarters. The energy in downtown was more his speed than the relaxed atmosphere at the estate. When he'd been younger everything in town closed at nine during the week and six on Sundays. Even though it was after ten there were people on the street coming and going from the downtown restaurants, coffee shops and bars. Jackson Falls was growing, and he liked being in the middle of the changes.

A silver Volvo was parked right outside his garage, and the lights glowed behind the closed custom blinds of his windows. Byron's hands tightened on the steering wheel. He took a long, deep breath as he pulled in behind the car. Rolling his head back he counted to ten and prepared himself.

He'd given Yolanda a key to his place right after proposing to her. They'd decided not to move in together before the wedding but agreed giving each other free access made their relationship more believable. They hadn't exchanged keys with the expectation of the other person popping in, unannounced, whenever they wanted.

"Which means she's pissed," he grumbled to himself as he cut the engine.

He got out of the car and entered his place through the garage. The house was quiet except for the sounds of the television in the den. Byron slipped off his shoes and set them on the shoe rack by the door next to Yolanda's beige pumps. He dropped his keys on the kitchen counter and went into the connected den.

Yolanda sat on the corner of his couch and flipped channels on the television. She didn't look at him as he entered. She sat stiffly, her shoulders rigid and her finger pressing hard as she changed channels.

"What's wrong, Yolanda?" Byron asked. He rubbed his eyes and fought not to sigh. He wasn't in the mood to figure out what bothered her. Might as well get straight to the point.

"I don't know, Byron. Why don't you tell me what's wrong?" She didn't look at him. She jabbed the buttons on the remote so hard he'd be surprised if they didn't get stuck.

"I've had a long day. Something came up with the campaign, and I'm trying to fix it."

Yolanda tossed the remote onto the coffee table and stood. "What's her name?"

"Whose name?" he asked, keeping his cool. He didn't think Roy would have told Yolanda about the blackmail or the problem with Zoe. Byron hadn't mentioned anything to Yolanda because he'd wanted to know exactly what they were dealing with before bringing her in.

Yolanda crossed her arms. "The woman you're seeing."

Byron rubbed his beard and looked to the ceiling. "I'm not seeing anyone," he said slowly.

"We promised we wouldn't start anything like that. Especially during this campaign," she continued as if he hadn't spoken. "Now you're disappearing for a day, your campaign manager doesn't know where you are and you return at—" she checked her watch "—after ten and you expect me to believe you aren't seeing anyone else."

He held up his hands in a "hold up" gesture. "Come on, Yolanda—"

"No, you come on!" She pointed a finger at him. "We are in this to win. We made a deal to do everything necessary to get you to the Senate. If you mess this up because you can't keep your dick in your pants—"

"I'm not sleeping with her." He cut in before she got going.

Yolanda was used to arguing her case and winning. It was one of the reasons he'd originally been attracted to her. They'd debated the outcome of a recent legal case on their first date and with every articulated cut she'd made to his argument, he'd wanted her even more. He still couldn't believe what started out as a no-strings-attached fling had turned into an engagement. That he was following in his grandfather's footsteps and marrying for convenience and political ties.

It's not as if you'd rather marry for love.

Yolanda's chin lifted. "Who is she?" she asked in a cool, detached voice.

Yolanda was angry, but she didn't look hurt. Her voice didn't waver. Her shoulders didn't slump in defeat. He'd seen that same look on her when she deliberated a case and was faced with an unwanted problem she had to solve.

Byron pointed toward the chair. "You're going to want to sit down for this one."

She eyed him coolly for several long seconds. Her eyes narrowed when he didn't back down under her glare. She finally lowered to the edge of the couch. Byron sat next to her on the chair.

"I was in Greenville, South Carolina, today. I went there to see an old college friend. Her name is Zoe Hammond."

"Why did you go see an old college friend?" Yolanda's voice dripped with sarcasm. "Did you have to plan your next reunion?"

"I went there because thirteen years ago she told her abusive boyfriend I was the father of her child, and in order to protect her, I went along with it."

Yolanda slid back. Her jaw slowly fell open as if she needed time to process the words. She closed her mouth, pointed at him and parted her lips to say something, then closed her mouth again. She took a long breath and tilted her head to the side. "Come again?"

He understood her confusion and disbelief. The story was outrageous, but Yolanda knew him well enough to realize he wouldn't joke about something like this. She listened as Byron told her the truth. Starting from the day Zoe ran to him for help and ending with asking Zoe to come to Jackson Falls to reveal Lilah as his daughter. She only interrupted him to ask a few clarification questions. By the time he finished, Yolanda had leaned forward, elbows on her knees, and her forehead in her hand.

She shook her head and groaned. "If ever there was a time I wished I hadn't quit smoking this definitely ranks among the top ones."

"I was going to tell you."

Her head lifted. She frowned at him. "When? Right before you had a press conference revealing a baby that isn't really yours?"

He deserved that, even if he wouldn't have waited that long to tell her. "I was going to tell you tomorrow. First, I had to figure out what was going on."

"You don't have to do this. Just tell the truth. Let everyone know the kid isn't yours and we can move on."

Byron shook his head. "You don't know her ex. He was involved in organized crime, and he's scheduled to get out soon. If I tell the truth, it's going to make headlines and possibly put her in danger."

"So our campaign has to suffer just to protect her?" Yolanda asked incredulously. "I didn't sign up for this, Byron."

He took her hand in his before she could get up and start pacing. "You knew the type of person I was when we agreed to do this. You know I can't just leave someone out in the cold like this. I made a promise to Zoe. Besides, you of all people should understand the type of risk she'd take by backtracking her story now. You've volunteered at the women's shelter. You've seen the way some guys never let go of a perceived wrong. If I tell the truth now and something happens to her... I wouldn't be able to forgive myself."

Yolanda slipped her hand away from his. "Byron, how can we possibly spin this to make it sound better?"

"We'll figure out something, but I can't do it without you." He was a Robidoux. If his family was good at anything it was making things go the way they wanted. He realized doing this was going to make his campaign harder, but he also knew he could make this work. He'd find a way to protect Zoe and Lilah, win the Senate seat and keep Yolanda happy. He'd maneuvered his way out of tough situations before. None as tough as this, but he didn't doubt his abilities completely.

The can't-do-it-without-you must have worked because Yolanda's shoulders relaxed and the frost in her eyes melted into the calculating gleam that had drawn him to her in the first place. "You can't keep secrets like this from me. The promises you made to her were over a decade ago. You recently promised me that we would be a team. We'd work together to make this campaign a success. Hiding things like this is not a partnership."

Byron slid closer to Yolanda. "You're right. There's nothing I can say to make keeping you in the dark better."

He met her eyes and tried his best to look chastised. He was tired, and wanted to go to bed, but he made the effort in order to get Yolanda to go along with this. She blinked prettily and leaned forward until her lips nearly touched his.

"Do you still love her?"

Byron jerked back. Love? Where had that come from? Byron Robidoux didn't play the love game. "What? No. Of course not. I didn't love her then. We were friends. That's all."

The lie slid easily off his lips. He'd told himself that enough over the years that saying the words no longer felt like a kick to the gut. He didn't want to think about Zoe being the first and only woman to work her way into his heart. The first and only woman to break it.

Yolanda raised a brow. "Just friends wouldn't do all that you did for her."

He met Yolanda's gaze dead on. "There is nothing for you to worry about. I have to get ahead of this story before Carlton comes out with something worse, and I'd prefer to do it without putting Zoe's life in danger. Will you stick by me while I do this?"

She searched his face before nodding. "I will, but first you have to make another promise."

"Anything." Relief flooded his voice. He hadn't been sure Yolanda would understand or agree. He should have known she wouldn't give up the opportunity for the future they'd envisioned because someone like Carlton threatened them.

"Promise me that if at any moment you start to feel anything for this woman other than friendship, you'll tell me straight up. I'm willing to accept an affair after we've made it to the Senate, but not before, and not one that's going to make me look like an idiot."

For a second he thought about what it would be like if he and Yolanda had chosen each other for love instead of mutual benefit. They had fondness, and obviously there was chemistry, but every time he expected her to show any signs her feelings were more than superficial, she displayed cold pragmatism. The realization sent another wave of relief. He didn't want Yolanda falling in love and expecting more from him. Not when he knew he could never trust her with his heart. Yolanda was too calculating to see love from him as anything other than a weakness.

"Nothing is going to happen." He articulated each word. His gaze and voice unwavering. He needed her, and the part of him that tried to spark to life after seeing Zoe would eventually understand that he couldn't afford to fall for Zoe again.

"Promise me. The second you feel anything. Tell me," she reiterated.

"I promise you." When she nodded he took her hand in his. "And there will be no affairs. Not before or after."

The risk of scandal was too great. He wouldn't go this far and agree to do everything possible to win the Senate seat to give it up for a quick thrill. The attraction between him and Yolanda would have to be enough. If it faded, then hopefully she'd be willing to work with him to rekindle things.

She smiled at him. A small knowing smile right before she lifted her hand to his cheek. "Let's just get through this campaign, okay?"

He chuckled softly at her patronizing tone before kissing the inside of her hand. He didn't need to rethink his words. As much as he loved his father, Byron remembered the hurt his mother had tried to hide whenever Grant visited his mistress. His now fiancée. When Byron asked his mom why she allowed it, her only answer was that she couldn't give their dad everything he needed. No matter how much she said she was okay with Grant's infidelity, Byron never wanted to put that look in another woman's eyes. If he married Yolanda, it would be with the goal of never humiliating her.

He leaned in and kissed her softly. As their lips brushed, a vision of Zoe from earlier filled his brain. That and a quiet whisper of uncertainty. Even if Byron forsook all temptation on his part, Yolanda never made the promise to do the same.

CHAPTER SIX

AFTER WORKING LATE all week to complete the items Miranda asked for after her presentation and rearranging schedules, Zoe was able to drop off Lilah at her best friend Julie's house Saturday morning before making her way to Jackson Falls. The girls had met in fourth grade and had quickly become best friends. Zoe had gotten to know Julie's mom, Victoria, and they developed a deep friendship. Victoria was also the survivor of an abusive relationship and understood how important is was to know and trust the people her kid was around. With little to no relationship with her mother and her sister living far away, Victoria and Julie were the family she and Lilah had created.

Byron had given her directions to his family's estate in Jackson Falls instead of his campaign office. She was buzzed in through the gated drive and gasped as the house came into view down the long, tree-lined drive. She'd known Byron was rich, but damn. She hadn't known his family lived in a modern castle. *Did he live there by himself?*

The home reminded her of one of those English countryside estates she'd seen in movies. The symmetrical multistory stone structure featured rows of tall windows along the front. Columns framed the door. What could only be described as possible additional wings with tall chimneys jutted out in perfect symmetry on the left and right side of the main part of the home.

She parked and prayed her SUV didn't leak a drop of oil on the pristine white, circular drive. She'd left early enough to drop off Lilah and not feel rushed on the interstate, which had her arriving before midday. When she'd called Byron to let him know she was coming, his reply had been pleasantly surprised and relieved, but not excited. Not that she blamed him. One lie she'd told was still affecting him years later. He'd texted her the address and said they'd meet this morning. She wasn't sure if the rest of the family expected her or what she was about to walk into.

The door was answered by an older black woman who could be anywhere between forty and sixty. Her dark brown hair was closely cut in a stylish fashion, and a kind smile graced her face. She wore a light blue button-up shirt with the name Sandra stitched on the right side and a pair of khaki-colored slacks.

"You must be Zoe," the woman said. "I'm Sandra, the head of housekeeping for the Robidoux family. Mr. Byron and the rest of his team are expecting you."

Mr. Byron? Zoe's stomach flipped and her hands became sweaty. He wasn't just Byron or Pretty Ricky here. He was Mr. Byron. The owner of this estate. A potential future senator for the country. The other day he'd still reminded her of her old friend, and she'd been nervous but confident she could trust him in this process. Now…now she wondered if Future Senator Byron Robidoux was still the same guy she'd once trusted.

"Thank you, Sandra," Zoe said. Her voice came out light and reedy. She cleared her throat. *Do not let them intimi-*

date or overrun you. "Where are we meeting?" Her voice was clear and stronger with the question.

"This way," Sandra said. She led Zoe down the hallway to a thick wooden door. Sandra knocked two times before turning the handle and entering without waiting for a response. "Ms. Zoe Hammond is here."

If butterflies weren't having a disco party in her stomach, Zoe would have chuckled at the formality of being announced. Zoe thanked Sandra again and took what felt like the longest step of her life by crossing the threshold into the room. An honest-to-goodness conference room. Complete with gleaming dark wood table, bookshelves on the wall filled from top to bottom, a huge flat-panel television along another wall and a window that overlooked what Zoe assumed was the backyard terrace.

She did chuckle at this. A conference room in a house. Who did that?

Four men sat at the shining table. Three she recognized; one was a stranger. Mr. Robidoux hadn't changed much in the thirteen years since she'd last seen him. He was still the spitting image of Byron twenty years in the future. His eyes were still sharp, calculating and clouded with distrust. He'd said she wasn't right for Byron, but he would go along with his son's wishes to make him happy. A few days later he'd sat next to his wife as she laid out all the reasons Zoe should walk out of Byron's life. No word of Byron's happiness had been mentioned during that meeting.

Byron stood along with Dominic, the private investigator she'd met a year before. The fourth guy glanced at her, his watch, then back to his computer.

Alrighty then. Apparently, she already had an enemy.

"Am I late? I didn't realize you were meeting at a set

time," Zoe said unapologetically. Byron knew she was on her way and was driving several miles. If he wanted to meet at a certain time, he should have told her.

Byron shook his head. "You aren't late. We've been in here since early morning. Come in and have a seat."

Zoe nodded and went to the table. A silver tray filled with fresh fruit and pastries sat on the buffet beneath the television. Next to it was a tray covered with crystal goblets filled with a variety of liquids varying in shades from dark brown to amber and clear. A minibar in a conference room.

"Do you want something to drink?" Byron asked.

She most definitely wanted something to drink, but she wasn't about to dull her senses with alcohol. Not when she felt like she'd just walked into an interview for a job she wasn't sure she wanted. "Water if you have it."

Byron immediately moved to the tray, opened a bottle of water, and poured it into a glass. He wore a short-sleeved blush-colored button-up tucked into navy slacks. The top few buttons were open, and a gold watch gleamed on his wrist. Even on the weekend he managed to look like he could be working in the office.

"You remember my dad," Byron said, handing Zoe the glass.

Zoe nodded and took a sip of the water. "I do. Hello, Mr. Robidoux." She couldn't lie and say it was good to see him again. She'd thought her burden on the family was over the day she'd walked away from him and his wife. She'd never expected to or hoped to be in front of him, once again needing his family's assistance.

"Zoe, welcome back," he said formally.

Byron pointed to Dominic. "You know Dominic."

Byron pointed to the guy who'd given Zoe the evil eye. "This is my campaign manager, Roy Bouknight."

"Nice to meet you, Roy."

"Likewise," he said, sounding as sincere as a telemarketer with a once-in-a-lifetime deal.

Zoe looked around the room then back at Byron. "I thought we were just going to talk."

"We are, but I need the entire team here."

The entire team. Her teeth clenched and her hand tightened around the straps of her purse. She glanced at the other men in the room. Men who were ready to plan her future. Her gaze shot back to Byron. "Have you also already come up with the plans for what's next? Did you really ask me up here just to tell me how Lilah and I are going to be paraded around by your campaign and what rules I'll need to follow?"

She'd forgotten how the entire team behind the Robidoux family had tried to intimidate her before after Byron asked her to marry him until this very moment when faced with the same thing.

Byron's eyes widened. "Zoe, no, of course not. I've got an uphill battle even without the threat of blackmail. We've spent the morning talking about all the challenges I face. Now that you're here, we're ready to talk about what will work for you and Lilah."

Zoe watched him for several seconds. She looked for but didn't see any signs that he'd lied. His gaze didn't waver. Tension started to seep out of her body. Slowly, she put her purse on the table and pulled out a chair.

"Okay, let's talk." She sat down.

Byron settled into the chair next to her. They didn't touch, yet she was completely aware of him beside her.

Could smell the hint of his cologne and a brush of the heat of his body. Zoe shifted her chair a little bit away from Byron and focused on his campaign manager.

Grant's eyes were sharp and observant as he looked from her to Byron. "Well, since we are going to go with the story you…*concocted* back in college…" A huff accompanied the word *concocted*. "Of course you should be here for the discussion."

Zoe's spine stiffened. Grant spoke as if she'd made her decision for fun. Not because she'd been afraid. Or because the second she'd seen the plus sign on the pregnancy test she'd known Kendell's promise that she'd never be able to leave him was true. Or that when Kendell found her crying over the test and his hand balled into a fist as he said *It better be mine* that she realized his suspicions were her way out.

Byron leaned forward and spoke before Zoe could. "The story we both agreed to," he said in an unflinching voice.

She threw him a grateful look. Byron had been there that night. He'd seen the truth of her situation and understood her decision hadn't been a plot to trap him. To hear his unwavering support even after everything that happened sent warmth through her chest.

Grant held up a hand. "Fine. The story you two concocted. We need to make sure we do a few things. Anyone who doesn't currently know doesn't need to. We'll have to work on a plausible story that won't make voters turn against Byron." His eyes flicked to Zoe. "Or hate you."

"Why do we care if they hate me?" Zoe asked. This was Byron's campaign and she wasn't the fiancée. What voters thought about her shouldn't matter.

"Because if they hate you that dislike will spill over to

Byron. We need something that will make them sympathetic to you both." The last part came out like a concession he didn't quite agree with.

She hadn't considered that. She wasn't sure how any of this was supposed to work, but voters liking her hadn't been something she'd considered. She took another sip of water to try and calm her fluttering stomach. She turned to Byron. His eyes were calm and reassuring. Zoe took a steady breath. That was why she was here, to find out all the ramifications of going forward.

"Then what do you suggest?" Zoe asked the question of Byron instead of his father.

Byron's hand lifted as if to reach for her arm or shoulder and squeeze it the way he used to. A beat later he rested his hand on the table near hers. He leaned forward, his gaze steady. "That's why I wanted to wait on you to discuss ideas. This affects you, too."

"Do what I told you," Grant's booming voice interjected. Both Zoe and Byron jerked back and focused on him. Grant nodded before continuing. "Go with a version of the truth and tell everyone she ran off and disappeared. You found out years later that she had the baby."

Zoe's hand balled into a fist on the surface of the table. "I didn't run off. I realized marrying Byron wasn't the right thing to do."

"No truer words were ever spoken," Grant mumbled.

Roy coughed and looked through some papers. Dominic flinched and glanced out the window. Zoe's teeth clenched. She couldn't believe he would sit there and act as if her leaving Byron after everything he'd done for her had been another whim. Zoe swallowed and took a deep breath.

Arguing with Grant and flying off the handle would play right into his hands.

"Of course you'd think those words were the truth. I got them from you and your wife the night before I left." Zoe said the words clearly. Deliberately.

Grant didn't look a bit chastised. His chin lifted a little and he studied her. Measured her up. She was here to do Byron a favor, not to get in good with his father.

Byron rocked back in his chair. He ran a hand over his beard and glared at his father. "You convinced her to leave? You and Mom?"

When Grant didn't immediately answer, only stared at Zoe in challenge, she guessed that even though she'd alluded to this when she talked to Byron, he hadn't brought it up with his dad yet.

Zoe turned from Grant and gently touched Byron's forearm to get his attention. Confusion swirled in the light brown depths of his eyes. She nodded. "They convinced me to leave. They weren't wrong, Byron. We both agreed to that the other day."

"We knew you'd get over her quickly," Grant said. "And we were right. You did."

The triumphant words punched Zoe's heart a little. She hadn't expected Byron to cry and pine over her after she left. Sure, he'd said he loved her, but he'd never lacked female companionship and hadn't admitted his feelings until after she'd come to him for help. She'd assumed he was feeling an abundance of affection and protectiveness after she ran to him for help. The tiny, romantic part of her heart she tried to ignore had wondered if Byron's love had been real. Grant's words snuffed out the last little bit of nostalgia she'd had about the true meaning behind Byron's promises.

Byron drummed his fingers on the smooth surface of the table. He looked from Grant to Dominic and Roy then finally at Zoe. Tension radiating off his body. He closed his eyes and breathed in and out through his nose. "Get out," he said in a low, controlled voice.

Zoe's eyes widened. "You're kicking me out?"

Byron shook his head. "Not you." He opened his eyes and pointed at his father and the other two men on the other side of the table. "Everyone else. Out. Now."

Roy sat up straight. "Hold up, Byron, I know your dad may have upset you, but we've got to figure this stuff out."

"We will figure this out. I'm sure you've got a dozen ideas and are ready to tell me exactly what to do, but right now I need a moment alone with Zoe." His eyes never left his father's. "Everyone. Out."

Grant's eyes narrowed. Zoe didn't move as the two men stared at each other. Dominic stood first. He motioned with his head toward Roy and then toward the door. The campaign manager huffed and shook his head before standing and following Dominic out of the room. The room was silent after the two men left. Byron and Grant glared at each other. Zoe sat still, her body tight and her breathing ragged. She didn't like being alone in a room with not one, but two, angry men.

"Son—"

"Dad," Byron said, his voice sharp. He held up a hand and took another long breath. "Not now. Right now I need you to go." His voice lost some of its edge but was still firm.

Grant rose stiffly to his feet. He ran a hand down the

front of his blood-red button-up shirt then straightened the collar. After one last irritated glance in Zoe's direction he left the room.

Silence filled the space and sucked all the air out of the room. Zoe had removed her hand from Byron's arm. He sat still, eyes closed, nostrils flaring with his deep, heavy breaths. Zoe licked her lips and tried to ignore the frantic beating of her heart. Was he mad at her? Byron had never lashed out or hurt her, but he was clearly furious. She hadn't been in a room with a furious man in over thirteen years. Her stomach quaked and her palms sweated. She eased her chair slightly away from his.

Byron's head snapped her way. She didn't know what he saw in her face, but his eyes widened. He slowly backed his chair away from her, got to his feet and walked to the windows overlooking the terrace. As soon as the distance was between them, Zoe breathed easier.

"I didn't mean to scare you," Byron said, his voice apologetic.

Zoe hadn't meant to show how much they'd affected her. She hadn't expected to be frightened so easily. She closed her eyes and pressed a hand to her temple. Embarrassment heated her face. Years of self-defense and therapy were supposed to have shown her how to channel her fear. Figure out how to assess and escape potential volatile situations. Not immediately turn back into the frozen, scared rabbit she'd been all those years ago.

"I didn't realize I would react that way," she said, instead of denying her fear. That was the other thing she wouldn't do anymore. Hide her own discomfort to make someone else feel better.

He turned his head to the side and glanced at her over his shoulder. "I'll be mindful of that in the future."

She didn't want him to treat her as if she would run scared if he ever raised his voice, but she appreciated that he understood and wasn't telling her she overreacted or needed to calm down. They were both getting to know the other person again. "Thank you."

Byron looked back out the window. "Why didn't you tell me what my parents said before you left?" His voice wasn't accusatory, just curious.

She'd considered telling him because she'd known exactly what he would say and do. He'd get angry with his parents for trying to protect him. Insist they were wrong and that the two of them getting married was the right thing to do. He would have convinced her to stay, and she never would have learned to stand up on her own.

"Some of what they said was hard to hear, but when they were done, I couldn't disagree with them." She sighed and sat back in her chair. "I think the entire thing was your mom's idea. Grant had already told me he was willing to go along with what you wanted, but he didn't contradict her when she said my leaving was for the best."

Byron turned away from the window and watched her. "I'd like to disagree on that, but if I'm honest with myself I know it was her idea. Dad was confused and frustrated when I called and told him, but he understood when I finished explaining. Mom, on the other hand…" Byron ran a hand over his face and let out a humorless laugh. "She wasn't happy at all."

"I didn't think you'd care," she admitted. "I thought a part of you would be relieved."

His eyes sharpened. "Relieved?"

"I came to you with a bruised face and a bunch of drama. Kendell's gang ties ran deep. So deep I think even his mom was involved. You were this awesome, confident, cocky guy who wanted to do something great with his life and possibly save the world. You deserved better than hiding my secret."

She hadn't believed she deserved Byron's help. That she wasn't worth his sacrificing future happiness. Though she never regretted telling the lie and escaping Kendell, she couldn't bring herself to accept anything else from him.

"I deserved better? You say that as if you didn't deserve to be loved by me." His reply held a hint of frustration.

"Honestly, back then, I didn't think I deserved that." She couldn't sit as memories of how low her self-confidence had been came rushing back. How she'd believed love only came with pain, embarrassment and subjugation. She got up from her seat and walked to the other side of the table. Her hands clenched the back of one of the soft leather chairs.

"I grew up in a pretty fucked-up household. My mom always said if a man didn't hit you occasionally, then it wasn't love. I needed time to deprogram that stuff from my brain. I needed to stand on my own two feet, love myself enough to accept real love when it finally came along."

His brows drew together. "Finally came along? There you go again pretending as if my feelings weren't real."

She scoffed instead of acknowledging the stirring in her stomach from the echo of disbelief in his voice. An echo of something she'd heard the first time he'd confessed he loved her and she'd laughed because she'd found the idea unbelievable. "Come on, Byron. We know you didn't really love me. We were friends. It was a little bit of attraction, tossed in with my hero worship and some affection."

He ran a hand over his face and looked skyward before letting out a dry chuckle and shaking his head. When he looked at her again, his eyes were hot with determination. He slowly stalked toward her. Zoe's breathing stuttered, but not from fear. Sparks crackled across her skin as he drew closer. He didn't crowd her, but he stopped close enough for her to see hunger in the depths of his light brown eyes. A hunger that tightened her nipples and sent slick heat pooling between her thighs.

"What I felt for you wasn't hero worship, a small bit of affection, or a little bit of attraction." His voice was low and resonated with emotion. "Neither was the pain I felt when you walked away."

Everything stopped as the truth of his words sank into her, settled around her nerve endings and scattered foolish yearning through her veins. Not once in the time they'd known each other had Byron ever embraced her as anything more than a friend. Once he'd brushed a brief kiss across her forehead after they'd won a grant for one of their projects. She'd stayed up late into the night swearing she could still feel his lips on her forehead and dreamed about his lips on her mouth, neck, back and other places. The next time she'd seen him she'd had to fight the urge to find out if reality was anything like her dreams. The same urge pushed her now. She wanted to step closer to him, press against the strength of his body and be encircled by the warmth of his arms.

She took a small step toward him. Byron slid just a little bit closer. Their breathing resonated in the quietness of the room. Her gaze dipped to his full lower lip. One more step. If she took that last step, if she closed the distance, would he pull her into his arms?

Only one way to know for sure.

The door opened. "There you are," a woman's voice cooed. "Your daddy told me you were in here meeting with the latest fire we need to put out."

As if doused in ice water Zoe nearly jumped back from Byron. He blinked as if waking from a trance before looking over her shoulder. For a second she saw disappointment flash across his features, before the confident smile he always wore lifted his full lips.

"Don't talk like that, Yolanda." His smile remained but his voice was serious.

Yolanda sidled up next to Byron, slid her arm through his and rested her hand on his forearm just enough for the diamond on her ring finger to catch the light.

The fiancée.

Could she be any more foolish? She was no better than Lilah. Getting caught up in romantic ideas of second chances and happily-ever-afters. Byron was engaged. She'd do well to remember that and not get swept away by declarations made long ago.

"I'm sorry. You know I'm only teasing. You must be Zoe." Yolanda's voice was warm, her eyes smiling, her lips lifted in a beautiful smile.

Zoe felt sick to her stomach. She would not be that woman. The woman who came into an ex's life and fucked everything up just because of a wild thought that she deserved a second chance. Besides, Byron had never been her ex.

"I am." Zoe's voice was husky, and she cleared her throat before holding out her hand. "It's great to meet you.

Byron has told me so much about you. It's great to see my old friend so happy."

He was happy. He was in love. He was getting married.

Yolanda's head tilted. "I'm the lucky one." She grinned up at Byron. Her eyes bright with adoration. "So have we come up with a plan? As soon as Byron told me about the blackmail, I immediately said we needed to contact you and find a way to make it work. Neither of us wants you to come into any trouble. We will find a way."

Zoe glanced at Byron, but he stood stiffly next to Yolanda. He avoided eye contact with Zoe and placed a hand over Yolanda's, which still rested on his forearm.

"Thank you." Zoe's stomach soured even more. She couldn't believe she'd almost threw herself into his arms. He couldn't even look at her. He had to think she was ridiculous, sliding close to him and probably begging him with her eyes for a kiss. Now he couldn't even look her way. This is why she hadn't had a relationship in years. She didn't know jack about having a healthy one.

"Good," Yolanda beamed. "Let's call the rest of the team in here and get to work."

CHAPTER SEVEN

It ONLY TOOK two hours to come up with a story. Byron could thank Yolanda for that. She kept them on task and cut short any potential nuclear meltdowns between Zoe and his father. He had to give her credit. She was great when it came to figuring out a plan and avoiding distractions. That was one of the reasons he'd known they'd be great together. She took his abstract ideas and helped form them into a coherent plan. He should be bursting with pride and confidence about the future they'd build.

Except you almost kissed Zoe.

He hadn't been able to get that thought out of his mind. Not only had he almost kissed her, he'd spilled his feelings like he'd swallowed some truth serum, too. He couldn't believe he'd done that! He could barely look Zoe in the eye. The last thing he needed on top of everything else was for Zoe to think he wanted to sleep with her. Doing anything with Zoe would complicate the situation. He'd promised Yolanda there was nothing to worry about between him and Zoe. His life already a jumble of complications, he didn't need to add anything more.

"Why don't we take a break," Yolanda said. "I'm getting hungry, and I'm sure Zoe is tired after driving all the way to Jackson Falls this morning."

They'd just come to a truce of sorts. The story they told would be a version of the truth. Zoe and Byron had been young and in love. Byron asked Zoe to marry him, but she'd believed they were too young. After she'd left, she found out she was pregnant and chose not to tell Byron so he wouldn't feel obligated to marry her. Now someone had found out the truth and tried to blackmail Byron for something he didn't know. Close enough so they didn't have to remember too many parts and not bad enough to make everyone hate Zoe. They just had to wait for Zoe to talk things over with Lilah and agree to the plan.

"I could get out of here for a few minutes," Zoe said, her voice tired.

Guilt ran through Byron. This meeting could have waited. He shouldn't have gone immediately from her arrival to this. "I'll order food. Zoe, Feel free to walk the grounds. If you want to rest, I can have one of the guest bedrooms ready for you."

She shook her head. "Walking the grounds for a few minutes will do me some good."

Yolanda stood. "I'll go with you, so you won't get lost."

Byron stiffened, but stopped himself from disagreeing. He'd been about to offer to show Zoe around. Yolanda taking her was better. He'd already proven being alone with Zoe wasn't the smartest thing for him to do. Yolanda, as intuitive as she was, may have picked up on that.

Dominic agreed to pick up whatever food Byron ordered. Roy cut out to handle phone calls. Byron asked Grant to stay behind. Their earlier conversation wasn't over.

"I suppose you asked me to stick around so you can tell me how horrible of a father I am for sending Zoe away all those years ago," Grant said, sounding bored.

Grant walked over to the drink tray and poured whiskey into two glasses. He held up one glass in Byron's direction. Byron walked over and took the glass.

"I don't think you're a terrible father," Byron said, not bothering to hide his annoyance. "I do believe you're so busy thinking you know what's best for everyone in the family that you don't stop to think all the consequences through."

Grant took a sip of his drink. "I thought through the consequences. I figured one day if you found out I'd tell you the same thing I would have told you back then. Zoe is a nice girl—"

"Woman."

Grant sighed. "Nice woman, but she isn't the woman for you. I get the appeal. You've always wanted to do what's right and she was in a bad situation. That can cloud your judgment and make you overlook a lot of other things."

"Other things like what?" Byron asked in a tight voice.

Grant shifted his stance and stood straight. "Things like the fact that she never chose you. She was with someone else. Got pregnant by someone else. Was in love with someone else. It didn't matter how much of an asshole that man might be. She chose him. Not you."

Byron's jaw stiffened. Grant was good at using the truth to gut someone like a fish. A truth Byron couldn't deny.

Grant continued in his direct tone. "If she would have wanted you, then she would have left him for you or accepted your foolish proposal instead of letting me and your mom convince her to leave. Get mad at me all you want, but that doesn't make anything I said less true. It's why I never thought she was good enough for you." He grabbed Byron's shoulder. "You're a Robidoux. My son. You didn't have to settle for being her second best."

Byron pulled away and downed the whiskey in the glass. The smooth alcohol masked the burn of bitterness caused by his father's words. As much as he might want to argue or bring up all the things that made the situation between him and Zoe different—the way they used to talk late in the night, how they paired well together on projects, the many times they flirted with just enough truth in their voices to hint of what could be—none of that changed the fact that after each of those encounters she went back to Kendell.

"You should have trusted me." Byron searched for lingering anger with his parents' intervention, but only found resentment for the foolish kid he'd been.

"We trusted you to act like a young man who thought he was in love would act."

"Whose idea was it to send Zoe away? Yours or Mom's?"

Grant lifted the glass to his lips. He took a small sip, his brows knitting together, his eyes avoiding Byron's. "Mine."

Byron closed his eyes and shook his head. "You're lying."

"I don't have a reason to lie to you."

"If you weren't lying, you'd look me in the eye with your admission. It was Mom's idea, wasn't it?"

"I don't want you to think badly about your mother," Grant said sincerely. "She was a great woman. All she ever wanted was to give you kids a better life."

"Did she pay Zoe to go away?" Byron asked hesitantly.

Byron knew his mother had been a great woman, but he also knew she'd been just as stubborn and ruthless as Grant. She'd taught him the importance of giving back to the community, how a charming personality got a lot more than an arrogant one, and how to cut your enemies with a touch so soft they didn't realize how far you'd sliced until they bled out on the floor. She'd been beautiful, bold and brilliant, which meant she wouldn't have hesitated to write a check to make Zoe disappear.

"She tried," Grant admitted. "Zoe refused the money."

The knot in Byron's chest eased. He'd never thought Zoe had been interested in his family's wealth. If anything, she'd seemed to accept his being rich as just another character trait and not something extraordinary. As if his having money was no different than someone else liking cereal for breakfast.

Byron pulled his thoughts from the past and met his dad's eyes. He looked up to Grant more than anyone else in the world. Unlike his older sister Elaina, he didn't want to fight their dad on everything, nor did he believe their dad was on a mission to run their lives the way India believed. Byron accepted his father for who he was: a smart businessman who would do anything to protect his company and family legacy. He wanted his dad to be proud of him.

"You don't think I should go through with this, do you?" he asked.

Grant took another sip of his drink. "No. I don't."

"You aren't fighting very hard to talk me out of it."

"That's because I don't think I would be able to talk you out of it. That girl does something to you. I don't like it, but hell, I know a little bit about not being able to get the wrong woman out of your system," Grant said wryly.

Byron quirked a brow. His dad was currently engaged to his longtime mistress. As hard as it had been for Byron to accept the woman who'd taken his mother's place years before she'd passed away—as hard as it still was—Byron hadn't seen his father this happy in years. He considered pouring more whiskey but put the glass down instead. He needed a clear head from now until the end of the campaign.

"She's not in my system. I promised to help her. Not helping her now could put her in danger."

"Could." Grant pointed a finger at Byron. "Not *will*. There are no guarantees. Things might have seemed bad years ago, but I promise you if that boy she used to date has spent thirteen years in prison he's probably moved on from the girl who cheated on him in college."

Byron shook his head and scoffed. "He's had nothing but thirteen years to think about it."

"Nonsense. He moved on just like you did. But if you want to help her, and if the public for some strange reason buys this misguided young love story you've concocted, then having a kid in the campaign might be a good thing."

Byron heard the calculation in his dad's voice. Already Grant was thinking of ways to spin this situation to their benefit. "We're not using Lilah in the campaign."

"The hell we aren't. You dragged Zoe up here, you're claiming Lilah as your own, you have to show the voters you're making up for lost time with your daughter. The last thing we are going to do is have you put us through this only to have *absentee father* thrown in this." Grant downed the rest of his drink.

"She doesn't live here. She can't be expected to participate in campaign stuff," Byron argued even though the logic of what his father said couldn't be denied.

His dad shrugged and checked his watch. "Figure it out. She can come up for weekend appearances. They can just stay here at the estate whenever we need them for something. I'll go let Sandra know we'll need two rooms ready for them." He chuckled drily. "She can have India's old room. I guess your sister will be moving in with her *husband* when she gets back." Grant shook his head and walked toward the door. "Your mother would be cursing every one of you out if she were here to see this fiasco."

Byron watched his father walk out in silence. How was he supposed to convince Zoe to come here more often? She didn't want to be in the campaign. Now he had to persuade her somehow to accept a room in his family's estate during the campaign. He'd barely gotten her to agree to this.

The door opened and Yolanda breezed in. Byron glanced over her shoulder. "Where is Zoe?"

"Oh, I left her with Elaina."

Byron's stomach dropped. "You what?" He walked toward the door. Elaina was an acquired taste on a good day. Zoe had never met her, and he could imagine the cold reception and thinly veiled insults his sister was potentially throwing Zoe's way. She'd mocked him for being silly back in college when he'd first told her about Zoe and had been the first person to assume Zoe would try to blackmail him with a birth certificate with his name on it after he announced his Senate run.

Yolanda placed a hand on his arm and stopped him. "Where are you going?"

"To get Zoe away from Elaina."

Her grip on his arm tightened. "No, you're not. Zoe is a big girl and she can handle your sister."

"Elaina doesn't like her," he said.

"I don't like her," Yolanda said easily. "But you trusted her with me."

He frowned and eyed Yolanda. "You don't like her? Why not?"

Yolanda stepped closer and brushed her hands across his shoulders. "Because I saw the way you looked at her when I walked in earlier. Oh, don't bother to deny it."

He wouldn't deny it, but he also wasn't going to admit to anything. "Yolanda, we were talking. Things got intense."

"Just remember what I said, Byron." Her eyes were steady as they stared into his. "Don't sleep with her. Don't mess this up. I love what we have. I don't want to back out, but I need to know right now if you want to back out."

His head drew back. "Why would I back out?"

"The public loves a second chance romance. Are you thinking of replacing me with her?"

As much as his body reacted to Zoe, and despite how much he'd wanted to press his lips to hers earlier, the thought of replacing Yolanda with her hadn't crossed his mind. His dad was right. Zoe was in his system. He didn't think straight when it came to her. Then and obviously not now. What he felt for her was not what legacies were built on. He was adding a new level to the Robidoux empire.

She never chose you. Never loved you.

He'd rather rip out his heart and put it in a blender than open himself to the pain of allowing himself to fall in love with Zoe again. Zoe had wanted his help. She'd never wanted him.

He slipped an arm around Yolanda's waist and pulled her against him. "I don't want out. You and me, we're in this together."

CHAPTER EIGHT

YOLANDA TOOK ZOE through the house and to a garden on the side. The entire time they walked, Yolanda talked about the antique pieces and unique paintings on the wall, gave a history on the Robidoux family and spoke graciously with any of the staff members they came across. She was completely nice and the perfect hostess, but Zoe felt there was also an underlying meaning.

This is my space. Don't get too comfortable.

She'd been given no direct hints, threats, or ultimatums, but Zoe received the message.

They'd just exited onto the side terrace where Yolanda had begun an explanation of why the former Mrs. Robidoux used to love it out here when the terrace door opened.

"Oh, please, Yolanda, no one wants to hear how well you know our family," a cool female voice said.

They both turned to face the woman who'd joined them. She was dressed impeccably in a peach A-line sundress that hugged her curves. Wavy, dark hair was swept to the side in a ponytail, and large brown sunglasses shaded her eyes. She held a champagne glass filled with what looked like a mimosa in her right hand.

Yolanda stiffened next to Zoe for a second before her smile relaxed again. "Zoe, this is Elaina. Byron's older sister. Elaina, this is—"

"The damsel," Elaina finished with a small lift of her full lips.

Zoe's chin lifted. Heat filled her cheeks. If she had any misunderstandings about how Byron's family might view her, Elaina just made them crystal clear. They thought she was weak and helpless. She'd just have to prove them wrong. For now Zoe tried to remind herself why she shouldn't get into a fight with Byron's sister.

Yolanda coughed delicately. Zoe swore she heard a chuckle beneath the cough. "I'll just leave you two and check on the food."

Yolanda hurried back into the house. She moved so fast Zoe had a sneaking suspicion she wanted to leave Zoe alone with Elaina. Maybe the two were friends, and now that Yolanda had given the subtle *you don't belong* talk, Elaina would finish it up with a *hurt my brother and I'll hurt you* discussion.

Elaina glanced over her shoulder at Yolanda as she left. As soon as the door closed, she strolled over to Zoe. "Don't trust that one as far as you can throw her," Elaina said.

The words struck Zoe speechless. That was not the next statement she'd expected. "Yolanda has been very nice to me the entire time." Zoe kept her voice even. She didn't know the politics of the Robidoux family and wasn't about to pick a side before getting the lay of the land.

"You know the saying, keep your enemies closer? She's going to make sure the two of you are best friends before this is said and done." Elaina took a sip of her drink. "There will be lunches and shopping outings where the press just happens to catch you two together. You'll be paired up for campaign events to talk about how great my brother is—which he is, by the way." Elaina pointed at Zoe.

"She'll even make the perfect stepmother to your daughter. She's probably already sent in the request to have her inducted into Jackson Falls's Young Debutante Program and picking out dresses for her debut."

"Say what now?" Zoe shook her head. "What the hell is the Jackson Falls Young Debutante Program? My daughter is not a young debutante, and Yolanda isn't her stepmother."

Elaina raised a perfectly manicured brow. "But she will be if Byron marries her."

Zoe's mouth snapped shut. She hadn't thought about that, either. After only a few hours in Yolanda's company, Zoe could already picture her doing everything Elaina insinuated. Zoe wanted to help Byron, and she wanted to make sure Kendell never had a reason to try and take Lilah away, but did that mean she wanted to succumb to the influence of Byron and his family?

Zoe headed back toward the house. "I can't do this."

The cool tips of Elaina's fingers wrapped around Zoe's wrist as she tried to pass. Zoe froze, opened her hand, quickly twisted out toward Elaina's thumb and freed herself. Zoe's heart rate increased even though she hadn't been afraid. Maneuvering from unwanted grips was second nature after years of self-defense classes. She waited for Elaina to scoff, ask what her problem was, or run off to tell Byron his fake baby momma was paranoid.

Elaina slipped off her shades and took a step back. Her eyes widened as if impressed. "You can do this if you're smart." Elaina nodded her head toward the yard. "Walk with me?" The words weren't a command.

Zoe licked her lips then nodded. The grounds outside the Robidoux estate were just as beautiful as the inside.

A wide green lawn was surrounded by tall pine trees and flowering azaleas that were too symmetrical to be considered completely natural. The entire place was structured beauty. Everything had a place; everything served a purpose and the purpose was to increase the grand illusion.

Is that what would be expected of her? That she play her part, play it well and lift Byron up even if doing so buried her? She didn't want that life. She hadn't found independence only to be dictated to and told how her schedule would run. She'd raised her daughter to be self-sufficient. She couldn't bring her into the lap of luxury and expect her to think all her problems would magically disappear if she conformed to the Robidoux ideal.

"I made a mistake," she said. "I'll tell Byron not to worry. If anyone comes and asks me I'll…" She let her voice trail off and glanced at Elaina. Did she know the true story? Should she tell her if she didn't?

"Don't worry, I know the truth," Elaina said. She stopped walking and faced Zoe. "Byron told me everything right after my parents sent you away. If there is one thing this family knows how to keep it's a secret. I won't reveal yours."

Relief mingled with curiosity. Just how many secrets did the family have?

They took a stone pathway toward the back of the house. "I didn't say all of that about Yolanda to scare you or make you change your mind."

"Then why did you say all of that? Or is that how you typically welcome visitors?" Zoe didn't bother to hide her sarcasm.

"Because you need to know what you're up against," Elaina replied in a voice similar to the one Zoe used whenever Lilah tried to get smart with her. "My brother, bless his heart, has a good heart, noble intentions and a drive to win, but he can be naive when it comes to some things." She looked Zoe up and down, giving Zoe a pretty good idea that Elaina considered her one of those things. "He'll see you and Yolanda becoming friends and believe everything is great. He won't realize she's taking over everything in his life until it's too late."

Though Elaina's voice was calm and practical, Zoe got the hint. "You don't like Yolanda."

"I know Yolanda. I've known her for years. She's smart, well connected and will do whatever it takes to rise to the top. Including latching on to my brother and using his ideals to grow her own interests." Elaina started walking again.

Zoe moved quickly to block Elaina's path. "Look, I'm not trying to get involved in whatever you two have going." She wasn't about to jump in the middle of whatever turf war Elaina and Yolanda may have going on.

Elaina's lips curved up slightly, her eyes lit with amusement. "You like to push back, don't you? That's good." Her eyes turned serious. "I just want Byron to be happy. Yolanda won't make him happy. Being elected to the Senate won't make him happy."

"You don't know that." From the moment Zoe met Byron he'd talked about his plans to run for public office. When she'd found out he was running for Senate she'd been happy to hear he was still following his dreams.

"I know Byron. He's seeing a vision of what he thinks is the right path even if he has no idea what he's about to get into." Elaina cocked a brow and finished her drink. She turned away from Zoe and continued down the path.

"I still don't understand what any of this has to do with me," Zoe said, following. "I'm not here to try and change your brother's mind about what he should or shouldn't do. I came here to help him out."

And secure a little more protection for herself. She didn't care if the idea was selfish. She had to be selfish after years of not taking care of herself. She'd do whatever she needed to do to protect Lilah and keep her real father away from her.

Including dealing with Yolanda?

She'd have to talk more with Byron about that before making a final decision and announcement. If he agreed to keep Lilah out of things, then that would keep Lilah out of Yolanda's influence. The two of them could get along for public appearances, but Yolanda wouldn't necessarily need to be seen with Lilah.

The walkway ended at a large patio. Zoe recognized it as the one the conference room looked out over.

"I'm not asking you to change his mind," Elaina said. "Byron is a grown man and he can make his own decisions. What I am asking you to do is keep your eyes open. Pay attention to what you're being asked to do and why. You've entered the big leagues now, damsel, and unless you're ready to fight for yourself, they—" she pointed to the window on the other side of the patio, "—will eat you alive."

"I'm no damsel." Zoe took a step closer to Elaina.

Elaina lifted her chin, and her eyes brightened with interest. "No need to puff up at me. I know you have claws. They've been hooked in Byron for years." She leaned in closer. "If you want him all you have to do is sink them in a little deeper." Elaina winked, turned gracefully and strolled back the way they came.

Zoe clenched her teeth. She wanted to scream. This family was going to drive her crazy. What did that even mean? If she wanted him? There was no getting Byron. She hadn't believed back then that he'd been serious about their getting together, and she wasn't about to get involved in a twisted situation with him, Yolanda and Elaina.

She'd had a moment of weakness earlier when she'd wanted to kiss him, and she was still a little weak because now she couldn't stop thinking about what his kiss would have felt like. Would his body be just as solid and strong against her as it looked? This was all one-sided, though. Byron wasn't helping her because he still felt something?

He looked like he wanted to kiss you, too.

Her lips lifted with the forbidden thoughts as she walked toward the glass door on the right of the patio that should lead to the conference room. She froze before opening the door and watched as Byron slid an arm around Yolanda's waist and pulled her into an embrace.

The blood rushed from Zoe's head. Zoe spun around and placed a hand on one of the wrought iron chairs on the patio to steady herself. She closed her eyes and took several deep breaths. She'd been daydreaming stupid thoughts again and deserved to feel foolish. Thinking about Byron's kiss when he was giving just that to the woman who deserved it. The woman he loved and was marrying.

No more believing in fairy tales or fantasies. Byron hadn't changed from the guy he'd been in college. Charming, handsome and charismatic as always. There wasn't anything between them except the flicker of sexual attraction that had always been there. No matter what Elaina may have thought, Zoe's supposed claws in Byron were nothing but scratches that had long healed over.

ZOE STAYED FOR dinner because she didn't have a reason not to. Lilah could spend the night with Julie and Victoria, so there wasn't a need to hurry back. Zoe also wasn't enthusiastic about turning around and making the three-hour drive back home after driving up that morning.

Zoe hadn't given her final answer, she wanted to make sure Lilah was okay with moving forward, and Zoe needed time to think things over. Byron's family made preliminary plans for a joint statement and press conference to announce everything. After the work was done, and a delicious dinner prepared by the family's personal chef, the family planned to congregate in the upstairs sitting room.

Zoe took that as her cue to leave. She took the moment to go into one of the downstairs living areas and call Victoria to check on Lilah before getting back on the road.

"How are things going up there?" Victoria asked after greeting Zoe.

Zoe hadn't told Victoria where she was going. She'd only mentioned a family emergency and the need to keep Lilah out of things for a while. Although she agreed with Grant about the need to keep the number of people from knowing the truth about Lilah's parentage, Zoe wanted nothing more but to confess her confusion and frustration with the entire situation with someone, and wished she could unload everything to her friend.

"They're going okay, I guess."

Concern immediately filled Victoria's voice. "Do you need anything? If Lilah needs to stay one more day that's fine. I'm happy to help."

Zoe smiled, appreciative of her friend's immediate offer of support. "Thank you, but I've already asked for enough."

"That's what friends are for. Will you be back tomorrow?"

"No, I'm heading back that way now." She checked her watch. It was almost nine, but the drive was only three hours. "I should get there around midnight."

"Zoe, don't you even play with me. You left early this morning and now you're trying to drive back tonight. No, ma'am. Get a hotel room, get some rest and then come pick up Lilah tomorrow," Victoria said, using what Zoe would call her "mom" voice.

"I asked you to watch her for the day. I honestly didn't expect things to take this long." An oversight on her part. She'd expected to talk things out privately with Byron, not have the entire family-planning session on the next step. She should have remembered how much oversight his father had on family affairs.

"I'd rather not spend the next three hours worried about you falling asleep and driving into a ditch on the way back. Find a hotel. Stay the night. Lilah will be fine."

Zoe covered her mouth and yawned. The idea of a bed versus three hours in a driver's seat and a long stretch of highway fought a short battle. "Maybe you're right. I'll see if I can find a hotel. Let me talk to Lilah."

"Good!" Victoria sounded pleased. "Hold on a second." She called Lilah's name. A few seconds later her daughter was on the phone.

"Hey, Mom! Did you say yes?"

Zoe rolled her eyes at her daughter's enthusiasm. "Can you not forecast our business to everyone?"

"I didn't say anything, and Ms. Victoria went upstairs to take the clothes out of the dryer. It's just me. Did you say yes?"

Zoe sighed and shook her head. "I said I'd talk to you before saying yes. If you agree to the plan, then we'll release a statement and possibly do a press conference."

"Yes!"

"But don't forget, this doesn't mean anything more than making sure you're safe."

"I know, Mom. I get it. We're not going to be a family."

Based on the way Byron pulled Yolanda into his arms earlier, no, there was no chance of them being a real family. The quicker Lilah understood that, the better. "We aren't going to be a family. This is politics. I've met Byron's fiancée and they're in love. He's happy. We can appreciate his willingness to still help, but at the end of the day he's doing this so that he and Yolanda can have a happy future together." She kept her voice firm and hoped Lilah understood every word.

"Okay," Lilah grumbled.

Zoe never liked to dash her daughter's dreams, but this was one that needed to be swiped out of existence before it took hold and made things worse. "Now, I'm getting a hotel instead of driving back tonight."

"You mean I get to spend the night?" The joy came back to Lilah's voice.

"Yes, please don't drive Victoria crazy."

"I won't! Love you, Mom! Have a good night, okay?"

"Oh, you're done talking to me?" Zoe said with a laugh.

"I've gotta tell Julie I'm staying the night. We can watch movies like we planned."

Zoe laughed, happy to give a little to make her daughter happy. "Okay, but remember we still aren't telling anyone the whole story. Not even Julie. I still need to think things through. So promise me you'll keep this just between us."

"I promise," Lilah said solemnly. Her daughter understood when Zoe was being serious and thankfully respected her concerns.

"Tell Victoria I'll call her in the morning."

"I will. Bye!"

Lilah hung up and Zoe chuckled as she stared at her phone. She hoped Lilah remembered not to get her hopes up too much about this situation.

You and Lilah both.

She blew out a long breath and pulled up the travel app on her phone. "Now to find a hotel room."

"Just stay here." Byron's voice came from the door.

Zoe turned quickly toward the door. Byron came in, his strides long and relaxed. Her gaze followed his movements. Regardless of her pledge to keep things platonic between her and Byron, Zoe had to admit the man looked good. He commanded the room and filled it with his self-assurance and poise. He could have been so much more arrogant, but he wasn't, which was part of the reason people were drawn to him.

"I can't stay here," Zoe said automatically. "I'll get a hotel room."

Byron went to the minibar and poured a drink. Did the family have one in every room? He turned to her and held up the goblet and raised a brow. Zoe needed to find a hotel. She should book a room, get a good night's sleep and prepare to make her way back home in the morning. Except, this was the only time they'd been alone since earlier. A lot had been said with so many people around them. She needed time with him to talk about what they were doing without the input from everyone else.

"Yes, please," she said.

Byron turned back to the bar and poured her a drink. "No hotel. We've got plenty of room. Stay here. Sometimes I pick a spare bedroom and stay over instead of driving home."

Zoe raised a brow. "You don't live here?"

Byron shook his head then brought the drink over to her. "No, this is the family center, but I've got my own place downtown. Elaina moved back home after her divorce. India stayed here when she finished touring, but I'm pretty sure she'll be moving out soon." Byron sank down onto the couch.

Zoe settled next to him. She turned to her side on the couch and faced him. "What about Yolanda?"

He shrugged and sipped his drink. "What about her?"

"She won't care that I'm staying here?"

Byron smiled his charming smile. "She doesn't live here either, but I'll call and let her know."

"Did she leave?" Zoe tried to sound disappointed, but from the way Byron chuckled she must have failed.

"She had to get home and handle some things."

She wanted to ask where Yolanda's home was. If Byron was calling her did that mean they didn't live together? The idea made her feel a kernel of satisfaction she didn't deserve to feel.

Instead of focusing on his relationship with the super-perfect Yolanda, Zoe chose to change the subject. "Where is India? I'm surprised I didn't meet her with the rest of the family."

Byron held up his glass and studied the brown liquid. He sat back against the cushions of the chair and stretched out his long legs. "India eloped."

Zoe's eyes widened and she grinned. "Oh, my God! Really? When?"

"The night of my primary win."

"Who did she marry? Did you know it was coming?" Zoe was amazed by people who eloped. The romantic notion of being so in love that waiting for a traditional ceremony was unacceptable. The urgency to just be married and start a new life with someone as soon as possible. Would she ever feel that way?

"The eventual marriage was expected, but not the elopement." He turned his head and met her eyes. "She married my best friend Travis."

Zoe hesitated. "Oh." She wouldn't have expected Byron to be against his sister dating one of his friends, but then again, she didn't have a brother and wasn't sure if that broke some man-code law.

"And Elaina's ex-husband," Byron added with a tight smile.

Her jaw dropped. "Ooh." She cringed and leaned in closer. "Seriously?"

Byron nodded slowly. "Seriously." He took another long swallow of the drink.

"How did that go over?" Was that one of the reasons Elaina seemed so tense?

"It was a shock…that wasn't really a shock," he said slowly. "In hindsight, I guess I should have realized Travis and India had more of a serious connection. Even before he married Elaina."

"Then why did he marry Elaina?"

Byron shook his head and sipped his drink. "Let's just say there was family pressure involved. He and Elaina used to hook up when they were young. They got in some trouble and got married. It only lasted a few years before they split. When India came back to town Travis and India's old friendship sparked up, which led to them realizing they loved each other."

"Wow. And everyone is cool with that?"

"We're getting used to it. They're happy. Really happy. In our family someone deserves to be happy." He sounded sullen and almost regretful.

Was he not happy? She thought about Elaina's words earlier about Byron doing what he thought would please him. That wasn't the Byron she remembered. In college Byron was completely confident in his choices and assured of his future. He'd never let anyone push him into a decision. She couldn't imagine he would be doing something deep down he didn't believe in.

"Are you happy?" When Byron frowned at her she realized she may be delving too deep. "I mean with all of this. With the plans we made today? With still having to deal with a lie I told years ago."

She watched him closely. Sure, he'd come to her and insisted on carrying the lie through, but what were his motivations? Was it really just to win his election? Was a part of it because he still cared?

What I felt for you wasn't hero worship, a small bit of affection, or a little bit of attraction.

"You didn't tell a lie. From here on out, what you said back then is nothing but the truth," Byron said, his voice calm and controlled. "Doing what we're doing has multiple benefits. The biggest of which is getting ahead of potential rumors. Political campaigns can be dirty, and by handling this up front it'll make it easier to win down the road. I'm not seen as a family man. My family helps but having you and Lilah seen as family is actually beneficial."

Zoe took a long sip of her drink, the heat of the whiskey burning away the disappointment of his words. She couldn't forget his ultimate goal. Winning. Doing whatever it took to come out on top. Byron was a fighter, so she wasn't surprised he'd chosen to fight a blackmail attempt and use the situation to strengthen his appeal. Turn a negative into a positive.

"I'm worried about Lilah," she admitted. "She's not used to this lifestyle. We've never been a part of anything this visible. I've spent a lifetime trying to protect her and now I'm throwing her in the limelight."

Byron sat up and put his drink on the table. He turned and faced her, his eyes and face serious. "Whatever you need during this process let me know. I know I'm asking a lot of you and her. I'll provide security for both you and Lilah throughout the entire campaign."

Zoe fought back the warmth spreading through her chest at his offer to help. He would do anything to make this easier for her and Lilah. That was the kind of guy he was. She appreciated his assistance, even if she didn't deserve it.

"We don't need security." The refusal was automatic. She didn't want to accept anything else from Byron or his family. They were already doing enough. She could look out for her and Lilah.

"Zoe." He held out a hand as if to touch her knee but curled his fingers in on themselves and pulled back. "I'm not making the offer to exert control over your life. I don't know who's behind the blackmail. We aren't sure who was originally looking for you. Until we get answers to those questions, having someone watching out for you and Lilah would make me feel better."

"Having a security guard following me and my daughter around will bring extra attention to our family, disrupt our lives and frankly is unrealistic. The school I chose for Lilah has security and my job is locked down tight."

"But—"

"But if things start to really get hot for us, and if I notice there are more people trying to get close to me and Lilah, I'll let you know and we can talk about security."

Everything he said was true. She didn't know if her threatening email was a fluke or tied to this. She'd already freaked out when he'd argued with his dad, and twisted away from Elaina as if she were made of acid. If she mentioned the emails the family might think she was paranoid. She was, but she didn't want them to know. Plus, she wasn't ready to have men in black suits following her around. If the campaign became overwhelming for her and Lilah she'd consider the offer for extra protection.

Byron's lip quirked up. "Fair enough." He chuckled softly.

"What's funny?"

"You. You always were a fighter. Independent." He rested his elbow on the back of the couch and propped his head on his fist. Humor danced in the gold flecks of his eyes.

Zoe glanced away, unable to accept the admiration also reflected in Byron's sexy eyes. "Not always." There was a time she took whatever was dished out to her. When she didn't think she deserved something happier.

"Yes, always. Do you remember when we worked together on that after-school volunteer project?"

Zoe thought back and grinned. She hadn't been into volunteering and community service when she'd started college. Back then she'd only cared about going to class, passing and partying. A school project required her to volunteer, and that was how she'd met Byron. The rich guy who also wanted to save the world.

"I do," she said slowly as she tried to remember the details. "We had to come up with a project for the after-school program at the local high school."

"I wanted to create a program that taught kids interview skills, and you fought me to add on that fashion show."

Zoe laughed and lightly pushed his shoulder. "It wasn't a fashion show. Knowing how to dress, get a haircut, have clean nails, all of that is part of making a good impression at an interview. You just wanted to do a lecture on potential interview questions. I made the program fun."

"You added a fashion show," he teased.

"And what did you tell me after we took the kids through the program?"

"That you were right," he admitted with an overexaggerated sigh. Then he smiled at her. "I was impressed. The way you got that store to bring in clothes for the kids to try on, and the nail and hair salon to help out, too."

"Of course I was right." Zoe took a quick sip of her drink. The heat of the alcohol only increased the fire simmering in her belly from the way he looked at her. Zoe put her drink on the table and faced forward. "It turned out great. The kids had fun. They got to practice an interview."

"You irritated the hell out of me."

She pointed her finger at him. "That's because before me no one else challenged you. Everyone was all *Oh, it's the rich guy. Let's just nod and say yes.*"

"I'd been challenged before," he said. "I was more irritated that you thought of the grooming portion before me."

"Ah, the truth comes out. I upstaged you."

"Yep. It's one of the reasons I asked you to help with my other projects. One thing I know is that no matter how smart I am, there are lots of other smart people in the room. I surround myself with smart people and you fought for your ideas."

That was one of the things she appreciated the most about Byron. He was cocky, rich and wanted to win, but not at the expense of ignoring good ideas from other people on his team. "I thought you were just a glutton for punishment. I lived to drive you crazy."

"You drove me crazy, too." His eyes met hers. The fondness in them pulled at her midsection.

Zoe cleared her throat and looked away. "Well, glad to know I did succeed at something." She rubbed her sweaty palms across her jean-clad legs. "I better stop and find a room."

Byron's fingers brushed her arm. "Stay here. Please."

Where he touched her tingled. The sensation hummed through her body. Reminded her of the way she'd eased closer to him earlier. Pulled her to do it again. She needed to go.

"We can talk some more. Reminisce about old times," Byron continued.

The look in his eye and the soft plea in his voice made up her mind. They could talk more. There was no harm in that. "I'll stay."

His shoulders relaxed. "And will you go through with the plan? You asked if I'm okay, but are you?" Byron watched her closely.

Zoe couldn't use Lilah as an excuse. Her daughter was all for it. Ultimately, this was her decision. The fallout, good or bad, would be on her.

"I'm okay."

He relaxed and nodded. "Good." He glanced away and scrunched his nose.

Zoe's eyes narrowed at his nervous tick. "What else?"

He waved a hand. "Nothing."

She raised a brow. "You know I can tell when you have something to say, right? Just spill it."

He shrugged before glancing at her. "We can set aside rooms just for you and Lilah. That way you won't have to worry about finding a hotel whenever you visit."

Zoe shook her head before he even started. "No, Byron, that's not necessary. Besides, I don't plan to be up here a lot."

"Then it's not that big of a deal. Besides, the least we can do is give you a place to stay. Plus, after the announcement the safest place for you and Lilah when visiting—" her eyes narrowed and he held up a hand "—*if* you visit, is here at the estate."

She wanted to argue against it, but again the suggestion made sense. She didn't plan to come up often. Once the announcement was made, she wouldn't need to visit much. She ignored the small voice whispering in the back of her head that staying at the estate would mean more time with Byron like this.

He doesn't live here. Stop fantasizing and focus on what's important.

"I'm good as long as we both agree to keep Lilah out of the limelight as much as possible," she said firmly. "If we do this it doesn't mean you or your family can dictate what we do with our lives. We're only a family on paper. Not in reality."

Disappointment flickered across his face before he nodded and held out his hand. "Agreed. This benefits us both. That's the best way to move forward and keep things clear."

Zoe slid her hand into his. Ignored the heat generated by his touch, and the question in her brain of whether or not Byron needed the reminder to keep distance between them as much as she did. "Agreed."

CHAPTER NINE

BYRON WAS FINISHING his Monday morning planning meeting with the volunteers at his campaign office when Travis and India strolled through the door. His body tensed. India gave him a shy smile. Travis watched him with a steady, confident gaze. Byron looked away from them back to the volunteers gathered around him.

"That's all for now, everyone. Thank you again for your support. I couldn't be here if it wasn't for your support and belief in me. I won't let you down. The time is now."

"The time is now!" the group chanted back. They clapped and cheered.

Byron smiled and answered some of the specific questions his lead volunteers had. In his periphery he watched Travis and India talk to some people in the office. The family hadn't told anyone about the elopement. He didn't hear any exuberant congratulations, so he assumed they'd been smart enough to hold out on sharing their happy news.

After giving the last bit of directions, Byron met his sister's and friend's gazes. He stiffly nodded toward his office and went inside without waiting for a response. He leaned against his desk and crossed his arms as he waited for them to enter. India came in first, her gaze wary as she watched him. Travis followed and closed the door behind him.

Travis stood next to India and placed an arm around

her shoulder. India looked relaxed and content, as if they were just back in town from a weeklong vacation instead of a whirlwind elopement. Her yellow blouse and cream-colored pants as bright as the sparkle in her eye. Travis appeared equally stress-free in a tan shirt and dark pants. Maybe love had that type of effect on people.

His sister leaned into Travis's side. They were a united front. Prepared to handle any hits the family threw at them. Byron had to admire their commitment. A small seed of envy sprouted in his stomach. He and Yolanda would always be a team, but they'd never have the emotion underneath that India and Travis had.

"The happy couple has returned," Byron said after a few seconds of tense silence.

India bit the corner of her lower lip. "Byron, you only asked us to wait until the primary was over."

"I did." He rubbed his jaw. His beard was getting thick. He'd have to shave it off soon or else Yolanda would shave it herself. "I didn't think that meant you'd run out during my primary party and elope to Vegas. I thought you'd believe me when I said I supported your relationship. I thought you'd understand I'd be willing to stand beside you and show everyone how happy I am to see my baby sister and best friend engaged."

"We knew that," India explained.

"If you knew that then why did you run off and get married in secret? Why would you two disappear and make it look as if the family wouldn't be supportive? Why elope and make it a potential scandal to manage?"

Travis's body stilled. They were equal in height, but Travis was lean and sleek. His stare was direct when he answered Byron. "This wasn't about you, your family, or any of your expectations."

Byron straightened. "Obviously not. You didn't give a damn about how this played out."

"No. We didn't," Travis said, unapologetic. "I still don't give a damn how this plays out. You're my closest friend, and I'll always have your back, but when it comes to my life and what makes me happy, I'm not going to let another Robidoux tell me how to live or what steps I can and cannot take."

"I don't want to tell you how to live or what steps to take," Byron argued. "I didn't give either of you grief about being together. I stepped up for both of you. I want you to be happy. The least you could have done was talk to me. Tell me what you planned. You could have gotten married alone in Vegas if that's what you really wanted, but shit, Travis, I'm your friend. You didn't have to hide this."

India placed a hand on Travis's chest before stepping forward. "We weren't trying to hide it. And, yes, we should have said something. But Byron, we love each other. We didn't want to wait another minute. We respected you and the family and kept quiet as promised. I know we hurt you, and I'm sorry about that, but please understand we never meant to make things harder on your campaign."

Byron looked into India's pleading eyes and sighed. One of the problems with being angry with India was that he couldn't stay mad at her for long. The tension eased out of his neck and shoulders.

Byron moved closer and placed a hand on India's shoulder. "Next time, will you come to me first? Don't spring any more surprises, okay?"

India beamed and hugged him. "No more surprises."

Byron couldn't possibly not smile back when faced with his baby sister's pleasure. He hugged her back. After they broke apart, he held out his hand and shook Travis's.

"We good?" Travis asked.

Byron was still irritated, but he wasn't willing to toss out a long-standing friendship over this. He couldn't blame Travis for seizing an opportunity to be happy. He held out a hand. "We're good."

Travis shook his hand. "And there won't be a next time." He reached out and pulled India back to his side. "No more marriages for me. I've found my forever wife."

India practically melted into Travis's embrace. The seed of envy grew and spread through Byron's gut. "Okay, I support you guys, but can you please save the hugging and kissing for when I'm not around?"

India pointed a finger at him. "Hey, you never bothered to hide the hugging and kissing you did with the women you dated."

Byron put a finger in front of his lips. "Shh, we're not talking about that anymore. I'm a settled man. Getting married."

India's eyes dimmed. "How is Yolanda?"

Byron tried not to let his sister's displeasure with his engagement add fertilizer to the envy growing in his stomach. India had gotten lucky and found someone she could not only love but also trust. Everyone wasn't destined to find that.

I'm in love with you, Zoe.

No, you aren't. Don't be ridiculous.

He pushed the old memory aside. His dad was right about Zoe. He had something safe with Yolanda. He cared about and admired her. They made a great team. She knew what she wanted. His grandparents had started with the same foundation and found love. Maybe not the fairy-tale love, but a practical love had been the backbone of their family.

"Yolanda is great," Byron said, infusing his voice with confidence. "She even took the latest development in stride."

"Latest development?" Travis asked. "You mean us?"

Byron shook his head. "I wish your engagement was the only unexpected thing that would have happened the night of my primary win."

India's eyes widened. "What happened?"

Byron glanced at the door and window. He trusted his volunteers, but he wasn't going to spill this information until the press conference on Friday. They'd chosen to formally announce everything at the last minute. No preparing the press or giving Carlton time to spill the information before Byron's camp did.

"A discussion for later at the estate," Byron said. India's eyes narrowed. He saw the argument forming on her lips. Byron leaned in and said softly in her ear, "You're an aunt."

Her jaw dropped. "What the hell does that mean?"

There was a quick rap on his office door before it swung open. Elaina strolled into the room not bothering to look up from the paper in her hand. "Byron, I've got some ideas about Friday. I do not like this news release."

She saw India and Travis and froze. She meticulously folded the paper and held it primly in front of her. "Oh, welcome back." Her voice was calm, friendly, even to people who didn't know her well.

Byron noticed the way her hand clenched the paper. Her hard swallow and the long breath in and out through her nose. Elaina had accepted that Travis and India were in love, but Byron wasn't convinced she liked it very much.

"India and Travis just got back in town," Byron said. "They came by to make sure things were okay with the campaign and the family." Byron watched Elaina closely as he talked. Elaina didn't show her emotions often, unless she was irritated or angry, but he'd learned how to read her. She deflected, methodically showed no facial expressions, or froze over more whenever she was upset.

"Why would there be anything wrong with the family or the campaign?" Elaina asked in a light tone. "The only thing that happened was my baby sister ran off and eloped with my ex-husband. It's not as if running off would make it appear as if they had something to hide." She smiled sweetly at India and Travis. "Does it?"

India's back straightened. "We don't have anything to hide. We just didn't want our wedding to be a big Robidoux family production."

Elaina nodded. "Understandable. You never were one for big productions." She turned her gaze to Byron. "Can I talk to you alone, please? I have something important to go over with you."

India stepped forward before Byron could answer. "Is it something we can't hear?"

Byron wasn't sure it was possible, but Elaina's expression became even more bland. The calm, unfeeling expression of a doll. "It's something related to one of our holding companies that is still confidential. While I appreciate your interest, you don't work for our company and therefore, it would be inappropriate for you to be involved in the conversation. Byron, on the other hand, still occasionally offers legal advice."

Elaina delivered her speech in a perfectly calm and rational tone of voice. Yet, Byron felt the cut. India's lips tightened but she nodded stiffly. Travis wrapped an arm around India's shoulder.

"Let's leave so they can talk," Travis said.

They walked toward the door. Elaina stepped out of their way. India stopped in front of Elaina. When she opened her mouth to say something Elaina held up a hand.

"I'll see you at the house later. Both of you. We have to toast your marriage." Elaina's voice was bright and brittle.

India relaxed and smiled. "I'd like that." She glanced back at Byron. "And hear the you're an aunt story?" She raised a brow, then she and Travis left.

"You told her already?" Elaina asked as soon as the door closed behind India and Travis.

"No, I'm waiting until we're away from the office." He sat in the chair in front of his desk and pointed toward the door. "I thought you were okay with her and Travis?"

Elaina hadn't given any indication previously that she was going to cause problems with India and Travis's relationship. She'd been remarkably low-key about the entire situation ever since the big reveal and subsequent fallout. Byron shouldn't have assumed her outward behavior was the truth.

With a sigh, Elaina gracefully sat in the chair next to him. "I am okay with them being together, but can I at least get a bit of a grace period with accepting the elopement and marriage?"

Her lips pursed in a slight pout. She felt comfortable again. He hadn't appreciated before how much more of herself she showed when the two of them were alone. Not enough for him to say he knew her deepest secrets, but more than she relaxed around anyone else in the family.

Byron placed a hand over hers that still clutched the sheet of paper. "Are you going to be okay?"

Elaina pushed back her bangs and smoothed her ponytail. "I am okay." Anyone looking at her would believe her. Her tan suit was impeccable, her back straight. Byron squeezed gently and she met his eyes. Her hand loosened its death grip and she patted his with her other. With another deep breath, Elaina relaxed before pulling away. "Now, can we get to the reason I came here?"

Deciding not to push, he twisted his wrist in a "go on" gesture. "Please. In fact, it would be great to hear about something not related to the challenges my campaign faces."

He hadn't heard from Zoe since she left, but he'd thought about her too many times since. Roy offered to handle communicating with her before the press conference. Byron agreed. His schedule was busy and there were a lot of appearances he needed to prepare for, but that didn't keep his mind from wandering to Zoe dozens of times in an hour.

"I'm coming to you because my next steps may be considered a slight challenge to your campaign."

Byron groaned. "Come on, Elaina. Please don't add to the already huge mountain I have to climb."

"Calm down. I'm just giving you a heads-up. I doubt it'll be a problem, but I'd rather you know in case someone asks a question."

"What are you doing? You said it had to do with one of our holdings?"

She lifted a shoulder. "That was just to get rid of India

and Travis. Daddy is letting me acquire businesses we have a major stake in under one holding company. We don't exactly see eye to eye about which companies should be a part of Robidoux Holdings, but our disagreements have been manageable. So far. I came here because I'm thinking of purchasing a business."

He waited for her to elaborate, but Elaina just watched him as if that was enough of an explanation. Suppressing a sigh, Byron settled back in his chair. "What business?"

"A production facility." She held up a hand. "And before you ask, I'm not telling you what kind until I'm sure if I want to buy it or not."

"That doesn't sound like it would be a problem for me."

"It shouldn't, but there may be pushback if I purchase. Which is why I'm telling you now."

"Are you about to buy some company and put hundreds of workers out of business?" He'd like to think Elaina wouldn't be so coldhearted, but he'd lived with her for over thirty years. She would be that ruthless.

Elaina rolled her eyes. "Seriously, Byron, don't be dramatic. If I do this, I'll be taking a business that still has viability and making it profitable again. No massive layoffs required. Later, if it makes sense, I might consider bringing it under the fold of Robidoux Holdings."

Byron studied his sister. Outwardly, she was calm and collected, but her eyes were hard and serious. Bringing all of the companies the family had invested in under one holding company wasn't easy, but Byron couldn't imagine anyone but Elaina doing so. He'd figured this was another way for her to increase the power of the company she would ultimately take over one day. He didn't understand her need to start something separate.

He leaned against the desk and crossed his arms. "Why?"

"Because I can," she said, enunciating each word. Byron held up his hands. Elaina did things her own way, and typically for a good reason.

Her lips lifted in a small but pleased smile. "Fine. Knowing Daddy, he'll get annoyed and say I'm not focused on Robdioux Tobacco or Robidoux Holdings, but he won't put up much of a fight. He'll want to keep any potential family squabbles out of the news. I doubt anyone on the political circuit will care about me buying a company, but you never know. I'm telling you now ahead of time, because I love you and expect for you to be on my side."

Byron chuckled. "Why wouldn't I be on your side?"

"Lately it seems as if nothing is going my way. I'm not going to assume anything," she said drily.

Elaina could be cold, calculating and mean, but she loved him and the rest of their family. She'd nursed him when he'd gotten the flu in high school and their parents were away, fought a kid who'd dared bully her baby brother in middle school, and told him to grow a pair when he'd been heartbroken after Zoe left. She always had his back and he'd always have hers.

"If you want it, buy the business. I'll support whatever you do."

CHAPTER TEN

Zoe walked into Miranda's office Monday morning with the report she'd requested in hand. She'd busted her tail to compile the information before going out of town Friday and had stayed up most of the night polishing it after driving back from Jackson Falls. Everything in her life was on the verge of being shaken up. She needed one thing to go right. She wanted this promotion. Not just to keep her daughter in school and safe, but because this job was the reason she'd been able to give Lilah a stable home. She needed her own stability knowing she was about to walk into the whirlwind of a political campaign.

Miranda looked up from her laptop and smiled at Zoe. "Good morning. Come on in and have a seat."

Zoe crossed the thin blue carpet to Miranda's desk. The office was large with no windows since it was in one of the corners of the manufacturing facility. Miranda had brightened up the room with large framed prints of abstract artwork on the walls.

Zoe held out the folder with her report. "I got the information you asked for after my presentation last week."

Miranda's eyes brightened. "Good. Let me take a look."

Zoe sat in the hard, wood chair across from Miranda's wide metal desk. Miranda opened the folder and flipped through the pages. Zoe clasped her hands together in her lap and watched. She hadn't expected Miranda to look at the report now. What if she hated it? She would have much preferred to find out later and not get an up-close-and-personal view of her reaction.

"Zoe, this looks good," Miranda said slowly as she continued to skim the papers. "Really good."

"I focused on the lessons learned from the few accidents we had. In many cases we immediately changed procedures or increased training. Chances of it happening again are low."

Miranda nodded and closed the folder. "This is exactly what I wanted to see. One thing I've learned is that if you focus on the good and don't bring up any challenges you faced people tend to question you harder. If you talk about what went wrong and how you recovered from that it'll make a much bigger impact. Remember that in the future. You're going to face a lot of scrutiny in a director's position."

Zoe sat up straighter. "Have you all made a decision?" Hope sprang in her chest. Was she getting the job?

Miranda smiled but shook her head. "Not yet, but we are meeting on Thursday to discuss our thoughts. We hope to announce our choice soon after." Miranda tapped the folder. "I'm not trying to be presumptuous, but this follow-up information does work in your favor."

Zoe fought not to grin. She didn't want to assume the job was hers. If they met on Thursday, then they would hopefully notify the candidate on Friday. The excitement bubbling inside her made it almost impossible to sit still. This Friday she could have finally reached her career goals and have a director position.

Then it hit her. Friday was the day of the press conference. That was the other reason she'd come to Miranda's office. She needed Friday off to drive back to Jackson Falls and stand next to Byron as they told the world he was her child's father.

"That's good to hear, Miranda. I'm just happy to be considered," she said.

"Of course we're considering you. You've been with the company for years. Loyalty from employees like you is one of the reasons we've been so successful for so long."

Zoe licked her dry lips. "There is something else I wanted to ask you about."

"Sure. Hit me."

How much to tell? If she said nothing and there was a media fallout from her press conference with Byron, the interest in Zoe might spill over to the company. Valtec wouldn't be ready to deal with any questions directed their way. If she told Miranda everything, she ran the chance of word getting out before the press conference.

"I was hoping to take Friday off. I've got a family emergency I need to take care of in North Carolina."

Miranda's brows drew together. "North Carolina. I wasn't aware you had family up there. Is everything okay?"

Zoe swallowed and nodded. "Everything is fine. It's just Lilah's father lives there. He's running for public office and wants her there for an event."

That was enough of the truth to keep Zoe from feeling guilty.

Miranda leaned back. "Her father? You've never talked about him before."

"We didn't get along for a few years, but things are different now. I know it's short notice, but she's looking forward to going, and I promised to try and take her."

Miranda immediately shrugged. "No problem. What we

do here is important, but not as important as the people we live with at home." Miranda leaned forward and tilted her head. "Will you be heavily involved in his campaign?"

Zoe heard the calculation in Miranda's words. The unspoken question: How many more days off will you need to be part of a political campaign? "No. It's just this thing and that's it."

Miranda relaxed a bit. "Good. We don't discourage political involvement with our employees, and with the campaign taking place in another state I don't see there being any potential conflicts. Just remember to keep anything related to the campaign out of the office."

"Absolutely," Zoe said, nodding.

"Sounds good." Miranda stood.

Zoe took the cue and got up, as well. "Thank you, Miranda. I'll have my cell phone if something comes up on Friday. Don't hesitate to call."

"You enjoy the time with family. I'm sure we'll be okay."

Zoe left Miranda's office and hoped Byron's campaign wouldn't affect her job. It shouldn't. Jackson Falls was hours away and in another state. No one in South Carolina would care about the latest senator from North Carolina. Would they? Even if there was media interest it would more than likely be focused on Byron and what he could do for the people voting for him.

Zoe ignored the ever-present knot of uncertainty in her stomach since Byron showed up at her job last week. One press conference, one quick statement and that was it. Byron would clear his name. Lilah would be safe from interference from her real father. Zoe would come back to work and get that promotion.

The little pep talk worked. By the time she went back to her office she was smiling and cautiously optimistic. She'd left her cell phone on her desk. There was a notification on her email icon. She picked up the phone and checked her messages. Byron's campaign manager promised to send her more information about what to expect later that week. The email wasn't from Byron's campaign.

From: debtcollector10@zmail.com
To: Hammond.zoe@gomail.com
Subject: BITCH
You are a lying bitch. You've tried to hide the truth. It's coming out and then you WILL pay for what you've done.

The words ran together. Zoe's hand shook so hard she dropped the phone. Her head swam. Slowly, she sank into the seat behind her desk. That did not read like a prank or an accidental email. A cold sweat broke across her skin. Someone was mad at her, and Zoe had a feeling they meant every word they'd sent.

ZOE'S NERVES WERE wound tight by the time she picked up Lilah from school. Her eyes scanned the line of other parents picking up their children. No one looked unfamiliar. No one seemed to pay her any more attention than usual. Still, the hairs on the back of her neck stood up. She was being paranoid, but an email calling her a lying bitch and saying she would pay for what she'd done was cause for paranoia.

She tried to hide her anxiety when Lilah got in the car. Thankfully, her daughter was obsessed with the last-minute paper their teacher had assigned and was on a rampage about the unfairness of the world. Zoe gave the obligatory nods and grunts of agreement as Lilah lamented about the unfairness of a teacher's supreme rule. Tomorrow she'd worry about course correcting her when it came to her teachers. Today she had to figure out what to do about the emails.

They got home and Lilah changed clothes for her archery practice. Typically, Zoe would drop her off and run errands while Lilah practiced. Today she sat on the sidelines of the archery studio with the other parents and watched her child.

Who could be sending her threatening emails? Of course, the obvious answer was her ex-boyfriend. Kendell had tried to keep in touch with her when he'd first gone to prison. He'd sent her letters and she'd gotten more than a few collect calls when he had the chance to call. She'd only accepted one. After he'd told her they were meant to be together and that when he got out they could start over she hadn't accepted another call. She'd changed her number and moved to Greenville, South Carolina.

How could he have gotten her information? Her mother, Dahlia, had moved to Canada five years ago with her new boyfriend and barely talked to Zoe. Another guy who had the same toxic approach to relationships as Zoe's father had. Molly, her sister, moved to Arkansas shortly after Zoe graduated college. She was married and happy with a job at the Walmart corporate offices. They talked occasionally, but just like Zoe had tried to forget her past, so had her sister. The last thing Molly said to Zoe before she'd moved away and started a new life was that Zoe was stupid for not marrying Byron and accepting his money and help.

Molly wouldn't have told Kendell how to find Zoe, but

if he'd managed to find Zoe's mother… A cold knot formed in Zoe's stomach. Her mother had liked Kendell. She'd accused Zoe of doing him wrong. Her mother might let Kendell know how to find her.

When the instructor pulled the kids together to talk about their form with the bow, Zoe got up and walked away from the practice. She hadn't talked to her mom since the year before when Dahlia had a layover in the Atlanta airport and decided that was close enough to warrant a quick call to her daughter.

She dialed her mom's number and waited for her to answer.

"Zoe?" Dahlia answered the phone as if she was unsure Zoe was really on the other end of the line. "Honey, what do you want?" The question wasn't asked with concern about hearing from a child unexpectedly. Instead, Dahlia asked as if Zoe frequently called begging for something and she didn't have the time to be bothered again.

"Yes, it's me," Zoe replied, trying not to sound irritated. Now that her mom was off living her new life with her new boyfriend, she acted like she'd fulfilled all obligations to her children.

You girls are grown now. You don't need to be pestering me for anything anymore. Dahlia's words after she'd called Zoe to tell her she was moving to a new country.

"Is everything okay? How's Lilah?" Dahlia at least sounded somewhat interested in her grandchild.

"Lilah is fine. I'm calling because…well, I want to give you a heads-up."

"Heads-up about what? Hurry up, honey. I'm meeting Bill for lunch. You know how he doesn't like it when I'm late."

Bill, Zoe's wannabe stepdad. He owned a chain of furniture stores and was the distant cousin of the owner of an NBA team. Zoe wasn't sure how her mom met him. She wanted to be happy for her mom, but she'd seen Bill call her mom stupid when she'd spilled a glass of water and Dahlia just chuckled and waved it off the way she'd done with Zoe's father. That was all it had taken for Zoe to know she'd never like Bill.

She glanced around to make sure no one was in earshot. "Byron Robidoux is going to publicly claim Zoe as his daughter. I don't think it'll be a big deal, but just in case, I want you to be prepared."

Dahlia was quiet for a few minutes. "Why would it be a big deal? You told me he was the father." Dahlia's voice held the same skepticism it had years ago when Zoe first made the claim.

"I did, but you know how it is with these rich families. Sometimes people want more of a story." She didn't want to tell her mom Byron was running for Senate. Dahlia might insist Zoe demand more from him. "I just need to make sure things will go smoothly."

"Why wouldn't they? He's the girl's dad. You're finally being smart and getting what he owes you. Remember, I'm the one who said you were dumb for not suing him for child support."

"Mom, I'm not going there right now." She tried to be calm, but some of her frustration bled through. "He's here now, and we're good. What I don't need is for Kendell to pop up asking questions or trying to push his way back into my life."

"Isn't he in jail?"

"He is, but his time is about up." More than about up. He would be out of prison in a few months.

"Really? It's been ten years already," Dahlia said as if she couldn't believe how fast time had flown by.

"It has, so I'm making sure he doesn't try to get back in our lives. He hasn't contacted you or anything?"

Kendell always turned on the charm when he was around Dahlia. When Zoe confessed to her mom about the way he liked to fight, Dahlia only snickered and shook her head.

It isn't really love if you don't fight every once in a while. What? You'd rather he didn't care and let you act and talk to him any type of way? Be happy with what you got.

"I haven't talked to him since right before he went to jail," her mother said as if that was a bad thing. "That whole thing was a setup. Kendell is a decent guy. Kind of reminded me of your dad on his good days."

He'd reminded Zoe of her dad, too. She'd realized much too late that being with a guy who was like her father wasn't a sign of love.

"Yeah, that was the problem," Zoe muttered.

"There you go being silly. Kendell had a temper, but you knew how to control it."

"That's the thing, Mom. I shouldn't have to worry about controlling his temper."

Dahlia sighed. "You young girls now. Don't know a thing about standing by your man and being his helpmate. That's why none of ya'll can keep a man."

Zoe rubbed her temples. She was in no mood to debate with her mom about this. Zoe eventually accepted that she and her mom would never see eye to eye about what was acceptable in a relationship. She only wished her mom would realize she deserved a lot more than what she accepted. "Look, I just want to make sure Kendell isn't trying to worm his way back into my life after all this time."

She wouldn't tell Dahlia about the emails. Her mom would tell her she was being silly again.

"You should at least talk to him. I mean, the boy did love you and you cheated on him with Byron. Not that I blame you much. Byron is fine as hell. Are you two together now?" Her mom's voice perked up with the question. She was probably calculating the benefits of a daughter dating a millionaire.

"No, we're not together. He's engaged to someone else and very happy. We're doing this for Lilah." In a way that was the truth. Sure, it was one more half-truth on top of a mountain of half-truths. One slipup and the entire mountain might crumble and crush them all. "But if Kendell finds out about me reuniting with Byron, he'll get upset and may reach out to try and start trouble. Promise me you won't talk to him or give him my phone number or email address. Please, Mom, do this for me."

She didn't beg her mom for anything, but she was willing to beg for this. If there was even a small amount of love Dahlia had for her then maybe she would do this one thing.

Dahlia sighed. "Fine, fine. If you don't want to talk to him, I won't tell him anything. But that doesn't mean he can't find you if he wants to."

A truth Zoe would prepare for. "Thank you. Look, I've got to go. Take care, okay?" She didn't like the decisions her mom made and hated that she pushed her daughters toward accepting toxic relationships, but she couldn't not love her. She wanted her mom to be happy. Maybe one day she'd realize that putting up with a man who didn't appreciate her wasn't the key to happiness.

Maybe Dahlia heard the concern in Zoe's voice because when she spoke again her voice had warmed slightly. "You too, Zoe. And if you know what's good for you, you'll steal Byron away from that fiancée or at least get child support."

Typical Dahlia Hammond. "Bye, Mom." Zoe hung up without waiting for an answer.

As frustrating as the conversation with her mom had been, Zoe had gotten some good information from it. Kendell hadn't been in contact with her mom. Dahlia wouldn't have hesitated to let her know if she had spoken with him, considering she still liked him. That didn't mean Kendell wasn't behind the emails. They could still be a prank or meant for someone else.

After the practice Zoe went over to thank the coach. Coach Riley taught archery at Lilah's school, but the older man's love for the sport and talent with making his own bows had resulted in his opening an archery studio.

"Is Lilah doing okay?" Zoe asked while she waited on Lilah to finish talking with some of her teammates.

Coach Riley's gray eyes beamed with pride. "Yes, she's great. One of the best archers on the team," he said in his deep Southern accent.

"That's fantastic. She's really excited about the upcoming competitions." The team had a few local competitions before they moved on to the state competitions and hopefully the regionals.

"She's already garnered some interest," Coach Riley said, grinning.

"Really? How?"

Coach Riley slid a variety of arrows into a leather carrier case. "Just earlier today I had a guy call me. Says he's a scout for the University of Georgia and he wanted to know more about Lilah and the date of the next competition so he can come watch her."

Zoe's stomach dropped. "How did he know about her?"

"Says one of his recruiters saw her at a competition the other month and was impressed." He pointed a finger and grinned. "If she keeps practicing, she could get a scholarship. Great, huh?"

"Yeah, great," Zoe said. She tried to smile as he walked away. A sinking feeling overwhelmed her. She glanced to Lilah, laughing and talking with teammates. A recruiter looking at her daughter would be great, but Zoe had been at the last competition. No recruiters were there. One of the other parents had checked. Sure, the organizers could have kept things quiet, but those types of things usually got out.

She swallowed her panic and hardened her resolve. Regardless of the strings attached or the demands, she would go to this press conference and connect Lilah to Byron forever. If someone was looking for her and her daughter, she'd be damned if she let that person get anywhere near her child without a fight.

CHAPTER ELEVEN

By Friday Zoe was a nervous wreck. An unscheduled audit had kept her too busy to think about the results of the job interview. Any other week this happened she would have spent Friday going over any deficiencies noted and coming up with an after-action plan in anticipation of any concerns. Luckily, the deficiencies were minor, but she still didn't feel right about not being there to handle any follow-up questions that may come up.

Lilah, on the other hand, was beyond excited to be going to Jackson Falls to finally meet Byron. Once Zoe had given her his name, her daughter had become an excellent internet sleuth and pulled up anything she could find on Byron and his family. The entire way up she talked about how impressive it was that the Robidoux family had taken a small tobacco farm and turned it into a multimillion-dollar company with various holdings across multiple sectors.

Hearing the pride in Lilah's voice only made Zoe remind Lilah that Byron's family wasn't their family. To which Lilah would just roll her eyes and say "I know, Mom" before going on another tangent about how interesting the family was. Zoe didn't know how to stop Lilah's growing hero worship without pulling out of this deal completely, but thoughts of the email she'd gotten and the "recruiter" asking questions about Lilah kept her foot steady on the gas.

They arrived at the Robidoux Estate early and in the middle of activity. Zoe and Lilah were quickly ushered into the downstairs family room where Byron, his family and his campaign manager were located. There was a buzz of multiple conversations as the group went through the details for the press conference.

She and Lilah walked through the door and her eyes scanned the room. Byron looked up just as she spotted him sitting next to Yolanda. When their eyes met, flutters went through her stomach. Nerves, it had to be nerves.

He stopped talking and stood. His gaze went from her to Lilah and then back to her. In a second he crossed the room to them.

"Good, you made it," he said, his deep voice warm and welcoming.

She held out her hand to shake his. Byron opened his arms to hug her. They both paused, laughed awkwardly, then Zoe leaned in for the hug. His body was solid and warm beneath the expensive white dress shirt he wore. More flutters overtook her midsection. She quickly pulled back.

"Right on time," she said brightly. Maybe too brightly. Her face heated and she turned to Lilah. "This is my daughter, Lilah."

"Our daughter," Byron said, his voice steady and insistent.

She fought back the warm and fuzzy feelings his words elicited. He was doing this to help his campaign. He'd only said that to remind her to stay on script from here on out. That was all.

"Right. Lilah, this is Byron Robidoux. Your f-father." The word nearly stuck in her throat. Not because she didn't want to say them, but because if she could turn back time, she would have made so many different decisions.

None of that mattered now. They were here. She had Lilah and wouldn't trade her for anything. All that mattered was the future.

Lilah stared at Byron with wide, uncertain eyes. "Um… hi." She shifted closer to Zoe and stared at Byron then over his shoulder to the roomful of people watching them.

Zoe put a reassuring hand on her back. "Lilah was just wondering if she'll have to say anything today."

Byron shook his head. "Not at all. We sent out a statement this morning. The phones have been ringing constantly ever since. The press conference will just be me talking, you'll say a few words and then Roy will shut things down. We won't take any questions and will get right back in the car and return here."

Zoe's body froze. "I need to talk?" She hadn't expected to talk, but she guessed that made sense.

Yolanda came up on Byron's left. "Byron, don't overwhelm them. They just got here." She was beautiful in a dark green skirt suit. Her hair fell in a smooth sheet to her shoulders. Her makeup understated but flawless. Her eyes flickered across Zoe's slim-fit jeans and Valtec T-shirt.

"Give her and—" Yolanda glanced at Lilah "—Lilah, right?" When Lilah nodded quickly, Yolanda gave her a reassuring smile. "Give them a minute to rest. Roy can go over Zoe's statement with her after they get a moment."

"We do need to change," Zoe said. She had a pair of navy pants and a light blue blouse and Lilah's cream-colored dress from Easter.

"We've set up two bedrooms upstairs for you and Lilah

to use," Byron said. "If you need anything else don't hesitate to ask."

"You didn't have to do that," Zoe said, then remembered his promise to have rooms ready for her and Lilah whenever they came up. Again, she fought back any pleasure about his making the offer.

He's only trying to make things go smoothly.

"Whatever you need just let me know. I'll do what I can to get it for you." Byron's eyes never left hers. Though he'd spoken a generic offer of assistance, all of the tension and worry that had Zoe's stomach in knots released. The fervent tone and direct stare added more to his words. Turned them into a vow that resonated deep in her chest. Yes, he was doing this to help his campaign, but the Byron she'd known in college would do anything for her. That part of him wasn't completely gone. The realization both warmed her and made her stomach clench. She didn't know what to do with that type of loyalty.

Yolanda shifted closer to Byron and placed a manicured hand on his forearm. "Byron, we need to go ahead and leave for the press conference."

Byron blinked then frowned at Yolanda. "Shouldn't we all arrive together?"

Yolanda shook her head. "There's so much we need to check beforehand. We should make sure everything is set and ready. Let Zoe get prepped while we get things together." Yolanda turned back to them. Her smile was wide and made her go from beautiful to radiant. "Lilah, I can't wait to get to know you better."

"You're his fiancée?" Lilah asked, sounding a little awestruck by Yolanda's warm welcome.

"I am. Soon I'll be your stepmother." She reached over

and placed a hand on Lilah's arm. "I know we'll eventually become friends." She patted Lilah's arm.

Zoe shifted closer to Lilah and wrapped her arms around her daughter's shoulders. Yolanda pulled her hand back. Elaina's warning rang in her head. Yolanda may have given Zoe the passive-aggressive "back off" treatment when it came to Byron, but Zoe was going to be direct with laying down her boundaries.

She met Yolanda's gaze dead on. "I'm sure we'll *all* become good friends, and I'll be here to make sure Lilah gets through this unscathed."

Yolanda's chin rose along with one brow. Her gaze sharpened as if seeing Zoe for the first time. "And we wouldn't have it any other way." She turned to Byron. "Are you ready?"

Byron gave Zoe a questioning glance. Zoe knew if she asked him to stay, he would. She wanted him to stay. Wanted him to sit with her as Roy prepped her and Lilah. Wanted to know his thoughts about how the day would go. Wanted him to strategize with her the way they used to back in college on projects.

Yolanda wiped a piece of lint off Byron's shoulder. Zoe hated the tightening in her midsection every time Yolanda touched Byron. She dropped her eyes to her daughter. She was here to protect Lilah, not rekindle her friendship with Byron or act like the jealous ex-girlfriend.

"I'm good," Zoe said. "Go ahead. It'll give me and Lilah a chance to catch our breath after the drive."

Byron's eyes narrowed. He opened his mouth probably to insist on staying when Yolanda spoke. "See. All set. Let's go so we can make sure everything is okay."

"Fine." Byron eyes met Zoe's. "We'll talk more later."

Byron left and Zoe and Lilah were ushered upstairs to change before meeting the rest of the family. She wasn't sure how Byron's family would react to Lilah, but to her surprise they all wrapped her in like one of their own. Byron's younger sister India introduced herself and immediately got Lilah in a discussion of her archery lessons while Roy went over Zoe's statement. Zoe listened to his strategy but kept an eye on Lilah and the rest of the family.

Not long after that they were piled into a limo and driven to the location for the press conference. Zoe noticed Elaina insisted on driving herself instead of riding in the car with the rest of the family, but once they reached the location of the press conference, which was right outside Byron's campaign headquarters, she and the rest of the family were nothing but smiles and goodwill.

Years of looking for real emotions behind false smiles gave Zoe the truth. Grant's fiancée, Patricia, and India didn't talk to each other. Elaina spoke with India and Travis, but she was stiff and kept her answers brief. Byron and Grant avoided eye contact for too long. Yolanda flowed between each of the family members with a smile and gracious word, but when Zoe caught Elaina's gaze after Yolanda walked away, Elaina rolled her eyes and shook her head. Zoe didn't want to, but she chuckled and glanced away quickly before getting caught. There was a lot at play beneath the surface with this family. She hoped she could shield herself and Lilah from most of the dysfunction.

"You sure you're okay with this?" Zoe asked right before they were to go out and address the crowd of reporters.

Lilah took a shaky breath and nodded. "I am."

"We can leave. I'll get up there and tell the truth and we can walk away." Doing so would mean moving away from

Greenville to make it harder for Kendell to find her. But she'd do it if Lilah was really upset about this.

"I want to do this." Lilah leaned into Zoe. "They're so… polished. You know. Sophisticated and put together. Are you sure they want me?"

Zoe wrapped an arm around her daughter's shoulders and pulled her in close. Lilah didn't look beneath the surface for the truth. She just saw a glamorous family that was taking her in. *I will not let them hurt her.*

"We wouldn't be here if they didn't."

Lilah smiled and Zoe squeezed her closer. Roy called them all together for a last-minute briefing and then they were outside in front of the cameras. So many cameras. Some from national news channels. Zoe swallowed hard.

Elaina slid up next to Zoe and whispered, "Welcome to the jungle."

Zoe's head whipped toward her. Elaina's smile was calm and plastic, but her eyes held a touch of warmth. Zoe's heart beat faster with every flash and click of a camera. In what felt like slow motion she turned toward Byron at the podium. Her life was about to change forever.

Byron glanced over his shoulder at her and smiled a reassuring smile. He winked as if everything would be okay. The movement so Byron-like that Zoe chuckled, breathed and relaxed. They'd get through this. Together.

Byron faced the crowd. "Thank you for coming today for this important and exciting announcement."

BYRON NEEDED A few minutes of quiet and possibly a drink. The press conference had gone better than he expected. Most of the reporters there had accepted the story they'd presented of young love and rash decisions that ended in a reunion story everyone was happy with. They'd already gotten calls from the major networks asking for an on-screen interview to talk about how their family was reacting to the news. Byron turned them all down. Claiming the family needed time to get to know each other before bringing in the media.

He'd spent the entire day answering calls, doing phone interviews and planning his next campaign stops. From now until the end of the campaign he would barely get a moment alone or time to breathe. He would have typically gone home and enjoyed the quiet. Instead, he roamed the halls of his family's estate in search of Zoe. He hadn't gotten a chance to talk to her except for the brief moment that morning. He knew he wouldn't be able to rest until he'd spoken to her and made sure she was okay.

He checked all the common rooms downstairs and hadn't found her. The house was unusually quiet for so much to have happened today. He expected Zoe and the rest of his family to be all together in the downstairs sitting area discussing the topics of today.

When he checked the upstairs family room, typically reserved for close family and not outside visitors, he found Lilah sitting alone on a couch scrolling through her telephone. Surprised, Byron looked around then down the hall to see if Zoe was close by. She'd stuck by her daughter's side for the entire day. Byron wouldn't have expected her to be alone.

"Hey, where's your mom?" Byron asked as he came into the room.

Lilah dropped her phone in her lap and sat up straight. "A-aunt Elaina wanted to show her something in her room. They should be right back."

Byron raised a brow but didn't voice his question aloud. Elaina had hovered around Zoe a lot more than he'd anticipated. He'd have to figure out what Elaina's motives were with linking up with Zoe.

"No one decided to keep you company?" Byron walked over to the minibar on the side of the room.

"I actually enjoyed the quiet. It's been kind of a crazy day." Lilah was still in the cream dress she'd worn for the press conference. Her braids were pulled back from her face in a tight ponytail. Though excitement still brightened her voice, she rubbed her eyes and muffled a yawn.

"I can't argue with that. Soda or juice?" He held up a can of cola and a bottle of apple juice.

"Juice, please."

Byron grabbed the bottle, put ice in a glass and took it over to Lilah. "So how are you doing?"

Lilah twisted off the cap and poured juice over the ice. "I'm good."

Byron sat on the couch and faced her. "No, really. How are you? This is a lot. Your mom told me you know the real story, but if you have any questions, or if things feel weird let me know. We kind of went into this to protect you. That doesn't mean you're okay with the changes."

Lilah took a sip of her drink. Her brows knitted together as if trying to figure out the right thing to say. Byron waited patiently for her to speak.

"I am okay. More than okay. I mean, this is kind of fantastic," she said in a rush.

He blinked, surprised by her enthusiasm. "Fantastic? Really?"

"Yeah, when Mom told me what you did for her, she didn't tell me your name. I wanted to know who you were.

I wanted to thank you. For saving my mom." Lilah raised a shoulder and glanced away after speaking.

Byron was blown away. He'd expected her to be overwhelmed, maybe annoyed by the interruption in her life. He wasn't prepared for gratitude for upending her life. "You don't have to thank me. Your mom was in a bad spot. I was happy to help her."

"But no one just does something like that for a friend. I don't care what anyone says. What you did was amazing. I wished you were my real dad. Now you kinda are." She lifted her shoulder again and smiled shyly.

Byron didn't know what to do with that. The trust shining from her eyes. He didn't deserve all of that. He added the weight of her expectations to the ones he'd taken on the night he'd won the primary. Lilah had gifted him with her trust. He wouldn't take it for granted or do anything to kill the light in her eyes. This is what it felt like to have a family, a child who looked up to you. He'd never thought about fatherhood except in the abstract. Something that would happen one day. That day was here. He couldn't screw this up.

"Not kinda," he said. "After today I am. If you ever need anything don't hesitate to call me."

Her face lit up and she grinned. "Seriously?"

"Seriously. This isn't just for the press conference or until the end of my campaign. You're a part of the Robidoux clan now, and we always look out for family."

There was a knock on the door. Byron looked over his shoulder. Patricia stood at the door. "Lilah, your mom is down at the pool house with Elaina. They asked if you'd join them."

Lilah's eyes widened. "There's a pool house?"

Byron chuckled. "There is. Down the stairs out back and to the right."

She jumped up, then hesitated and glanced at him. "Are you coming?"

"I'll be down in a minute."

She grinned, downed the rest of the juice, put the glass on the table and hurried out the door. Byron chuckled as she left. They hadn't had that kind of enthusiasm in the family in years.

"She's going to bring a lot of joy into the house," Patricia said.

"I agree." Byron stood and went back to the minibar. "Drink?"

Patricia wrinkled her nose and shook her head. "No, thank you."

She'd changed after the press conference earlier into a yellow linen suit. Her salt-and-pepper hair was pulled up in a soft twist. She looked regal and striking. Nothing like the woman who'd started working for their family as the head cook twenty years ago. Back then she'd worn a chef's suit, her hair pulled back in a tight ponytail, and even though she'd smiled she also held herself stiff and away from the family.

His dad started seeing Patricia around the time his mom was diagnosed with breast cancer. Byron didn't know if the affair started before or after the sickness. What he did know was his mom had quietly condoned the relationship.

Love is fleeting and not what dynasties are built on. If you remember that, your heart will never be broken. His mom's words when he'd confronted her about Grant's affair.

"Where is Dad?" Byron asked as he mixed together an old fashioned.

"He's in our room on the phone. Some problem with one of the holdings. I told him to let Elaina handle it, but…"

Grant and Elaina were in the middle of a shaky truce right now. Byron chose to stay out of that. "Let him handle it, then." He finished mixing his drink. "I think I'll see what's happening at the pool house." He was tired and needed time to relax, but he wanted to see Zoe.

"Before you go, can I offer a quick word of advice?" she asked.

Byron's head titled to the side. "On what?"

Patricia didn't offer him or anyone else in the family advice. He'd been the first out of all the siblings to accept her relationship with their dad. Not because he'd approved of it, but because he'd realized his dad wasn't going to give her up. If he wanted a relationship with Grant, then he had to deal with Patricia. His relationship with her was cordial, not close.

"On Lilah." She took a step closer. "Be careful there. Kids can become attached easily, and you don't want to hurt her in the long run."

Byron did a double take. "Hurt her? How will I hurt her?"

"I understand why you're doing this. I think it's admirable, but she's not your daughter." Patricia lowered her voice as she spoke the last part. "One day you and Yolanda will have kids. You'll be a senator, and your life will be pulled in multiple ways. You might not be able to give her the attention she's craving."

"After today she is my daughter," he said firmly. "Whatever life I build with Yolanda will include Lilah."

He and Yolanda hadn't talked much about how they'd incorporate Lilah into their family. Zoe wanted him to be more hands off, and he'd respect that, but he meant what he'd said to Lilah. If she needed him for anything, he'd help her. Regardless of what Yolanda thought.

Patricia smiled at him as if he were a kid who said he could ride his bike to the moon. Part *how sweet* and part *bless your heart*. "You say that, but will Yolanda agree with that?"

"Yolanda knew what she was getting into when we talked about this. We're good."

More so, he didn't appreciate Patricia stepping in, trying to offer advice. She was the last person he'd go to for help navigating ways to build a relationship with a child. She hadn't tried to build one with them, just their father.

"Now, if you'll excuse me." He turned to walk away.

"This is exactly why your mom didn't want her in your life." Patricia sounded exasperated.

Byron froze and spun back. "Excuse me? How would you know what my mom wanted?"

"Because I talked to her about you and Zoe," Patricia said casually.

"You talked to her? Why would she talk to you?" He'd rarely seen his mother talk to Patricia.

"I was her friend."

Byron stared for a stunned second before he laughed. She actually sounded like she believed those words. "Friend? Is that what you call it?"

Patricia's mouth tightened, but she didn't look away or back down. "There are different types of friendships. Your mom understood your father had needs she couldn't provide."

Byron slashed his free hand through the air. "Please, don't even try to tell me my mom pimped you out to my dad."

Patricia flinched and tugged on the edge of her shirt. After a deep breath she spoke in a steady voice. "I'm not saying that, but what I am saying is she was a smart and practical woman. She knew you would do anything for Zoe including get so blinded by what you thought was love you wouldn't see the future. She's not here to help you now, but I can't stand by and not say anything."

Byron took two steps forward and pointed. Her audacity to say something so ridiculous made years of holding his tongue bubble to the surface. "You know what? You can. You can stand by and say absolutely nothing about me, my life, or anything I plan to do. Your advice is not wanted or needed."

He turned his back and walked out. Anger and frustration fueled his steps. He could put up with a lot of things, but if Patricia thought she could give any input on what he did she'd lost her damn mind. She wasn't his mom, would never take the place of her, and an engagement to Grant would never change that.

CHAPTER TWELVE

ZOE WOKE UP early the next morning. She checked on Lilah, who'd slept on the pull-out sofa in the pool house's living room and was still knocked out. The day before had been busy, so much so she hadn't put up a fight when Grant offered her and Lilah the pool house for their stay. Instead of waking up Lilah, Zoe showered and dressed then left the pool house to search for coffee in the main house.

The early-morning sun was still rising over the trees on the edge of the expansive lawn. The air was cool with a hint of the heat that would come later that afternoon. Movement on the edge of her periphery caught her attention. Zoe turned in that direction, and her breath stuck in her chest.

Byron jogged toward the house wearing nothing but a pair of red basketball shorts and black running shoes. He spotted her and changed direction to come her way. Sweat glistened on the chiseled muscles of his chest, arms and shoulders. Zoe clenched her teeth. It was either that or watch him with her mouth open and tongue hanging out.

"Hey. You're up early," Byron said between deep breaths.

Zoe's fingers itched to touch his chest. To trace her fingertips across the glistening lines of muscles of his upper body. She shoved her hands in the back pockets of her jeans. "Yeah, I'm used to getting up early for work."

"You used to hate getting up early." Byron grinned and wiped sweat from his brow. "I always had to drag you out of bed on weekends for our volunteer work."

Byron would show up early at her dorm room on Saturdays when they'd volunteer, coffee in hand and music playing. He would literally drag her from the bed, shove the coffee in her hand and give her twenty minutes to meet him outside.

His smile sent a funny feeling through her stomach. Zoe licked her dry lips. "You know a lot of things change in fourteen years."

"I guess they do."

His gaze flicked over her body quickly before he looked away. Heat flashed through Zoe's midsection. Some things didn't change. The undercurrent of attraction between them obviously hadn't gone away over the years.

"Where are you coming from?" she asked.

"I spent the night here. Decided to get up and jog through some of the trails leading back to the old tobacco fields."

They'd stayed up late the night before. Elaina had hung out with them and answered all of Lilah's questions about the family. Mr. Robidoux hadn't joined them, and Zoe got the feeling Byron's dad accepted the new situation but didn't like it. Regardless, she'd had more fun last night than she'd expected. She'd thought Elaina would be standoffish, and while she couldn't say Elaina was exactly warm, she had been courteous and helpful.

Her gaze lowered to his glistening chest. "I'm glad you stayed over," she said, her voice a little too husky.

Zoe cleared her throat and jerked her eyes away from his half-naked body toward the main house. She searched her scrambled thoughts for a good reason why she'd said that. The bad reason was getting to see him like this.

"I need to talk to you and didn't want to do that in front of everyone."

"What's up?" Byron shifted his weight to one side with his hands on his hips. The muscles in his arms flowed with the easy movement.

Zoe met his eyes. Maybe if she focused on something other than his body she wouldn't be so…distracted. He smiled. His full lower lip surrounded by the sexy beard was even more tempting in the early-morning light.

Stop ogling him and get to the point! "I've been getting emails," she blurted out.

"What kind of emails?"

"The kind that call me a lying bitch and say I'm going to pay," she said quickly.

Byron immediately straightened. His eyes sharpened. "From who?"

She shifted from one foot to the other. "I don't know. I asked someone in my company's IT department to see what they could find and only traced it to the city the email originated from. I thought it was a prank, but there's been too many of them coming."

Byron stepped closer. His focus completely on her. "How many?"

"Four or five." She twisted her hands together in front of her. They were trembling and that made her want to kick something. No, it made her want to kick whoever sent the emails. She hugged herself to stop the shaking. She was safe. Lilah was safe. That was all that mattered. "I was going to ignore them. I thought they'd go away."

"When was the last one?" Byron's voice remained calm.

He watched her closely and she could tell he was already thinking of what to do next.

"Earlier this week," she answered.

He nodded. "Send over the email. I'll ask Dominic to check things out. Between him and Jeanette I'm sure they'll figure out what's going on."

Jeanette was the private investigator who worked with Dominic. Zoe had met her the year before when Byron originally sought her out. She'd liked Jeanette and believed her when she'd offered to help Zoe in any way she could.

"That's not all," she said.

"What else?"

She hoped he understood her concerns and wouldn't think she was overreacting. She could be pessimistic, but ignoring her instincts when she was younger had only led to her digging a deeper and deeper hole to fall into. "The other day at Lilah's archery practice one of her coaches mentioned someone called to ask questions about her. They said they were a college recruiter."

"But you don't believe that?" he asked hesitantly.

"I might have if there'd been recruiters at her last match. There weren't any. I understand people may have taken video that could have gotten back to a college recruiter, but it came the same day I got the email. It just doesn't feel right."

Byron stepped forward and placed the tips of his fingers on her elbow. "We'll look into that, too. If you feel something is off, then I trust you."

Her shoulders relaxed as the weight of holding everything to herself lifted. She'd kept her fears wrapped up inside for so long. Her mom always told her she worried too much. Kendell used to laugh and tell her she was stupid whenever she doubted something. God forbid she ever say "told you so" when her intuition was right. Byron had always trusted her instincts. He'd never mocked her or easily dismissed her.

"Thank you, Byron."

She wanted to hug him. In college she'd wrapped her arms around his neck and hugged him tight whenever he'd helped her with a project or gave her good news about one of their programs. She leaned slightly forward. His fingertips slid from the side to the back of her elbow as if he wanted to pull her into his embrace.

"I think you should stay in North Carolina. At least until we find out what's going on."

She frowned and stepped back. His fingers brushed her skin as his hand fell away. Accepting a room occasionally if she came to Jackson Falls to help with his campaign was one thing. Living there was something completely different. "I can't stay in North Carolina. We don't know how long it'll take to find out what's going on, if anything."

"I want you here." His eyes both determined and pleading.

Zoe's breath stuttered. A tiny flare of excitement shot through her heart. "What?"

Byron blinked and slid back. He did his nervous nose twitch thing before running a hand over his face. "My family and our resources can better protect you if you're close."

The practicality of his words snuffed out her excitement. He still thought she was too helpless to take care of herself. "Lilah's school is in Greenville. So is my job, and I'm up for a promotion. I'm not giving up my life just to come up here and be taken care of by you." She wasn't about to lose her independence again.

He shifted his shoulders. "It's not me taking care of you," he said in a rush.

"Then what is it? Why else would you want me here?"

"Because I…" His mouth snapped shut. Byron took several deep breaths and shook his head.

Zoe's heartbeat stuttered. She stepped closer and leaned her head to the side to catch his eyes. "Why, Byron?" She wasn't sure what she wanted or expected to hear. She couldn't leave everything behind and be dependent on Byron. But something inside her desperately wanted to hear a reason other than because he believed she couldn't take care of herself.

"Because it'll be good optics," he said in a voice that sounded too much like his father. "We've announced that Lilah is my daughter. If you're closer, it'll give us better opportunities for public appearances at various events."

"Good optics?" The disappointment in her chest was exactly what she needed. A cold, uncomfortable reminder that at the end of the day Byron was all about winning. Always had been, always would be. It was why she'd never believed him when he'd said he wanted to be with her. Byron hadn't liked Kendell and she'd known his interest in her was mostly about stealing her from Kendell.

"Yes. That and I can keep you both safe."

Zoe crossed her arms over her chest. "I don't need you to keep me safe," she shot back. She let anger cover her disappointment. "I promised not to keep anything from you as we moved forward and that's what I'm doing. I can take care of me and Lilah."

She moved to go around him toward the house. She needed coffee. Caffeine would clear her head. Maybe then she'd stop expecting more out of this situation. Long fingers wrapped around her forearm.

"Zoe, wait—"

She extended and twisted her arm while simultaneously turning until her hand wrapped around his wrist. Byron froze. Several moments passed as he stared at her wide-eyed. His heavy breaths matched hers. Beneath her fingertips his pulse raced.

Zoe quickly released him and crossed her arms. "Look, I understand. You want to win the election. My old lie has come back and now you're having to deal with it. I appreciate everything you're doing, and we'll do what we can to help you win. But I'm not giving up my life in Greenville. I built it, and Lilah is happy there. Thank you for agreeing to ask Dominic to look into the emails and stuff, but don't ask me to move here for you."

Byron continued to study her. Something shifted in his gaze. Concern blended to admiration and finally acceptance. He took a few breaths then nodded. "Will you at least accept the security detail I offered before?"

She wanted to say no, but the sick feeling she had when she'd heard about the phone call to Lilah's coach along with the emails shut her mouth. She nodded. "I will."

The corner of his lip lifted. He reached out but stopped right before his fingers would have brushed her chin. "Always a fighter." His hand dropped away.

Her skin tingled as if he had touched her. A sensation she felt down to her core. Zoe swallowed hard. "I'm used to fighting you and winning."

"It's because you've got me at a disadvantage."

She raised a brow. "Oh, really?"

"I have a weak spot when it comes to you, Zoe. Always have. Always will." His voice sounded bittersweet.

Zoe drew in a breath. Byron had a weak spot for her? She couldn't believe it. They were old friends, he wanted to help her and he wanted to win the Senate seat. Those were the reasons why he'd agreed to help her. If there were other reasons, if he still cared the way he'd once claimed, she wasn't sure if she'd be able to get through this.

"Byron, I...we..."

He nodded toward the house. "Come on. Let's see what's for breakfast." Byron turned and went toward the house without waiting for an answer.

CHAPTER THIRTEEN

"ZOE, HAVE YOU gotten the after-action report for the OSHA inspection?"

Zoe froze in the middle of raising the turkey sandwich she'd brought for lunch to her mouth. Thirty minutes. That was all she'd hoped for. Just thirty minutes of quiet so she could eat her sandwich and get on with her day. Instead, John Bailey had come straight for her in the break room and ruined the few minutes she'd had to rest.

Even though a week had passed, she still couldn't believe they'd hired John for the director position instead of her. Ten years between busting her ass at OSHA and climbing the Valtec corporate ladder only to be overlooked and the job given to John. They'd never say so, but Zoe knew she hadn't been chosen because of the drama that had erupted in her personal life. Turns out the media was interested in a story about a potential senator from North Carolina having a kid show up out of nowhere.

She'd sat down with Miranda and asked for feedback on why the company had gone in the direction they'd chosen.

Although we were very impressed with your programs and the improvements you've introduced, he's got more managerial experience than you.

Managerial experience. Code for less drama and the easier choice. She currently managed three inspectors and had managed a team of four before coming to Valtec.

Zoe lowered her turkey sandwich, ignored the rebellious grumble of her stomach and turned to John hovering at the end of the table where she sat in the break room.

"I've done the after-action report and emailed it to you right before I came in here for lunch." Zoe kept her voice moderate. Tamped down the frustration bubbling up inside her.

John looked from her, to her sandwich, and back to her. "Did you?" he asked as if she was trying to trick him out of his family fortune.

He pulled his cell phone out of his back pocket. Zoe took a quick bite of her sandwich while he pulled up his email. She didn't doubt he would find something else for her to work on since she'd already completed this task. Whatever managerial experience John had he must have learned from the Micro Managers School for the Insecure. The man questioned everything, oversaw every task and butted in on the simplest items. Zoe was pretty sure he'd install an intercom in the bathroom if it meant he could check in on employees throughout the day.

"Oh," John said, sounding disappointed. "I guess you did send it."

"I promised it to you before one o'clock." Zoe took another bite of her sandwich. Maybe, just maybe, he'd let her eat her lunch in peace.

John stuck the phone back in his pocket. He crossed his arms and watched her with a frown. "What about the training programs that are supposed to start next week?"

"The presentations are ready," Zoe replied and sipped from the can of sparkling water in front of her.

"Ready? Already? Are you sure?"

She nodded. "Very sure. I used the presentation from

the previous year and updated it with all the new information I have."

John immediately shook his head. "No. That won't work."

"Why not?" She bit her tongue instead of saying it had worked for the previous seven years.

"The employees get bored when it's the same old stuff presented every day. I need a new presentation."

"The regulations haven't changed. The focus isn't the presentation. I've worked out an interactive way to reinforce the intent of the regulations." Something else she'd done for the past few years, which earned her favorable reviews from employees whenever she taught a class.

"Nope. Not going to work. That's why they chose me in this position. They wanted new ideas. Something fresh. You play things too safe, Zoe. Send me the presentations then come to my office. We'll go through the slides and see how we can update it with any new information."

"That's exactly what I said I would do."

He waved off her words. "You'll leave too much old stuff. Come on. Let's get a start now."

She pointed to her sandwich. "I'm at lunch."

He shrugged and looked at her as if she was making a ridiculous point. "So bring it with you. It'll be a working lunch. You're an exempt employee anyway. You're expected to work through lunch." He turned and went to the door. "Chop chop." He snapped his fingers with each word.

Zoe flinched and gritted her teeth. She glanced at the other people sitting around the conference room. Saw the looks of solidarity and sympathy. Years of giving one hundred and ten percent only to have to report to John? Was this what the next several years of her life would be like?

Pushing aside the depressing thought, Zoe got up from the table and put her half-eaten sandwich into her lunch bag. No need to bring it with her. Knowing John, he'll have her constantly working on the presentation and she wouldn't even get a chance to take a bite. As she went back to her office to send John the perfectly fine presentation, she questioned her life choices.

ZOE SCOOPED OUT a heaping spoonful of red beans and rice and dumped it onto her plate. She glanced at the mound of rice, then the pot and scooped out another spoonful. Her growling stomach approved.

"Zoe, seriously, leave some rice for the rest of us," Victoria teased.

Zoe's cheeks heated. She dropped the second spoonful and moved on to pierce a grilled chicken breast and added it to the mound of rice. "I missed lunch today."

Victoria frowned. "John again?"

Zoe just sighed and added a roll to her plate. Lilah and Julie had made their plates and were already laughing and whispering over their food in the dining room. Zoe took her plate of food to the kitchen table then went to the fridge.

"You guessed it." She opened the fridge and pulled out a can of sparkling water.

Victoria flipped her long faux locks over her shoulders. Her dark eyes sparked with a you're-better-than-me look. "I don't know how you can stay there after they passed you over."

"I need the job, the money, the security," Zoe said. All three things were true, and for the first time in her life she felt pinned in by the responsibilities of adulthood.

Hook up with a guy who will take care of you forever. You may have to put up with some shit, but it's worth it.

Her mother's advice rang through her head. She'd started the early years of her life like that. Had let Kendell handle her car payment, buy her books and take her on shopping trips while accepting his jealousy and occasional slaps as the shit she'd have to put up with. Now she was independent. She paid for everything herself. Answered to only herself. While she did not want to go back to a relationship like she had with Kendell, she wished she could snap her fingers and make all the reasons she had to stay at Valtec disappear.

"I'm vested," Zoe said. The word everyone at Valtec used once they'd been there five years or more. If she stuck it out until retirement, she would get retirement benefits. If she left she'd have to start all over somewhere else.

Victoria came over and sat across from Zoe. "Vested in what? That guy's bullshit? You deserved that position. Start looking and get the hell out of there." She took a bite of her rice.

The idea of looking for a new job scared Zoe. What if they didn't pay her what Valtec paid? What if she went there and worked for someone worse than John? What if she was fired because she was a newer employee and was in worse shape than she was in now?

She shook her head. "I don't know. I've got too much going on right now. I'll think about it after the weekend."

"What's this weekend?"

Zoe shrugged but avoided Victoria's see-all gaze by cutting her chicken. "Another campaign event."

"Another one? Zoe, you've spent the past two weekends in North Carolina already. I thought after the announcement you'd be done. Do you really have to keep going up there?"

"I don't, but I like to try and help out." Even though Byron had approached her about going public she was the one who'd come up with the lie in the first place. If she would have handled her situation herself, he never would be in this position.

"Mmm hmm..." Victoria stabbed at the grilled vegetables on her plate.

"What's that supposed to mean?"

Victoria held up a hand. "Nothing. I'm staying out of it. What's the event this weekend?"

Zoe decided to let that go. "Campaign dinner. They want the entire family there." Victoria raised a brow and Zoe continued quickly. "I'm not really family, but they want people to see that I'm getting along with Byron and his family. He's getting some bad press after the reveal."

Even though she hadn't revealed the entire truth to Victoria, she had reiterated to her friend that she was not family. She didn't want to consider herself as family. If she did, then she'd think too much about how it felt when Byron looked into her eyes for too long. How he still made her laugh. The way her body awakened whenever she got a whiff of his cologne. She had to be the outsider before she started having insider thoughts.

"Who wants you to get along with everyone? Byron or the fiancée?"

"The fiancée," Zoe admitted. "She's nice enough. She's been super supportive during this entire thing and she's great with Lilah."

Victoria leaned in. "But..."

"But I don't know. I think it's weird because it's a forced friendship. I'm sure I'd like her either way."

Except Yolanda wasn't the type of woman Zoe would have pictured Byron with. He dated all types of women when they were in college, so Zoe couldn't say he had a specific type. But something about Yolanda didn't seem like she was right with him. She was ambitious, smart and pleasant enough, but one thing was missing. All the women Byron typically went for were crazy about him. Yolanda wasn't crazy about Byron. Yolanda didn't look at Byron like she couldn't wait to be alone with him. Byron didn't look at Yolanda as if he knew most of her secrets and couldn't wait to uncover more. They looked like a couple in some 50s sitcom: perfect with no passion.

"Well, go with your gut. Just because she's nice doesn't mean you two have to be friends."

"Oh, I am well aware of that." Zoe stabbed a piece of chicken and quickly cut it into smaller pieces.

"And while you're up there politicking, maybe use your new connections to help you find a way out of Valtec."

Zoe stopped cutting her chicken. "What do you mean?"

Victoria gave her a don't-be-dumb look. "You know what I mean. You've been helping them. They can help you, too."

Zoe waved a hand and shook her head. "I can't ask them for a job."

His parents had thought she only wanted Byron for his money. She didn't doubt his dad still believed she was out to play Byron. Asking for more help would only fuel that suspicion.

"I'm not saying ask for a job. Just see if they can put in a good word for you somewhere else. You're connected to a rich, influential family now. If they can help you get from under John's obnoxious thumb, then go for it."

"I don't want to owe them anything."

"Would Byron expect anything back if he helped you?"

He wouldn't. Zoe had thought more than once of his suggestion that she move to Jackson Falls. He said he'd have an update on the emails when she came to town this week. She dreaded the answer. Either someone she knew was behind them and really wanted to make her pay, or she'd been the victim of a prank and had freaked out and scared Byron for nothing. Even if it was the latter, Byron would give her a reference if she looked for another job. He wouldn't help with the expectation of being owed something.

"He'd be chill about it."

"Then think it over while you're there. Valtec told you with their decision exactly where they want you to stay in their company. Use the new changes in your life to level up."

Zoe took a bite of the savory red beans and rice and nodded. The logic of Victoria's words sank in. Not wanting to be considered as trying to use Byron wasn't the same as asking for a reference. She'd try to see what she could find on her own first. It wasn't as if any potential employer who bothered to look her up wouldn't see she was connected to the Robidoux family. She just hoped the connection that was supposed to make her life safer didn't further hinder her future.

CHAPTER FOURTEEN

BYRON STOPPED BY the estate on his way home from a campaign appearance in Raleigh to drop off paperwork for his dad. It was after ten and he knew Grant and Patricia were still out at a fund-raiser, which was why he'd chosen to swing through late instead of going straight home even though he was ready to be in his space.

He'd barely spent a night in his own bed since the press conference. Every day was another speech, luncheon, or town hall meeting where he had to combat the rumors that refused to die that he was a playboy millionaire with dozens of secret children out there. After fighting to save his reputation constantly on the road, he was in no mood to come to the family estate—a place that once meant refuge—and argue with his dad.

Grant went along with the decision Byron made to introduce Lilah as his daughter, but the topic was still a sore spot. Like a sprained ankle he didn't want to put too much weight on, he avoided his dad to avoid the pain. Add on Patricia's random interest in playing consoling mother toward Byron, the sprain might turn into a fracture he wasn't sure they'd recover from if he told her to mind her own damn business like he wanted to.

Byron went upstairs to his father's study. The familiar scent of the signature Robidoux Tobacco cigar hung in the air. That and the scent of the floral perfume Patricia wore. When he worked at Robidoux Tobacco, Byron would lounge on the leather sofa in his dad's study and update Grant about his day, ask advice, or strategize with him about how they'd negotiate a business deal. He hadn't done that in a long time. Patricia now caught up with Grant in his study. She'd taken over his lounging spot.

He dropped the paperwork in Grant's leather executive chair. He'd lost his spot on the couch, and the family had new lawyers who handled things for them after Byron left the company, but every now and then Grant still asked him to look over some items. The idea of refusing never entered his mind. The company was his legacy, too.

He left the study and went downstairs. His stomach rumbled, so he made a beeline for the kitchen. Sandra mentioned there was pie in there when he'd arrived. A slice would hold him over until he made it home and ordered food. Yolanda wasn't coming over tonight, so he could finally get one night alone to himself.

Voices on the other side of the cracked door of the conference room caught his attention. Byron stopped and frowned. The lights were on. That room was only used when the family had major business to conduct away from the corporate offices. Grant and Patricia were gone. Elaina was off doing something. She slipped off a lot lately without telling the family where she was going. He doubted one of the servants would be using the room, but stranger things had happened.

Byron pushed open the door and his eyes widened with surprise. Zoe sat at the conference table. A laptop in front of her with paperwork spread out around it. She held the phone to her ear and nodded at whatever was being said on the other side.

"John, I've got it. The presentation will be ready first thing Monday morning." She was silent for several beats. Her head fell back, and she raised a fist toward the ceiling. "It's late and there's nothing else we can do tonight. Let me make these changes and get the draft back to you." More silence. Her middle finger popped free of her fist and she pulled the phone away from her ear and flipped off the device.

Byron grinned and leaned against the door. He shouldn't eavesdrop, but it was his family's house. Zoe's thick curls were twisted down against her scalp. The ends of the twists brushed the back of her neck. She wore loose-fitting gray sweatpants with a dark blue tank top that didn't cover the straps of her black bra. He was instantly taken back to college. Finding Zoe studying late into the night. *Procrastinator* was the perfect word for her. He'd have to drag her away to take a break after she'd spend several hours binge studying.

She put the phone back to her ear and nodded. "Exactly. I will get the updates to you before noon tomorrow. You know, it wouldn't hurt for you to take the weekend to, you know, relax."

Zoe leaned forward and pinched the bridge of her nose. "Yes, John, I do care about the quality of our work. Don't worry. Tomorrow at noon. Goodbye."

She tossed the phone on the table with a long groan. Byron knocked on the door. Zoe jumped up and faced him. Her eyes widened and she sat up straighter.

"What are you doing here?"

Byron chuckled and strolled into the room. "I need a reason to be here?"

She smiled but rubbed her eyes. "You don't live here, so actually the question isn't out of line."

He pulled the seat next to her out of the way and leaned against the edge of the table facing her. "According to my dad I'm always welcome."

"I better inform him to reconsider that before you move back in."

Her big brown eyes met his as she teased him with a beautiful smile that brought out the dimple in her cheek. His breathing stuttered. Something stirred deep in his midsection. He understood the reaction wasn't one he should be having, but he could never walk away when she looked at him like that.

"He doesn't have to worry about me moving back in. I have no plans to move back home."

Zoe leaned forward, rested her elbow on the table then propped her head in her hand. "Really? No elaborate dreams of living in your dad's basement and playing video games all night?"

He chuckled and rubbed his beard. "I don't know. If I lose this race, maybe I'll consider the basement backup."

She lightly bumped his thigh with the side of her fist. "You're going to win."

He sighed and gripped the side of the table instead of reaching out the way he once would have, wrap his fingers lightly around her wrist, see how long she'd let him hold her. He wasn't ashamed to say he'd tried to steal her away from Kendell. And every time Zoe let his fingers caress her skin a second longer than necessary, he'd thought he was getting closer to changing her mind about him.

Except her mind had never changed.

Byron looked away from her soul-stealing gaze and

tore his mind from the past. "I'm getting beat up on the campaign trail."

"But you're handling it all well," she said, sounding impressed.

"I'm trying, but it's not easy."

"Did you expect it to be easy? I know you always got what you wanted without problems but becoming a United States Senator doesn't just fall in your lap." She pointed toward his lap. Her fingernails were painted a light gray color.

A vision of her soft, manicured hands touching his lap invaded his brain. Her hand squeezing his thigh. Easing up to brush against his dick.

Byron shifted and cleared his throat. *Campaign. Focus on the campaign.* "I know that. I didn't expect it to be easy. I knew I'd have to fight to win voters' trust. I even expected to get beaten up."

"Then what is it?" The teasing left her expression and she watched him with interest. As if she not only wanted to hear what was bothering him but was also ready to help.

He didn't know if there was anything anyone could do to make the campaign easier. He'd expected a backlash after the announcement. Questions about his credibility and rumors about his dating history. The level of negativity aimed at Zoe was not something he'd been prepared for. Neither had he been prepared for how much every negative comment angered him. The story of her keeping the child a secret was one they'd all agreed on, but he hated hearing voters call her names. He played up the star-crossed, too-young-to-understand lovers angle, and had just today been warned by Roy to cut back on that.

Play up the sympathy vote. Let them hate her a little and love you a lot. It'll work great.

"It's all of the time away from home. I'm tired and you know how much I like to get my beauty rest," he said to Zoe. He wasn't sure how much she knew about what was being reported about her in the media. He didn't know how to approach the subject without making her feel uncomfortable. Regardless of what happened on the campaign trail he didn't regret helping her.

Zoe rolled her eyes. "Okay, Pretty Ricky. You're such a rich boy."

He chuckled. "I know it."

Once her laughter died down, she asked. "They're giving you a hard time about me, aren't they?"

He shook his head. "It's no big deal."

She leaned back in her chair. "It is a big deal. I know it. I've seen the reports and I know what they're saying. And you know what?"

He lifted a brow. "What?"

Zoe shrugged. "I don't care. They can say what they want about me. I know the truth. I'm more concerned about how it's affecting your campaign."

"My campaign is stronger than this. Honestly, a lot more people are supportive of us reconnecting than are mad about what you did."

"The ones who aren't happy are just louder," she said with a cute twist of her lips.

Byron chuckled then sobered and met her eyes. "Seriously, I knew this wouldn't be easy. When I win, things will be just as hard if not harder. I signed up for this and I won't complain. Besides, I wouldn't change anything we did. I couldn't turn my back on you like that."

Zoe's lips parted slightly. The look in her eye made him want to clasp her hands until their fingers entwined. Let her know not only with words, but also with actions that he meant everything he said.

She sat up straight and looked away. She ran a hand over the twists on her head. "Did you hear anything about the emails?"

Heat prickled Byron's cheeks. What the hell was wrong with him when it came to her? He slid away. "Dominic traced them to a library in Memphis. He's working on pulling surveillance video to try and narrow down who's coming and going."

Her brows drew together. "Kendell doesn't have ties to that city."

He wasn't so sure about that. Dominic's initial dive into Kendell's background had revealed he had traveled to Memphis for some illegal gun sales. That was years ago, and the person Kendell sold to wasn't there anymore, but it was enough to make Byron want Dominic to keep digging. "Once I find out anything more, I'll let you know immediately. Have you gotten any more?"

She shook her head. "They've stopped. Thankfully."

"Good." He'd be sure to thank Dominic for stopping them. He wouldn't worry her about the emails now. Not until he knew there was something worth worrying about. He pointed to the papers on the table. "What's all this?"

Zoe huffed out a breath. "Work. I've got an important presentation on Monday. My new boss wants to make sure everything goes perfectly."

He raised a brow. "New boss?"

She ran her fingers over the keys of her laptop. "I didn't get the promotion."

She'd mentioned the promotion when he'd first brought up the idea of her moving to Jackson Falls. Even though she hadn't made a big deal about things, he'd known she was excited about the opportunity. She'd later made an offhand comment about how the raise would help her pay for the increase in tuition at Lilah's school.

"Damn, Zoe, that sucks." He immediately regretted the words. Maybe he should have said something supportive or inspirational.

Zoe laughed drily. "It sucks so much."

Byron relaxed as the level of comfort he and Zoe used to have flowed between them. They'd never offered superficial words of support or comfort. Their relationship had always been built on telling the truth and saying what they felt. Which is why he felt more comfortable with his next, more direct question. "What are you going to do about it?"

She sighed, leaned an elbow on the table and rubbed her temple. "I'm not sure yet. My friend Victoria said I should start looking for another job. I may do that, but I've got time and good benefits with Valtec. I'm thinking about transferring to another facility. Valtec has operations all over the world. I don't have to stay in Greenville if I want to move up."

The idea of her going away, of losing contact with her again, made him want to offer up a position at Robidoux Tobacco or one of their holding companies. He tamped down the thought. He would not get upset about the possibility of something happening. He'd wait and see. Valtec had an operation in North Carolina if he wasn't mistaken. Maybe she'd end up closer. Even if she didn't, he shouldn't care about how close she was. They weren't anything more than friends.

"If you're thinking of transferring let me know. I can make some calls."

She looked as if she was about to argue then took a deep breath and met his eyes. "Honestly, that would be great."

The relief and appreciation in her voice made his chest expand. "That's what family does. It's not that big of a deal to make a phone call."

"Still, I appreciate the offer." She was silent for a second. Her eyes scanned the laptop and papers in front of her. "I should get back to this." She shuffled the papers on the table.

He should let her get back to it, but he wasn't tired anymore. Besides, if he left her there, she'd work all night and get no rest before having a long day with his campaign tomorrow.

Byron shook his head. "No, it's time for you to take a break."

ZOE LOOKED UP at Byron leaning against the conference table. He had to know how good he looked. With his dark blue tie loosened around his neck, tailored dark pants and that perfectly trimmed beard he could be the spokesperson for sexy business casual. If that was a thing. If it wasn't, all a modeling agency had to do was see him at this moment. His light brown eyes sparked with mischief and the upward tilt of his lips tempted her to walk away from the table and follow him to fun.

Zoe rested against the high-backed soft leather chair until it rolled back slightly. Just a little bit of space to hopefully counteract the magic he created. "Just like college. You're trying to distract me from my work."

He pressed a hand to his chest and widened his eyes innocently. "I'm just trying to help you out. I was on the way to the kitchen for something sweet. Come on. You can't tell me you don't want something sweet."

She wrinkled her nose. "The only thing in there is lemon meringue pie." Byron hated lemon meringue pie.

Byron cringed. "What the hell? Why?"

"Your dad was craving it and Patricia indulged him. Or that's what Elaina told me earlier before she left."

Byron straightened and held out his hand. "Come on. Let's make a run."

Make a run was Byron's code for going to a convenience store and buying as much junk food they could carry. That was how they'd survived judging all night dance-a-thons, studying for their statistics exams, or her favorite, when Kendell had gone out of town and she'd gone to Byron's off-campus apartment to watch all eight Harry Potter movies in one day.

"You can't be serious. It's getting late." She looked at the time on her laptop. Not even eleven yet. She wouldn't be going to bed for at least another two hours, but she shouldn't drop everything to hang out with Byron like she used to.

"When did that stop us before?" Byron asked with his lets-have-fun smile that always tempted her.

Not once. Her resolve weakened. "What about Lilah?"

"Where is she?"

"In the pool house."

Grant suggested she and Lilah would be more comfortable in the pool house whenever they were in town. Zoe didn't think he'd made the suggestion because he cared about their comfort, more like to further remind her she wasn't really a part of the family, but she did prefer the pool house. She didn't want to be in the main house with the rest of the family. She didn't know where to go and what to do in the main house. The pool house felt more like their own space. She'd only come into the conference room because she needed to spread out. That and Lilah had been watching a horror movie that would only distract Zoe.

"She'll be fine. We have a house full of servants. You have a cell phone. Plus, we'll be back in a flash." Slowly, his long fingers slid around hers. His touch was soft and hesitant. Zoe should have pulled away. Especially since the feather-light caress of his hand on hers made her breasts feel heavy and her breathing quicken.

She didn't pull away. Byron's grip firmed. He cocked his head in the direction of the door. "You know you want to. Afterward you can get right back to working on your presentation."

She bit her lower lip. Byron didn't wait for her to think of reasons to say no. He tugged on her hand and Zoe stood. He kept her hand in his as he led her toward the door.

"Let me check on Lilah first," she said.

He stopped and faced her. "Sure. Meet me at the front door."

Zoe nodded and pulled her hand back. He didn't hesitate to release her, which she appreciated while also wondering if she would have resisted if he'd eased her closer to him, wrapped her in his arms, kissed her.

She turned and hurried to the pool house. The entire way she listed the reasons why she didn't need to go anywhere with Byron. But the biggest reason had nothing to do with leaving Lilah or working on the presentation. It was the way he'd looked at her when he said he couldn't turn his back on her. For a split second she'd thought he felt more than friendship or empathy toward her. Elaina's words teased her: *If you want him all you have to do is sink in a little deeper.*

Lilah was asleep and when Zoe shook her to say she was running to the store, her daughter mumbled "okay" then pulled the blankets over her head. She should text Byron and tell him she wasn't going to go. Instead, she grabbed her purse and rushed back to the main house.

Fifteen minutes later they walked through the door of a convenience store not far from the Robidoux Estate.

"I can't believe we used to find this fun." Zoe grinned and looked at the aisles of chips and candy. A soda fountain station with a multitude of various drinks and slushies took up one wall while hot dogs and sausages rolled on metal wheels across from them.

"It's still fun. Let's go." Byron placed his hand on the small of her back and guided her toward the massive fountain drink station.

Zoe grabbed the largest cup and immediately filled it with a mixture of all the sodas in the fountain. Byron followed suit but stuck with a mixture of the fruity drinks. They joked and laughed as they wandered down the snack aisle. They approached the register armed with not only their drinks but a variety of candy, salt and vinegar pork skins and Moon Pies, too.

"Hey, you're Byron Robidoux." The attendant with a name tag that read Gary pinned to his shirt pointed at Byron before ringing up their items. "You're running for Senate, right?"

Byron nodded and held out a hand. "I am. It's nice to meet you, Gary."

Gary pumped Byron's hand up and down. "Tell me why I should vote for you."

Zoe blinked at the direct question before crossing her arms and looking at Byron. She'd expected him to hesitate or maybe be thrown off, but instead, Byron nodded and met Gary's direct gaze before answering his question. Zoe listened as he talked about his plans to improve health care, address student loan debt and increase national security. Other patrons came over and listened as Byron spoke passionately and sincerely about how he'd like to make change. When he finished Gary was grinning.

"You got my vote," Gary said. "Can I take a selfie?"

Byron chuckled. "Sure."

Gary pulled out his cell phone, turned his back toward Byron and held up his phone so the camera faced him and Byron. Byron didn't hesitate to pull Zoe close to his side for the picture. Zoe grinned and wrapped her arm around Byron's waist. He was hard and hot against her side. Her entire body burned, and she fought not to squirm or press closer to him while Gary took several shots.

"Thanks!" Gary finally said. "I knew you were cool."

"I'm glad you think so," Byron replied.

"You know, you two make a cute couple," Gary said and rang up their items.

Zoe opened her mouth to deny it, but then stopped and waited for Byron to say something instead. He glanced at Zoe, gave her a half smile and shrug then looked away.

They rode back with light casual conversation, but Zoe couldn't help but think about what the attendant had said. Calling them a couple. How many times had people mistaken them for a couple in college? How many times had she wondered what it would be like to really be with

Byron? To believe he wasn't just interested in her because she challenged him or because he'd wanted to "steal" her away from Kendell.

Today their relationship wasn't about her challenging him and she wasn't with anyone else. She felt something between them. Something she didn't want to admit was there.

They both reached for their drinks in the center console of the car. Their hands touched. Byron stopped talking midsentence. Zoe froze. The space inside the car constricted for the duration of a heartbeat.

Zoe rested her hand more firmly on her cup. "What were you saying?" Her voice was slightly shaky.

Byron left his hand on his cup. "I was saying…tonight was fun."

Zoe smiled and glanced away. "Yeah. It was."

They didn't pull their hands back for the rest of the ride. A charged silence filled the car and all too soon they were back at the estate. Byron parked in front of the house.

Zoe put her hand on the door. "Are you coming back in?"

He shook his head. "Nah. It was a long day. I should get home. Yolanda called earlier. I need to call her back."

Zoe's smile stiffened. She remembered when his phone rang. He'd silenced it and put it back in his pocket without a second look. She may be free, but he wasn't. "Yeah, you should get back."

She opened the car door. Byron's hand wrapped around hers. Zoe froze and turned back to him. She could easily break the contact. She should break the contact. She didn't.

He slid his fingers through hers. Zoe's pulse pounded in her ears. Heat flowed like lava through her chest, down to her midsection and pooled at the juncture of her thighs. She struggled to breathe. She hadn't felt a rush of desire this strong in years.

This yearning wasn't good. A part of her didn't care. That part urged her to grab his face and pull that oh so kissable lower lip between her teeth. That part knew Byron wouldn't push her away if she did.

"Zoe, I..." His voice was deep, rough and heavy with longing.

As much as she wanted to know if she really could have Byron, she wasn't the type of person to play the side piece. He was engaged. She'd already noticed the way Yolanda watched them whenever Zoe came up for campaign appearances. She continued to smile and be friendly, but the woman was smart. She had to have noticed the way Zoe could barely keep her eyes off Byron. They couldn't do this.

Zoe pulled her hand out of his quickly before she went with the urge. "Good night, Byron."

She heard his rough, "'Night, Zoe," as she rushed out of the car.

CHAPTER FIFTEEN

ZOE COULDN'T DENY that Byron's campaign dinner was outstanding. The donors who'd payed one thousand dollars a plate to be here were some of the most influential people in the state. The speeches were made, additional donations were agreed upon and the brokering of unofficial deals started. Now the party was in full swing. The band played music that had people on the dance floor, and the alcohol flowed freely.

Yolanda had been at Zoe's side during the entire event. The two of them acted like long friends. They put on a great show for everyone about how accepting they were. Yolanda told everyone who listened that she was thrilled to learn Byron had a child. That they were blessed to have Lilah as a part of their family. Zoe did her part by saying she was happy to no longer keep the secret and introduce her daughter to his father. The level of cooperation was all very admirable and adult of them.

The only problem was with every smile, every slip of Yolanda's arm through hers as if they were sisters, every comment about how splendid it was that they were getting along, Zoe wanted to scream. Not just a scream of frustration, but a soul-deep scream of agony. She wasn't sure how she'd continue to do this. She didn't want to ruin Byron's chance to win, but last night with the talk about his campaign, the moment he took her hand and the trip to the convenience store, Zoe realized something she hadn't wanted to admit.

She wanted Byron. Not as a friend. Not as the person helping her protect Lilah from her ex. Not just for one night to see what things would be like between them. She wanted a full-blown relationship. She wanted to see if the sparks between them could translate into something meaningful. Basically, she wanted something that could never happen.

"What's wrong with you? You look like someone punched you in the kidney." Elaina's cultured Southern belle voice broke into Zoe's thoughts.

The two of them sat at the head table for the family. Byron and Yolanda were across the room, arm in arm, smiling and laughing as if they were deeply in love. For all she knew they were in love. She was the one tangled up in a very awkward and unwanted attraction.

But was it one-sided?

The thought teased her from the moment she'd gotten out of his car. The way he'd held her hand. The look in his eye. Was it real or just her projection?

Zoe avoided Elaina's gaze. "Nothing's wrong."

Elaina turned in her seat so she faced Zoe. She was stunning tonight in a designer black dress. Her hair fell in a thick wave to her shoulders, makeup flawless and a perfume that had even made Zoe lean in for an extra whiff. "Then why are you scowling?" Elaina placed her elbow on the table and leaned toward Zoe. A champagne flute filled with the sparkling liquid rested between her fingers. "And why are you scowling while looking at my brother and his fiancée?"

Zoe jerked her eyes back to Elaina. Damn, her gaze did

keep drifting to Byron and Yolanda. "They make a beautiful couple. They're perfect for each other."

"Do you really think that?" Elaina asked as if Zoe said she believed elephants were great at basketball.

"Yes. I'm happy for him. That he's happy and he's in love."

Elaina grunted and sipped her champagne. "He loves her about as much as Yolanda loves him."

Zoe glanced around. The rest of the family wasn't at the table and there were no donors there to overhear. "What do you mean?"

She knew she was gossiping. Gossiping wasn't a good look, but she couldn't help it. Her attraction for Byron wasn't going away, and she was clinging to anything.

"I mean they're only doing this for the votes. Byron needed a wife. Yolanda fit the bill. Voila, the perfect political power couple."

She frowned and shook her head. "He wouldn't do that."

"He would. Once you have your heart broken it's hard to trust in love again." Elaina frowned at her glass then downed half of her drink.

What I felt for you wasn't hero worship, a small bit of affection, or a little bit of attraction. Neither was the pain I felt when you walked away.

She'd ask who broke his heart, but Zoe already knew the answer. She glanced back at Elaina, who continued to frown at the empty glass on the table. Her gaze indicating her thoughts were somewhere else.

Zoe got the feeling Elaina wasn't just talking about Byron. "Did you have yours broken?"

Elaina blinked and focused on Zoe. "What? Of course not. I'm talking about Byron."

Zoe placed a hand on Elaina's arm. "It's okay if you ever want to talk to me. I know it may be hard to talk with your family, but if you need an ear, I'm happy to lend mine."

Zoe wasn't sure if Elaina had any close friends. She doubted Elaina had anyone to talk to. India was kind of off-limits and Byron, while she loved him, was still her brother and had loyalties to the family.

Elaina stiffened. Zoe waited for her to say she was being ridiculous or to shove her hand away. Instead, Elaina's eyes shimmered. She looked away and reached for the water goblet on the table, causing Zoe's hand to fall away. "I may take you up on that."

Before Zoe could respond, Elaina's phone chimed. Zoe's chimed a second afterward. Elaina picked up her phone and frowned. "Oh, crap."

"What?" Zoe asked.

Elaina looked up from her phone at Zoe. "Get ready because tonight just got a lot more interesting."

She held her phone face out. The picture from last night with Zoe and Byron and the gas station attendant was on Elaina's phone. Along with a headline that read: The fire is still hot between candidate Byron Robidoux and his old flame!

Zoe snatched her phone off the table. Sure enough she'd gotten the same notification. She'd signed up for new alerts so she could be on top of the latest stories just like the rest of the family. Not only was it the one selfie with Gary, but also several other shots of her and Byron talking, laughing and touching hands in the store. She looked up at Elaina, who shook her head.

"This is about to get messy," Elaina said, sounding almost delighted.

Zoe looked away from Elaina to the rest of the family. They were all checking their phones and glancing at Zoe then Byron and back. Zoe's gaze jerked around the room. More people checked their phones. Her heart rate accelerated.

Okay, this wasn't that bad. They hadn't done anything wrong. They'd just gone for a late-night run for snacks. Nothing nefarious about that. At least not on Byron's part. She was the only one who'd realized she wanted more than their pretend relationship.

A man Zoe recognized from Yolanda's public relations team walked up to Yolanda and whispered something in her ear. Yolanda nodded and excused herself from the group. Byron nodded at the guy but didn't look as Yolanda walked away with him.

Zoe watched them as they walked toward the exit of the ballroom. The man held out his phone. Yolanda looked at the screen and frowned. Something cold snaked through Zoe's midsection.

Zoe stood abruptly. "I need to tell Byron." Before Yolanda said something and made things worse.

"Believe me, he'll know soon enough." Elaina stood. "I'm going to distract Daddy so he doesn't go over there and try to lecture Byron on the importance of appearances. He's good at that." Elaina headed toward Grant.

Zoe slipped through the crowd to Byron's side. On the way she could hear the hushed wave of whispers and feel the intense scrutiny as people studied her. Every vibration and chime she heard of a cell phone made her stomach twist. Byron's night was about to be ruined.

She smiled at the group of donors he spoke with and tapped on his shoulder. "Byron, do you have a second?"

When he looked at her the smile on his face froze. Concern filled his bright eyes. "Sure. Excuse me," he said to the group and followed her. Once they were out of earshot he asked, "Is everything okay?"

She nodded and grinned. "We've got a problem," she said between clenched teeth.

He chuckled. "Then why are you smiling and nodding?"

"Because there's something in the media and you need to know about it. Is there somewhere we can talk?"

His smile didn't falter, but his eyes sharpened. He nodded toward the exit. "We have the room next door for the family."

"Let's go there."

He didn't argue and led her out of the ballroom. Once they were out of the room he frowned. "Okay, you're worrying me."

"It's about last night," she said. "When we were at the gas station. The picture the attendant took was leaked to the media. They're saying you were out with an old flame. I'm worried it'll look bad."

Byron frowned for a second as if he couldn't recall what picture then waved his hand. "Is that all? Don't worry. It was nothing. Just us going out to grab some snacks. We can clear everything up."

His words knocked the air out of her like a shove to her chest. Had he really felt nothing?

"Are you sure?" she asked. "We all got notifications. I'm worried some of the donors will see and worry."

"About what?" He walked toward the door of one of the rooms adjacent to the ballroom.

"That there's something between us."

Byron stopped at the door. He stood with his back to

her for a few never-ending seconds before he looked at her over his shoulder. "There's nothing there."

She'd seen it. The nervous nose twitch he did. Her heart rate sped up. He had felt something. Zoe moved until she stood right beside him. "Isn't there?"

His shoulders stiffened. He turned and faced her. His eyes filled with frustration. "I'm not in the mood for games, Zoe. I've been here before."

"I haven't been here. Everything is new and I don't know how to react," she admitted.

Before he could answer, the door to the room opened. Yolanda came out. She took one look at Zoe then Byron before stepping back in the room. "Come inside."

Zoe and Byron exchanged glances. He walked in first. Zoe pressed a hand to her stomach and followed. She couldn't believe what she'd been about to do. Byron had a fiancée. He didn't need her jumping in and making his life even more complicated.

Once they were inside, Yolanda crossed her arms over her chest and lifted her chin. She watched them with narrowed eyes.

"Do you really expect me to believe you're not sleeping with her?" She pointed at Zoe. "I've known this was coming from the first day I saw you two together."

Zoe took a step back. Her mouth fell open and she shook her head. "No, we aren't sleeping together. It's not like that."

Yolanda sniffed. "For now."

Byron ran a hand over his face. "Really, Yolanda, I thought we were past this."

Zoe's eyes widened as she looked from Byron to Yolanda. "You've talked about this?" She'd suspected

Yolanda noticed the way Zoe felt about Byron from the start, but not that she'd brought it up to Byron.

"I thought you understood everything I told you," Yolanda said. "We'd keep our affairs discreet."

Zoe couldn't believe a word she was hearing. Elaina had warned her Byron and Yolanda weren't as happy as they seemed. There was no way Yolanda could love Byron if she wanted him to keep his affairs discreet. Zoe wouldn't stand for Byron having an affair if they were together.

"I'm not having an affair," Byron countered.

"Yet, you're spending every night she's in town at your dad's estate. You're taking pictures with her late at night at gas stations. The report from the attendant says you two said you were together." Yolanda spoke quickly, but her voice didn't rise.

"It was just a night out. It didn't mean anything," Byron said, but his voice wasn't convincing. Not even to Zoe.

"It means something," Yolanda said calmly. She pulled the ring off her finger. "I'm making the choice easier for you."

Zoe shook her head. "Yolanda, wait. Don't do this."

"I should have done this the moment you came back into his life." She walked to Byron and put the ring in his hand. "This is better."

"No. I can't have this. Not right now," he said. "How do I explain this?"

Yolanda lifted a shoulder. "You're a smart guy. You'll figure it out." She nodded to a member of her team and pointed to the door.

"Yolanda, don't end things because of a picture."

Yolanda's lips lifted and she placed her hand on the side of Byron's face. "It's not just the picture. I'm getting out before you realize what you really want." She looked at Zoe. "Then have to deal with the consequences." Her hand dropped and she squared her shoulders. "Besides, my leaving isn't your problem. The real problem is figuring out how someone found out about your late-night trip, why they sought out the clerk and why they're trying so hard to ruin your life." Yolanda walked past Byron to the door. "I know how to recognize a sinking ship when I see one. I wanted to be tied to a winner. That's not you. You can have Roy call me later to arrange our joint statement." She motioned for her assistant to follow her out the door.

CHAPTER SIXTEEN

"How can we trust Byron Robidoux in the Senate? The man has more drama than a daytime soap opera. Secret babies are only part of his tumultuous personal life. His *close* relationship with this woman he claims he didn't know had his child has now cost him his fiancée. I don't care how much he denies it. Byron Robidoux is exactly what we knew he was. A rich playboy who decided to run for a higher office on a whim."

Byron picked up the remote and turned off the television. Silence filled his living room and he tossed the remote onto the couch. If only he could shut off the lies spewing from Nelson McLeod's mouth. His opponent hadn't wasted any time taking advantage of Byron's broken engagement.

Byron couldn't blame him. His life was unfolding like a daytime drama. Yolanda hadn't come out and said she and Byron broke up because of Zoe. Not after she'd put on such a great show of her and Zoe getting along. Instead, she offered just enough insinuations about making room for everyone to be happy and her wish for Byron to have all the best with his new life.

He couldn't even get mad. He'd chosen Yolanda because she was good at spin and strategy. How could he have expected her to do anything less?

The doorbell rang. Byron groaned and ran his hand

over his face. He was not in the mood for company. He'd debriefed with Roy. Listened to his dad tell him how to handle the bad publicity. Come up with a statement that convinced voters to trust him despite the activities in his personal life. He was spent, and no one should have a need for him at all tonight.

He picked up his cell phone and pulled up the app connected to the camera at his door. He was prepared to tell whomever was on the other side to fuck off. Especially if it was a reporter who thought they'd snag the next scoop on him. The words were forming on his lips when the image of Travis on the other side of the door with a brown paper bag in his hand filled his screen.

Sliding his phone into his back pocket, Byron strode to the front door. "Come on in."

Travis held up a six-pack. "I thought you could use a drink." He crossed the threshold.

Byron chuckled and rubbed his now-smooth chin. He'd finally shaved the beard. He needed all the help he could get with being a likable candidate, so he'd finally caved to the people who said he looked more professional without the beard. "I need something a lot stronger than beer."

Travis held up a brown paper bag in the other. "I've also got whiskey."

Byron took the bag from Travis and pulled the bottle of Johnnie Walker out of the bag. "See, that's why I like you."

They went inside where Byron grabbed two glasses and put ice in a bucket. He and Travis settled at the high-top card table next to the built-in bar.

"I didn't expect you over," Byron said as they sipped their drinks.

"Because of the drama with the media, or because I eloped with India?"

"Both," Byron admitted. He and Travis hadn't hung out since he and India eloped. Granted, Byron was out of town most of the time on the campaign trail, but where he'd once go to Travis's place to hang out or ask his friend to meet him at a bar for drinks after a stressful day, he didn't anymore. He went to the estate if Zoe was there. Yolanda was right about that.

"Where do you want to start?" Travis asked.

"There's no need to rehash the thing with India. I said I was cool with you two and I mean it. Congratulations."

Byron held up his glass. Travis hesitated a second then clinked his glass with Byron's. He meant what he said. He had more things to be worried about than Travis marrying the woman he loved. On the list of fucked-up things with his family, Travis and India's genuine love for each other wasn't one of them.

"So Yolanda wasn't as perfect as you thought," Travis said. A hint of I-told-you-so in his voice Byron wished he could get angry about.

Byron frowned and lightly hit his hand on the top of the table. "How did you see it? How did I miss it?"

"I didn't see this. I never thought you should marry her, but that wasn't because I thought she'd leave you hanging like that."

"Yolanda is smart. All she ever wanted was to win. To have political influence without actually serving."

"Then why break up with you?"

Byron lifted a shoulder and sipped his drink. "She said she was on board. In the end, she thought Zoe was a threat. She wanted to get out and control the optics of her moving on. We both know having Zoe back in my life made this road to the Senate harder."

"What are you going to do now?"

"Keep campaigning. Keep pushing uphill. I can't afford to bow out of the race and let McLeod win. He'll do everything he can to support pushing our state back three hundred years."

He had a challenge ahead of him. Good thing he wasn't afraid of challenge. Giving up wasn't an option.

"I know you're going to keep campaigning. I mean what are you going to do about Zoe?"

"What are you talking about? Her number of campaign appearances might need to go down until this stuff with Yolanda dies down, but otherwise I don't see anything changing."

He wasn't going to hide her or take back the statement he'd released. There was still the matter of the emails to her, and Yolanda's last words. Who was trying to make things harder for him and Zoe?

Travis sighed and shook his head. "You're not usually this slow. You wanted a wife to make you appear like a family man. Yolanda has left and created a mess when she did. You obviously still hold a torch for Zoe. Kill two birds with one stone."

"What? Nah." Byron scoffed. "I'm not going to replace Yolanda with Zoe."

"Why not?"

Why not? Two words that carried so much temptation. "Because, it wouldn't be good optics. Despite what Yolanda said the public isn't going to accept me getting a new fiancée right after we split."

"Yes, they will," Travis said confidently. He leaned back and sipped his drink.

"It'll feed the rumors that something is going on between us."

"And? Look, I haven't been around you two a lot, but I've been around enough to know you're feeling her. What was between you hasn't gone away. I say go for it. People love a second-chance romance."

The idea sent a ripple of anticipation through Byron. The same ripple he'd felt when he'd looked into Zoe's eyes in his car the other night. He wasn't naive enough to pretend as if he and Zoe weren't attracted to each other, but he needed more than attraction. He'd be better off single than reinvesting his heart into the idea of a relationship with Zoe. The last thing he needed was another failed relationship during this campaign.

"People love the idea of reunited lovers in books and movies. Not in real life." Byron tapped his finger on the edge of his glass. The hum of energy sparked by Travis's suggestion still buzzed in his system even as he tried to ignore it. "Plus, Zoe and I were never lovers in real life. She never chose me."

"So you're not denying you still like her."

Liked her. Wanted her. Thought about her. Constantly. "She's cool. I like her, but…"

"But what?"

After all these damn years she still had her hooks in him. He'd pulled her into his life when he didn't need to. She never would have sought him out because he was running for Senate. She would have stayed out of his life and lived hers. Yet, he'd insisted on finding her. If he'd left well enough alone…

Then the person looking for her would have found her.

If he hadn't looked for Zoe, Carlton would have found her and given her location to whomever sought her out. A person Byron believed was connected to Kendell. He'd gotten Dominic to intercept her emails so she wouldn't see them anymore while he searched for the source. She'd be dealing with this on her own if he hadn't looked for her.

"We're helping each other out. That's all," Byron said.

Travis met Byron's eyes. "I get it. Being with her is complicated and she broke your heart."

"She didn't break my heart."

Travis smirked. "Sure. Your stance on never falling in love just magically happened after she left you."

"I was like that before." He'd dated women without thoughts of the future before meeting Zoe. Zoe was just the one woman he'd wanted more than a casual affair with.

"Byron, stop trying to talk yourself out of doing what you want. I get it, the campaign would be harder, but what do you really want? Go for it. Go for her."

Byron felt a sensation in his chest. The same sensation he'd experienced whenever she looked at him as if she felt something, too. The instinct to take her in his arms and ask her to be with him.

He already knew how that would end. He'd confessed his feelings to her once before and she'd turned him down. He'd be setting himself up for disappointment again.

"I didn't bring her back into my life for this."

"Are you sure? Because if you believe one hundred percent that Zoe isn't into you then cool. But if you have any indication she could feel the same, don't let another thirteen years go by wondering what could have happened. All I'm saying is let her know you're interested. Open the door and see if she walks through it. After all these years shouldn't you at least try to shoot your shot?"

HE WAS WASTING his time. The thought went through Byron's head over and over since talking to Travis earlier. Still, he found himself picking up the phone and calling Zoe later that evening. He hadn't talked directly to Zoe after the need to amicably break up with his convenient fiancée arose. They'd been in damage control ever since. He hadn't made it to the estate for the remainder of the weekend because of that. Byron wasn't sure when Zoe would be back.

"Byron? Is everything okay?" Her voice sounded distant as if she was on speakerphone.

"Yeah, everything is good. I just wanted to check and see how you were doing." He cleared his throat. "Did your presentation go well?"

In the middle of all the damage control he hadn't gotten to ask Zoe how things had gone for her when she'd returned home. If the presentation she'd been working on so hard before he'd pulled her out for the night had impressed her boss or not.

Her deep sigh echoed through the phone. "Presentation went well."

"Then what's wrong?"

"Let's just say I have to do some of my own damage control here," she said. "John has expressed concerns about my current situation and how it's affecting my job performance."

Byron closed his eyes and pinched the bridge of his nose. "Damn, Zoe, I'm sorry."

"You know what, it's not your fault. Part of this is because I didn't want to deal with my past."

"But it wouldn't be coming up and threatening your career if it wasn't for me."

"Well, this is just another reason to search for better opportunities." Her voice was optimistic if strained. "I may need that good word you mentioned before."

"Anything. Just let me know." There he went trying to fix things for her again without question. Yolanda was right. He didn't think straight when it came to Zoe. "Are you in the car?"

"Yeah, Lilah had archery practice tonight. I just dropped her off and I'm on my way home to work on some things until she's done."

"Is Lilah okay? After everything that happened?"

"She is," Zoe said. "She thinks it's all exciting and can't wait to get back up to Jackson Falls again. I told her what Roy said. That we should lay low for a while."

That was the plan, but Byron didn't want to lay low or push Zoe away. "Don't worry about Roy. Visit whenever you want."

"Thanks, Lilah will appreciate that." He heard the smile in her voice. Maybe Lilah wasn't the only one who would appreciate that. "How are you doing?" she asked.

His fiancée dumped him because she felt he was still in love with Zoe. He and Zoe had never finished that conversation they'd had right before his life got scrambled. "Not too good." He needed to know what she'd meant when she'd said she was in unfamiliar territory. He knew he couldn't start a new relationship right now. Not with his breakup so fresh. He'd be killed by the media and no one would focus on the issues. Yet, he had to know. "I can't stop thinking about that night."

"Me either. Wait…what the hell?" Disbelief filled Zoe's voice.

Byron stiffened. "What's wrong?"

"There are police and fire trucks everywhere," Zoe answered, sounding distracted. "I can't get down our street because—"

A siren blared and cut off the end of her sentence. When she spoke again her voice trembled. "Oh, my God. My house is on fire!"

CHAPTER SEVENTEEN

SHE HAD NO HOME. Even though she'd watched in horror as the firefighters tried to save her place and seen the ceiling collapse, Zoe still couldn't believe it. Her safe place, her refuge, was gone.

Her hand clenched into a fist and pounded against the balcony railing. In the weeks since the fire her life had been chaos. She'd taken a leave of absence from work. John hadn't batted an eye and struggled to show an ounce of sympathy as she made the request. She had no clue where she'd work, but she doubted she'd go back to Valtec.

To her surprise, Grant insisted Zoe and Lilah move permanently into the pool house on the estate. As much as she wanted to deny, Zoe didn't have anywhere else to go. Victoria would take her in, but on the heels of her past coming up, the media had taken an interest in the fire at Zoe's home. She refused to bring drama to her friend's doorstep. She'd agreed to the move at least until the fire investigation was done and she figured out what to do next. The fire marshal hadn't suspected foul play, but between the emails and increased scrutiny in her life Zoe didn't think the fire was an accident. Without the sanctuary of her home she felt exposed and uneasy.

The other thing Grant insisted on was the family taking a sabbatical. Things were too hot in the media. They needed time to plan. She'd been in such a state of shock she hadn't thought to say no when Grant told her the entire family was spending a week at their vacation home in the Smokey Mountains. The thought of a break away from everything, the campaigning, the realization her house was gone, the way John practically pushed her out the door at work, made her agree instantly.

In hindsight, a week in a mountain home with the Robidoux family was probably not the way to relax and think things through.

The sliding glass door connecting the room next to Zoe's with the balcony opened and Lilah came out. "Mom, are you okay?"

Zoe took a deep breath. She was so not okay. She was frightened, angry and more than anything she was tired. She buried all that deep and turned to give her daughter a reassuring smile. "I'm admiring the view. It's beautiful up here."

Lilah came to stand next to her at the balcony. Their room overlooked nothing but mountains and trees. The view was breathtaking and peaceful with not a sign of another home as far as the eye could see. If only she could hide up here forever.

"It is pretty," Lilah said. She leaned her head on Zoe's shoulder. "Can we stay up here?"

Zoe wrapped an arm around her daughter's shoulders. "We can't." She squeezed Lilah closer to her. "But while we're here we'll figure out how to pick up the pieces and keep moving forward."

"T.J. asked me to be his girlfriend," Lilah said, referring to the boy who'd asked her to his party the day Byron showed up.

Zoe blinked several times. She'd forgotten about T.J.

in all the changes in their life. That seemed like a lifetime ago. "He did? When?"

"Right before we left. I told him we could stay friends. I don't have time for a boyfriend. Not right now. Besides… I wasn't sure if we'd be going back."

Zoe heard the question in her daughter's voice. "I don't know yet. Do you want to go back?"

Lilah's shoulders lifted and lowered. "I don't know. I miss my friends and school, but I like Byron. I like having a family. Now that Yolanda's gone…"

Zoe dropped her arm from Lilah's and faced her daughter. "Don't start that. Not right now."

Byron had been great ever since the fire. He'd gotten off the phone with her and driven straight to Greenville the same night. He'd been beside her every step of the way. She didn't want to lean on him, didn't want to become dependent on anyone after years of fighting to stand on her own, but he didn't offer help in a way that made her feel she owed him. He treated her as a partner and damn if that didn't make it harder for her to forget the ache in her heart when he was near.

"But Mom—"

"Not now, Lilah. I'm not saying that again. We've got enough to worry about right now. Okay?"

Lilah let out a long sigh, but she nodded. "Well, I came out to ask if you wanted to go with me and Aunt Elaina."

"Go where?" Elaina had been a godsend. She'd entertained Lilah and kept her spirits up as any true aunt would. Zoe couldn't thank her enough but doubted Elaina would accept thanks. She'd probably roll her eyes and tell Zoe she was being ridiculous.

"Some boutique store," Lilah said excitedly. "She says if she doesn't get out of here she's going to hit something."

Zoe smiled. She'd been surprised Elaina made it this long without saying that. The only family member Elaina seemed comfortable around was Byron. She understood the need for an escape. "I don't want to go, but you can."

Lilah grinned. "Thanks. Grandpa and Ms. Patricia are out, and I think Aunt India and Uncle Travis went sightseeing."

"Everyone needed a break, huh?" Herself included. She'd spent most of the day in her room and on the balcony. Byron was off for a campaign appearance. The family could take a break, but with the race heating up as it was, he couldn't afford to do the same. He was supposed to join the family later that night.

Zoe went back into the bedroom. Lilah followed her. "I think so. If you're going to stay you should get in the hot tub."

Zoe sat on the bed. "Why?"

Lilah shrugged and pulled on the edge of one of her braids. "You look tense. No one is here. Take a few minutes to relax."

"I think I'm just going to take a nap."

Lilah leaned in and kissed Zoe on the forehead. "Mom, it's three in the afternoon and you're too old to take a nap. Grab a book and relax in the hot tub. For me, please."

Zoe poked Lilah in the belly button and grinned. "I'm not too old for anything."

Lilah laughed and grabbed her purse off the chair. "Fine. See you later."

Zoe waved at Lilah as she swept out the door. She lay back on the bed and hugged a pillow to her, instantly realizing she wouldn't be able to sleep. Her mind wouldn't rest. Not with all the problems going through her head. She'd just sit there going over all the things she needed to do. Find a job. Find a home. Figure out why her house burned down.

Zoe jumped up from the bed and pulled open a drawer. Ten minutes later she'd changed into her bathing suit, grabbed a towel and was downstairs going to the outdoor hot tub. The house was quiet, and Zoe was thankful for that. She found herself relaxing at the thought of the warm water and soothing jets in the hot tub.

She opened the door to the back and froze. "What are you doing here?"

Byron's head shot up. He lounged in the space she planned to relax. His arms stretched out along the edges. He'd had his head back and eyes closed when she'd come out on the deck.

"I thought you were going out with Elaina and Lilah," he said.

"Lilah told me she was leaving and said I should come down here. She didn't tell me you were here."

"I just got back. Elaina suggested I relax while the house was quiet."

They stared for several seconds then they both started laughing. "I think we've been set up," Zoe said.

"I think so." Byron's eyes softened.

Zoe fought not to squirm. Heat spread through her midsection. The bubbles from the water popped against his bare chest. He was golden brown and glistening in the afternoon sunlight. Her nipples hardened and gooseflesh tightened her skin. "I can come back."

He shook his head and slid over. "No need. Come on. There's plenty of room."

Sense said go back upstairs and relax with her book. Convenience said she'd already changed and was down here. "If you're sure." She crossed the deck and stopped at the edge of the whirlpool.

Zoe sat down her towel and slipped out of the flip-flops she'd worn down. Her entire body was cognizant of Byron's gaze on her. She'd put on a black two-piece halter-style bathing suit. Not very suggestive or sexy, but she was aware of every inch of bare skin. Skin that tingled for his touch.

She eased into the water. The hot tub was big enough to comfortably fit four. Byron moved to the opposite side, giving her plenty of room. Still, with his long legs stretched out, their feet touched. He moved his feet quickly. Zoe couldn't believe how much she wished he hadn't.

"I take it campaigning hasn't been great," she said, trying not to wonder what type of shorts he wore beneath the bubbling water.

Byron shook his head. "It's rough as hell. McLeod won't focus on the issues. Every point I make he counters with a personal attack."

"From what I've researched, you can hit him back with personal attacks." McLeod had come after Byron for bad family values when he'd been married three times, each time with a woman he'd been having an affair with. His business dealings were shady, but voters didn't have time to focus on that if he kept deflecting to Byron's faults.

"I can," Byron replied slowly.

"But you won't?" Byron wasn't deceitful or a dirty

player, but she also didn't know him to not use every advantage available to him to win.

"I didn't say that. Dad gives money to groups who are more willing to handle personal attacks."

Zoe's brows rose. "You let other people do the dirty work."

"I didn't think I'd be okay with that, but when he came for you and Lilah all bets were off." His voice hardened. "No one comes after my family. Not unless they're ready for the consequences."

The determination in his voice sent a thrill through her. A man with fight in him had always been a turn-on for her. Usually with disastrous results. Byron's fight would never be directed at her physically or emotionally, and that made him even more sexy.

"We aren't really your family."

She said the words for herself. For someone not used to having reliable people around, Byron's open acceptance of her was tempting. Too tempting.

"We agreed you were." Byron's voice was still as sincere as before. "Don't be surprised when I treat you like family." His lips spread in a sexy smile.

Zoe rubbed her hands over her thighs, which were slick beneath the warm water. "It's a fantasy. One for the outside world, but not us. We have to stay focused."

She had to stay focused. He was fresh out of an engagement of convenience. Her life was in limbo. She couldn't get lost in fantasies of really being Byron's family.

He dropped his arms from the edges of the hot tub and shifted one seat closer to her. His brows drew together. "Focused on what?"

His foot brushed hers again. Electricity shot up her leg

and sizzled across her skin. Her sex clenched. She pulled her foot away. "Focus on reality. That this is politics for you and protection for Lilah and me."

Silence stretched between them. His unwavering gaze consumed her even though she refused to look his way. If she looked she knew what she'd see. She'd seen that same look in Byron's eyes before. A look that promised everything she'd always been too afraid to believe in.

Byron slid even closer. One arm stretched along the back of the hot tub until the tips of his fingers barely brushed her shoulder. "What if…this isn't just politics for me?"

That made her look at him. His nose scrunched up the way it did when he was nervous. The look was in his eye, but it wasn't like before. He didn't look cocky, no hint of the swagger that constantly cloaked him. He looked as if he was just as afraid to make this leap as she.

Her heart danced like the bubbles in the hot tub. She struggled to breathe as she watched him. Her skin felt flushed. Not from the water, but from the craving simmering in his eyes. "What else could it be?"

His eyes closed for a second before he spoke in a rush. "Despite my better judgment I keep coming back to you."

The frustration in his voice gave her pause. "Your better judgment?" That was not the romantic declaration she'd expected.

Her defensive tone must have been infectious. Byron's shoulders straightened and he turned sideways to face her fully.

"Yes, Zoe, my better judgment. I loved you in college, but I sat back and respected your relationship with a man who didn't deserve you. I did that because it was your decision who you wanted to be with. When I told you how I felt you laughed it off and went back to him. That shit hurt like hell, but it didn't stop me from helping you when you needed me. I don't regret a thing. Then or now, but I know some of what Yolanda said is true. I still care about you. I'll always care. I don't expect you to feel the same, and I don't want you to be with me because you think you owe me something. I just need you to understand—" he pointed at her "—that a part of me—" he slapped his hand to his chest "—feels like an idiot for pining after you for years, knowing you don't feel the same."

They sat in stunned silence. Zoe couldn't do anything but blink and stare. Her brain tried to catch up as her heart beat faster, harder. After all this time? She hadn't believed he'd loved her then because she hadn't thought she was good enough for a guy like Byron. She wasn't that girl anymore. She didn't view life through the lens of battered self-confidence and shame. She saw him fully now. Even more so, she saw herself fully. Saw the things she wanted and was no longer afraid to go after. That was why the attraction she'd tried to brush aside before refused to be pushed aside now.

He looked away first. "I'll let you relax alone now." He moved to sit up.

Zoe shot forward and grabbed his wrist. "Don't."

Byron watched her hesitantly. "Don't what?"

She licked her lips. "Don't go."

"Why?" He didn't look as if he wanted to stay longer after that huge confession. His shoulders were rigid. His eyes wouldn't quite meet hers. "I don't want to just be your savior. I'll always help you and protect Lilah without ask-

ing anything in return. So don't go there with me if gratitude or pity is involved. We both deserve better."

She understood why he'd think that. A big part of their
friendship had been about her turning him down or laughing off his confessions of having feelings for her. Then
she'd gone to him and asked for something huge, and he'd
done it without question. She didn't want to think about all
of the screwed-up emotions that made her turn away from
Byron before. Not right now. Right now she only knew she
didn't want him to leave. If she let him go now, they may
never get this moment back. He'd get elected, maybe pick
another Yolanda to pretend to be happy with. She'd have
to watch and remember this day, this moment, when she
let him walk away.

Zoe didn't have the perfect answer as to why he should
stay, but she did have the answer to the question of whether
or not she wanted him. She slid onto his lap before she
could think about what she was doing. "Don't go."

His gaze never left hers as she moved. She couldn't
look away if she wanted to. Her heart was lost in the
bright depths of his eyes. Her knees settled on either side
of him. Their skin gliding easily over each other in the
warm water.

Byron's hands grabbed her waist. "Zoe?" Her name
was a question on his lips. His eyes burned with need and
desire. The proof of what his body wanted grew long and
hard against her sex. Yet, he hesitated. This was her call.

She answered the question by pressing her lips against
his. The feel of their lips together filled something in her
she hadn't known was empty. Not once had she and Byron
kissed before, yet she felt as if she were coming home. She
placed her hand on the side of his face, angled his head

to the side and slid her tongue across his oh so kissable lips. Byron immediately opened to her, and her tongue slid over his.

She tried to get closer. The hard tips of her breasts were flattened against the solid planes of his chest. His hips pressed up as his strong hands pushed her hips down. The hard ridge of his dick pushed against her core. Zoe gasped. Desire rushed through her bloodstream, heightening her senses and making her light-headed.

Their bodies slid and glided against each other. Water spilled over the sides of the hot tub onto the deck below as they urgently kissed and twisted to get closer. Byron jerked on the string of her top before pulling it down to reveal her breasts. He cupped her breast, lifted the full mound and wrapped her hard nipple in the soft heat of his enticing lips. Each firm tug of his mouth against her sensitive nipple sent an answering demand to her brain. *Closer. Harder. More.*

Get closer. Kiss harder. Take more. Zoe's trembling hands reached down and slipped beneath the waistband of his shorts. Her fingers wrapped around his rigid length. The warm water eased her movements as her hand caressed up and down before her thumb circled the top.

Byron's lips slipped away from her breast. His head fell back and he gasped. Satisfaction filled Zoe like a balloon. As if feeling her gaze, Byron's head popped up. His hand grasped the back of her head and he pulled her in for another soul-claiming kiss. Wet fingers slid into her hair and opened her up to him. She relaxed and gave everything he demanded. Her trust in him and her comfort almost as much of an aphrodisiac as the thought of his hands on her body.

His other hand lowered to the edge of her bathing suit and pushed it aside. Warm water caressed her swollen folds before his skilled fingers spread her open to his touch. Her hips bucked. Her legs spread farther. The tips of his fingers skated across her sensitive clit. The water, her desire, they both had her more than ready when two of his fingers pushed slow and deep inside her.

Zoe gripped his shoulders. She bit her lower lip, but when his mouth claimed her other breast she cried out. Her pleasure echoing in the stillness of the mountains. Byron shuddered. A low moan rumbled through his chest. Her body shook. Her brain blanked out and the only focus was the wonderful things he did to her body. *Closer. Harder. More.*

Zoe's eyes cracked open just as his lips slipped away from her hard nipple. He sucked his full lower lip between his teeth as he watched her with open adoration. Emotions squeezed her heart so tightly she knew this moment would stay with her for the rest of her life. The warmth of the water, his fingers inside her, the glide of his skin across her, and the devotion in his eyes took her over the crest almost instantly. Pleasure burst across her skin, through her veins and within her soul. She convulsed around him as a short cry burst from her lips. Byron silenced her cry with another searing kiss.

They held each other. Panting as the steam of the hot tub rose around them. The hum of the motor and the background sounds of nature the only noise as the realization of what they'd just done hit her. Zoe's mind tried to process the implications, but it was mush and her body still buzzed from the aftermath of her orgasm.

The back door opened. Byron stiffened. Zoe's heart jumped into her throat, and she looked over her shoulder.

Grant stood frozen in the doorway. Dressed in a robe, eyes wide and a towel in hand. He glanced from her to Byron then shook his head. "Get yourselves cleaned up. The rest of the family will be here soon." He went back in and firmly closed the door.

CHAPTER EIGHTEEN

"So I HEAR we have to clean the hot tub."

Byron closed his eyes and shook his head. He straightened from the pool table in the game room and glared at Elaina at the door. She only stared back as she leaned against the door frame with a glass of wine in her hand and a smirk on her face.

"You can leave now," Byron said.

Elaina's smirk morphed into a sly smile. "It's true," she said gleefully. "You did." She hurried into the room and rested her hip on the edge of the pool table. She wore dark leggings, a burgundy tunic and black flat shoes. She looked more relaxed than he'd expected with her spending the days strategizing with the family. She sipped her wine, and Byron realized the wine was probably the reason for his sister's improved mood.

"Why do you care what I did or didn't do?" He wasn't going to confirm or deny anything. Even though heat spread through his cheeks.

Zoe had rushed out of the hot tub and upstairs to her room without a backward glance at him. By the time he'd gone inside, his dad was pacing back and forth in the living room while Patricia sat solemnly on the couch. Travis and India returning was the only thing that saved him from whatever lecture Grant had prepared. By the time Lilah and Elaina were back in the house it was easy for

Byron to avoid his father altogether. He guessed Zoe was doing the same thing with him since she hadn't come out of her room.

"Normally, I wouldn't care who you have your fun with," Elaina said.

"Then why are you here?"

Elaina raised a finger. "I will care about where you have your fun, if that fun is taking place in a shared space."

Byron gripped the pool stick and pushed back his frustration. "Again, why are you here? Is it to tease me? Okay, you've succeeded. Go do something else."

"Plus, I kind of care now," she said begrudgingly.

Byron ran a hand over his chin and swallowed a sigh. "If you're here to tell me I shouldn't be with Zoe then tell me something I don't already know."

He'd had time to think about things after the embarrassment of getting caught by his dad in a hot tub had time to settle. He'd spilled his emotions out to Zoe, she'd kissed him and they'd come close to having sex. Not once did she admit her feelings for him. Once again, his feelings were out there waiting for her to accept them.

That was one of several reasons he shouldn't be with Zoe. The breakup with Yolanda was too new. He wanted to win this election. His entire life had been dedicated to getting here. Serving the public. Furthering the family legacy. A scandalous relationship could ruin that.

Still, he didn't regret what happened, nor could he say his body didn't ache to do more.

Elaina blinked and her head shot back. "That's not what I'm here to tell you."

"You're not?" He'd avoided the confrontations with his

family. He already knew what they were going to say. Or at least he thought he'd known.

"No. I'm here to say you've finally made the right choice. Yolanda was good on paper, but I never liked her. Obviously, my instincts were right. She left as soon as things got hard." Elaina sounded pleased with herself for knowing Yolanda wasn't the right one for him. "You still need a wife and family to make you more palatable to the voters. Go with the woman you actually want."

Byron put down the pool stick and rested his hands on the edge of the table. "Hold up. Are you telling me to marry Zoe?"

"Not right away, of course," Elaina said as if he was being silly. "You've got to introduce your relationship with her over time. Maybe a few more public appearances together, with Lilah there, obviously. You both talk about how great things are now that you're reunited. Play up the years of regret and how happy you are with your family. Make the public fall in love with you two, so that by the time you're officially together they'll cheer."

Byron brought a hand to his temple. Disappointed but not surprised at the suggestion. That was the family way. Find a way to spin a negative into a positive. "You want me to exploit our relationship for the win?"

Elaina tapped the edge of the pool table with a long, manicured nail. "I want you to use what's happening to your advantage. Don't be naive. You wanted to marry her years ago. Mom realized it wasn't right and separated you two. Now you're back with her and you both obviously want to be together. This way you get the best of both worlds."

"I'm not going to do that. If Zoe and I decide to be together then it'll be because we both want it. Not because it'll help me win."

A disgusted grunt came from the door. They both turned. Grant shook his head before coming in and closing the door behind him. He'd changed into a cream-colored short-sleeved linen shirt and matching pants. His hair looked wet and curly as if recently showered. Byron guessed Grant had to settle for a relaxing shower instead of a stint in the hot tub.

"You always were the romantic of the family," Grant said in a noncomplimentary way.

"Excuse me?" Byron asked.

Elaina took her glass of wine and crossed the room. She sat in one of the leather chairs along the wall and watched with a slight smirk on her lips. Guess he'd be getting no help from her.

"You always thought the world was a good place and that as long as you did good then things would work out. Your mom fed into that fantasy and you sopped it up."

"It's not a fantasy. I do try to make things better if I can and I try to live my life in a way that I can be proud of." Yes, those were lessons his mom taught him, but they were lessons he still believed in. He appreciated what his family built for him and wanted to make a way for others to build their own legacies while also preserving his. He would never feel bad about that.

"Were you proud when you decided to marry Yolanda when you didn't love her?" Grant asked casually.

"Don't bring Yolanda into this." Byron picked up the pool stick and circled the table. He couldn't focus on the balls or practicing his shots. He just needed to hit something instead of lashing out at his dad.

"The hell I wont," Grant argued. "You chose her because she was most likely to clean up your image as the guy who could get any woman he wanted. You didn't love her, and you made a political decision. Now, when your sister is making a smart suggestion, that you build a family image with the woman you want a family with, you decide to claim a moral high ground. Step off that high horse, Byron. You're a Robidoux and you want to win. Stand there and tell me that you don't see the value in using your relationship with Zoe to get you to the Senate."

Byron aimed at the green ball. He could hit it into the hole with no problem. An easy shot. Almost as easy as his dad tried to make marrying Zoe sound. "It won't work." He hit the ball and watched it roll smoothly into the pocket.

"Why not?" Elaina asked casually before taking a sip of her wine.

Byron clenched his teeth. He shouldn't have said anything. He'd absorbed his mom's lessons, but he'd also absorbed his father's. Already the pros and cons of marrying Zoe were drifting through his mind. "People will view her as the other woman."

Grant pointed at him. "Not if you play this right. Slowly introduce her to the public. Start by focusing on being a father to Lilah and then let it gradually grow."

Elaina snapped a finger. "That's what I said."

"Will you two stop talking about my life like you're winning points in a political game?"

Grant stepped forward and placed his hand on the end of the pool stick, stopping Byron from aiming at another shot. "Your life is a political game. The moment you announced you were running for Senate you put your life on a game board. Every move you make is up for scrutiny and debate. You know this is a good idea. You know it makes sense and it'll win you political points if we work it right. So why don't you tell me the real reason you're hedging."

The real reason. He couldn't put political hopes on a situation that was too close to him. With Yolanda it was one thing. He wasn't in a position of being hurt.

Byron left the pool stick on the table and stood. "I don't have time for this."

They didn't try to stop him from walking out. His dad probably thought it was just another emotional decision. It was, but not for the emotions his dad would suspect. Grant probably didn't realize how unsure Byron felt after what happened that afternoon. That he wasn't sure if he wanted to put too much of himself into this.

He rounded the corner and stopped suddenly. Zoe leaned against the wall. Her arms were crossed. She stared down at the floor. He said her name and she looked up at him.

"Well, what did you all decide?" Her voice was calm, but there was a guarded look in her eye.

Byron ran a hand over his head. "We didn't decide anything."

She pushed away from the wall. Her arms still crossed tightly over her chest as if shielding herself from him. "It sounds like your family has the perfect way to deal with the Zoe problem. Just like before."

"It's not like that." Except it was. In a matter of a few hours his family had already crafted a plan to deal with the latest threat. If he didn't take the upper hand, his dad would take control and push Byron and Zoe together without a thought to all the baggage between them that needed unpacking.

"Look, forget them and what they said," Byron said.

"This is something you and I need to figure out. No one else."

Zoe opened her mouth then shut it. She ran a hand over her hair, which was twisted into a curly puff at the back of her head. She nodded and waved a hand. "Fine."

The heavy disappointment in that single word settled like a boulder on his chest. "Let's go somewhere and talk?" She was not *fine*.

"Mom." Lilah's voice came up the stairs. "Want to play Uno with me and Auntie India and Uncle Travis?"

Byron shook his head. They needed to finish this. Now.

Lilah called again. Zoe took a step toward the stairs. "I'm coming," she said then turned back to Byron. "We'll talk later. When there isn't so much going on."

She turned and hurried down the stairs. The sound of Lilah and India greeting her drifted up. Byron cursed and rubbed his temples. He took a long breath. There were too many damn people in the house. He didn't know how he'd get her alone again, but before the night was over he and Zoe were going to talk. There was too much between them that they couldn't keep ignoring. He did like to win, and right now he wanted to win her heart.

ZOE TOSSED BACK the covers and reached for her phone on the nightstand. She clicked the power button on the side. Bright light illuminated the room. She flinched and blinked until her eyes adjusted. One fifteen in the morning.

She put the phone back on the nightstand and sat on the edge of the bed. She'd feigned a headache and gone to bed immediately after the Uno game. She was procrastinating and she knew it. A character flaw that she kept saying she'd correct but knew she never would.

Sighing, Zoe stood, slid on the slippers next to the bed and left the bedroom. The house was quiet. She'd listened as everyone had gone to their rooms and settled in for the night an hour before. She tiptoed down the stairs. Her heartbeat faster with each step she took.

The only light on was in the living room. Byron sat sprawled out on one of the couches in a white T-shirt and dark green pajama pants. He looked up from the book in his hands, a mystery novel, when she stood at the back of the couch.

"I didn't think you'd come back down." His voice was soft and slightly relieved. His brown eyes appeared more golden in the muted lamplight. He turned on the couch to face her.

Zoe licked her dry lips. "I wasn't sure if I would."

She'd known he would be down here waiting on her. She understood just as much as he that they needed to talk. Not just about what happened in the hot tub, but also the suggestion his family made. She believed Byron hadn't said everything he'd said earlier that day as part of some plot to put her in the spot Yolanda vacated, but she didn't trust his family to twist anything between them into something not resembling the healthy relationship she both wanted and finally realized she deserved.

His hand covered hers on the back of the couch. His touch warm and steady. "Sit down."

Zoe hesitated for a second then came around. Byron swung his legs off the couch so she could sit next to him. Her stomach was a tangle of knots. She didn't know the best place to start untwisting them.

She settled on starting with the most immediate situation. "Your family made a good point earlier. I also heard your reply. You said no, but you were considering what they said."

Byron slid closer to her. "My family is always going to try to find the angle that benefits us the best. I can't change them, but what I can do is promise you that I'll never make any decision that affects you without talking to you or considering your feelings. I don't care about the points they made. All I care about is what's right for us. What I said earlier hasn't changed."

She believed him, and that further twisted the knots in her stomach. She hadn't put her trust in anyone other than herself for years. She knew Byron and didn't doubt he meant what he said, but doubt still whispered in her ear. The only way to silence the voice was to face her fears head-on.

Zoe met his eyes and watched him closely. "I trust you, but I don't know if this is the right move. How will things work out? Will we eventually hurt each other?"

He didn't look away. Calculation didn't cloud his gaze nor did it filter into his voice. "Zoe, listen to me. If we do this then it's because we both want to make this work. Not for the election and not just to protect Lilah." His hand squeezed hers. "What do you want? Tell me and I'll make it happen."

No matter how hard she'd worked to be okay with going after what she wanted without fear and accept the good things in her life, expressing her wishes out loud still made her feel as if she were that girl whose mother humiliated her in front of a class for daring to be proud of doing well. She thought of the way Byron treated her. Not just recently, but the unwavering friendship, encouragement and support he'd offered when they were friends. The way he was so patient and sweet with Lilah. How he looked at her as if she was special and worth his love.

"I never believed you when you said that before."

His body stilled. He tried to pull back, but her hand tightened on his. She took a long breath and tackled the second knot between them. "I didn't believe you because I didn't think what you offered was how relationships were supposed to be."

His brows drew together. "I don't understand."

"That's because you never met my parents. All they did was argue and fight. It wasn't anything for my dad to slap my mom just to end an argument. My mom would hit back. Then they'd be in each other's arms again later that day. My mom told me and my sister that people in love acted that way. My dad spoiled her with clothes, money, jewelry and they both seemed to thrive off that life. I thought that was what real love was. Not the fairy-tale stuff on television. Kendell gave me what I grew up seeing. By the time I realized my view of relationships was screwed up and I needed out, I got pregnant. Then my only focus was getting away from him and giving my child better than what I had."

Byron's attention wasn't the only thing that helped her come to that conclusion. Getting away from her parents, seeing other women in college thrive and not put up with similar bullshit, and the slow realization that Kendell's offer to pay for her bills, books and other items was his way of slowly gaining more and more control over her life. All that helped her realize things needed to change.

"Later, when your mom accused me of taking advantage of you, I couldn't deny it."

"I knew what I was doing," he said firmly.

"I know you did. I knew that if I married you all of my problems would be over, but I really did need to find out who I was first. Who I was and what I wanted. I couldn't be with you if I didn't learn to love myself again."

"And now?"

Zoe let go of the fear and doubt and said words she'd been too afraid to speak for too long. "I want you." She leaned into him. "I want us."

The light that came into his eyes made joy explode in her heart. He placed his hand on the back of her head and pulled her in until their foreheads touched. "You have no idea how long I've wanted to hear you say that." His voice trembled.

Her stomach clenched. "Seriously?" Insecurity and doubt made her voice weaker. How could he be that emotional just for her?

His eyes never left hers. "Seriously."

Zoe ignored the voice in her head that wondered if she could live up to the adoration in his eyes. For now this was enough. She pressed her lips to his. "I want you, Byron Robidoux."

His head slanted and he kissed her harder. Zoe opened her mouth and let him deepen the kiss. The flame of passion he'd ignited earlier that day flared to life. Her hands slid over his strong shoulders and down his arms. His body trembled and he pressed into her as if he couldn't get enough of her.

Zoe broke the kiss. Byron's lips trailed across her cheek to her neck where he lightly nipped then sucked. Desire shot straight to her sex where slick heat pooled.

"Come to my room," she said in a thick voice.

Byron shook his head. Zoe's heart dropped. There was

no way he could kiss her like that after she poured her heart out and then send her to bed alone.

"My room is closer," he said with a sexy smile.

She smiled so hard her cheeks hurt. Byron stood and took her hand. She grabbed his and followed him to his downstairs bedroom. As soon as the door closed, they were in each other's arms. He undressed her slowly. He reverently kissed every inch of skin he revealed. His lips and tongue traced decadent patterns across her skin. She wanted his lips on her breasts, her stomach, the aching spot between her thighs. Zoe twisted and tugged to get his clothes off faster.

By the time they lay naked on the bed Zoe thought her body couldn't take any more. Byron pulled her into his arms until the front of her naked body was flush against his. The next kiss was slower. His long legs tangled with hers as his hand ran down her side and back up.

He pressed her onto her back and cupped her breast in his hand. He took the hard tip into his mouth and sucked deep. Zoe arched her back. Her hips lifted off the bed as a low, desperate moan vibrated through her chest. His other hand lowered to the junction of her thighs. His fingers gently spread her open and slid across her slick sex.

Zoe gasped and dug her nails into his shoulder. Her legs opened wide and Byron didn't hesitate. One long finger slid deep inside her. His mouth never lifted from her breast and he worshipped her nipple while his fingers sent her to heaven. But his finger wasn't enough.

Lowering her hand, she wrapped her fingers around his dick. He was so thick and hard, just the thought of him filling her made her moan, "Byron."

"Mmm hmm," He moaned, sounding pleased with himself.

He slid down her body. His teeth nipped at her thighs right before his tongue brushed over the sting. Her legs spread wide; he didn't hesitate. His firm tongue ran across her slick core. Zoe reached down and dug her nails into his shoulders. She tried to bite her lip to hold back her cries. It had been too long. Too long since anyone touched her, kissed her like this. Too long since she'd felt pleasure. Too long since she'd felt cherished.

Her leg shook. "Byron!" His name was both a plea to stop and go on forever.

One long finger pushed inside her, then two, then those wonderful lips of his closed over the pearl and tugged softly. Her body convulsed. Her fingers dug deeper into his shoulder. Her cry filled the room.

He pulled away to get a condom and was back in her arms before any of the heat left her body. Zoe opened her arms and pulled him back to her. Byron lifted one of her legs over his hip and slid into her with one long, exquisite stroke. Zoe's head pressed back into the pillow. Her eyes shut as bliss took over her body.

His lips brushed her jaw, her neck, her cheeks, but always came back to her lips. There was no rush or urgency to his movement. He took a hold of her heart and soul with each long, deep thrust and tender kiss.

He pressed his forehead against hers. "Zoe." He whispered her name. Her name on his lips, spoken as if he were in the center of paradise.

He pushed deep, filling her and pressing against her sensitive clit. Zoe's body shook from another wave of rapturous pleasure. Happiness, pleasure and affection squeezed her heart so tight she knew he was forever imprinted there.

CHAPTER NINETEEN

BYRON WOKE UP with Zoe next to him and couldn't stop a smile from spreading across his face. He turned onto his side and pulled her back against his front. She moaned softly and snuggled against him.

The night before had been everything he'd imagined and more. He had no other words to describe it. For the first time he didn't feel as if they were in a one-sided relationship. Knowing Zoe not only wanted him, but also trusted him, was a gift he didn't deserve, wouldn't refuse and would always cherish.

She'd given hints about her parents' relationship before when they'd hung out, but the night before was the first time she explained how their relationship impacted her. He could relate. He'd grown up in a house where relationships were bartered and sold like goods at a flea market. Back then he'd thought his protection was all Zoe would need to love him. Now he could see the arrogance of that thought. He hated the years they'd lost, but those years had given them both time to realize what they truly wanted out of a relationship.

Zoe sighed softly and her backside shifted. His dick thickened and his blood heated. She was soft, warm and smelled so damn good. His hand cupped her breast and her nipple hardened. Images of lifting her leg, sliding in and starting their morning off right made his smile widen.

His cell phone rang. Loudly. The accompanying vibration made the harsh interruption worse.

Zoe groaned and buried farther into the covers. Byron glared at the offending device across the room. He wanted to ignore it more than anything in the world, but couldn't afford to in the middle of a campaign.

"Make it stop," Zoe moaned and pulled the covers over her head.

"I've got it." Byron reluctantly jumped out of bed and hurried across the room to silence the phone. He hoped it was a call he could send to voice mail, but Dominic's number on the screen killed that dream. "Shit, I've got to take this."

"Go outside," Zoe mumbled from beneath the mound of covers.

He grinned despite his irritation. "Always so bossy." Zoe's sleepy chuckle came from the bed. He answered the phone. "Hold on a second," he spoke into the phone. He scanned the floor, found his pants and hurried to put them on. He crossed the door leading to the balcony.

"Then come back and finish what you started."

Byron froze at the door and looked back. Zoe was still under the covers. Just imagining her warm and naked beneath was enough to make up his mind. He was getting to the point of this call with Dominic really quick.

He slipped out the door and put the phone to his ear. "What have you found out?" The crisp mountain air chilled his skin and snatched away any lingering drowsiness. The thought of getting back in bed with Zoe was even more tempting.

"The fire marshal's report says it's an electrical fire."

Dominic jumped straight to the chase. "Did Zoe ever have any electrical problems in her house before?"

Byron leaned one hand on the balcony and stared out at the mist clinging to the mountains. "I'll have to ask, but I doubt it. I was there and she has a newer home. It had to have been built within the last few years."

"Hmm…well, the report says it started in the garage. Maybe something she left plugged up."

"Zoe is too cautious to just leave things plugged that shouldn't be. Did you check the surveillance video?"

"Not yet, but I'm putting Jeanette on that. We just need the footage from the alarm company."

Byron nodded. "Get it. Let me know if you find anything." He hesitated before asking the other question he didn't want but had to. "Any more emails?"

Dominic offered to have any further emails from the account that sent threatening messages to Zoe forwarded to him instead. Byron quickly agreed. Zoe had enough on her plate without being subjected to that mess. If it turned out to be a prank, then he and Dominic would deal with the asshole who thought calling a woman a lying bitch was funny. If it wasn't a prank…he'd deal with that, too. Until they figured out who was behind them then she didn't need to get them.

"Yes, two more."

"What did they say?"

"More of the same. Threats to get back at her and that she'll get what she deserves for lying." Frustration entered Dominic's voice. "Except this time they didn't originate out of Memphis. This time the emails were from Charlotte, North Carolina."

"Shit!" Byron rubbed his temple. They were getting closer. "Where in Charlotte?"

"Another library. Jeanette's team is already tracing it. What are you going to tell her?"

Byron looked back at the door. He thought of everything Zoe had just gone through. The loss of her house and job hadn't broken her, but she was nearing a breaking point. He couldn't throw this on top of everything else.

"Nothing yet."

"You sure?" Dominic asked, sounding unsure.

"I am. Until we find out the person, Zoe doesn't need any more trouble in her life."

"You're the boss," Dominic said. "Do you want me to look further into the fire?"

"I'll tell her what the fire report said, but I won't worry her about your investigation unless you find anything. Besides, she's staying at the estate for now. She and Lilah are safest there."

Despite what the report said, something didn't sit right with Byron. Not to say a newer home couldn't have an electrical fire, but Zoe hadn't mentioned having troubles. He didn't want to borrow trouble, but he'd rather be sure.

"Yes. Let me know if you find out anything."

"I will."

The call ended. Byron shivered, partially from the cold morning air and from the phone call. Now the emails were coming out of Charlotte. That was too close to Greenville and Jackson Falls for his liking. He called the head of his security team and requested they increase patrols around the estate and continue to shadow Zoe and Lilah. Then he went back inside.

Zoe was still in bed, but she'd pushed the covers down to the tops of her breasts. "Everything okay?"

He dropped his phone on the dresser and crossed the room. "That was Dominic." He sat on the edge of the bed. "He got the fire report."

Zoe sat up quickly. "And?"

"And it's saying an electrical fire. Did you have any problems before?"

Zoe frowned and twisted her mouth. "No. Everything was checked before I bought the house. There were no electrical issues."

"Something in the garage maybe?"

"I mean… I have a deep freezer out there, the battery panel for the internet and the breaker box, but still. Why would it just burst into flames?"

Worry seeped into her eyes. A line formed between her brows and she twisted the covers between her fingers. This was exactly what she didn't need.

He placed his hand over hers. "Hey, look at me." When she did he smiled. "It'll be okay. Right now you're safe, Lilah is safe and you're going to stay that way. I've got you."

Her shoulders relaxed slightly. "I know, but… I don't like depending on you to bail me out again."

He shook his head. "No buts. This is just temporary. Valtec didn't appreciate you. I know you'll find something better. You've got a place at our estate until you find someplace else." Even though he didn't want her to leave he knew trying to hold her there would make her bolt. "And even though you don't necessarily need it, you've got my shoulder to lean on. I promise you, Zoe, I'm not going anywhere."

Her eyes softened and she let out a long, slow breath. "You're right. I'll get through this."

"You will."

"Did he say anything else? Did he find out about the emails?"

"He's still working on those." Not exactly a lie, but he didn't want to see the fear come back into her eyes. He wasn't going to let anyone hurt Zoe. Not if he could do anything to protect her.

He could tell she wanted to ask more, so he leaned in and kissed the side of her mouth. "No more bad thoughts. Not after the night we just had."

Her frown morphed into a smile that brought out the dimple in her cheek. "It was a good night."

Byron flipped back the covers and slid in beside her. "And this morning is going to be even better." Zoe's giggle as he pulled her into his arms washed away the vestiges of guilt from keeping secrets trying to worm their way into his heart.

CHAPTER TWENTY

Zoe roamed the downstairs hall of the Robidoux Estate for the third time that morning. She went from the music room, to the sitting room, and ended in the sunroom after grabbing another chocolate chip cookie from the cookie jar. Just like the two previous trips, nothing had changed.

Lilah had started at a private school the Robidoux children had all attended. No waiting period or strenuous application required. Grant had made sure of that. Lilah said she liked the school, their award-winning archery team helped, but Zoe knew she missed her old friends. Thankfully, there was video chat. Lilah spent almost every afternoon swapping updates with Julie on everything about both her old and new school.

Grant and Elaina were each off making decisions and solving problems at Robidoux Tobacco and their new holding company. Byron was once again out of town for a campaign appearance. Everyone had something to do except her.

She'd kept busy for the first few days after the trip to the mountains, searching for a demolition contractor to clean up the debris from her home, filling out the insurance paperwork and reviewing the footage from her camera system of right before the fire. There wasn't anything suspicious on the video, but her neighbor, Mrs. Morgan, swore she'd seen someone around the house. Zoe tried to reassure herself that Mrs. Morgan always thought she saw people who weren't supposed to be there. That no one would really burn her home down. That the fire report was correct, and it was an electrical wiring problem.

That was another reason she needed a job. More time sitting meant more time coming up with conspiracy theories.

She sat in the sunroom looking out over the neatly manicured backyard. Bright sunshine filtered through the fluffy white clouds in the sky. This was the first time she'd ever had leisure time. She didn't have to rush to work, answer to a shitty boss, or worry about Lilah's safety. She could relax and enjoy life. The only problem: now that the business with the fire was taken care of she was bored out of her mind.

Zoe sighed and pulled her cell phone out of her back pocket. She needed a job and she needed one yesterday. She'd started applying after they'd returned from the mountains, and she checked her email and voice messages every hour. Hoping for some indication someone out there needed her.

Sounds from the kitchen caught her attention. She didn't get too excited about the possibility of a distraction. Sandra, the main housekeeper, was nice to Zoe, but she also didn't make any attempt to hide her discomfort with having Zoe try to help around the house. She might as well go back to the pool house and scour the internet for more jobs until Lilah came home and she could ask her daughter about every detail of her day under the guise of being a concerned parent and not because she was starving for conversation.

"I grabbed another cookie, Sandra," Zoe said as she

came into the kitchen. Instead of Sandra, Elaina stood at the counter. She poured coffee into a mug with one hand and frowned at her cell phone in the other. In her stylishly cut tan suit with her thick hair pulled up into a sleek twist, she reminded Zoe of the type of businesswoman she'd strived to be. Poised, polished and professional. Zoe's hand tightened on her cell phone. The need to check her emails again an obsession.

"Oh. I didn't know that was you." Zoe brushed the cookie crumbs off the old Valtec Safety Week T-shirt she wore. She had opted for jeans instead of leggings today, but she still felt like a lazy loafer standing next to Elaina.

Elaina's eyes jerked toward Sandra. "Of course you didn't. I don't typically come home during the day."

Zoe had spent enough time with the family to know Elaina's bark was worse than her bite. Elaina typically gave a smart-ass reply to a question or statement when she wanted to be left alone. Unfortunately for Elaina, Zoe was bored and in no mood to leave anyone alone.

"What are you doing here, then?" Zoe went over to the island and leaned her forearms on the cool marble surface.

"Working." Elaina put the pot back on the fancy stainless-steel coffeemaker. She picked up her mug and headed toward the door.

"Come on, Elaina, throw me a bone," Zoe said, not caring if she sounded like she was pleading. "I've sat here for several days with nothing to do while everyone else is busy. Pretend I'm one of your work colleagues and not just Byron's…" She didn't know what to call herself. Friend, lover, fake baby momma?

Elaina did a slow, graceful spin on her high heels to

face Zoe. She raised a brow, and interest sparked in her eyes. "Girlfriend?"

"Current partner," she countered. She and Byron hadn't labeled what they were doing. Between his frequent travel and the infrequent moments they could snatch together when he was in town, she sometimes wondered if things would last past the election. What if she found a job somewhere else? Would she really stay in Jackson Falls forever? She didn't want to think about that too much. "What are you working on?"

Elaina sighed and came back into the kitchen. She sipped the coffee before focusing on Zoe. "I'm thinking of acquiring a company."

Elaina said *acquiring a company* with the same casual indifference as Zoe would say she was buying a pack of socks. "Really?"

"Why not?" Elaina asked, sounding offended.

"You work for Robidoux Tobacco and your dad put you in charge of consolidating a bunch of other companies. Why would you go buy another company?"

Understanding cleared the fight from Elaina's eyes. "Because I need my own assets. Assets outside of the family. If I'm going to do that then I need to start somewhere."

"Okay, that makes sense." Zoe had spent every year since having Lilah trying to stand on her own. She understood the drive to build your own, as well, instead of relying on other people. "Is there anything wrong with the company?"

"Nothing's wrong with it. The business model is sound and there's a market for the goods."

"But?" Zoe heard the hesitancy in Elaina's voice.

Elaina let out a sigh and sat on one of the stools by the

counter. "But the manufacturing facility is plagued with problems. They've missed deadlines due to high turnover and safety concerns. If that can be corrected then I could make it work, but I don't know if it's worth my time."

The words rushed out of Elaina. It was the first time Zoe had seen the otherwise self-confident woman unsure of herself. Elaina probably didn't have a lot of people she could discuss her concerns with. Business advisers and lawyers were one thing, but sometimes you just needed a friend to listen to your thoughts. Zoe hadn't seen or heard Elaina mention a friend.

Zoe perked up, the flash of an idea brightening her mind. "I can help."

"You? How?"

"That's what I did with Valtec. I worked in risk management. If you're serious, I can visit the facility, identify the risks involved, figure out what's leading to the high turnover and give you a report on what would be needed to turn things around."

Elaina wrapped her hands around her coffee mug and assessed Zoe. "Can you really?"

Zoe was pretty sure other people had doubted themselves when Elaina asked that question in that tone of voice, but she didn't. "I can. Why do you sound doubtful?"

She shrugged. "A lot of people overpromise and under deliver."

"Believe me on this. I can help you." Zoe didn't doubt she could do it. Even though she'd considered looking outside risk management after leaving Valtec, a few weeks of doing nothing were enough for her to not be choosy.

"How long will it take you?" Elaina's eyes didn't waver.

Her voice before wasn't warm but it became assessing and more direct.

Zoe sat up straight. She felt like she was on a job interview. Which she kinda was. She fought the urge to straighten her T-shirt. "Where is the facility located? Can you get me access to information?"

"It's located in Raleigh, and yes, I can get you information and access to the facility."

"How soon do you need the information?"

"I'll need a report in a few weeks," Elaina said, her voice a challenge.

Zoe nodded and filled her voice with the confidence coursing through her. "I can do it."

Elaina narrowed her eyes. Eyes the same whiskey-brown color of Byron's. "You don't even know what you're walking into but you're ready to offer something in a few weeks."

"What else do I have to do?" she said honestly. Helping Elaina was better than waiting for an employer to call, waiting for Byron to come back in town, or creating theories about what else could have burned her house down.

Elaina lifted a shoulder. "Sandra did mention to Daddy that you're roaming the halls like a lost kitten."

Zoe's mouth fell open then she snapped it shut and raised her chin. "I am not."

The corner of Elaina's lips lifted. "Don't feel bad. Doing this for me will be good for us both."

"So you're going to let me help?"

Elaina hummed for a second then nodded. "Yes. I'll let you help. You'll actually be doing me a big favor."

Zoe clenched her fists and did a mini-pump. "Thank you, Elaina."

"Thank me now, hate me later. Just ask my administrative assistant, Gwen. Apparently, some people think I'm difficult to work with."

Zoe lifted a shoulder. "A lot of people think women who are direct and straight talkers are difficult. After my last boss, I think I can handle you."

Elaina leaned back. Humor flashed in her eyes. "And once again you prove you're no damsel. I guess I can see why Byron likes you." Elaina stood and brushed a hand across her flawless suit. "I've got to get back to the office for a meeting with Alex the Asshole. I'll email you the details. Come by tomorrow morning and we can talk."

She stood and nodded. "Sounds great." Zoe had heard the phrase "Alex the Asshole" enough to know she didn't want to touch that subject with a six-foot pole.

Elaina turned, stopped and faced Zoe again. "One other thing. I don't want anyone within the family to know what I'm doing."

"Why not?"

A devious gleam flashed in her eyes. "Because, I'm going to buy one of my dad's companies."

BYRON CAME BACK to town the next evening, so Zoe decided to go to his place instead of waiting for him to make his way to the estate. She was looking forward to seeing him. The media storm after the end of his engagement only intensified after the fire at her place. Byron spent even more time on the campaign trail. They'd barely agreed to be together before responsibilities kept them apart.

She stood on the other side of his door anxiously waiting. She needed to give him a heads-up about working with Elaina. More than that she missed Byron. She couldn't wait to wrap her arms around him, be wrapped by the strength of his arms holding her, feel his full lips pressed against hers.

Her grin faded when his door opened and Roy stood on the other side. He seemed just as surprised to see her as she was to see him. "Oh, it's you."

"Were you expecting someone else?"

Roy shook his head. "We ordered food, but you know what, it's a good thing you're here. Come on in."

Zoe followed him inside. Byron sat at his dining room table. A stack of papers and multiple laptops covered the surface. The television was on a cable news station where analysts discussed upcoming congressional and senate races. A few of the staff members from his campaign office buzzed around the space, passing papers, bringing cups of coffee and working on the laptops.

"You're still working," she said, surprised.

Byron's face lit up when he saw her. He immediately stood and crossed the room. The top buttons of his shirt were unbuttoned and a paisley tie hung loosely around his neck. He pulled her into his arms and brushed his lips across her cheek. "I wasn't expecting you."

Any guilt she might have felt about interrupting his work evaporated as she breathed in the rich scent of his cologne. "Elaina told me you were back in town. I thought I'd come by and see you," she said once they pulled apart.

"I'm glad you did," Byron said. "I missed you."

Roy sat in the chair Byron just vacated. "I told Zoe it's good that she's here. She can help us as we work this out." Roy's fingers scrolled across his iPad screen.

Zoe frowned at Byron. "Work what out?"

Byron shook his head. "It's nothing."

"We're coming up with the best way to introduce you as Byron's new love interest," Roy said. "What appearances you'll need to make. The best times to showcase you both in public. With you here we can take into consideration any ideas you have."

Zoe stepped back from Byron. "You're strategizing about our relationship?" She'd known they would have to be careful about how they introduce their relationship. He'd promised to include her on any decisions that affected her. Not for him to discuss their relationship with Roy and the rest of his team without her.

"No, no. That's not what's going on," Byron said, shaking his head. "Even though I did well on the campaign trail, there are still a lot of people asking about you and Yolanda. It's taking away from the issues." A crease formed between Byron's brows the way it always did when he was thinking about his next moves.

"I didn't realize it was such a problem." After the fire she hadn't focused on the reports on the campaign. A part of her wanted to ignore that she may be viewed as the woman who destroyed his perfect engagement. Though Byron had mentioned what the reporters were saying before, he'd never sounded as if she was a complication.

He gave her an encouraging grin and rubbed her back. "That's why we're coming up with a plan. Something that will work for everyone."

His voice was reassuring, but unease was a cold, dead weight in her stomach. She'd always been something his campaign needed to fix. A problem that required a good story and plan to sway voters. This get-together was no different from the first day she'd walked into the conference room at the Robidoux Estate and they'd strategized the introduction of Lilah as his daughter. But today it bothered her more. Why had she believed anything would change just because she and Byron had slept together?

"You know, I think you guys can handle things." Zoe walked backward toward the door. "I think I'll just go."

Byron gently placed a hand on her elbow to stop her. "You don't have to leave."

Zoe tensed up. Not from his touch, but from the urge to run away as if a hot fire was beneath her feet. Byron wanted to win. He'd always been about winning. Eventually, he'd have to get back into the game of working out a way for their relationship to help him win.

She tried to convince herself this wasn't him going back on what he'd said in the mountains. That he cared about her. He listened to her. That she was not just Yolanda's convenient replacement.

"I'm sorry, it's been a long day," she said, trying but not succeeding in hiding her irritation. "I'm not really in the mood to strategize. I'll let you all work and maybe we can figure out the best times for me to be seen with you in public later."

"You know what," he said, "it has been a long day." He looked over his shoulder. "Roy, let's call it a night."

Roy threw up his hands. "We just got started."

"We can talk about things tomorrow." Byron's voice was firm.

"But—"

"No buts. Everyone out." Byron's tone held no room for argument.

Roy took in a long, frustrated breath through his nose before nodding and standing. The other campaign aids followed his lead. The doorbell rang as they gathered their things. The food they'd ordered. Byron sent the food away with them.

"You didn't have to get rid of the food," Zoe said as they stood awkwardly in his living room after everyone was gone.

"I can find something to eat." He lowered to the end of the couch and pointed to the other end.

Zoe lowered herself onto the other end. "I didn't mean to cause a problem."

"You didn't cause a problem. I am tired. The campaign can wait."

Zoe looked over at the papers still stacked on his table then at the television where talk of national campaigns was still the topic of conversation. His campaign couldn't wait, but he'd paused things for her. Her doubts eased and she settled into the couch. "Why are you so good to me?"

"Because I never want to give you a reason to ever think I would hurt you."

The simple honesty in his voice unraveled the doubts that had wrapped around her heart. "I'm not jumpy around you. I know you won't hurt me."

His shoulders relaxed. "Will you tell me why you were upset?"

After his confession she felt foolish for reading so much into him doing his job. She didn't like Yolanda, but Zoe would have to adopt some of her traits. She'd have to learn how to be a good campaign partner. Which meant she'd also have to be honest with Byron about her concerns.

Zoe licked her lips. Her palms were sweaty. This was Byron. He wouldn't make her feel ridiculous for being uncomfortable about something. He never had. He watched her calmly. Nothing but concern in his eyes. No irritation, sneering, or impatience. He really was a guy she could relax and let her guard around.

"This entire thing with the campaign," she said slowly. "Planning our appearances and introducing our relationship to the public."

Byron slid across to her. "I know. It's not ideal, but we have to be prepared. Right now McLeod's team is working hard to paint you as the real reason for my breakup with Yolanda."

"Aren't I?"

"You're not. She made her own decisions."

"Only because I came back in your life. If you wouldn't have helped me you would have married her. Then you would have been happy. Not planning ways to introduce your relationship in a positive light. No worrying about me messing things up."

Byron rubbed his hands together. "Messing things up? How are you going to mess things up?"

"I don't know how to be the perfect candidate's girlfriend. My past isn't perfect. I'm homeless. I've lied. You have to have sessions with your political team just to come up with a plan to introduce me without making things worse. While I can't regret the decisions I made to protect Lilah, I also can't help but realize you'd be better off if I'd never been in your life."

Byron took a long breath. "Would it have been easier to marry Yolanda? Yes. That's why I picked her. Would I have been happy with her?" He shook his head.

"You seemed pretty happy when I first saw you." She remembered catching them kissing that first day at the estate.

"That's the image we portrayed. We were always about making people believe we were a love match. I thought

I was doing what was right. That not marrying for love would protect me from feeling the way I felt after you left thirteen years ago."

Zoe was struck by the unguarded emotions in his voice. She remembered something else from that first day. The hurt he couldn't hide when she'd said what he'd felt was attraction mixed with adoration. When she'd brushed aside his feelings as trivial.

"I would have married her, but I wouldn't have been happy. When I asked her I thought it was the right thing to do. My mom said having all the money in the world didn't mean a thing if you didn't do something with that money. That giving back and helping others were the way to make things better." He leaned back on the couch and stared at the ceiling. "She volunteered for everything. Every cause out there she gave money, but giving money isn't enough. When I told her that the people who made the laws were the ones who ultimately made the difference, she said then make the laws. I've been on that path since high school. Student council in high school, volunteering in college, going to law school and defending those less fortunate with my practice, and making it to the state house."

"She was so proud of you," Zoe said. She'd never forget the determination in Virginia's voice as she laid out all the reasons Zoe should leave Byron. She wasn't taking no for an answer, and Zoe saw the love for her son was the reason why.

"She was," Byron said with a small smile on his face. "But I also learned from my father. My dad says if you want to succeed you have to win and you win at any cost. My grandfather married a woman he didn't love but who had enough money to help him expand our tobacco production. My parents met young, loved hard, but they both were ambitious and stubborn. Their only goal was to raise kids who were strong enough to take over the business. They did, and that's why I didn't care about marrying Yolanda without loving her. The one time I let love rule me…" He sat up and met her gaze. "That's when I was ready to deviate from everything I planned and marry you."

Zoe rubbed her temples. "Gee, thanks." She tried to laugh it off, but his admission stung. Loving her hadn't been what he wanted.

Byron gently wrapped his fingers around her wrist and pulled her hand away from her face. "I'm not saying this right. I'm not trying to make you feel bad. I'm telling you this because even though I hate the circumstances that brought you back in my life, I don't regret having you back in it. I've done everything because it was expected of me or because that's what I was supposed to do. Being with you was the first time I wanted something not for the family legacy or how it would further my career. I wanted you because of you and being with you made me happier than I'd ever been. It hurt when you left, and I never wanted to hurt like that again. I thought things would be better for me if I took love out of the equation, but having you back proved I can't suppress those feelings. I don't want to pretend to be happy with someone else when I have the chance to be happy with you."

Zoe sucked in shallow breaths. Why was it that in all the fairy tales the heroine was lifted by the love of the hero? She didn't feel lifted. She felt weighted. She wasn't worth that much love. She couldn't hope to live up to his expectations. How would her heart survive watching the affection in his eyes slowly die away as he realized she wasn't as great as he thought?

Don't let him find out.

She could try to be the woman he deserved. The partner he deserved. First, she'd have to make him understand she wasn't Yolanda and didn't want to be.

"I told you about my parents. How they fought and how I thought love was supposed to be that way."

He nodded. She waited for him to tell her she was foolish for believing that. He just held her hand and waited for her to finish.

"I didn't know how to do relationships. I still don't know if I've got it figured out. I haven't dated a lot of people since having Lilah. I was too afraid they'd turn out like Kendell and only make things worse for her. What I do know is that I'm ready to try." She interlocked her fingers with his. "I'm ready to try with you."

A WEIGHT LIFTED off Byron's chest. He'd been unsure about where they stood ever since returning from the mountains. Time apart and the political realities of their relationships had done that. Then, when he'd seen her face as Roy rambled on about the right way to introduce her, he'd seen her withdraw. Saw the uncertainty in her eyes. He never wanted her to feel insecure when it came to him.

"Then we'll try together," he said.

She smiled, but doubt clouded her eyes. As much as he wanted her to trust him and see him as more than just someone who wanted her in his life to make winning easier, he also knew making the uncertainty in her eyes disappear would take time. He wanted to pull her into his arms and kiss away her fears, but that wasn't why he'd kicked everyone out. He'd gotten rid of his team so they could spend time together.

"How about I order food."

She laughed. "You just sent away the food you ordered."

"That was the food for them. I'll order us something. You pick out a movie or television show we can watch."

"Any movie?"

"Any movie." He leaned in and kissed her quickly. Zoe followed him when he pulled back. The doubt in her eyes now erased with a playfulness that he loved seeing in her eyes.

"I'll be right back," he said.

She grabbed his tie. "Where are you going?"

"To change clothes."

Her eyes lowered to his chest. Desire flashed in them. He wanted to push her back on the couch, rip off her pants and make love to her until the stress of the campaign washed away. Byron took a steadying breath before he did just that. He wanted to reassure her of his feelings. Not jump on her or make her think he wanted her body.

Zoe licked her lips. "Don't take too long."

"I won't." He kissed her quickly then jumped up from the couch before he pushed her back and did exactly what he wanted.

Spending time together. That was what they needed right now. He had to build her trust in him. In them.

He went into his bedroom and jerked the tie over his head. He tossed it on the bed as he headed to the closet. Once in there he pulled off his shirt and slacks and put them in the basket of clothes for cleaning. He'd slipped out of his underwear and was opening a drawer for a pair of shorts when there was a knock on the closet door.

Byron spun around. His hands instinctively covered his dick at the unexpected interruption. Zoe leaned against his closet door. Her full lips were lifted in a devilish grin.

"Sorry, but I'm hungry," she said.

Her gaze slowly traveled over his naked chest, stomach and stopped where his hands covered himself. The heated look in her eye said she was hungry for something other than food. Blood rushed to his groin. His hand wouldn't cover his reaction for long.

"What do you want me to order?" His voice was hoarse. He cleared his throat. Tried not to look as if he was ready to pull her to the floor of his closet.

She strolled through the door. The tip of her tongue dipped out to the corner of her mouth. Her gaze had once again dropped to his hands. A vision of her tongue gliding across the head of his erection flashed in his mind. Making it harder to hide it.

"You've already got what I want."

She'd made her way across the closet to him. She stopped in front of him. The heat of her body and the sweet, fruity smell of her perfume intoxicated him. "You can't just say stuff like that and kiss me then walk away."

"Zoe, I—"

"You're trying to be a gentleman and I appreciate that." She ran her fingers across his chest. "Except you forgot one thing."

Her touch reverberated through his body. "What's that?"

"I've never been into gentlemen."

The words made Byron pause. No, she hadn't been into gentlemen. Zoe had gone for the bad boy. Is that what she wanted from him? To not be the nice guy?

Before the unsettling thought could sink in and fertilize

his insecurities, Zoe pushed his hand aside and wrapped her fingers around his dick. She lifted on her toes and kissed him softly. All reasons to stop and talk this out fled. Byron went with his instincts. Tonight he'd give Zoe what she wanted.

His hands cradled the sides of her face. He slid his tongue over her lips. She opened to him without hesitation. He'd forever feel blessed to have her trust. The fabric of her T-shirt and jeans brushed against his skin. He wanted her naked. Just as naked as he was so he could feel as much of her as possible.

Zoe wrapped her arms around his neck. The heavy fullness of her breasts pressed against his chest. He wanted more than just to feel her; he had to see her. His hands slid down the sides of her body to rest on her hips. In a quick motion he lifted her up. Zoe's long legs wrapped around him. The heat of her sex seared him through her pants.

The urgency of too many days on the campaign trail and too many nights without her in his arms had him hurrying across the bedroom. He wanted to gently lay her on the bed and savor every inch of her body.

I've never been into gentlemen. Maybe she hadn't been. But this was one night, and he was the one gentleman who'd change her thoughts on that forever.

He tossed her on the bed and grinned as she bounced. Her delighted squeal made him harder.

"Get naked," he said. His voice was unrecognizable. Deep and rough with the desire coursing through his system.

Excitement flashed in her eyes. Byron stood next to the bed. His pulse raced harder with every article of clothing she pulled off. He thought he'd drop to his knees and worship her when she wiggled out of her jeans. By the time she was naked he was ready to explode, but Zoe had other things on her mind. When he moved to get on the bed, she came forward and wrapped her hand around his erection. A wicked grin lifted her lips before her lips closed around him.

Byron's mouth fell open. Words wouldn't form. His brain turned to mush as her mouth took him to places he'd never been before. His fingers dug into the loose curls of her hair. He started to pull back, but Zoe moaned deeply and renewed her efforts. Emboldened, Byron gripped her hair but didn't pull. He looked down to gauge her reaction. Any hint she needed him to pull back and he would; it would damn near kill him, but he would. Zoe looked up at him. Desire and devilment bright in her gaze.

The look in her eye almost took him over the edge. His toes curled and his leg shook. Byron pulled back before he climaxed. He placed a hand beneath her elbow and helped her to her knees. Then he kissed her long and thoroughly. He may not be the "bad boy" Zoe once craved, but he would find a way to become the man she deserved.

He grabbed a condom from the nightstand. His hand slid between her thighs. She was slick, hot and ready. Byron laid her back on the bed, covered himself and slid in deep. Zoe's tight heat hugged him. His heart beat so hard he thought it would explode in his chest. He brushed the hair back from her forehead and looked into her eyes.

The light glistened off her dark skin. Her lips were parted and swollen from his kisses. The trust in her eyes the most beautiful thing he'd ever seen.

He'd been a fool for thinking he could have married Yolanda with Zoe in his life. Zoe was perfect for him.

The only person he'd ever wanted. The only person he'd ever loved.

Everything he felt was too hard to convey with words. He just knew he'd move a mountain to keep her safe. "Making you happy is all I want to do."

Her eyes glistened. Her soft hand cupped his face. "I don't deserve you."

Byron slid his hips back then pushed forward. Zoe's lids lowered. Her mouth fell open and she sucked in a breath. "You deserve everything I can give you and more, Zoe. Never forget that."

Her leg trembled and she bit her lip. He repeated the movement until he pressed against the sweet nub of her clit. "Do you hear me?"

She nodded. Her entire body shook. Her eyes lost focus. His hips shifted back and forward but not as far. "Say yes. Tell me you believe me."

Her hips lifted and tried to pull him deeper. "Yes. I believe you."

He gave her what they both wanted. Thrusting in and out with long, slow strokes. Byron buried his head in her neck and breathed in her scent. A contentment he'd never known before infiltrated all the way to his bones. He'd be happy to remind her at any time.

Her eyes closed and her hips rotated. Byron shuddered and lost himself in the rhythm of their lovemaking. He wouldn't get caught up in her believing him now. He had time to convince her that his feelings were real.

CHAPTER TWENTY-ONE

"LET'S DO SOMETHING different today. Just the three of us," Byron said to Zoe the next morning.

She glanced up from her cell phone and raised a brow. She looked so damn beautiful sitting at his kitchen table, wearing nothing but one of his T-shirts and a pair of his boxers. Her thick hair was pushed away from her face with a black band. She had one leg bent with the foot in the chair and the edge of the boxers rode up, giving an enticing glimpse of smooth skin.

"The three of us?"

He jerked his eyes away from her thigh and met her eyes. "You, me and Lilah."

Zoe sat up straighter. "I thought we agreed not to get Lilah's hopes raised too high. She already has fantasies of us becoming a family."

Byron didn't have any problems with Lilah's wishes. Zoe wanted to ease into things, and he didn't blame her for being hesitant. Convincing her he wanted more than just political benefits would take time. Time he was willing to put in. Coming on too strong too soon would only push her away. He had to play things cool.

"She's been cooped up in the house with my family all night," he said. "This isn't about getting her hopes up, but about getting her out of the house."

"Don't you have campaign stuff to work on? I did interrupt your plans."

"That stuff can wait. I want to spend some time with you. Both of you." He did have a lot of campaign stuff to do. The plan to introduce Zoe as his girlfriend so soon after breaking things off with Yolanda was going to be tricky, but today was part one of showing Zoe he was willing to put her first.

Zoe studied him for a few seconds before she nodded. "Okay. What do you have in mind?"

"I'd like to show you around Jackson Falls."

She chuckled. "Why? We've been here for a while."

"You've been in town for weekends to help with the campaign and to relocate, but have you really been around the town? Seen what makes it great?"

He wanted her to fall in love with it the way he had. Maybe if she saw his hometown as something more than the location of his campaign headquarters, she'd also begin to see herself there long-term. In his life long-term.

She lifted a shoulder. "I guess you're right." She looked back at her phone. "Especially since I'm going to be working with Elaina."

Byron froze in the middle of turning to get a cup of coffee. He slowly spun around to face her. "Come again?"

She looked up and her eyes widened. "It was one of the reasons I came over last night. Elaina mentioned buying a company, but she has some concerns. I offered to do a risk assessment for her."

The same company Elaina had mentioned to him weeks ago? The one that might cause a stir during his campaign? "Did she tell you what company?"

"She doesn't want the family to know."

Byron closed his eyes. That couldn't be good. "Is she about to fire hundreds of people?"

"What? No! She's looking at one of your dad's companies. I told her I wouldn't say anything, but I can't do this without letting you know."

Byron pinched the bridge of his nose. Just the thought of the fallout between Elaina and Grant was almost enough to kill his happy mood. "Why go after one of Dad's?"

Zoe lifted her shoulders. "She said she wanted to build her own legacy. I don't know the reasons, but I do know I need something to do. Working with Elaina could be fun."

"Elaina fighting with my dad could prove deadly." How was he going to handle them fighting in the middle of the campaign? Maybe he could convince Elaina to change her mind. Or at least wait until after the election.

"Please, Byron, stay out of it." Zoe's voice interrupted his mental strategy session. "Let them fight out whatever they need to. I'm tired of sitting around the estate waiting for someone to call me back. I can do this."

"I can make some calls for you." He'd offered to do that before. She hadn't said anything, and he'd assumed she was taking the time away from work to get thing straightened out with the house. He didn't want her in the middle of whatever Grant and Elaina had brewing.

"I don't want calls. I want to do this on my own. I thought about starting a consulting company. If I can give Elaina a risk assessment that helps her make a good decision, then other people may hire me for the same thing."

The hope in her voice killed any arguments he may have had. She'd lost her job and her home. If working with Elaina could help her get her bearings again, who was he to stop her? "Fine. I'll stay out of it. But work at your own risk. If my dad and Elaina get into it, then he won't care that you just did a risk assessment."

Zoe lifted her hands. "I'm willing to deal with your father for this opportunity."

"Then I wish you well." He'd pray the company Elaina wanted wasn't one his dad would care about losing. "Now, can we get Lilah and I can show you my town?"

Zoe's grin made his heart flip. "Sure, let's pretend we're tourists." Zoe put her phone down and stood.

"Great." He walked over and kissed her softly. "I promise it'll be more fun than it sounds."

AN HOUR LATER they'd dressed, picked up Lilah and were back in downtown Jackson Falls. Byron took them to his cousin Ashiya's high-end consignment store, Piece Together. Ashiya's hazel eyes widened when the three of them walked through the doors.

"This is a pleasant surprise. What brings you in this morning?"

"Well, Zoe's been attending a lot of my campaign events and I thought why not buy a dress from one of the best stores in town." Byron hugged his cousin.

Ashiya laughed and squeezed him. "Thank you for thinking of my place." Ashiya grinned at Zoe. "All right, Zoe, what are you looking for?"

Considering Zoe hadn't realized she needed a new dress for Byron's campaign events, she wasn't looking for anything. Instead of saying that, she smiled at Ashiya.

"A suit, maybe," she said. "Do you have anything?"

"I've got a great selection." She grinned at Lilah. "I even have a section for teens. Come on, let's check that out."

Lilah practically bounced on her feet with excitement. Zoe glanced a Byron but he waved her on.

"Go ahead. I'll wait."

Zoe and Lilah followed Ashiya through the store. They picked out several outfits to try on. Ashiya made suggestions for what would work based on Zoe's and Lilah's body types and style comfort level. Before long, Zoe and Lilah were in the dressing rooms trying on clothes while Byron answered phone calls.

"You and Byron make such a cute couple," Ashiya said. She was in Zoe's dressing room helping her into a suit. "I'm so glad you two were able to get back together."

Zoe glanced around, even though they were alone in the dressing area. Lilah had insisted on having her own room. "It's not official. We're keeping that information just in the family."

"I understand, but it is true, right? You two are back together?" Ashiya asked with the pointed Robidoux stare.

"We're seeing how things work out during the election."

"And after the election? I mean, it's obvious the two of you love each other."

"It's not obvious," Zoe said defensively.

Ashiya laughed and helped Zoe zip up the back of the emerald green dress she'd tried on. "I spend most of my time observing what's going on with the family. I've seen Byron date a lot of women, and I've never seen him look at someone the way he looks at you. Plus, the fact that he was willing to put his campaign in jeopardy is further proof. He's in love with you."

"I wish he weren't," Zoe blurted out.

Ashiya froze in the middle of sliding the jacket that matched the dress off the hanger. "Seriously? Why?"

Zoe focused on her reflection in the mirror. She smoothed out the material for the dress. "I just mean Byron would be so much further in his campaign if he didn't think he was in love with me. He'd be better off. He and Yolanda would be together, and he would be higher in the polls."

Ashiya sucked her teeth and waved a hand. "Girl, please. He wouldn't be happy, and he would have married someone he didn't love. Not to mention she walked away just when things heated up." Ashiya chuckled. "You've got to be stronger than that to survive in this family."

"She wouldn't have left him if it wasn't for me."

Ashiya grunted. "Believe me, she might have left him eventually. Regardless of what you say, I think Byron being in love with you is good. Love isn't easy and he's proving he's willing to go the distance to be with you. What could possibly be wrong with that?"

I'm afraid to love him back.

Loving Byron back meant being his perfect match. Always having to think about the optics of whatever decision she made. Being under constant scrutiny. She'd hate every minute of it, but she'd do it anyway because Byron would want her to. The person she'd finally found and grown into would disappear because she wanted Byron to succeed and she would do whatever she needed to in order to help him succeed. She'd lose herself to be what he needed.

"I still think he'd have it easier without me," Zoe said, avoiding Ashiya's gaze.

"I promise you, Byron doesn't think that."

"Ashiya, I'm having a problem ringing up this customer's discount. Can you help me?" one of the ladies working with Ashiya called on the other side the door to the dressing room.

Ashiya squeezed Zoe's shoulders. "I'll be right back."

Zoe smiled and nodded. After Ashiya left, she stared at her reflection in the mirror. She didn't recognize the sophisticated woman looking back. The woman who looked like a senator's wife. No one would look at her and see the single mother who'd escaped an abusive relationship and rebuilt her life. No one would ever know her story.

There was a knock on the door. "Let me see," Lilah said.

Zoe opened the door and held out her arms. "What do you think?"

Lilah tilted her head to the side and rested a finger on her chin as she studied Zoe. "I like it. You look the part."

"The part?"

"Senator's wife," Lilah said with a grin.

Zoe narrowed her eyes and pointed at the door. "Not now, Lilah. Grab what you want and let's go."

Lilah sighed. "Fine, but I can pretend."

Lilah walked out. Zoe looked back at the reflection of the senator's wife in the mirror. She was willing to stand next to Byron for now. She'd have to keep her heart out of the line of fire. She couldn't lose herself again. Not even for Byron. That was the only way she would be sure to come out of this unscathed.

CHAPTER TWENTY-TWO

AFTER HIS COUSIN gave them discounts on whatever they wanted in the store, they ate lunch at Frank's Fish and Chicken. The owners still treated him as if he were family after he'd chosen them to cater one of his earlier campaign events. Afterward, Byron took Zoe and Lilah to the museum of art where India performed once a quarter and some of Travis's paintings were featured.

"You really do a lot to support local businesses," Zoe said after they finished lunch and were on their way back to his place. Since he lived downtown, they'd walked to the museum instead of driving.

"Small businesses are just as important as large ones. Plus, many of these people I've known all my life. It's great to see them take their dream and make it thrive."

Lilah walked to Byron's left, and she looked at him. "Is that why you're running for Senate? So you can help local businesses?"

"It's part of the reason. My family's success started because of the tobacco farming. I still want to protect the interests of the agricultural industry. Running for Senate, and hopefully winning, will give me a better opportunity to do that."

"My social studies teacher said if you want to have the biggest impact on your hometown then you have to work locally," Lilah said. "She said most people ignore local politics and only listen to the talking heads on cable news instead of listening to the local politicians who slowly chip away at their rights right under their noses."

Byron's brows rose. "Sounds like your social studies teacher is smart."

"She made us read some of the council minutes and watch video of a meeting. She's right. So much stuff happens there."

Byron wrapped an arm around Lilah's shoulder. "Maybe you should run for local politics one day."

"Maybe I will. I think I'd like it better than national stuff. You're getting hammered, and the press really doesn't like me or Momma," Lilah said.

Byron glanced at Zoe, who wore a worried expression. He stopped in the street and turned Lilah to face him. "The media doesn't like your momma because they don't know the truth behind her story. Your mom is strong, smart and brave. She did what she had to in order to protect you."

Lilah smiled at him. "I know that. Everyone knows the media will go for juicy stories." Her eyes grew serious. "As long as you like me and my mom. That's all that matters to me."

"Lilah, I—" He broke off.

He'd been about to say he loved her and her mom. The realization was like a kick to the chest by someone wearing six-inch stilettos. A sharp truth he wasn't ready to admit or even acknowledge. Loving Zoe was not in the cards for now. Falling in love could turn into a disaster. She might wake up one day and realize she didn't want any of this.

He went with the politically correct answer. "You have nothing to worry about. I know the truth. I have nothing but respect and admiration for your mom and what she continues to do to protect you."

Lilah beamed, which he guessed meant she was satisfied with what he said. He glanced at Zoe. She smiled at him but looked away quickly. Maybe she was okay with the answer, too. She had insisted on his not getting Lilah's hopes up about them.

"Let's get back to my place, put down some of the stuff we bought and finish our debate on what movie to see later today."

Lilah laughed. "Sorry, you're outvoted. We're going to see the new Keanu Reeves movie, right, Mom?"

Zoe nodded. "Keanu in a romantic comedy? Uh…yeah!"

The mother and daughter high-fived and Byron knew he was outvoted. He didn't care. As long as he got to spend more time with the two of them. Today had been good. Just what he needed. Time away from the campaign. Time to relax and just enjoy. Tomorrow all his responsibilities would still be waiting for him. He'd pick up right where he left off last night, but today he was going to pretend as if he and Zoe were in a relationship with no questions about the future, Lilah was his wonderful daughter and he was enjoying a day with his family. Tomorrow he'd worry about how to make this fantasy day into a reality.

"Thank you for today. It was fun."

Byron looked over his shoulder at Zoe lounging next to the pool at his family's estate. They'd gone to the movie and ended the day at the pool. Lilah had gone inside to update her friend on all the fun she'd had. In her absence, Byron asked Zoe if she'd cared for a margarita and he'd used the outdoor wet bar to make their drinks.

She opted against wearing a bathing suit and sat next to the pool in a tank top and shorts. Byron and Lilah had changed into swimwear and had done a few laps in the pool.

"I want to take you and Lilah places," he said. "Show you both all of the things you've dreamed of seeing."

He poured the frozen drink into two glasses and took one over to Zoe. She accepted her drink with a grateful smile.

"I don't need all of that. I enjoyed seeing your hometown through your eyes."

Byron sat on the edge of her lounge chair. He pulled her feet into his lap and gently massaged one. "You used to dream of traveling. You talked so much about seeing different places and visiting every corner of the world. I'd love to be the one to take you there."

Zoe ran a finger around the rim of her glass. "I dreamed of that when I wanted to escape my family. That was back when I thought getting away to some new location would be the answer to all of my problems."

"You wanted to escape?" He'd viewed her dreams of traveling and visiting new places as an example of her free spirit.

"My family. My life," she said. "My parents weren't the best role models and did the best they could with us, but I hated going home. I'd have to worry about who was the latest woman my dad cheated with. Watch my mom get angry and throw all of his stuff out. They'd argue, then fight. If it wasn't cheating it was something else. Every day my sister and I had no idea what we'd be walking into."

"I can understand why you would want to escape."

"College was my first escape plan," she said. "I started

without declaring a major and not knowing what I wanted to do with my life. I just wanted to be away from home." She looked over her shoulder at the pool house where Lilah was safe inside talking to her friend. "Lilah was my second. One time my mom said when you have a child your thoughts about life change. Things you never thought you'd say or do aren't even a question. I think that's why she put up with Dad for so long. As soon as we were out of the house she left him. I thought she would do better, but her new guy…" She wrinkled her nose and sipped her drink.

"Not much better."

"The only good thing I can say about him is at least he doesn't hit her."

"My parents often used the excuse of doing what's right for us for the things they've done." Byron considered the way Grant coerced the marriage between Elaina and Travis, separating him from India. How his mom convinced Zoe that leaving was the best. Who knows what else they'd done for the sake of the family.

He glanced at Zoe and thought about how he was keeping the emails a secret from her. He didn't agree with the decisions his parents made, but he understood their reasoning. "No one wants to see the person they love suffer."

"No, you don't." Zoe stared at the still water of the pool. "Kendell's control kept getting worse. He'd have people show up at the places I volunteered to make sure I was really there, take my car keys to try and keep me from leaving my place and giving me less money so even if I did go somewhere I couldn't do much."

Byron remembered times Zoe asked him to pick her up somewhere because her car was broken down, or her not eating when they went places because she was dieting. He felt stupid for not recognizing what was going on.

"I hated that guy," Byron said in a tight voice.

Zoe let out a soft laugh. "Tell me something I didn't know. It's why I thought part of the reason you wanted me was because you didn't like him."

Byron tickled the bottom of her foot. "That was only a small part."

Zoe giggled and pulled her foot back. She lightly kicked him. "But it was a part."

Byron took hold of her foot again. He squeezed gently. "I'll admit my male ego couldn't understand why you would choose that guy over me. I wanted to treat you better than he did."

"Did you pine for me like the guys in the throwback R and B songs?" Her eyes were teasing and her dimple was out.

"Oh, you like the idea of that, huh?" He tickled her ankle. She jerked her leg back but he didn't let go. He watched her and tilted his head to the side. "It didn't start like that. You were my rival when we first met. I grew to respect you and couldn't believe we became friends. Later, I feel in love with you." His voice became serious. "It was never just about the physical attraction or trying to steal you from him. You seduced my mind and once you took up residence there you never moved out."

Zoe slowly sat up. "Never?" She tried to sound teasing, but there was a breathless quality to her voice.

Admitting to feelings he'd ignored for years wasn't easy. After everything they'd shared, his stomach still clenched. A part of him wanted to tease and deflect. Except the look in her eyes and the emotion reflected there pushed him. Byron's gaze didn't waver. "Never."

She licked her lips and stared down into her melting drink. "Sometimes I'd wonder what would have happened if I'd married you. I want safety. I want Lilah to have stability, and you would have given that to us, but…"

"But what?" Had that been the only reason she'd wondered?

Her eyes met his. "But I also missed you. I always felt safe when I was with you. Sometimes I'd let myself fantasize about what it would be like if I'd married you. I'd picture us happy. You being awesome with Lilah. Seeing the love in your eyes again and knowing it was just for me." Her voice trembled as if it was just as frightening to admit her feelings.

"I can be all of that if you'll let me."

"What if you change your mind?" she asked hesitantly.

He tugged lightly on her foot. "What if *you* change *your* mind?" When she frowned he softened his words with a half smile. "Zoe, I offered you my heart and you walked away once. It's scary as hell, but I want to believe we're older and wiser. I can't promise you anything more than you can promise me. But what I will promise is to always be truthful. To always let you know how I feel. To always make sure you're never in the dark about my feelings. Can you promise the same?"

The uncertainty left her eyes. "I promise to try."

The words were quick, but the conviction in her voice felt real. "Then that's what we'll have to trust right now."

She took a long breath before leaning in and kissing him. "That sounds good to me."

A flood of memories of the night before, and her body

tight against his, rushed him. He pulled her over onto his lap. "Come home with me tonight." He murmured the words against her lips.

She moaned softly. "I can't leave Lilah again."

"Then I'll stay at the estate. You can find me when she's asleep," he said between kisses. He'd do whatever he needed to get another night in her arms.

Zoe shook her head, but he kissed her again until she let out a sexy whimper. Her margarita hit the floor and her hands wrapped around his shoulders. The door to the pool house opened. Lilah squeaked. "Oh, my God! I knew you two would fall in love again!"

CHAPTER TWENTY-THREE

ZOE REVIEWED HER checklist as she made her way to the front office of TJA Manufacturing. She could understand why Elaina wanted to buy the place. The company was housed in a former textile facility that now processed hemp. With the increase in uses not only for the fibers but also the oil, the facility had the potential to generate a huge profit. Due to a series of accidents the plant was behind on production. Zoe went over the accident reports and the training records. The previous management didn't care about meeting or keeping employees up-to-date on the latest safety regulations.

The new plant manager, Mr. Dickerson, was trying, but hadn't been able to get the owners to invest in the changes.

Zoe knocked on Mr. Dickerson's door and entered after he waved her in. "I've finished my walk-through."

Mr. Dickerson was a tall white man with a bulky figure that reminded her of a bodybuilder or football player with blond hair thinning at the top. When she'd first arrived, his blue eyes glared at her through his glasses. She didn't need to be told he wasn't happy about her arrival. For a moment she'd second-guessed herself as he eyed her skeptically. Then she'd remembered all the work she'd done at Valtec and OSHA before that. The improvements she'd made and efficiencies that resulted from her hard work. Valtec may not have appreciated what she had to offer, but

Elaina was giving her a chance. She'd squared her shoulders, looked Mr. Dickerson dead in the eye and told him what she would need in order to complete her assessment. Surprisingly, he hadn't pushed back and had given her what she wanted with no problems.

He motioned for Zoe to sit in the visitor's chair across from his desk. "What do you think?"

"There are things we can do to increase production like updating the equipment. That would not only improve morale but also increase employee safety."

He shifted in his chair and eyed her warily. "That's great to hear, but I don't know if this will help. I've asked for changes for months and they keep saying there aren't enough funds to make any changes. I think they're planning to shut the place down."

He looked at her as if she had the answer. Zoe wished she did. She wasn't sure how Elaina had gotten her this visit, but she had a feeling Mr. Dickerson thought Zoe worked for the owners. She wasn't going to alarm him by mentioning Elaina was considering purchasing the facility.

"I don't know what the future holds, but I do know the problems you have aren't insurmountable. I'll be sure to make that clear in my report."

Zoe hoped Elaina purchased the place and turned it around. Not only did the facility have potential, but if Zoe helped correct some of their deficiencies then she'd have more credibility, too. The idea of being a risk management consultant had taken hold since her talk with Elaina, and Zoe wasn't sure she'd be able to shake it.

Mr. Dickerson nodded. "That's all I can ask, I guess."

"Thank you for your time." Zoe held out her hand to him.

He took hers in a firm grip and shook once. "I'll walk you out."

After Zoe was back in the car, she turned on the ignition and pulled out her cell phone. She turned the air-conditioning on blast to combat the sauna inside the car from the hot sun. Her phone battery was nearly dead. Lilah had snatched the car charger the day before. She sent a quick text to Byron, letting him know she was leaving Raleigh before dialing Elaina's number. Elaina answered on the second ring.

"Well, is it worth the effort?" Elaina went straight to the point instead of greeting Zoe.

"It is. Are there problems if you buy it, yes, but nothing that can't be resolved. It's also going to take a big investment. Equipment needs updating, training programs need to be implemented. You may even need some facility upgrades. Most of the problems come from a lack of maintenance."

"I can handle all of that," Elaina said with the confidence of a Robidoux.

Zoe couldn't help but smile. Maybe she'd borrow some of Elaina's confidence and put it toward her idea to start her own business. "I have no doubt you can."

"My dad's not doing anything with it," Elaina said, sounding disgusted. "He won't even miss it or care."

"Does he know you're the one making the offer?"

"No, I'm working through a liaison. He has a partner, but that partner will be fine once I purchase the place and turn it into something." Elaina's voice held a warning.

Zoe put the car in gear and drove out of the parking lot. "I won't tell your dad anything, but I did give Byron a heads-up. I don't like being in the middle of your family fight."

Zoe was already too engrained in the family and couldn't see an easy way out. Lilah was convinced Zoe and Byron were in love after seeing them kiss. While Zoe hadn't planned to keep her relationship with Byron a secret, she wasn't sure how to manage her daughter's expectations. Instead, she'd gotten wrapped up in the comfort of being with Byron and let her guard down, and now Lilah's happiness was at stake. Zoe didn't want to see her daughter's disappointment if Zoe and Byron didn't work out.

"You're already in the middle, and you're already a part of our family's power plays," Elaina said.

"Which is why I feel a little weird about helping you take your father's company after everything he and Byron have done."

Elaina laughed as if Zoe was being foolish. "Don't think my family hasn't looked for ways to use you to further their own gains. That's what my dad does and encourages."

Zoe had sat through enough strategy sessions to know Elaina was right. "Byron is trying to help me." He'd stopped the emails from coming after realizing they were from a spamming site. Given her time to get back on her feet after the fire. He didn't have to do all that as part of their deal.

"Byron is also an opportunist," was Elaina's matter-of-fact reply. "I don't doubt that he cares about you and Lilah, but he still released photos of the three of you out and about having a fun family day this past weekend to bump his campaign numbers."

The traffic light turned red and Zoe slammed on the brakes. "What photos?"

"The photos are gracing the front page of our newspaper and reported on multiple news channels. You're a happy family reunited. Most of the reports are eating this up like candy. The expected few are saying you stole him from Yolanda. So before you jump on a high horse and tell me it's wrong to snatch my father's company from him, remember that my family will *always* do what's in their best interests. If you're going to be a part of this family, you'll have to learn to look out for yourself. Do this with me. Once I turn this company around you can do it with me somewhere else or for another company. Build your own wealth, and no matter what happens between you and Byron, you'll never have to depend on him for your future."

Zoe didn't have an argument for that. The light turned green and Zoe eased into traffic getting on the interstate. Her hands gripped the steering wheel. Byron released pictures of them? He'd said he wanted a day of just the three of them. No politics and no pressure. Only to turn around and use that day to look better in the media.

She couldn't believe she'd been blinded by her emotions again. Byron may care for her, but he fought to win, and he'd do whatever he needed to win. Including using Zoe and Lilah to further his political chances.

Loving a man is the hardest thing you'll ever do. No one can hurt you the way he can. Zoe remembered the day her mom had told her those words. The day after Kendell hit her the first time. The day she'd convinced herself she'd made the mistake and deserved the punishment. The first time she'd wondered if her life would be easier if she never fell in love.

Time to get back to building her own legacy. "I'm in."

"LOOKS LIKE WE just beat a huge pile up on 40," Byron's driver, Wesley, said through the intercom.

Byron looked up from the speech he was editing to meet Wesley's eyes in the rearview mirror. "Any injuries?"

"Not from what the news reports are saying. It's holding up traffic for hours."

Byron frowned. "Zoe was in Raleigh today." He reached into his jacket pocket and grabbed his cell phone.

"She may have missed it, too," Wesley said, sounding confident.

A recent text from Zoe said she was leaving Raleigh. She could have just missed it, be blocked by it or worse, a part of it. "I'll call her and check."

"Hello?" Zoe answered in an exasperated tone.

Byron's stomach clenched. "Are you okay?"

"I would be if this traffic would move. Ugh!"

Byron relaxed and smiled. She was never patient when it came to traffic jams. He kept any hint of humor out of his voice. "I take it you're behind the accident. It's a huge pile up that's going to hold up traffic for a few hours."

"Hours! No. I've got to pick up Lilah. She's joined the archery team at the school, and they have practice tonight. I can't leave her there."

He motioned to Wesley with his hand. "You're not. I'll pick her up." Wesley nodded.

"You're in Jackson Falls? I thought you were out of town?"

"I was, but I wanted to come home. I missed you." He had an appearance early the next day and it would have been easier to stay overnight, but he'd wanted to see Zoe and Lilah.

"You missed us?" Her voice sounded dubious.

"Of course I did. Why wouldn't I?"

She was quiet for a heartbeat. "Yeah…look, if it's no problem, will you get Lilah? We'll talk later."

Worry creased his brow. Dread slithered through his midsection. He didn't like the way she said *we'll talk later*.

"Do we need to talk about something?"

"Dammit, just cut me off. Asshole," Zoe said, frustrated. "Look, my cell is dying, and I need to pay attention to the road."

He wanted to finish the conversation. He glanced at Wesley in the front seat. He'd save this for later. "That's fine. Pay attention to the traffic there. Come home safely, and I'll get Lilah. We'll see you later and talk then. Okay?"

She sighed in frustration. "Fine." She ended the call without another word.

Byron stared at his phone in confusion. What was that about? Things were going well with them. They'd finally gotten to a place where he felt like they could trust each other.

"Picking up Lilah now?" Wesley asked.

"Yes, head to her school." Byron's cell phone rang again. Roy's number lit the screen. Byron immediately had an idea of why Zoe might be upset.

"Did you release those pictures?" Byron said instead of greeting his campaign manager.

When Roy admitted one of the staffers had taken pictures of him, Zoe and Lilah when they were downtown that weekend, Byron had been irritated, but he knew his staffers were always on the lookout for good visuals. He'd thought he made it clear to Roy not to use the pictures.

"Your dad called and said you gave the okay," Roy said defensively. "Good thing he did, because I'm getting calls with people wanting to interview you. The immediate response is positive. The family angle is helping. That and the way you eviscerated McLeod's latest attempt at a policy promise to bring more jobs and you're up."

"My dad doesn't have final say so in anything to do with my campaign," Byron said through clenched teeth. He'd expressly told Roy he didn't want the pictures released. He'd like to eviscerate Grant. "I didn't want them released. The day I spent with Zoe and Lilah wasn't a campaign stunt."

"Everything you do is a campaign stunt. Are you in this to win or not? We both know how McLeod fights. You don't have time to play the nice guy, Byron. Your dad made the right call."

Byron punched the back of the passenger seat. The smooth leather gave way, but the frustration building inside him didn't. "I don't give a damn if it was the right call. When it comes to anything related to *my* campaign, I make the final call. If you do anything again without consulting me first, I will fire your ass. Do you understand?"

Byron didn't care if Roy was the best campaign manager in the state. Roy could get Byron to the White House if he ever aimed that far. But his political career was his. Not his father's. If Roy was going to work with Grant behind Byron's back, then he was better served working with someone else.

"I got it," Roy said, sounding chastised. "I'm sorry."

Byron clenched his fist but didn't hit the seat again. He would save the anger for his father. "I'll deal with my dad. I'll see you in the morning for the speech in Durham." Byron hung up.

Now he had to clean this up. He'd considered telling

Roy to release the photos. The pictures looked good. He'd known they would play up the family angle he needed. The temptation had been real and strong, but he'd also known releasing the photos without talking to Zoe wasn't the right move. Leave it to his dad not to give a damn about Byron's decisions and push for the win.

He considered calling Grant, but that was a conversation that needed to happen in person. Byron channeled his anger by sharpening the points against McLeod in his speech for the next day. The idea of verbally murdering his opponent was a minor balm to his ragged emotions.

He'd calmed himself down by the time they pulled up in front of Lilah's school. The faculty knew him since his family had all attended and gave generously to the alumni association. He stopped in the main office to speak with the administrative staff, talk about his plans for the area and snap a few pictures.

Lilah's eyes lit up when she saw him. His heart swelled with pride as the coach complimented Lilah on her archery skills. She was a smart kid. Smart and talented. He had to tamp down his visions of future gold medal winner glory with him and Zoe cheering Lilah from the stands. He wouldn't push her the way Grant pushed him. Whatever Lilah wanted he'd help her achieve. He may not be her biological dad, but he'd be a good father to her.

They got into the back of the car and Wesley guided them through traffic toward the Robidoux Estate.

"Sounds like someone is the coach's new favorite team member," Byron said.

Lilah grinned and twisted the end of one of her braids. "He said he wouldn't give me any preferential treatment just because I was a Robidoux. Which meant I just had to show him preferential treatment isn't needed. I don't think he realized just how good I am."

Byron held out his hand for a fist bump. "That's my girl. Let them underestimate you and then knock them off their feet."

Lilah bumped her fist to his. "You know it."

"When's the first competition?"

"In two weeks. I'm excited and nervous. It's a regional event, so my old school is in the competition, too. It'll be weird going against my old teammates."

"That's understandable. Just remember it's not personal. It's okay to talk to them and wish them well."

Lilah opened her mouth to reply but something crashed into Byron's side of the vehicle. The world spun, the sound of glass breaking, and metal crunching blended with Lilah's frightened scream. The car was hit again, and everything tilted. Byron barely had time to register the second hit when the car flipped and fell.

CHAPTER TWENTY-FOUR

IN TRUE HOW-could-this-day-get-any-worse fashion, Zoe's day went from irritating to multiple bottles of wine required. The accident on the interstate held up traffic for two hours. In that time she managed to run over something sharp because as soon as she made it past the accident her tire went flat. She'd never replaced the spare after it had gotten a nail in it six months before, which meant she had to sit on the side of the interstate for another hour while she waited for roadside assistance to show up and change her tire. Her phone died somewhere in the middle of all that. She'd have to remember to get her car charger back from Lilah immediately. When she borrowed the phone of the roadside assistance guy and called Byron to tell him she was running late, his phone went straight to voice mail.

She was in no mood for anything else to go wrong in that day, which was why she groaned when she finally walked into the Robidoux Estate and was immediately greeted by a worried look on Sandra's face. Something was off. The house was normally quiet, but tonight it was too quiet to have so many cars out front. The entire family was there, yet the place was silent as a tomb.

"What happened?" Zoe asked, expecting to hear there was a problem with Byron's campaign, Robidoux Tobacco, or that Grant had called an unwarranted family meeting to discuss whatever new idea he had.

"There was an accident," Sandra said. She reached out and took Zoe's purse and car keys.

Zoe's heart jumped. "An accident? Is anyone hurt? Who?"

"The family is in the upstairs sitting room. Everyone is fine, but it was Mr. Byron and Miss Lilah."

Zoe slapped a hand to her chest. Panic weighed her down. "Lilah?"

"Is fine. They're upstairs," Sandra said in a patient voice.

Zoe didn't wait to hear anything else. She took the stairs two at a time. She was out of breath by the time she burst through the upstairs living area. Lilah sat next to Byron on the couch. She was in the clothes she wore for archery practice. There was a bandage on her forehead. She popped up and ran across the room toward Zoe.

"Mom, where were you?" Lilah slammed into Zoe's arms.

Zoe hugged her daughter tight. "I'm so sorry, baby. The accident on the interstate held me up, my tire went flat and my phone died." She pulled Lilah back so her eyes could scan her daughter. There were a few scratches on her face along with the bandage, but otherwise she looked fine.

"What happened?" Zoe's voice shook.

"A car ran into us." Lilah's eyes were wide. She spoke in a high, rushed voice. "It knocked us off the road and into a ditch. Byron was great, Mom. He kept his cool, cut the seat belts and pulled us out of the car. Once he got me on the side of the road he went back and pulled out Mr. Wesley. He saved our lives."

Zoe pulled Lilah back into her arms and looked at Byron across the room. His face was solemn. Beneath that she saw something else. He was angry. She didn't blame him. She wanted to hurt someone, too.

"Did the other driver stick around?" Zoe asked.

Byron shook his head. "It was a hit and run."

Zoe clenched her teeth. Who would do something like that and just drive away? She wanted to scream and ask a thousand questions, but instead she hugged Lilah tighter. Her daughter was fine. She'd gotten out of the car with a few scratches. Byron was okay. Things could have been worse. She would take this small blessing.

Elaina stood from where she sat on Byron's other side. "Lilah, let's go get you changed and cleaned up while Byron gives your mom and update on what happened."

Zoe slowly let go of her daughter. Lilah smiled and nodded at Elaina. "Okay." She looked back at Zoe. "You're coming back to the pool house?"

"As soon as I'm done here," Zoe promised.

Elaina came over and placed her hand on Lilah's shoulder. "I'll sit with her until you come over. Take your time."

"Thank you, Elaina," Zoe said.

Elaina nodded before wrapping an arm around Lilah's shoulders and leading her out of the room.

"We should get going, too," India said.

She and Travis sat opposite Byron. They stood and Byron got up carefully. Zoe's hands clenched into fists as she watched his stiff movements. He hugged his sister and then his friend. She didn't miss the grimace on his face when Travis patted his back.

"Holla at me tomorrow," Travis said. "Drinks on me."

"I've got a campaign event tomorrow," Byron said.

Grant quickly rose from the leather chair. He slashed a

hand through the air. "You can skip one damn event because of a car accident. I'll tell Roy to wait."

"No," Byron said in a hard voice. "I'll talk to Roy. You've done enough."

Grant's eyes narrowed but he didn't argue. He held a hand out to Patricia. She stood and took Grant's. Grant nodded stiffly. "Suit yourself."

Patricia moved toward Byron and placed a hand on his cheek. He jerked his head back and stepped out of her grasp. "Good night, Patricia."

She placed her hand on her chest. "Stay here tonight. Please."

Some of the stiffness left Byron's shoulders. "I'll think about it."

The family filed out of the room. Travis closed the door behind him as they left. She and Byron stared at each other for several long seconds. She was supposed to be angry with him. She was supposed to be telling him he couldn't use her and Lilah for political favor. That he couldn't say things about wanting to be with her and make things work if he was going to go behind her back and release photos of a day she'd thought was private and between them.

But when he shifted his shoulders as if to relieve tension and winced, none of the anger from earlier found a foothold. She was across the room and examining his face just as closely as she'd examined Lilah's.

"Are you okay?"

He gave her a half smile. "Stiff, but I'll be fine."

She placed her hands on his cheeks then ran them down over his shoulders. There were cuts in the shirt she knew should have been crisp and white. Now it was torn, dirty and spotted with blood.

"Lilah said you saved her life," Zoe said in a tight voice.

"I just got them out of the car. That's all."

"You went in a ditch?"

"It was a little more than that. We almost went into a creek. That's why I got them out so quickly." He took a shaky breath. "If the car had gone under water…"

She wrapped her arms tightly around his neck. "It didn't. We aren't going to talk about that."

Byron eased down on the couch with her still in his arms. "I'm fine. Seriously."

Zoe eased back to examine him again. "Did you go to the hospital?"

He nodded. "An ambulance came, but by then I'd gotten Lilah and Wesley out of the car. There are no broken bones, just a cut on her forehead."

Zoe placed a hand on her chest and let out a relieved sigh. "And you?"

"I didn't get checked out. Before you fuss, I'm going to the doctor tomorrow."

"So, no campaign visit. You'll take the day off and get some rest." She pointed at him.

He didn't argue with her the way he had with his dad. Instead, he took her hand in his and pressed her palm to his chest. "I promise. I'll get some rest. I just didn't want to give my dad the satisfaction of telling me what to do."

"Do you have any idea who could have hit you?"

Byron's entire body stiffened. "I don't. Wesley said a black SUV came out of nowhere. They t-boned us and knocked us off the road toward the creek. After we went over, they drove off."

A terrible thought sent icicles through her veins. "Was it on purpose?"

His jaw hardened. "I don't know."

She trembled but didn't want to think about that. "I've got to check on Lilah and make sure she's okay. Promise me you'll stay at the estate tonight."

"I should get home—"

Her fingers curled against his chest. "Promise me. Once Lilah is asleep, I want to see you again."

Byron nodded. "I promise."

WHEN ZOE WAS sure Lilah was asleep, she left their room to find Byron. Lilah had insisted on coming back to the main house after taking a shower and changing clothes. They'd sat in the upstairs family room talking about anything but the accident until Lilah finally fell asleep leaning against Byron's side. She'd woken up and complained when Zoe told her to go to bed, so Zoe pretended to be going to bed, too.

It wasn't often Lilah showed the tendency to want to have her mom by her side or needed her close in order to go to sleep. The fact that it took a damn car accident to get her daughter to feel this way made Zoe want to take Lilah's bow and play target practice with whomever hit their car. Seeing Lilah so scared not only angered Zoe, but it also scared her. There was too much happening, and it was all happening too close together to be a coincidence. She'd avoided trying to be overly paranoid, but she couldn't shake the feeling these incidents weren't just accidents.

Byron was still in the sitting room. He was alone and had stretched his legs out on the coffee table in front of the leather sofa. His head rested against the back of the couch and he breathed deeply. His eyes were closed. Zoe settled down next to him and rested her head on his shoulder.

He turned his head so his cheek pressed against the top of hers. "I wondered if you were coming back." His voice was a low rumble.

She slid an arm around his midsection and relished the feel of him next to her. "Maybe I should have stayed in the room. You're almost asleep."

He shook his head then wrapped an arm around her shoulder. "I wanted to wait up on you. I needed to talk to you."

"About the accident?" Had he come to the same conclusion she had?

"About the pictures. I didn't tell Roy to release them. That was my dad."

A knot in Zoe's chest loosened. She'd been willing to let the conversation about the pictures slide for the day. With everything going on that was the last thing she wanted to dive into. She was glad he understood she would be upset.

"Why did he do it?"

"For the typical reasons. To make me look good in the public eye."

"Did it work?"

"It did, but I wouldn't have let them be released without talking to you first. I didn't even know they'd been taken." He shifted and Zoe met his gaze. "One of my staffers saw us out and thought it would make a good visual."

Apparently, the staffer was right. Elaina was right. The Robidoux men would do whatever they needed to pursue their own goals. "Have you said anything to you dad?"

"My plan was to talk to him today but…"

He'd gotten knocked off the road into a ditch. "Yeah… I get it."

"I did talk to Roy. If he does something like that again

without talking to me first he's going to be looking for another candidate to support."

She didn't want to see Roy fired, but she understood Byron's decision. He trusted Roy with his career. He'd have to trust Roy wouldn't listen to other people instead of Byron.

"I'm surprised your dad didn't talk to you first."

"We haven't been seeing eye to eye lately," he said blithely.

"I noticed. It's because of me, isn't it?" Byron had always idolized his dad, but ever since she'd been here, they'd been at odds. Starting with the argument they'd had the first day she'd come to the estate.

"Actually…it's because of Patricia."

Zoe sat up and tilted her head to the side. "Patricia?"

Byron sighed and sat up. "Yep."

"Why? I thought she got along with the family." Zoe hadn't had much interaction with Patricia. Grant's fiancée was pleasant, but it was obvious her focus and loyalty were for Grant.

"We get along with Patricia because Dad wants us to get along with her. It wasn't easy when he started seeing her before Mom died. But when he kept seeing her and gradually made her a part of his daily life, it was either learn to accept her or constantly fight with him about her."

"What's changed?"

"After you came back, Patricia tried to warn me to be careful. She said she knew what my mom wanted and why she didn't want me to claim Lilah as my child. She pretended as if she was my mom's friend."

"Was she?" Zoe couldn't imagine it, but stranger things had happened in this family.

"Of course not. My mom tolerated Patricia because she

was sick and couldn't be there for my dad, but they weren't friends."

"Did your dad agree with her?"

"I haven't brought it up. Our unspoken rule in this family is not to question Dad on anything. He makes the plans and we go along with it. I can't live like that anymore. Especially not if he's going to expect us to sit back and take the same treatment from Patricia."

"Sounds like you're really mad at your dad for butting in, but instead it's easier to pick a fight about Patricia."

Byron's brows drew together. He sat up quickly. Zoe moved back.

"That's ridiculous. I'm mad she's acting like my mom."

"No, Byron, you're mad your dad told your employee what to do without consulting you. I know you look up to him. I know he's the person you've tried to emulate. He loves you, but you have to set the boundaries."

"But—"

"No buts. You're running for Senate. How are you supposed to handle major political and policy decisions if you can't even tell your dad to butt out? You've got to be the grown-up in this."

Byron's mouth snapped shut. He stared at her for several seconds before shaking his head and chuckling. "You see, that's why I love you. You always tell me like it is."

Zoe was struck speechless. He loved her? Nah, couldn't be like *love* love. He had to mean like friendship love.

She waved off his words. "That's what friends are for."

Byron took her wrist in his fingers and brought her hand to his chest. "You're not just a friend, and I'm not joking around."

"We just started sleeping together." Sex was the only

reason a guy thought he was in love so soon. It had to be. She thought back to her conversation with Ashiya and the pressure she'd felt of living up to the version of herself Byron saw.

Byron shook his head. "Us sleeping together has nothing to do with how I feel. We weren't sleeping together back in college and I felt similar."

She frowned. "Now is different?"

"Yes. You were amazing back then, but you're incredible now. If anything, I love you more."

Zoe pulled away from him. "Love isn't enough," she blurted out. "Love feels good, but it makes you do dumb things. It makes you put up with dumb things. I don't want to be in love."

Byron let her go. "Do you really believe that?"

The incredulous look in his eye, as if she were an oddity he couldn't figure out, made her cheeks burn. How could she explain this to him without hurting him again? How could she explain that love made her heart race for all the wrong reasons? Right now, in this moment, she believed in what she had with Byron. It was the future that frightened her. Falling in love meant not wanting to disappoint the other person, and eventually she would disappoint him. She supported him becoming a senator, but she didn't want to be a senator's wife. She was excited about starting her own business. She was still looking for a place to live. She didn't want her daughter to get completely sucked into the Robidoux's world. Love would make her lose focus, or worse, lose herself in an effort to fit the mold of perfect political partner.

She looked into his eyes. He looked at her as if she were

the key to his happiness. She didn't deserve that, but she was selfish enough to want it.

"I believe we've both had a long day and our emotions are high," she said.

"I'm serious—"

Zoe slid across his lap and straddled his waist. "Shh. I know you are." She kissed him softly. "Let's focus on today. You're alive. Lilah is okay. We get another day together. Please."

He met her eyes and she saw the argument churning in his gaze. "Zoe—"

She kissed him again before he could utter another word. "You're alive," she breathed against his lips. Her next kiss was longer, deeper and filled with all the joy of knowing he was okay after the accident. His body relaxed. His arms wrapped around her and pulled her close.

He could have been gone. He and Lilah could have both been gone. While she'd been stuck in traffic. Tears pricked her eyes. She kissed him harder. The fear, frustration and relief from the day made her movements urgent. She jerked on the edges of his T-shirt until he lifted his hands and she tossed it aside. She kissed each scratch and bruise on his chest and shoulders.

His kisses and touches became just as urgent as hers. His breathing ragged as his body trembled. She reached for the waistband of his pants. Byron lifted his hips and pushed them down. Zoe snatched up the edges of her nightgown. His fingers shoved aside the edges of her damp panties. Then they slid through the wetness pooling there. A low groan rumbled in his chest.

He raised her hips until the tip of his erection rubbed across her opening. She slid down on him hard. For several long seconds they clung to each other. Zoe squeezed around him, pulling him deeper. Byron's fingers dug into her hips. He lifted her slowly then lowered her quickly. Then repeated the movement faster this time. Until they were making love hard and fast on the couch. The fear and exultation of making it through another day fueled the fire between them.

She couldn't say the words he wanted her to say. Love had only led her down the wrong paths before. Loving Byron might make her ignore the way he deferred to his father, put up with the demands of his family, try to become the impeccable partner he'd originally had in Yolanda. She didn't want to love him, but she could show him she cared in other ways. When his body tensed, and he clutched her tighter as he climaxed, she kissed him deeper. He could have her friendship, her respect, her desire, but she wasn't sure she could give him her heart.

CHAPTER TWENTY-FIVE

BYRON SOUGHT OUT his dad the next morning. He found Grant in the kitchen, laughing and teasing the family's chef, Jules.

"Okay, now, you promised me bacon on Friday," Grant was saying with a grin.

Jules rolled her eyes then pointed a finger at Grant. "You know good and well I said if you ate all the meals I prepared this week you'd get bacon. How are you planning to stay healthy if you don't eat properly?"

Grant pounded his chest. "My heart is as strong as it was twenty years ago."

"Mmm hmm, I bet." Jules put several slices of bacon on the plate Grant held out.

Byron cleared his throat to get their attention. "Dad, can I talk to you for a few minutes?"

Grant turned away from Jules and eyed Byron with cool detachment. A look he'd seen Grant give to Elaina hundreds of times, even India on a few occasions, but rarely had he gotten the look. He'd never crossed his dad. This was the first time Byron could remember ever being on the outs with him.

"So you did stay the night," Grant said.

"I was tired, and it was a long day," Byron replied. He walked over to the counter with the coffeemaker. "Good morning, Jules."

"Good morning, Mr. Byron," she said. The teasing tone she'd had with his dad was replaced with the professional voice she used for the rest of the family.

"Regardless of the reason, I'm glad you stayed."

Byron poured himself a cup of coffee. When he faced his dad again Grant watched him as if he was unsure of what to expect. His face may be indifferent, but Byron heard the concern in his dad's voice. He'd been worried about him.

"Upstairs or down?" Byron asked.

"Let's go in the dining room," Grant said. He opened the pastry dish and pulled out a doughnut.

Jules tisked and shook her head. "I'm making you an egg white omelet."

"Give that tasteless mess to Patricia when she comes down. I'm eating this doughnut and I don't want to hear a word about it."

Unfazed, Jules picked and apple from the fruit bowl and placed it next to the doughnut and bacon. "Eat it."

Grant grinned and winked before going into the dining room. Byron followed. He glanced over his shoulder at Jules, who smiled as she made the omelet. Byron shook his head.

"Isn't that what got you in trouble one time?" Byron said as he and Grant settled at one end of the dining room table.

"What?" Grant picked up a slice of bacon and bit it in half.

"Flirting with the family chef. You keep it up and Patricia will wonder if she might lose you the same way Mom did."

Grant froze, his eyes narrowed and his chest puffed out. Byron only slightly regretted the words. Years of not pushing back against his father fought with the words he'd held inside himself for over a decade. He considered apologizing, then remembered Grant ordered Roy around without a consideration to Byron's wishes.

"Patricia has nothing to worry about," Grant said confidently.

"Did you say the same thing about Mom?" Byron countered.

Grant dropped the bacon and pointed at Byron. "Now, you listen here—"

"No, Dad, you listen. I'm not saying this to be disrespectful or out of spite. I'm saying it because I'm being honest. Patricia claimed she was Mom's friend. If she was and you slept with her then how am I supposed to know you won't sleep with Jules?"

Grant threw up a hand. "What the hell brought this on? This doesn't really have anything to do with me and Patricia."

"What, you're having a hard time believing I'd question you after I've gone along with everything you expect of me? You wanted me to go to the University of North Carolina, I did. You wanted me to become a lawyer and work for the company. I did. When you said I could do more if I got into national politics, I jumped into one of the biggest races I could. I've accepted so much of what you say and expect of me that even my own campaign manager thinks it's okay to take orders from you instead of me."

Understanding flashed in his father's eyes. He relaxed and resumed eating bacon. "Is this about the pictures?"

The way Grant sounded unfazed made Byron want to snatch the bacon out of his hand and toss it across the room. His dad really didn't care if Byron was upset, because Byron had never fought back on anything. He was tired of just going along with what his dad thought and believed. Holding back for years was the reason Grant believed he could go to Roy and override Byron's orders.

Byron pressed a finger on the table. "It's about more than the pictures. It's about how you really do think we're supposed to be okay with everything you say and do for us. No pushback. No questions. When I have to threaten to fire my employee because he listened to you instead of me, and when I see you flirting with our new chef right after you told us to accept your proposal to our previous cook, I think I have a right to ask some damn questions."

By the time he was finished his breathing was fast. His heart pumped wildly. His voice hadn't risen, but years of frustration and untapped anger clipped the edges of his words.

Grant meticulously dusted his hands off by wiping them together. Once done with that, he took a long breath and leaned back in his chair. "You don't have to worry about Jules being an upgrade, because I happen to love Patricia."

"Does that mean you didn't love Mom?" Piercing pain punctured Byron's chest. He scanned his memories of his parents together and couldn't come up with anything to suggest they weren't happy. They'd been loving, affectionate and damn formidable when it came to the Robidoux legacy.

"I did love her," Grant said, sounding sad. "But…"

"But what? When she got sick you couldn't deal?"

Grant's back straightened. "I stayed by her side through the entire ordeal. I made sure she had everything she needed." Grant said the words as if that absolved him of all wrongdoing.

"What if what she needed was a faithful husband?"

"Well, then she wouldn't have told me to seek comfort in Patricia's arms."

Byron drew in a sharp breath. "That doesn't make it right."

"I'm not saying that it does. Right or wrong, that's how it started. Once it started, well, it kept going. The day of your mom's funeral I knew she was the only person who would understand my grief."

Byron shook his head. "No, she wasn't. You lost a wife, but we lost a mother. We needed you here."

Grant's face tightened. "I gave you kids everything I could. I'm not good at the nurturing and the emotional stuff. That's what your mom was for. I'm here to make sure you reach your potential. To give you everything you need to have more than me. You want to get mad about Patricia now, or say I pushed you to do things you didn't want to do, fine. But look where my pushing got you. You're this close to winning this election." He held his thumb and forefinger a few centimeters apart. "This damn close. You know why? Because I released those pictures of you and Zoe. You're a fool in love with that woman and the public needed to see it. You went up in the polls. After word gets out about you pulling your kid and driver from the wreckage, you'll get another jump."

Byron hit the table with the side of his fist. "That's not how I want to win."

"How you win doesn't matter as long as you get what you want," Grant said easily.

"I don't know if I want this." The words burst out of Byron. A truth that shook him like an unexpected hit to the solar plexus. He wasn't sure if he wanted this life. The constant scrutiny. The questioning of his lifestyle and that of his family. The expectation to be a perfect role model, citizen and man.

"If you don't want this, quit."

Byron's head jerked back. "What?"

"You think I'm pushing you to run for Senate and you don't want to. Fine. Quit," Grant said with a wave of his hand. He leaned forward and lowered his voice. "But ask yourself if you're giving it up because you're really tired of me pushing you to be great, or if you're doing it because you think it'll make being with Zoe easier."

"She's got nothing to do with this."

Grant scoffed. "Son, if you really believe that then you don't deserve to win." Grant stood, grabbed the pieces of bacon off his plate and shook his head. "I'm going upstairs to my fiancée. You stay down here in your feelings and figure out what's really going on in your fool head."

Byron didn't look at Grant as he left. What had he wanted to get out of this conversation? Had he thought he'd get an apology from his dad for going behind his back and a promise to never butt into his life again? Now all he had was a stomach full of frustration, and no push in the right direction.

If he quit, what would he do? Be with Zoe and live happily ever after? He'd seen the panic in her face when he'd said he loved her. She hadn't said it back. He'd let down the people who'd supported him and worked for him on the hopes of Zoe loving him.

Byron clenched his hand around the coffee mug and took a long sip of the liquid. The heat of the coffee burned away any remaining softness. His dad was a cynical man but look where not being ruled by emotions had gotten him. Byron had been too accommodating, too eager to please, and look what he'd gotten? If he was going to win, now was the time to ignore his heart and make logical, not emotional, decisions.

CHAPTER TWENTY-SIX

BYRON RECEIVED DOMINIC'S report on the fire investigation two days later. The official investigation said it was an electrical fire. Something he hadn't believed considering Zoe's home was less than ten years old and had no prior electrical issues. After Zoe mentioned her neighbor's claim to have seen someone around the house, he'd been anxious to find out what was on her security cameras. Initially, the cameras hadn't caught any unusual activity, but after Dominic had the file reviewed, they discovered the file had been hacked and tampered with. If there had been someone in Zoe's home before, the proof had been erased.

He had to tell her. He'd spoken to Wesley after the accident. The car that hit them had done so deliberately. He hadn't wanted to tell Zoe it wasn't a random hit and run so he wouldn't scare her. He wasn't sure if the intent was to hurt him or to hurt Lilah. Things were heating up and whomever was behind this was increasing the intensity of their attacks. He couldn't leave Zoe in the dark.

He left the campaign office and went to the estate. He'd texted Zoe earlier and asked if she wanted to go to lunch, but she'd had lunch with Elaina. Now she'd be at home waiting on Lilah to get there.

He went straight to the pool house and knocked on the door. Byron glanced around at the bay windows and the door. It was time for her to move into the main house. The pool house was secure and protected on the grounds, but she and Lilah would be safer if they were closer to the family. Zoe liked her independence and the privacy of the pool house, but her safety was more important than privacy.

Zoe opened the door and blinked against the bright sunlight. Her hair was parted asymmetrical down the middle with two large flat twists that connected to a curly ponytail at the back. Her short-sleeved red button-up blouse opened just above her cleavage and dark patterned pants hugged her hips. After she'd blinked a few times and her eyes adjusted to the light, she grinned. Byron almost forgot what he was about to say, the brightness of her smile stunning him.

He wished he could tamper back his response. He'd said he loved her. She hadn't said the same. He hadn't said it again. Just because she looked at him with affection in her eyes didn't mean he could make assumptions about how she felt. He'd done that before, but damn if her smile didn't make him want to forget the past and just go with the emotions swirling through him.

"I didn't expect you until later tonight," she said, stepping back. "Come in."

Byron entered and pushed the door closed behind him. She immediately came into his arms. His mouth covered hers and he breathed her in. This was easy between them. He liked the way her curves cradled him, the sweet taste of her lips and the way her fingers curled around the lapel of his suit and pulled him closer as if she needed him just as much as he needed her.

"How is your shoulder?" she asked after pulling back.

He rolled his shoulder, which was still stiff and sore after the accident. "It's better."

Her brows drew together. "You frowned when you said that. It's still bothering you, isn't it?"

"Nothing I can't handle." He wrapped his arms around her waist and pulled her closer. "I'm not here to talk about my shoulder."

She grinned and kissed him again. "Then what are you here for?" Her hips shifted forward. "Lilah won't be here for another hour."

His dick stiffened. He wasn't there for that, either. Yet, his body didn't want to focus on the bad news he'd come with. His body said lift her up, take her to the bedroom and make damn good use of one of the rare moments they had alone together.

Zoe grinned against his mouth. Her hand lowered to cup the growing hardness between them. "Never mind. I think I figured it out."

Byron groaned and gently pulled her hand way. His body screamed for more attention. His head tried very hard to silence the scream. "Not that, either. I need to talk to you."

Zoe pulled back and met his eyes. Slowly, the sexy smile on her face faded away. She took a step back and frowned. "What's wrong?"

"Let's sit down."

"That bad, huh?" She shook her head and went to the couch. "Let me guess. Your dad found out Elaina is trying to purchase his company and now he hates me?"

Byron blinked and tried to process what she said. "Wait…she's going through with it?" After Zoe's inspection neither of them had mentioned the purchase again. He'd assumed the plan was off the table.

Zoe's eyes widened. "Oh, crap! That's not it?"

Byron pinched the bridge of his nose and settled next to her on the couch. "I actually hoped she'd change her mind."

"No, she can really turn things around if she does everything she says she will. I'm sorry. Now that she's getting closer to making the deal, I'm worried Grant's going to find out and kick me out. Plus, earlier today she was upset. I thought maybe she'd told your dad."

Byron ran a hand over his chin. "No." He sighed. Could nothing be easy with his damn family? He couldn't deal with that right now. "You know what? That's their fight. We've got bigger things to worry about than my dad and Elaina."

"Are you sure? Once the word gets out don't you think it'll look bad on your campaign?"

Just the idea of another media scandal he'd have to navigate made his right eye twitch. The only good thing is they could easily handle Elaina buying their dad's company as a planned transfer. Elaina's latest whim was nothing compared to having to face the person who'd doctored the security video at Zoe's home, and possibly rammed head-on into his car.

"My campaign is about to take a backseat to another problem," Byron said.

"What could possibly happen now?"

Byron met her eyes. "I don't think your house fire was an accident."

Zoe stared at him for several long seconds before her eyes narrowed. "What are you talking about? We got the fire investigation. It was bad wiring."

"I wanted to be sure, so I asked Dominic and Jeanette to do a separate investigation. Dominic had the surveillance video around your home checked. It looks like someone tampered with the video. He wasn't sure why someone would delete the footage of that day and replace it with old footage. Unless…"

"Are you saying someone set my house on fire?" Zoe stood up and paced back and forth.

"I can't say for sure."

Zoe glanced around the pool house. Her gaze guarded and suspicious. "And you didn't think to tell me? Byron, why would you keep this a secret?"

"I wanted to be sure." Faced with the hurt on her face he wished he would have said something sooner.

"Even if you wanted to be sure you should have told me you were suspicious. I thought Lilah and I were safe."

"You are. I'm keeping you safe."

She slashed a hand through the air. "No, you're keeping me in the dark."

Byron stood and placed his hands on her arms. She stiffened and his stomach twisted. She hadn't reacted negatively to his touch in weeks. "I didn't want to worry you. I just found out today and that's why I'm here telling you."

She crossed her arms over her chest. "Is there anything else I need to know?"

Byron sighed. "The emails…they haven't stopped."

Zoe stretched her arms until his hands fell away. She took three deep breaths and turned away. When she faced him she opened her mouth a few times as if trying to find the right words. "What do you mean? You said they weren't linked to anything? I haven't gotten any more."

Byron ran his hands over his pants and braced himself for her reaction. "That's because Dominic set it up so any emails from that address would go to another account."

"Are you kidding me?" Zoe exclaimed. "You broke into my email?"

"We redirected them." She turned away and pressed a hand to her forehead. Byron kept talking. Hoping she'd understand. "Dominic needed more time to try and track down where they were coming from."

She spun and pointed an accusing finger. "You told me they were coming from some spammer farm location."

"I didn't want you to be afraid."

She stepped forward. "I've been afraid my entire life. I've always lived in fear." Her voice shook. "I was afraid my dad would come home and fight my mom. I was afraid Kendell would slap me because I spent too long at a volunteer event with you. I was afraid he'd find out about Lilah and come back. My life is fear."

He placed his hands on her shoulders. "Which is why I wanted you to feel safe."

Zoe jerked out of his touch. "No, you wanted to leave me unprotected. You created a false sense of security, so I'd go along with things and be your perfect political partner."

Byron staggered back. Her words as much of a shock as a slap to the face. "That's not true. All I care about is your and Lilah's safety."

"No, you don't. Lilah and I were safe before. I handled things."

"Your house was set on fire. What if the two of you were in there? I have the resources to track down the threat."

She crossed her arms. "Have you?" Her voice was an accusation.

"Not yet, but we're close."

She scoffed and rolled her eyes. "What did I say. We're unprotected. I let my guard down because I thought I could trust you. I believed you would keep us safe, but you haven't done that."

He'd done everything in his power to try and protect her. How could she not understand that? "I'm telling you now so we can figure out what to do. First, you need to move into the main house."

"I'm not moving into the house. We're leaving." Zoe walked past him to the bedroom.

"Have you lost your mind? You can't leave."

She whirled on him. "Yes, we can and we are. I'll go someplace new. We'll start over. We did it once, we can do it again."

"Your face and Lilah's face are all over the news. You can't hide anymore. People will know you. You have to stay here. You have to rely on me." As soon as the words left his mouth he knew they were the absolute wrong thing to say. She didn't want to rely on him or anyone else.

Her eyes widened. Zoe shook her head. She backed up several paces. "No."

Byron wanted to rush to her and pull her into his arms. Instead, he held up his hands. He tried to keep his voice calm. "Zoe, I didn't mean it that way. It's going to be okay. I know this is a lot, but we can get through this. I can help you."

Her gaze focused on him. "Oh, my God," she said as if coming to a realization. She let out a shaky laugh. "I can't believe it. I tried so hard to stand on my own, but I'm right back in the same situation. I trusted you, and instead you kept me in the dark and controlled things so I'd have to rely on you. We can't hide. Everyone knows Lilah as yours. If I run, you'd send Dominic to find me. I'm trapped."

Byron watched the trust she'd had in him seep out of

her eyes. He felt like he was falling into a hole. One he'd dug and couldn't escape from. "You're not trapped. We'll figure this out together."

She shook her head. Tears filled her eyes. "I said I wouldn't be here again, but I walked right into this. I'm so stupid." Her hands clenched into fists.

"You're not stupid." He couldn't help it. He went to her and placed his hands on her forearms. Her flinch broke his heart. "Zoe, I love you. I only wanted to help."

Tears spilled down her cheeks. She pulled away and wrapped her arms around her chest. "I've heard that before. I'd say you don't love me, but isn't this what love is? Control. You have all the control over my life, my daughter, and if I try to escape, you'll just pull me back."

Escape? The word tore into his heart. No, this wasn't how things were to go. He wasn't trying to control her. He wasn't trying to force her into anything. He'd thought he was making things better. He'd thought he was protecting her.

"Zoe, I was only trying to protect you."

"I never wanted protection. I only wanted a partner." Her sharp words were like a razorblade across his heart.

"Zoe." He reached for her.

She jerked back and hastily wiped the tears from her face. Her eyes were cold as they met his. "Promise me you'll make sure Lilah gets extra protection."

"Of course, but Zoe let's talk some more. I need you to understand."

"No more talking. Right now the important thing is making sure Lilah stays safe. We'll move into the main house today. Will you please include me in any updates on the investigation?" Her voice was weak, defeated.

"Absolutely, we'll work together."

She shook her head. "No, we won't. You'll find out what's happening, come up with a plan and tell me what to do. You always wanted to be like your father. Apparently, you're just like him." With that she turned, went into the bedroom and slammed the door.

CHAPTER TWENTY-SEVEN

ZOE NEEDED A PLAN.

She stood with the rest of Byron's family in the background as he made another campaign speech. She smiled and nodded at the appropriate times. She clapped and cheered with the crowd. Not once did she let any of the anxiety inside her reflect on the outside. Years of practice hiding anxiety worked out like that.

Ever since Byron admitted he'd hidden the emails from her in the "name of love" she'd been anxious. The extra security around the estate, for her, and Lilah, no longer felt like protection. It felt like barriers. A part of her brain acknowledged Byron wasn't like Kendell. Byron would never hit her, nor would he fight with her and call her stupid the way her dad had done with her mom, but he still had control over her. She hadn't realized how much control until he admitted how much information he kept from her. Information she needed to know.

His people monitored her emails. He got reports on her movements. They watched her phone calls and reviewed her schedule. While he never once told her she couldn't do something or tried to change her plans, if he said something had to change his people would do so without a second thought to her. She'd handed over so much control of her life because she thought they were a team. She'd believed he'd seen the stronger person she'd grown into. Instead, he still saw the damsel Elaina had first called her. Someone who couldn't take care of herself without him. Someone weak and stupid. The same way Kendell had seen her.

She needed a plan. She needed to figure out how to get away and start over.

First, she'd continue to work with Elaina. She needed money. Lots of money. Byron had her too entrenched in his life for her to just up and leave as she'd done with Kendell. If she worked for Elaina, started her own business and was successful, she'd make enough to set up her own home. She'd play the part of accommodating baby mother to Byron during the campaign while building her own nest egg until she had enough to move away.

The speeches ended. The family clapped and joined Byron at the front of the stage. She shifted so Byron's immediate family surrounded him. She belonged on the periphery. She wasn't a part of their inner circle, and she never would be.

She left the stage quickly after the photos were taken of them and went to Dominic hovering at the edge of the room.

"I'd like to go home," she said.

Dominic frowned. "Byron said the family would be staying after the speech to do more talking."

Zoe clenched her teeth. She couldn't even make the decision to leave. "Did he tell you I had to stay, or can I leave?"

Dominic frowned, but he shook his head. "He didn't."

"Do you have to get permission for me to go home?"

He blinked as if that was ridiculous. "No."

That only eased the ache in her chest a little. "Then, let's go." She walked around him and out the door. Not giving him the chance to change his mind.

"Are you feeling okay?" Dominic asked as he followed her out. Once outside, they were immediately met by a dark-clad figure who was part of the security detail.

"I feel fine. I just don't want to be here," she said.

Dominic shifted from one foot to the other. "He loves you, you know. That's why he had me investigate."

Zoe glanced from Dominic to the bodyguard opening the door of the car that slid up to the curb. Another guard stood at the door they'd come out of and spoke into his earpiece. No doubt telling Byron right now where she was and where she was going.

"I know. I've been loved like this before." She got into the car.

Thankfully, the driver didn't talk to her on the ride back to the estate. It was a local campaign dinner. The election was ten weeks away. Their schedules were getting tighter. After Byron finally told her everything there was to know he'd forwarded her the latest emails. They were coming to her weekly now. Saying she was getting exactly what she deserved.

When she got home, she was heading upstairs when Lilah bounced out of the kitchen smiling with a handful of cookies in her hand. She saw Zoe and hurried over.

"You're back already? I expected you to be later," Lilah said. She handed a cookie to Zoe.

Zoe took it and wrapped an arm around Lilah's shoulders. "I thought you'd be upstairs in bed by now."

"I was upstairs reading and video chatting with T.J."

Zoe stopped before they went up the stairs and faced her. "Video chatting? You're still talking to him?"

Lilah lifted a shoulder. "Well, yeah."

"Why?"

"Because he's still my friend," she said as if Zoe was stupid. "And he says he still likes me." Lilah's eyes lit up. "I didn't think he would after I moved away and told him we should just be friends."

Lilah started up the stairs. Zoe stared, dumfounded. "You shouldn't be video chatting with him."

"Why not? I still video chat with Julie." Lilah took a bite of her cookie.

Zoe hurried up the stairs to catch up with Lilah. "That's different."

"How? I'm making friends up here, but all my real friends are back home. He's one of them. I can talk to them still."

"He may get the wrong idea. Or think you're still holding a torch for him. It's better to cut things off now."

Lilah stopped at the top of the stairs and gave Zoe and incredulous look. "Mom, are you serious right now? I thought you'd be okay."

"Why?" What about Zoe made Lilah think she'd be okay knowing her daughter was still chasing after some boy back home?

"Because you're finally happy."

"I've always been happy," Zoe argued.

Lilah shook her head. "No, you haven't. You've always been warning me about how terrible men are, and that I shouldn't get attached to anyone. But now you've seen that's not the case. Byron is great and you're happy with him. I thought I'd give T.J. the benefit of the doubt."

Zoe took Lilah's arm in her hand. "Don't give him the benefit of the doubt. Never let your guard down and don't give false hope where there shouldn't be any. You're too young to be thinking about a boy anyway. You should be focusing on making new friends and meeting new people up here. Not trying to hold on to some guy from your past. I thought I taught you better than that."

Lilah pulled away from Zoe and frowned. "You taught me to be smart. I'm not being dumb, Mom. He really is an okay guy. He's not going to hurt me."

"You think that now, but they always end up hurting you. Cut him loose now."

Zoe turned and stalked to her door. Lilah's footsteps followed. "How can you say that? Byron is perfect."

Zoe spun around and pointed. "No one is perfect. Especially not Byron."

"But he wants to take care of us."

Exactly why she never should have agreed to this plan. All the work she'd done to teach Lilah to stand on her own was washed away by Byron's Prince Charming persona. "I don't need anyone to take care of me and neither do you. We can take care of ourselves."

"I know that."

"Then quit thinking Byron is some knight in shining armor sent to rescue us. We're still in this on our own. Just you and me. Don't get swept up in this fairy tale and think it'll last. It won't."

"God, Mom, you're always like this!" Lilah yelled. "You always want things to be terrible when they aren't."

"I'm realistic."

"No, you're scared and you're angry and you think every guy is like my dad. Well, they aren't. There are some decent guys out there. You're going to ruin everything."

"I'm going to make sure we're independent and able to

take care of ourselves. You'll understand where I'm coming from one day."

Tears filled Lilah's eyes. "You won't be happy until I end up like you. Afraid and alone with no real friends. That's what you want. I can't wait until I grow up and move out."

"Well, you've got a couple of more years for that, so until then, deal with it," Zoe snapped back.

Lilah's eyes glistened before she turned and ran into her room. Zoe closed her eyes and took a deep breath. She tamped down the guilt expanding inside her. Pressed it down until it was just a tight knot in her chest. One day Lilah would understand. She was only trying to protect her. Words like *love* and *trust* were traps. She was better off alone. Lilah would be better off learning that from the start. Zoe didn't need protection or love. She could do both for herself.

What had her belief in a second chance with Byron gotten her anyway? A guarded escort home and her house burned down. She sucked in a breath and went into her room. To hell with love.

CHAPTER TWENTY-EIGHT

THE NEXT MORNING Zoe went downstairs for breakfast and was surprised to find Byron, Rob, Grant and Travis already occupying the dining room table. She stopped short at the door. Four sets of eyes landed on her, but only one made her breath catch.

Byron immediately stood. His mouth opening to speak. Zoe didn't want to hear anything he had to say.

"I'll eat in the kitchen," she said and turned to leave.

"Zoe, wait, you need to hear this, too." Byron's voice stopped her.

Byron looked too good for it to be so early after a long night at a campaign event. He was dressed casually in a lavender polo shirt and khaki-colored shorts. The soft material of the shirt clung to his shoulders and chest.

She shouldn't be noticing the way he looked in a shirt. Damn sure shouldn't be distracted by how good he looked. Except last night she'd dreamed about that last kiss they'd had before he'd told her of the secrets he'd kept from her.

"What is it?" As much as she wanted to walk out and not look back, she wasn't going to refuse any information he was willing to give. Even if he was only humoring her at the moment. It was only a matter of time before he'd go back to withholding information.

"My poll numbers are up," he said.

"Up is an understatement," Roy said excitedly. "His

numbers have skyrocketed. Ever since the video of Byron pulling Lilah and Wesley from the car went viral, people love him. He's even getting attention outside the state."

The urge to throw the plate of bacon and eggs she held along with her cup of coffee at Roy made her fingers grip the plate. "Good for you. Now everyone thinks you're a hero."

"I never asked to be a hero," Byron replied.

"It doesn't matter," Grant cut in. "What matters is what people think. Right now Byron is a hero who saves children and his employees from burning vehicles."

Byron scowled. "The car wasn't burning. We aren't exaggerating this story."

"What does this have to do with me?" Zoe asked before Byron and his dad could start debating.

"We want to have a campaign rally at the local high school," Roy explained.

Zoe lifted a shoulder and took a fortifying sip of her coffee. "Okay, I still don't get it. You plan rallies all the time."

"They want Lilah to attend," Byron answered.

Zoe shook her head and took a step into the dining room. "No. The agreement was Lilah wouldn't do campaign appearances after the first press conference."

Byron opened his mouth to respond but Grant spoke up first. "That was back when we didn't think her appearing would make a difference. This will make a difference."

Roy nodded. "He's right. If we put Lilah and Wesley on that stage with Byron, the public and the press will eat it up. It's just like when the pictures of the three of you surfaced a few weeks ago—"

"When you intentionally released pictures of me and my daughter," Zoe shot back.

"Semantics," Roy continued. "You can't deny the pictures had the desired effect. Doing this will get us major points going up to the election. We're running out of time."

Zoe glared at Byron. Hurt even more than she'd been before. "I can't believe you'd add this on top of everything."

She turned and stalked out of the room. Her eyes burned with tears she didn't want to shed. As angry as she was about him keeping the information about her house and the emails a secret, a small part of her understood where he was coming from. Byron had always had that misguided hero complex. Trying to do right for other people, but often in the wrong way.

Footsteps chased her. Her heart jumped into her throat. She knew it was Byron before he hurried past her and blocked her retreat into the kitchen.

"What?" she snapped. She avoided eye contact and blinked rapidly to hide the tears.

"I said no," Byron said. "Lilah isn't coming to the press conference."

"I guess you want a prize?" She didn't care if it took seeing her upset for him to say no. He should have realized Lilah was off-limits still.

"No, I don't want a prize. What I do want is for you to understand that I told them no before you came into the room. They were arguing against me. That's why I said it involved you and we needed your opinion. I needed you to back me up."

Zoe pressed her lips together. So what, was she supposed to thank him for doing what they'd agreed upon at the beginning? She wouldn't give him the satisfaction, even though relief made her shoulders sag.

"I don't want Lilah at campaign appearances. Especially

now that we know what happened to my house." Her eyes went wide. "How could they want that when they know about the threats?"

Byron shook his head. "They don't know about the threats. Dominic worked on this under my direction. I never told the rest of the family about anyone looking for you."

"No one knows? Not even your dad?" She would have expected Grant to be the first person Byron confided in.

"They don't. They only know Carlton blackmailed me. I came to you the other day to tell you about the emails so we could come up with the plan for how we'd move forward. I didn't want my family's opinion on what to do, especially when it directly affects you and Lilah."

Zoe pulled the cup of coffee closer to her chest. "Oh." She didn't have an immediate response to that. Nor did she want to acknowledge the satisfaction of knowing he'd come to her first. That he'd taken all of the heat for bringing her into his life without revealing all of the reasons he wanted to protect her.

Zoe frowned and walked past him. She would have expected he'd updated his dad or Roy on everything before coming to her. Byron kept pace with her as she went into the kitchen. Sandra and Jules glanced at them as they entered. Sandra's eyes narrowed as she looked between Zoe and Byron.

She touched Jules's shoulder. "Let me show you something in the garden. I believe Ms. Patricia mentioned wanting to grow mint."

The two ladies went through the sunroom outside. Zoe put her plate and coffee mug on the island. Byron stood next to her.

"Dominic told me what you said yesterday," he said.

"That I wanted to go home?"

"No, that you've been loved like this before. Zoe... I'm sorry." Regret was a heavy weight in his voice.

Zoe kept her eyes on the plate. "For what? For keeping me in the dark?"

"For treating you as if you couldn't handle knowing the truth. I should have known better. I do know better."

Zoe glanced at him from the corner of her eye. His voice was mellow. His tone humble. It was the first time she'd ever heard Byron sound humbled.

"You're amazing, smart and strong. You've taken care of Lilah without anyone's help for thirteen years. You built a life for yourself with no one's help. Instead of sulking about leaving Valtec, you're helping Elaina and starting your own business. You were right. I'm too much like my dad. I think I'm protecting or helping when I'm not. I apologize. It won't happen again."

"I'm not going to break, Byron. I haven't broken before." She'd been down, and she'd been afraid, but she'd always fought to survive.

"I promise you I won't make any decisions affecting you and Lilah without talking to you first."

She turned to face him. "It's not just about making decisions, Byron. It's about trusting me. Thinking of me as being just as capable as you. Not thinking of me as a damsel in distress you need to save. I never should have run to you back then." He'd thought she was capable before then. Respect, admiration and pride were the emotions typically reflected on Byron's face when they'd worked together. The night she'd run to him she'd seen the pity in his eyes and knew he'd never look at her the same way again.

He slid closer. "I'm glad you did. Do you think I don't realize how much you had to trust me to come to me when you needed help? I want you to trust me like that again."

She read the rest of his wish in his eyes. He wanted her to love him. *You're scared and you're angry and you think every guy is like my dad.* Lilah's words had haunted Zoe all the night before. She had looked for signs of Kendell in every man she met. Even Byron, who was the opposite of her ex. What would it feel like to trust someone completely? To relax and love without fear of manipulation?

"No more lies," she said firmly. "No more secrets. Promise me."

"I promise. No more secrets."

His voice resonated with conviction. His gaze didn't waver. His eyes begged for forgiveness. Zoe's chest filled with emotion. With just a look he turned her insides into mush. She wanted to believe him. Even more, she wanted to trust the look in his eye. Wanted to trust her own response to him. Instinct tempted her to let go and love him, but fear held her back. She couldn't trust her instincts. Not completely. Not so soon.

She nodded instead of speaking. With the feelings swirling around inside her she couldn't be sure she wouldn't blurt how much she wanted Byron to really be the happily-ever-after she'd never believed in. Byron eased even closer until the scent of his cologne wrapped around her like a comforting hug. Her body leaned into his. Her midsection tightened and she sucked in shallow breaths.

"Zoe." Byron whispered her name like a prayer. "I lo—"

Zoe lifted on her toes and kissed him softly. She didn't want to hear declarations she couldn't return. Didn't want to think about a tomorrow that wasn't promised. She still needed a plan. She still didn't want to sign up for the role of senator's perfect partner. Byron would love her and treat her like a queen, but the demands he'd place on her because of his position were another thing entirely. She'd been under the influence of one man; she wouldn't do that again.

Byron's hand gripped her waist. His head tilted at an angle and he pushed forward to deepen the kiss. Zoe pulled back before he could. If he kissed her the way she wanted him to she'd be lost. She couldn't afford to be lost. Not right now. No matter how much her body ached for him or her sex screamed for his touch.

"Thank you," she said. "For not giving in on Lilah, and for understanding where I'm coming from."

With effort she didn't know she had she pulled out of Byron's embrace. "I need to get to work." She cleared her throat. The hunger and acceptance in his eyes one of the biggest aphrodisiacs in existence. "We'll talk more later."

He licked his lips, maybe to get a lingering taste of her. The idea made her insides flip. "Later." He nodded.

Zoe took a deep breath and walked out of the kitchen. She hurried down the hall and back up the stairs to her room. A part of her yearned for Byron to follow her. She knew she wouldn't be able to pull away from him if he did. Another part of her was grateful he didn't. Byron's love would comfort and overwhelm her until once again she was following his lead and not noticing how much she'd lost of herself until it was too late.

"For the last time, we are not inviting Lilah to the rally," Byron said to his father.

They were in the upstairs family room getting ready

to leave for the rally at the high school. Grant had been on Byron's ass ever since he'd told him no. Not only did Byron agree with Zoe about keeping Lilah away from public events, but until they verified who was behind the emails and Zoe's house fire he didn't want to broadcast her whereabouts.

"Why not?" Lilah's indignant voice came from the door.

Both Byron and Grant swerved around toward her. Grant's eyes gleamed with potential. Byron's stomach sank.

Byron spoke quickly before Grant could pounce. "It's going to be a lot of people there. Your mom and I both agreed not to draw a lot of public attention your way. We wouldn't be able to control the photos taken of you."

"But if you let her come," Grant countered, "she could talk about how you rescued her from the car. It'll help you win the election."

Grant's words hit the target. Lilah's eyes lit up. "I want to help you."

Byron shook his head. "Lilah, no. You're staying here and that's that."

Lilah's eyes narrowed and she put her hands on her hips. She looked like a miniature Zoe ready for battle. "This is because of my mom, isn't it? She doesn't like you doing things for me, so she doesn't want me to go."

"We both agreed on this," Byron said.

"Only because she's scared. She thinks my dad is going to show up and try to hurt her again. Tell her it's not true. You said it yourself the emails had stopped. Once she understands it was just a prank and that my dad isn't going to come back, she'll ease up."

Lilah's words knocked the air from Byron's lungs. *You*

left us unprotected. He should have told Zoe the truth. If he had then Lilah would understand why they wanted her away from large crowds and out of the public eye. He had created a false sense of security.

"It's not that easy, Lilah," he said. He'd talk to Zoe and find out when she wanted to reveal the truth to Lilah. Dominic was getting close to finding out the person behind the emails, which would hopefully get them closer to the person who'd set the fire.

"It is that easy," Lilah said, stomping a foot. "I'm not a little kid. I want to help you win."

"Not like this," he argued.

Grant crossed the room and placed a hand on Lilah's shoulders. "She's making a good point, Byron. The people at the rally want to see her and Wesley."

"Wesley is going?" Lilah looked up at Grant. "So this rally is about you rescuing us?"

Byron pointed at Lilah. "I didn't rescue you." He pointed at Grant. "And will you stop twisting things around?"

Byron glared at his father. He hoped his dad understood the silent warning. *Don't use her in our fight.* Grant raised his hand and went over to the wet bar. Rile everyone up then retreat and let the dust settle. That was the Grant Robidoux way.

Byron turned back to Lilah. Dealing with her was easier. "You're not going. End of discussion. You're going to stay here and watch the rally on television. When it's over, me and your mom will come and talk about how we'll move forward. Okay?"

Lilah rolled her eyes before turning and stomping out of the room. *What the hell?* Byron gaped at the empty doorway. Stunned by his first display of teenage anger from Lilah.

"Let her go," Grant said. "She reminds me of Elaina. Probably shouldn't let her hang out with her *auntie* so much. Give her a little bit of time and she'll cool off."

Byron crossed the room to his dad. "You shouldn't have tried to manipulate her like that. She doesn't need to come."

"I don't see why not. You have her standing next to you looking up with the hero worship that shines from her eyes and I guarantee you'll win the election."

"It's about more than winning right now," Byron said through clenched teeth.

Grant set his highball glass down with a thud. "Excuse me? What is more important than winning? We've been involved in state politics for years. Now we have a good chance of influencing national politics, and you want to hold back because of some foolish feelings you have to Lilah's mother."

Byron rubbed at the headache starting in his forehead. "You wouldn't understand."

"Then you better start talking," Grant said.

Zoe walked into the room then. She pointed over her shoulder. "What's wrong with Lilah? She's been giving me the cold shoulder for the last few days, but that anger wasn't directed at me."

Byron momentarily forgot what he was thinking about. Zoe looked beautiful in a forest green short-sleeved suit. The pants fit her long legs and full curves perfectly. Her thick hair was free from the braids and twists she typically wore and framed her face like a curly cloud.

"She's mad at Byron," Grant answered.

Zoe's eyebrow lifted. "I didn't think that was possible."

Until that moment Byron hadn't, either. "I told her she couldn't go to the rally."

Zoe frowned and came farther into the room. "She knows she can't go."

Byron glared at his father. "Someone gave her the idea that if she went, she'd be helping me win."

Zoe sucked in a breath. "No. Why would you tell her that? She might do something rash."

Grant waved them off. "Will you two quit acting like that girl is a baby? She's thirteen and knows better than to get in a car with strangers. She'll be fine."

Zoe marched over to Grant. Anger flashed bright in her eyes. "Not when there is someone out there threatening her life and mine."

Grant laughed. "You're almost as dramatic as him."

Byron stared at his father. "She's not being dramatic."

Grant's dark eyes jumped to Zoe then back to Byron. The smile slowly fell from his face. "What are you talking about?"

Byron looked at Zoe. How much they revealed to his father was up to her. Zoe took a deep breath. "Tell him."

"Tell me what?" Grant asked.

"Someone has been sending threatening emails to Zoe," Byron said. "They said she's going to pay for the lies she told. We also think they're behind her house fire. Possibly even my car accident."

Grant's eyes widened. "Someone tried to kill you?" His tone was measured but rage threaded through his voice. His hands balled into fists on the bar.

"We don't know if the accident is related," Byron said. "But Dominic found evidence that someone tampered with the video just before Zoe's house caught fire. Her neighbor thought she saw someone at Zoe's place. It doesn't make sense that an electrical fire would start the way it did unless there was tampering."

Grant's face hardened. His sharp gaze snapped to Zoe. "Is it your ex?"

Zoe raised her shoulders. "We don't know. He's not supposed to be released for another month."

Grant pushed away from the bar. He paced to the window and back. "Why didn't you tell me this before?" Grant snapped.

"Because it wasn't for you," Byron said. "I wanted to be sure."

"He only just told me," Zoe said. She didn't sound angry anymore, but Byron heard the exasperation in her voice.

"What is the plan?" Grant asked.

Byron answered. "Increased security. We've already started that. Along with surveillance. Dominic thinks he'll have the person behind the emails within the week. If we can prove it's Kendell or someone related to him, then we'll go from there."

"What will you do?" Grant asked.

"Go to the police," Zoe answered.

Byron and Grant met each other's gazes. Byron saw the same calculation in his dad's eyes that went through his head. "There's no guarantee the police will do anything," Byron said.

"Then what are we supposed to do?" Zoe asked incredulously. "Ask him nicely to stop?"

Byron's shoulders stiffened. "I won't ask nicely."

Her lips parted and she leaned back. He meant it. He would do whatever he needed to make sure Kendell, and anyone related to him, understood Zoe and Lilah were off-limits. He'd tried to stay on the right side of the law all his life, but he wasn't naive. He knew Dominic and his father had other means of dealing with bad situations. Byron wouldn't blink an eye about blurring the line between right and wrong to keep her safe.

Before she could reply Elaina, India and Travis walked in. Roy followed behind them. Roy took in the family and rubbed his hands together. The excitement of another campaign event adding an extra bounce to his step.

"All right, are we ready to go rack up some votes?" Roy asked in his cheery voice.

Grant walked over to Byron and placed a hand on his shoulder. Byron met his father's gaze. Grant squeezed and nodded. "We look out for family." Grant looked at Zoe. "Since the start of this we agreed you're family. We'll work this out."

He let Byron go and faced Roy. "Let's do this. I'll go down and tell Sandra to keep an extra close eye on Lilah while we're gone."

Zoe's eyes were still wide. She moved to Byron. "Byron—"

He looked past her at the rest of the family. "Let's get out of here before we're late."

Uneasy looks passed between his siblings and best friend, but they didn't question the tension in the room. They turned and followed Grant out. Byron moved to go with them.

Zoe placed her hand on his arm to stop him. "Promise me you won't do anything stupid because of this."

Byron covered her hand with his. "I promise you I will do what I have to if it means protecting you and Lilah."

"Not if it means risking your integrity," she said.

"Byron, you've always fought to do things the right way. You're better than him."

Byron brushed his hand across her cheek. "Some things are worth fighting for. Even if it means fighting dirty."

Because he couldn't help himself, he lowered his head and brushed his lips across hers. He wanted desperately to pull her body close to his. Kiss her deeply. Tell her he loved her. Zoe sighed softly. Her full lips parting slightly against his.

They hadn't slept together since he'd told her about the emails. He wasn't sure where they stood with each other. What would happen after the campaign and if she still wanted the relationship they'd tentatively started. He had a sinking feeling Zoe didn't plan to be with him after the election. He'd lost her when he'd lied to her. The least he could do is make sure wherever she ended up after she walked out of his life again that she wouldn't have to look over her shoulder and worry about Kendell again.

He pulled back instead of kissing her deeply. The confusion in her dark eyes wasn't something he could clear up. He couldn't make her love him. She'd have to decide that for herself. "Let's go," he said before stepping away and walking to the door.

CHAPTER TWENTY-NINE

ZOE LISTENED AS Byron finished his speech at the campaign rally. Once again he'd wowed the crowd. His enthusiasm and dedication to improving things if elected were both refreshing and intoxicating. She knew Byron believed in everything he said. He was a good guy who wanted to help people and would be devoted to serving everyone in his district.

He was also willing to go against his own principles in order to keep her safe. The thought made her stomach churn and her chest swell. He was a good guy who would fight dirty if he needed to. She was drawn to his ruthless side, even if she didn't want him risking his future to fight her fight.

Elaina bumped her shoulder with Zoe's. "You all right?"

Zoe smiled and nodded. "Yes. He's doing great."

"He always does great," Elaina said as if the possibility of Byron not doing great was silly. "But something is different. What happened before we came into the room?"

Byron raised a hand and ended his speech with his catchphrase. "The time is now!"

The crowd clapped, cheered and chanted back the words. Banners waved, signs were held up and a few people wiped tears from their eyes. Zoe ignored Elaina's words and applauded along with the rest of the crowd. Wesley, whose broken arm was still in a cast, walked over to Byron.

Byron clasped Wesley's free hand and raised them up. The fervor of the supporters increased.

Grant was wrong. They didn't need Lilah there for people to view Byron as a hero. Not once did Byron talk about helping Wesley out of the car, but people knew what happened. Some signs and posters included pictures of Byron on the side of the road assisting Wesley after the accident, or Byron with a superhero cape around his shoulders.

"He's their hero," Elaina said, sounding a bit overwhelmed by the response to her brother.

"He is," Zoe said, though the words were bittersweet.

Byron was good at being the hero. She didn't like why he'd kept the threat against her and Lilah a secret, but she also understood. She also believed after seeing her reaction he wouldn't keep information from her again. The regret in his eyes and the apology on his lips weren't like the apologies she'd gotten from Kendell. Superficial ones only provided to try and appease her rather than acknowledge fault.

She trusted him to keep his promise. She trusted him to fight to keep her and Lilah safe even as he accepted her walking out of his life. And he had accepted that. She'd seen the bittersweet regret in his eyes as he'd pulled away from her before the rally. He knew she planned to leave, and he wasn't going to fight her on that.

The realization filled her with a light-headed hope she hadn't felt in years. The feeling was freeing and scary at the same time. She'd never trusted anyone to put her best interests before theirs. She'd trusted her parents to fight and make her home life unstable and scary. She'd trusted her sister to retreat within herself and escape without a backward glance whenever she could. She'd trusted Kendell to remind her why she needed him by playing on her insecurities.

She trusted Byron to only want to make her happy. Not because he wanted to sleep with her. Not because it would make him feel good. Not even so he could win this election.

"Something is wrong. Tell me what it is," Elaina said in a serious voice.

Zoe met Elaina's gaze. Her perfect Robidoux smile was in place and she continued to clap with the crowd, but her eyes were filled with concern.

"Would Byron do something illegal in order to protect the people he loves?" Zoe asked.

Elaina's eyes widened; her hands froze midclap. The reaction only lasted a beat before Elaina turned away and smiled confidently at her brother. Her outward appearance excited, but her shoulders stiff and her claps jerky.

All the confirmation Zoe needed.

Dominic came up on Zoe's other side. He leaned down to her ear. "Zoe, I need to speak with you."

Zoe frowned at Dominic. "Is everything okay?"

He shook his head. "Let's go behind the stage."

Cold sweat beaded on Zoe's forehead and upper lip. The worry in Dominic's eyes said he wasn't coming with good news. She clasped her hands together to calm their shaking and tried not to let her panic show as she followed Dominic off the stage to the back. As soon as they were out of the vision of the crowd, she grabbed his arm.

"What is it?"

Dominic's face was grim. "I just got off the phone with Jeanette. Apparently, Kendell was released early. He got out two days ago. Jeanette and her group of detectives immediately started tracking him. One of her people spotted him in Jackson Falls this morning. He's on his way to the estate."

Zoe's vision dimmed. The noise in the gym was too loud. The air too thick for her to breathe. She took a stumbling step back. Dominic placed an arm on hers.

"Zoe, it's okay."

She shook his hand away. "He's here? In town? He's going to the estate? Lilah is there."

She was there alone. None of the security guards or servants who worked there would protect Lilah the way Zoe would. None of them knew what precautions she'd put in place. They wouldn't know what to tell Lilah or give her the warning to be prepared.

"I've got to go." She scanned the back for an exit.

"Wait. Byron is done. We can leave together."

Zoe had no intention of waiting. "Then you can give him the update and he can catch up to me. I'm not going to just sit here and wait for something terrible to happen to my daughter."

"Nothing terrible is going to happen. We're watching the estate."

"I don't care who's watching. She's there alone and he's going to her. I won't let him get a chance to try and fill her head with lies, or worse, hurt her because he wants me to pay for what I did."

Zoe turned and ran toward the door. Dominic called her name, but she didn't turn around. She burst through the door into the full parking lot. She went straight for the vehicle waiting for the family and jerked open the door. "Back to the estate. Now!" she said to the driver sitting in the front.

She looked over her shoulder but didn't see Dominic

following. He probably ran back to tell Byron so he could come up with a plan. Well, she didn't need one of their plans. She'd thought about everything she would say or do if Kendell tried to come back into their life.

She pulled out her cell phone and tried to call Lilah. The phone rang once. Twice. Three times. Four times. Five.

"Hi, you've reached Lilah. Leave a message and I'll think about calling you back," Lilah's voice said with a sweet giggle.

Tears prickled Zoe's eyes. She squeezed the phone. "Lilah, sweetheart, please call me back. He's here, baby. You need to be prepared."

Zoe hung up and called right back. Again, she went through the series of rings before voice mail picked up. Zoe opened the text app and sent a hurried message.

Your dad is in town. He's coming to you. Get ready.

She prayed Lilah looked at the text or listened to her message. Lilah was mad, but she'd understand that if Zoe was calling constantly something important was going on. But as the miles diminished between the school and the estate with no answer, Zoe's hopes plummeted.

Maybe she's asleep. Maybe she's in the pool. Maybe she's in the kitchen and left her phone in her room.

All of the possible scenarios went through her mind. Anything other than her dad was with her and keeping her from answering the calls.

The car barely stopped before Zoe opened the back door and jumped out. She didn't bother going through the house. She'd check the pool house first. Though they moved into the main house, Lilah still preferred the pool house. She often went there whenever Zoe left for a campaign event. Zoe sprinted around the main house.

The door to the pool house stood open. There was no sign of Lilah outside by the pool. Zoe's entire body shook. Not just with fear, but with rage. She was sick and tired of Kendell and the fear he'd caused ruining her life. If, no, when she got her hands on him, she was going to kill him.

Noise came from inside the pool house. Steely determination went through her body. She crept to the door and slowly walked inside. The pool house was quiet. No sounds of the television or music. No mess as if there was a struggle. She wanted to call out, but she held back. She could sense someone was in there. Maybe it was just Lilah.

The living room was clear; so was the kitchen. Zoe went to the bedroom. She gently eased the door open to look inside. An arm wrapped around her neck. Panic tried to take over. She pushed it to the edges. Self-defense kicked in. She stomped on the foot of the person behind her. The man grunted and his grip loosened enough for her to flip him over her shoulder to the ground. A move she'd practiced a hundred times. She twisted the assailant's arm and planted her foot in the downed man's throat.

Kendell's surprised wide eyes stared up at her. For years she'd worried fear, regret, or panic would take over and make her forget the self-defense moves she'd learned when she came face-to-face with him again. The only thing she felt now was a cold, fierce need to protect herself and her daughter. She was not the scared woman he used to intimidate anymore.

"Where the fuck is my daughter?" Zoe said in a slow, measured tone between clenched teeth.

Kendell kept his arms stretched out to the sides. He relaxed his body and met her eyes. "I came to warn you."

"You've been doing that for months." She increased the pressure of her foot. "Where is she?"

He shook his head and tried to talk but the pressure she had on his throat blocked the words. She eased up enough to let him squeeze out, "She got here first."

"She who?" Zoe didn't trust anything he said.

"My mom. She wants Lilah."

Zoe frowned and tried to make sense of the words. His mom? Why would she want Lilah?

"How did you even get here?" Security was all over the estate.

"I came through…the back fields," he said in shallow breaths. "I pretended to be one of the landscapers."

Footsteps hurried inside. Zoe looked away from Kendell on the floor as Byron rushed through the door with Dominic and several of his guards. They stopped and took in the scene. Dominic raised a brow.

"We got an identification of the vehicle she's in," Byron said.

Relief swept through her, but she didn't let go of Kendell. Not until she knew what was going on and why his mom took her child.

BYRON COULDN'T BELIEVE his eyes. When Dominic told him Kendell was in town and Zoe had taken off to try and protect Lilah he'd almost had a panic attack. He'd had visions of her confronting Kendell and things getting out of hand. The threats in the emails kept replaying in his mind. He'd tried not to think the worst, that Kendell would hurt Zoe, but memories of her battered face and the fear in her eyes when she'd come to him that night years ago kept replaying in his mind.

What he hadn't expected was to find Zoe with her foot pinned against Kendell's neck while she held him against the floor. The fierce look in her eye would make him back away if this wasn't so important. She reminded him of a warrior ready to fight any enemy who got in her way. She was beautiful and strong, and he realized how wrong he'd been to underestimate her.

"Security cameras caught Lilah getting into a car we think she thought was a rideshare vehicle at the edge of the estate," Byron said.

Zoe's attention snapped back to him. "How was she even able to leave?" The sharp question was directed at Dominic.

"She snuck out the back of the pool house." Dominic's voice vibrated with frustration that meant someone was losing their job. "The security detail didn't get nervous until she didn't come back out. That's the same time one of the landscapers tipped us off about a stranger on the grounds."

"Why would she call a rideshare?" Zoe asked.

"My guess is to come to the rally," Byron said.

"Whose car was it?" Zoe's voice remained calm, but her gaze darted frantically back and forth to him, Dominic and Kendell.

Kendell tried to sit up. Zoe increased the pressure on his neck. He held his hands out and lay back down. "My mom."

Dominic scowled at Kendell. "There was an older woman driving the vehicle."

"Why didn't you stop her?" Zoe asked. "That was the entire reason to have protection."

Dominic looked regretful. "By the time my man realized she'd snuck out she was already halfway to the spot where she'd gotten in the car."

"What are you doing here, then?" Zoe glared down at Kendell.

"I came here to warn you both," Kendell wheezed.

"How did you know she'd be in the pool house?"

"That's the last place my mom had," he rasped out. Zoe must have increased the pressure on his neck. "She said you and Lilah were living here in the pool house."

Byron walked over to Zoe. He put a hand on her shoulder. "Let him up so we can talk." While Byron didn't care if she suffocated Kendell they needed answers first.

"We don't have time," she said. "He knows where she is."

"I do," Kendell said. "Let me up and I'll take you there."

Byron glared down at Kendell. "Why should we believe anything you say?"

Sweat trickled down Kendell's face. He kept his palms open wide and didn't move to fight Zoe's hold. "My mom wants to take Lilah out of the country. She begged me to go with her. I told her I'd meet her in Jackson Falls so we could talk. I'd hoped to get here first."

"Why would she want Lilah?" Byron asked.

Kendell looked at Zoe. "Because she knows she's my daughter."

Zoe's eyes narrowed. Her shoulder trembled beneath Byron's touch. "According to who?"

"Will you let me up?" Kendell begged.

Byron gently squeezed Zoe's shoulder. With a heavy

sigh, she moved her foot and stepped back. Dominic and the guys he'd brought with him tensed and stepped forward. Kendell noticed the attention on him and slowly eased up with his hands in plain sight.

"I didn't come here to hurt you or Lilah," he said. "I've had enough time to think of the mistakes I made. I didn't want to make another one."

Zoe's jaw clenched. Her body was stiff, and her eyes shiny. Byron could only imagine the fear coursing through her. The longer they talked the longer it kept Lilah away.

"If you don't want to make any more mistakes then tell us where she is," Byron said. "We can get the reasons why later. Lilah coming back is the most important thing."

The look Kendell gave Byron said he didn't care for him any more now than he had back in college. "She's at the Fairmont Inn on the edge of town," Kendell said. "She told me she'd be there for one night. Then she was going to leave for Texas and cross over the border."

"No," Zoe said.

Byron slid his arm around her shoulder. Thankfully, she didn't pull away. Instead, she leaned into him.

"That won't happen." Byron looked at Dominic. "Get people over to check out the hotel. Call the highway patrol and have them check the interstates for any sign of a vehicle that matches the description." Dominic nodded and pulled out his phone. Byron looked back at Kendell. "If you're lying…"

"I'm not," Kendell said, glaring. "I'm not going back to prison."

"If you are lying," Byron continued, not giving a damn about anything Kendell said, "you won't have to worry about going back to prison. There won't be anything left of you for prison."

Zoe stiffened next to him. He meant every word. For Kendell to threaten not only Zoe but also Lilah was despicable. Anyone who would willingly kidnap and hurt a child was the worst example of humanity. He wouldn't give Kendell the benefit of going back to jail if anything happened to Lilah.

Kendell continued to glare but nodded stiffly. "Still cocky as hell."

"Cocky and angry. You threatened my family. I don't respond well to that."

Kendell's jaw tightened. Zoe placed a hand on Byron's chest. The fear in her eyes was the same fear coursing through his veins.

"We've got to find her," Zoe said.

He understood what she didn't say. The time to fight with Kendell was later. Byron lifted and lowered his chin. "Let's go now. Kendell, you're in the car with me and Zoe."

Zoe's eyes widened. "You're going to let me go?"

He was surprised she'd even ask that question. "Why wouldn't I?"

"I thought you'd say something like it's safer for me to stay."

Byron shook his head. "I promised you I wouldn't leave you out. There's no way I'd try and make you stay behind."

Her eyes softened and the sheen of tears returned. "Let's go."

They left the pool house. The two guards Dominic hired frisked and flanked Kendell. He and Zoe followed behind them. Dominic was outside on the phone. He finished his call as they all left. He exchanged a look with Byron. All of Byron's requests had been handled.

Dominic drove the SUV while Zoe, Byron and Kendell sat in the back. One of Dominic's guards sat in the passenger seat, the other next to Kendell. Dominic glanced over his shoulder as they sped away from the estate toward the hotel Kendell mentioned.

"Jeanette has people there," Dominic said. "The car is parked there, and they've identified the room."

Byron nodded and reached over to take Zoe's hand in his. Her body trembled. She met his eye and squeezed his hand. They would get Lilah back. Once they did that he was going to make Kendell wish he were back in jail.

Zoe twisted in her seat toward Kendell behind them. "Why does your mom think Lilah is yours?"

"She is. Isn't she?" Kendell said with certainty.

Zoe's grip on his hand tightened. "Answer the question."

"She saw the two of you a year ago in Atlanta," Kendell said. "She said the instant she saw Lilah she knew you'd lied. My mom always believed you lied and that our breakup was the start of my downfall."

Byron's free hand clenched with the need to punch Kendell in the face. "Zoe had nothing to do with your downfall," he said between clenched teeth. "You made your own decisions."

"I know that. I was young and trying to be a man the only way I knew how. I'm not saying that's a good excuse or right, but it's the truth. As soon as I saw a picture of her…" Kendell met Byron's gaze. "She's not your daughter."

Byron would fight to the end of time to keep Lilah as his daughter. If Kendell pushed this he had little to stand on. He and Zoe weren't officially together. She'd lied about the paternity for thirteen years. Would they have a chance if Kendell pushed for rights?

No. A real father doesn't participate in a kidnapping.

"What do you want?" Zoe asked.

Kendell was quiet for several seconds. His voice was resigned when he finally spoke. "For her to be taken care of. I can't do that. My mom can't do that. She's still tied up in the life that got me put away. If Lilah is happy then I'm happy." Kendell looked out the window.

The knots in Byron's midsection tightened. He wished he had a reason to believe a word Kendell said. "Let's get her back safely then worry about what we do next."

CHAPTER THIRTY

"THEY ARE IN room two-twelve," Dominic announced as they pulled into the parking lot of the Fairmont Hotel. "One older woman and another man. No one else in the room. No other people associated with them at the hotel."

"She wants to keep this small and quiet," Kendell said. "That's what she told me. It'll be easier to get Lilah out that way."

Zoe's stomach rolled. She couldn't believe Kendell's mother was behind the kidnapping. That she was trying to take her grandchild. What did she hope to accomplish? Lilah wasn't a submissive child. She wouldn't just succumb to their demands and accept a new life forced on her.

Please don't let them hurt my child.

"We'll make it easy," Dominic said. "Kendell, go to the door. Gain access and we come in after."

"Are they armed?" Byron asked.

Zoe sucked in a breath and Byron squeezed her hand. He hadn't let go during the entire ride. He'd been so calm throughout the ordeal even though she knew he was just as worried as she was. His left eye twitched, the pulse in his throat raced and tension radiated off his body. Byron was good under pressure. His calm was the only thing keeping her from shaking every bit of information out of Kendell, who confirmed his mom was behind the fire and car accident. Both were attempts to hurt Zoe and Byron.

"We don't know," Dominic said.

"Then let's be sure of that before we go in," Zoe said. "I don't want her harmed."

"My mom carries a gun. The guy she's with probably has one, too," Kendell said matter-of-factly. "I'll make sure everything is clear before we go in."

"No, I don't trust you," Byron said. "Dominic can go in with you. Your mom doesn't know him, and you can say you brought him along."

Kendell's features tightened. Zoe sat forward and caught his eye. He better not argue about a damn thing concerning this. He scowled but nodded. "Fine," Kendell said.

They parked and Dominic's men got out first, followed by Kendell and then Byron and Zoe. Tension filled the air. Zoe's pulse beat in her ears so loud she couldn't focus on any other sounds. The Fairmont Inn was a cheap motel on the outskirts of town. Three stories tall with doors that opened to the outside landings. There were a few other cars parked there during the day.

Fear and anger rushed through her system as she looked up to the second floor. Lilah was in there. What had his mom done to her? Was Lilah scared and crying? Had she remembered what Zoe taught her? Stay calm and look for a safe way to get out. Lilah would just roll her eyes and say *I know, Mom.* Whenever Zoe used to remind her daughter of how to respond in a tense situation, Zoe had always hoped she was being overly protective, and Lilah would never be in danger.

Kendell and Dominic walked to the metal stairs leading to the second floor. They'd made it halfway when the door to room two-twelve burst open. Lilah sprinted out and continued to the stairs. Zoe let out a disbelieving breath.

Fear and pride increased the pounding of her heart. Lilah was a fighter.

Zoe and Byron both ran toward the stairs at the same time. Yelling came from upstairs. Dominic and Kendell reached the top of the stairs just as Lilah reached them. Without skipping a beat, Lilah elbowed Kendell in the stomach and rushed past him down the stairs.

Zoe's heart pumped. Byron got ahead of her and reached Lilah just as she hit the ground floor. Her eyes widened and she jumped into Byron's arms. He picked her up, turned and ran back toward Zoe. Dominic's two guards were past him in a flash and up the stairs. More shouting ensued.

Zoe didn't try to figure out what was happening on the second floor. Byron reached her side with Lilah, and the three of them ran to the car. Inside Lilah started crying and clung to Zoe.

"They were taking me to Mexico," Lilah hiccupped. "They thought they could tie me up, but I knew how to get out. I ran as soon as they looked away."

Zoe pulled Lilah to her chest and breathed in the smell of her daughter's hair. Byron sat on her other side with Lilah sandwiched between them. Byron's guards handled things outside. She didn't have to worry. Everything was okay. Zoe felt nothing but relief and thankfulness to have her family back together.

CHAPTER THIRTY-ONE

EVERYTHING HAPPENED IN a blur after they got in the car. Dominic and his people quickly subdued Kendell's mom and the man she'd brought with her. Zoe wasn't surprised to learn it was Carlton. The same guy who'd been looking for her from the start and blackmailed Byron.

Thanks to Dominic calling the cops they arrived shortly after. Arrests were made and everyone was taken down to the police station. They separated her, Byron and Kendell as they went through everything. Straightening out what happened didn't take long. Everything Kendell said about his mom turned out to be true.

Zoe wanted to talk to Kendell's mom. She wanted to look into the eye of the woman who'd terrorized her for months. Byron pulled some strings so she could. She kissed Lilah before going into the interrogation room.

Mira's eyes narrowed after Zoe entered the room. Her sharp, calculating gaze was just as Zoe remembered. Kendell had taken her around his mother often when they were dating. Once Zoe asked Mira why Kendell got so angry and possessive. The response she'd gotten was so eerily similar to what Zoe's mother used to tell her that she'd never asked again.

Jealousy is how a man shows love. You should be happy he loves you enough to care.

Even though she'd eventually realized what love wasn't, she also hadn't accepted what love was.

"I didn't think you'd want to talk to me," Mira said with a sneer. She lifted her hands, which were handcuffed to a bar on the table where she sat. "I won't be in these for long. Once the truth comes out, they'll let me out of here."

"The truth has come out, Mira," Zoe said calmly. "You came to town, kidnapped my daughter, then held her against her will at a local hotel. Not to mention the fire and car accident. I do plan to press charges."

"Just like you did with Kendell?" She sucked her teeth and sneered. "You always did like to ruin people's lives."

"I pressed charges because Kendell never should have hurt me like that," Zoe said calmly. She wasn't going to lash out the way Mira wanted her to. "He went on to make his other mistakes."

"You made it so he couldn't get a job, couldn't get recruited. The only thing he had left was crime."

Zoe lifted her shoulders. She didn't give a damn about how protecting herself from Kendell affected his life. "That wasn't my decision. Those were all his and that's why he ended up in prison. Not because of what I did."

Mira sat back in her chair. Disgust written over her features. "I guess you have to tell yourself something to sleep at night. That's okay. The world will know the truth. Your rich boyfriend's political career won't survive after this gets out and everyone will know you're a liar who kept a good man away from his child."

Zoe wasn't sure they could keep this secret anymore. A part of her didn't want to. She'd run from her past and hidden it for long enough. Her only regret was that living in her truth meant Byron's life would suffer even more.

"We'll deal with what happens," Zoe said with confidence she didn't feel. "I just want to know why. Why would you do this not to me but to Lilah? Why would you scare her like that?"

"Because she deserved to know."

"She does know," Zoe said. "I told her the truth a long time ago. She didn't want anything to do with the man who used to beat me."

Mira sucked her teeth. "He didn't beat you. He only hit you a few times. You young girls don't know how to handle the love of a real man."

Zoe closed her eyes. The similarities between Mira and her mother made her chest ache. Thank God she'd broken the cycle. She prayed Lilah never had to deal with something like this again.

"Those words are exactly why I didn't want you or Kendell around my daughter." She opened her eyes and met Mira's defiant gaze. "Lilah will know her self-worth and hopefully will never be in a situation like I was. She deserves better."

"You can't keep my son out of her life now. Regardless of what happens to me. Kendell is her father. He'll sue for custody."

Zoe swallowed hard. She didn't want to think about any demands Kendell might make now that things had come to a head. He may have come here to stop his mom, but that didn't mean he'd changed.

"And I will fight with everything in me to make sure you never step in the same room with her again." The one thing she could fight for. She didn't know if it was possible, but after this Zoe never wanted Mira anywhere near her daughter.

She turned and walked out without another word. Kendell waited for her outside the interrogation room. Time in prison had aged him more than thirteen years. He hadn't lost the tightly muscled athletic figure he'd had in college, but now lines bracketed his eyes and mouth. His movements were jittery, and his eyes darted around as if expecting something to come out and surprise him.

Zoe's hands clenched and she fought not to take a step away. He couldn't hurt her anymore. She wouldn't let him hurt her anymore.

"What did she say?" he asked.

"That she wanted the truth to get out. That now you'd fight me for custody." She went straight for the answer she wanted. She didn't want to extend any more of the time she had with him.

Kendell's brows drew together. Surprise flashed in his eyes. "I don't want custody."

"You don't?" Relief nearly made her knees weak, but she refused to let her guard down.

Kendell shook his head. "I'm not cut out to be a father. I just got out. I'm still trying to get used to living on my own terms. After this thing with Mom, I don't even know how my probation is going to go. A kid will just make things worse."

She didn't want to ask, but she had to know. "Do you want to see her, or have visitation?"

He shook his head. "Zoe has a dad now. He'll treat her better than I can. Both of you."

Byron wasn't perfect. He was arrogant, used to getting his way and determined to fix every wrong in the path of the people he loved, but he'd never hurt her or Lilah. "He will."

Kendell nodded and rubbed his hands together. His stance shifted and he glanced around. "Yeah, well, I'll sign whatever paperwork you need."

Byron came to the end of the hall. Worry flashed in his eyes as he watched them, but he didn't immediately rush to her side to save her. He saw she had this, and she appreciated that he let her deal with closing this chapter on her life.

"Leave your address and we'll get them to you," she said.

"Cool." He shifted from foot to foot.

Zoe only wanted to get away from him. "Goodbye, Kendell."

He opened his mouth as if to say something, then shook his head and walked away. He hesitated a second next to Byron then nodded and kept moving. Once he was out of sight Byron came to her side.

"Are you okay?"

She nodded. She only wanted to hold her daughter. "Where's Lilah?"

"In the waiting room with Dominic." Byron took her hand and immediately walked with her to the waiting room.

Lilah jumped up and ran to them. She wrapped her arms around Zoe then turned and hugged Byron. "Can we go home now?"

Zoe smiled and nodded. "Yes. Let's go home."

"The estate?" Byron asked.

Zoe shook her head. She didn't want to spend time with the rest of the family, getting them caught up and answering questions about what happened and why. She just wanted to be alone with Byron and Lilah.

"Can we go to your place?" she asked.

Byron looked surprised but didn't argue. "My place it is."

Once they got to Byron's place Zoe got Lilah settled in one of Byron's spare bedrooms while Dominic and the rest of Byron's security team set up outside. Even though there was no evidence Mira had any help, they didn't want to take any chances.

"Did Kendell leave?" Lilah asked. She lay on her side on the bed.

Zoe sat next to Lilah. She ran a hand over the braids on her daughter's head. "He did. Did you want to see him?"

Lilah's brows drew together as she considered, then she shook her head. "Not really. Mira said she was taking me to him and that we'd be a family."

"He's agreed to sign over full custody," Zoe said. "You won't have to see him again unless you want to later in life."

Lilah's lips lifted in a small smile and she nodded. "Good. Now Byron can adopt me and really be my dad." She closed her eyes.

Zoe kissed Lilah's forehead. The thought of Byron adopting Lilah and the arguments she'd once had about Lilah not getting her hopes up were nowhere in Zoe's head. The idea of being a real family no longer scared her. "We'll see."

She left Lilah's room and found Byron in his living area behind the bar. He held up a decanter of whiskey. "Drink?"

"Please," Zoe said. She went to the bar where Byron poured a drink into a glass for her.

"How's Lilah?"

"Okay for now. I told her Kendell is going to sign away any rights to custody. We can try to do it quietly. Maybe you can get Dominic to keep the records secure or something."

Byron frowned. "Why would we do that?"

"Because if word gets out about another lie it'll make things even worse for your campaign. I don't want this to get out and you lose because of it, but I also need to make sure Kendell has no rights to Lilah."

Byron placed his hands on the bar and gave Zoe a serious look. "I don't care if it comes out. I don't care if this costs me the campaign. If Kendell will sign over full custody to Lilah, then let him."

"You don't care if you lose? You've worked so hard and you're finally up in the polls."

"Some things are more important. You and Lilah are at the top of that list." He picked up his glass and walked toward the couch. "I'll call Roy tomorrow and let him know about what's going on. He'll come up with something and we'll deal with what happens."

Zoe stared in stunned silence. Too many emotions bubbled up inside her to identify. Relief, happiness, disbelief, but one overruled them all.

"I love you," Zoe blurted out. The words she'd fought against for so long could no longer be held back.

Byron spun around and stared at her wide-eyed. "Say what?"

Zoe put her drink down and walked to him. "I love you. I never thought I'd say those words to another man. I always thought love also meant pain and humiliation. That's all I'd ever seen or knew. When you came back in my life I was afraid I really hadn't changed as much as I thought. I was afraid of losing myself and being another victim, but Byron, you don't make me feel like a victim. You make me happy. You make me feel safe."

He approached her slowly as if he was afraid quick movements would make her take back the words. He didn't have to worry about that. She was completely confident in what she said.

"I only want to make you feel safe," Byron said. "I love you so much you will never know, but if my love ever makes you feel uncomfortable, tell me. We do things big in my family, including love. But my love is for you, Zoe. Your strength and determination. I don't want you to be anything other than the person who calls me out and keeps it real."

"Even if loving me will cost you what you worked for your entire career?"

"I can help people whether I'm in Washington or here in Jackson Falls. As long as I'm helping them with you then I've already won."

The love in his voice was like a thread that wrapped around her heart tying hers to his. If she could bottle this feeling and save it for the rest of her life, she would. She closed the distance between them and wrapped her arms around his neck. Byron lifted her off her feet and kissed her. The love in his eyes said she didn't have to worry about being anything other than herself with him. No matter what happened, he'd make her feel this loved for the rest of their lives.

CHAPTER THIRTY-TWO

"THE RESULTS ARE IN, and the winner of the dramatic and contentious North Carolina Senate race is Paul McLeod."

Zoe's warm hand slid into Byron's. He squeezed and looked at her. This time he didn't watch the votes come in at an elaborate watch party. There was one going on at the same brewery where the first one was held. His family was there along with his supporters. He and Zoe were prepared to make an appearance. He had to deliver his concession speech.

"How are you feeling?" she asked.

Byron lifted her hand and kissed the back. She looked exquisite in an emerald green one-shoulder cocktail dress to complement his navy blue suit. They matched his campaign colors. When Zoe suggested they slip out of the party and watch the results come in at his place he'd quickly agreed. He'd known winning would be hard. The press had ripped him and Zoe to shreds after word came out that he wasn't Lilah's biological father. Only the story of him and Zoe saving Lilah from a kidnapping had kept him in the running.

He'd expected to feel disappointment. Instead, he felt relief. "I'm surprisingly relieved." Shouldn't he feel disappointed?

"The campaign was hard on you. I'm not surprised," Zoe said.

"I worked so hard for so long to win. But all I can think about now is how great it's going to be to not go to Washington. No more questions about my personal life. I can be home more."

"Are you sure you're okay with that?"

He looked into Zoe's dark eyes. Now he'd be here to pick up Lilah after archery practice when Zoe was out of town working. She'd started her consulting firm, and with Elaina's recommendation was already doing compliance reviews for other businesses. He wouldn't have to spend half the year living out of town. They wouldn't have to pull Lilah out of another school and relocate to DC. His future was unplanned. For the first time he could decide what he wanted to do next. The realization was liberating.

He grinned. "I am."

"Then let's go to this party." Zoe grinned.

They arrived at the brewery. The music blared and he was greeted with cheers, backslaps, and well-wishes. He shook every person's hand and thanked everyone sincerely. They'd believed in him through the entire rough campaign.

When he took the stage and looked out over the crowd the same weight of responsibility he'd felt before pressed into his chest. "It was a long fight," he said into the microphone. "But at the end I am still thankful. This campaign showed me the meaning of family, loyalty and happiness. I may have lost this battle, but the war isn't over. I will always be here for the people of North Carolina. I will always fight for you, and to make things better. This loss isn't the end. It's the beginning. The time to give up isn't here. Now it's time to fight harder!"

The group cheered. Zoe stepped next to him and he wrapped an arm around her shoulder. He looked over the crowd. His eyes met Yolanda's in the back. She raised a glass. He nodded in acknowledgment. Grant stood next to Patricia. Pride in his father's eyes despite the loss. India and Travis smiled at him. Elaina was near them. Her arm around Lilah's shoulders as his soon-to-be adopted daughter waved at him.

Love and contentment filled him so much, tears burned his eyes. He'd thought he'd been happy when he'd won the primary months ago. Tonight he was happier than he'd ever been.

He and Zoe left the stage. Grant pushed through the crowd and slapped him on the shoulder. "You know Jackson Falls will be needing a new mayor next election."

Byron shook his head and grinned. "Not tonight, Dad. Let me just enjoy tonight."

Grant sighed but nodded. "I'm still proud of you, son."

Byron's throat tightened. He and his dad may not ever see eye to eye on a lot of things, but he would always love him. "Thanks."

Zoe's arm around his waist tightened. "How about we grab a drink before you two get sentimental."

Grant laughed and kissed Zoe's cheek. "You two don't party too hard." Grant winked then lost himself in the crowd.

Zoe looked up at Byron. "He's not going to be that happy when Elaina buys his company next week."

Byron shrugged. Truly unbothered by the potential family drama. "We'll worry about that tomorrow. Tonight I'd like to dance with the woman I love."

Zoe's huge grin brightened his world. "Still love me?"

With all seriousness Byron looked in her eyes. "Now

more than ever. Let's build whatever future we want together."

Zoe's eyes misted over. Her lips lifted and she nodded. "That sounds like a deal of a lifetime."

"Then I need to seal this deal," Byron said.

Zoe held out a hand. "In true Robidoux fashion with a handshake?"

He shook his head. "Nah. I can think of a much better way." He kissed her. As the crowd cheered again, Byron knew the love and trust reflected in Zoe's eyes was the best thing he could have ever received.

* * * * *

ACKNOWLEDGEMENTS

First, I have to thank my awesome group of writer friends. Thank you to Cheris, KD, Jamie and Kwana for encouraging and pushing me to do my best. You ladies rock! I couldn't have written this book without the support of my family, specifically my husband, Eric, who doesn't give me a side-eye when I talk out loud while trying to figure out a section of dialogue. Thanks to the awesome team at HQN! Michelle, Errin, Samantha and everyone else involved in getting the Jackson Falls books out in the world. You all are a great team to work with! Finally, thank you to the readers. You don't know how much each email or social media tag saying you're enjoying my books keeps me typing away at the laptop. I appreciate each of you taking the time to read, review and reach out.

Don't miss Careless Whispers,
the next sexy and irresistible book in
Synithia Williams's Jackson Falls series
featuring the Robidoux family!

CHAPTER ONE

ELAINA ROBIDOUX STEPPED into her sleeveless black sheath dress. She shimmied her hips as the cool material slid across her skin and she slipped the dress up. Reaching behind her, she struggled to grab the zipper before a larger hand pushed hers aside.

"I've got you, baby." Robert's deep voice flowed over her like the satin lining of her dress.

She'd promised herself she wouldn't let him see how happy she was they'd reunited. Wouldn't reveal how much she'd needed a win in the relationship department, but after the sexy afternoon they'd just had, she couldn't stop from grinning over her shoulder. "You've got me?"

He zipped her dress and ran his hands up and down her arm. "You know it." He pulled her against his chest and kissed her neck. "Can't you stay longer?"

Elaina glanced at the unmade bed in their hotel room. If only she could stay. These moments with Robert were the one good thing in her life. Robert was the one who'd gotten away. The guy she'd fallen in love with years ago when she was too young to appreciate a good guy over the allure of the bad boy. They'd debated books, movies and politics. He'd challenged her on everything without caring that she was a Robidoux, and most people let her get away with being demanding. He'd soon become the only guy she'd anxiously sit around waiting for him to call.

Then she'd gotten pregnant by the first guy who'd made her feel passion and soon after announced an engagement rather than besmirch her family's name.

Robert had moved on, married and divorced, and was now frequently visiting Raleigh, North Carolina, which wasn't far from her home in Jackson Falls, to follow up on potential business deals. She didn't know the specifics of his business dealings. They hadn't reconnected based on business. Their reconnection had been almost coincidental. She'd learned he was divorced thanks to a nostalgia-fueled trip down a social-media rabbit hole, had attended the conference he'd mentioned looking forward to, and they'd run into each other at the bar.

The coincidence had been the bar. She hadn't *known* he'd be there at that time, so her surprise had been genuine. His interest in reconnecting as welcome to her as ice water in a desert after being so unhappy in relationships for so long. They'd started their affair that week and kept it going off and on for months afterward.

After years of disappointments, she hadn't wanted to put too much anticipation in their reunion. Robert traveled to Raleigh often and Elaina came over whenever he was in town. Despite her efforts to keep things strictly physical, she was well and truly in a state of deep infatuation with Robert.

"I wish I could stay longer." Elaina eased her head to the side, giving Robert better access to her throat. "I'm expected home. Family stuff."

Her brother, Byron, had unsuccessfully run for Senate but easily won the race for Jackson Falls mayor two years later. Her brother's political career combined with her dad's business connections meant multiple requirements for the family to show support at some event or another. Today was a garden party for potential donors. Elaina would have to break multiple North Carolina traffic laws to get home in time to shower and change. She hadn't brought anything with her when Robert called the evening before to let her know he was in Raleigh and wanted to see her. She'd grabbed her purse and raced down the highway.

She would not think about how pathetic and lonely she would have accused anyone else of being for doing the same.

"Do you think you'll be able to come back tonight?" Robert's lips brushed across the sensitive spot on her neck. He was taller than her, with sandy skin and green eyes that used to mesmerize her. Her dad once called Robert a pretty boy. An assessment she attributed to her dad's usual attempts to push her in the direction he'd preferred.

Once they'd reconnected, she'd begrudgingly admitted to herself that her dad may have been right. Robert's suits were expensive, his car pricey and his tastes high-end. All things he didn't mind letting people know about but Elaina was willing to overlook, because he still didn't back down when they debated and the sex was amazing.

"I wish, but this thing will go late, and I do need to be in the office on Monday." She regretfully pulled herself away from him and walked to the dresser. She picked up her diamond earrings. "You'll be back next week, right?"

Did she sound desperate? She hoped she didn't sound desperate. Elaina Robidoux didn't chase after a man.

Tell that to your gas light.

She pushed aside the reminder. Her gas light had come on when she was ten minutes away from the hotel. She'd ignored it in her haste to get to Robert, which meant she'd have to stop on her way home.

Robert cringed and rubbed his hands together. "I don't know."

She slipped an earring into her right ear. "Okay, the following weekend, then?"

Robert shrugged. "I'm not sure when I'll be back."

Elaina stilled. "Not sure." Her voice didn't betray any of her sudden paranoia. She turned her back to Robert as she slipped the other earring into her ear.

"The investors I thought I'd have for my business venture didn't pan out." He paused for a heartbeat. "I don't have a reason to keep coming back."

No reason? Her heart raced and a cold sweat broke out over her skin. Elaina frowned as she lifted her multistrand gold necklace. "Oh, really?" she asked in a cool voice. She fastened her necklace and schooled her features to the bland expression she'd perfected before facing Robert again. "Does that mean the end of us?"

"It doesn't have to be," Robert said. His lips lifted into a nervous smile. "You know I want to keep this going."

"What are you proposing?" She crossed her arms and watched him while her pulse fluttered. She was being romantic. Of course he wasn't proposing something serious, but a part of her wished he'd ask her to move back to Atlanta with him. To start her life over. For them to get back what they'd lost when she'd been young, impulsive and ridiculously rebellious.

"I need seventy-five thousand dollars," Robert said.

Elaina blinked. Seventy-five what? "Excuse me?"

"Just to start out," he continued. He ran a hand over his curly dark hair. "If things go well, I can pay you back in a year. Though, you'll be a partner and might want to consider increasing your investment."

The request for money was so far from what she'd expected that it took several seconds for the audacity of the statement to filter through the confused fog in her brain. He was seriously asking her for money? "What exactly am I investing in? You haven't given specifics about your business."

Robert's eyes lit up. She recognized that look. Greed. He thought he had her on the hook. "I'm opening a beauty supply store."

"You can't be serious." Wasn't he in finance? At least she'd thought he'd said finance. Admittedly they hadn't gotten deep into discussions of their work in between the hasty, tear-each-other's-clothes-off meetups they'd had.

"I'm serious. I know a guy who has a hookup on premium hair I can get at a discount. He's been selling it out of his car for now, but once I get a storefront, he'll start supplying me. I've got another friend who has a connection with hair care products and supplies. I just need the initial money to get started."

Elaina held up a hand, her brain spinning with what she'd just heard. "You need seventy-five thousand dollars to set up a beauty supply store with hair and supplies you're buying from bootleggers?"

"None of this is bootleg stuff. It's the real deal. They just get it." He waved a hand and shrugged. "Before it leaves the truck."

Elaina pressed her fingers to her temple. Tension radiated through her neck and jaw. She was getting a headache. "I thought you were in finance."

"I was before my divorce. She took everything, and I'm

starting over. As much money as she used to spend on her hair," he scoffed and shook his head. "This was a good way to make my money back."

Elaina dropped her hand and studied him, but there were no signs this was a joke. No suppressed laughter or mischievous twinkle. His eyes were serious and eager. "Robert, I'm not giving you seventy-five thousand dollars to start a beauty supply store."

The excited gleam in his eyes dimmed. He took a step back. "Why not?"

"Because I'm not interested in investing in a beauty supply store."

"I guess that means you don't want to see me again, either." He lifted his chin and threw out the words like a challenge.

Elaina's spine stiffened. "Is that what this was all about?" She pointed to the bed. "You hoped I would give you money?"

"That wasn't everything," he said quickly.

Despite her irritation, a spark of hope flared. "What was the other thing?"

"I've always wanted to sleep with you," he said without flinching.

The words were like a kick to the gut from a champion kickboxer. Hard, fast and lethal. Her stomach muscles clenched, and she swallowed hard. Disappointment weighed so heavily on her she wanted to sink to the floor. But she wasn't the type of person to sink. Not in situations like this.

She straightened her shoulders and returned his stare. "Well, at least we both got that out of our systems." She picked up her purse. "Goodbye, Robert."

He hurried across the room and blocked her exit. "Come on, now, Elaina. What did you think this was?"

"Not an attempt for you to try to get money from me," she said in a cool voice.

"I wasn't initially going to ask you for the money, but you've got it. Your family's company is always looking for investments. Why not invest in me?" he asked like a petulant child.

"Helping you sell hair that your friend has in his trunk isn't that appealing." She sidestepped around him. "Don't call me again."

Robert's disbelieving laugh stopped her. "So, you're dismissing me again."

She spun around toward him. "Dismissing you? You're the one who threw out the ultimatum. Give me money or go?"

He held up his hands and dared to look offended. "I don't know why you're acting surprised, Elaina. You didn't want to give me the time of day when we were younger because you were caught up with that thug your dad took in. Now, because he left you and married your sister, you think you can just call me up, sleep with me and then we're going to be a couple. You're a coldhearted business-woman. I knew I was just an itch you wanted to scratch. You knew I wasn't looking for anything serious after my divorce. I thought we could at least grow this into a busi-ness partnership."

She watched him with her practiced dismissive stare for several seconds. She needed those seconds to control her emotions. Needed those seconds to keep the pain blast-ing through her like a grenade from coming through in her voice.

"And I'm not looking to be your bank. Good luck with your beauty supply store." She walked out of the room without a backward glance.

Her entire body shook with the effort to hold in the hurt, rage and embarrassment surging through her system. He had told her he didn't want anything serious after his divorce, yet she'd asked him to consider Raleigh as a place to restart. She'd come to his hotel room when he'd first visited. She'd ignored the infrequent mentions about searching for investors between pillow talk. All because she'd thought they'd pick up where they'd started.

She'd watched too many rom-coms on cable. The old boyfriend comes back, love is rekindled, and everyone lives happily-ever-after. She knew not to believe in fairy tales.

You're the oldest, Elaina. You have to be smarter. Never give more of yourself to anyone, because they'll try to take advantage of you.

Some mother's read bedtime stories to their daughters at night. Elaina's mother imparted advice on what it meant to be the oldest child and the responsibilities she'd one day have. Elaina had gotten some form of the same speech from her grandfather and her father. She was the one who'd one day take over Robidoux Tobacco, which later became Robidoux Holdings. She had to lead by example. She had to be smarter. She had to be stronger.

Elaina pressed the button on her key to unlock her Mercedes and slid behind the wheel. She turned on the air-conditioning to combat the stuffy heat in the car. Her hands gripped the wheel until her knuckles hurt. Her gas light mocked her.

"I'm tired of being strong." She whispered the words.

Too afraid to admit as much even to herself. Her cheek tickled and she swiped at the stupid tear that escaped her eye.

She took a shaky breath and shook her head. She didn't have time for a pity party. Her life was good. She owned her own business. She still stood to take over her family's businesses. She was healthy, rich and able. No one cared about her broken heart. Why should she?

"To hell with Robert," she said in a strong, confident voice before easing her car out of the parking space and searching for a gas station.

Don't miss what happens next in...
Careless Whispers
by Synithia Williams.

Available February 2021 wherever
HQN books and ebooks are sold.

www.Harlequin.com

Copyright © 2020 by Synithia R. Williams

HARLEQUIN
DESIRE

Luxury, scandal, desire—welcome to the lives of the American elite.

They made passionate music together.
Has this heartbreaker changed his tune?

Songwriter Eden Voss had the perfect man—sexy, charming, talented and *hers*. Until record executive Blaine Woodson broke her heart to save his fledgling label. Now music's bad boy is back, begging for her songwriting skills in his studio… and her lovemaking skills after hours. Eden vows to keep thing strictly business this time. But there is nothing professional about the heat still between them…

Available October 2020

Harlequin.com

HDBPAKA10

SPECIAL EXCERPT FROM

(H) HARLEQUIN

DESIRE

A tempting new music venture reunites songwriter
Eden Voss with ex-boyfriend Blaine Woodson, a record label
ecutive. He wronged her in the past, so they vow to keep things
·ictly business this time. But there is nothing professional about
the heat still between them…

Read on for a sneak peek at
After Hours Redemption *by Kianna Alexander.*

ging through the opening verse, she could feel the smile coming
·r her face. Singing gave her a special kind of joy, a feeling she
n't get from anything else. There was nothing quite like opening
mouth and letting her voice soar.

She was rounding the second chorus when she noticed Blaine
ding in the open door to the booth. Surprised, and a bit embarrassed,
stopped midnote.

His face filled with earnest admiration, he spoke into the awkward
nce. "Please, Eden. Don't stop."

Heat flared in her chest, and she could feel it rising into her cheeks.
aine, I…"

'It's been so long since I've heard you sing." He took a step closer.
don't want it to be over yet."

Swallowing her nervousness, she picked up where she'd left off.
w that he was in the room, the lyrics, about a secret romance
ween two people with plenty of baggage, suddenly seemed much
re potent.

And personal.

Suddenly, this song, which she often sang in the shower or
le driving, simply because she found it catchy, became almost
biographical. Under the intense, watchful gaze of the man she'd
e loved, every word took on new meaning.

She sang the song to the end, then eased her fingertips away from
keys.

Blaine burst into applause. "You've still got it, Eden."

"Thank you," she said, her tone softer than she'd intended. S looked away, reeling from the intimacy of the moment. Having him a spectator to her impassioned singing felt too familiar, too reminisc of a time she'd fought hard to forget.

"I'm not just gassing you up, either." His tone quiet, almost rever he took a few slow steps until he was right next to her. "I hear sing all day, every day. But I've never, ever come across another voice I yours."

She sucked in a breath, and his rich, woodsy cologne flooded senses, threatening to undo her. Blowing the breath out, she strugg to find words to articulate her feelings. "I appreciate the complime Blaine. I really do. But…"

"But what?" He watched her intently. "Is something wrong?"

She tucked in her bottom lip. *How can I tell him that being close to him ruins my concentration? That I can't focus on my w because all I want to do is climb him like a tree?*

"Eden?"

"I'm fine." She shifted on the stool, angling her face away from I in hopes that she might regain some of her faculties. His physical s combined with his overt masculine energy, seemed to fill the sp around her, making the booth feel even smaller than it actually wa

He reached out, his fingertips brushing lightly over her I shoulder. "Are you sure?"

She trembled, reacting to the tingling sensation brought on by electric touch. For a moment, she wanted him to continue, wante feel his kiss. Soon, though, common sense took over, and she sh her head. "Yes, Blaine. I'm positive."

Will Eden be able to maintain her resolve?

Don't miss what happens next in…
After Hours Redemption *by Kianna Alexander.*

Available October 2020 wherever
Harlequin Desire books and ebooks are sold.

Harlequin.com

Copyright © 2020 by Eboni Manning

HDEXPKA10